TORMENTED LOVE

"Torrie, you can't judge all men by what he did."

"Stop it! Just stop it!" Torrie's voice was strangled with unshed tears as she forced the words from her lips. "You're a horrible man."

"You're right, I am a man. Not a boy who's going to run away to lick his wounded ego with some other woman. Not a monster who's going to rape your luscious body. Just a man, Torrie." Every word brought him closer, until he was a few inches from her. Yet, a chasm separated them, a gulf littered with the sharp pieces of shattered dreams.

Her shoulders shook with an effort to keep her emotions under a tight rein. "What do you want from me?"

"I want you to realize it's natural to feel desire, it's healthy to cry. I want you to know how good it feels to be alive. You gave me my life, let me help you find yours."

DEBRA DIER

SURRENDER THE DREAM

To my parents: The lady who taught me to read and the man who always watched over me. I know you're watching now, Dad, and smiling in heaven.

Book Margins, Inc.

A BMI Edition

Published by special arrangement with Dorchester Publishing Co., Inc.

Printed in the United States of America.

FOREWORD

Your Gloria Diehl Book Club selections are chosen by an independent review board with members all across the United States. Board members are carefully chosen to represent all backgrounds, views, and reading interests. Any romance novel which bears the imprint *Gloria Diehl Book Club Selection* has been reviewed and recommended by the committee for its originality, reading interest, plot, and character development.

Chapter One

San Francisco, April 1897

Was he dying? Spence Kincaid didn't want to know. Still, there was no chance to escape into oblivion, not with a dozen finely honed stilettos stabbing in a slow, steady throb just behind his eyes. With a groan, he pried open his eyelids. Gold and red flames writhed before him, the fiery heat scorching his skin. No, he wasn't dying. He was already dead. And he hadn't risen to a better place.

As he blinked the grit from his eyes, the flames slowed their wicked dance, blossoming into huge gilt flowers splashed across a red satin wall, gaslight flickering on each golden bloom. Spence thought back on all those mornings spent in Sunday school as a boy, but he couldn't recall a single mention of red satin walls in hell.

He frowned at the gas jets hissing behind the grate on the hearth. The room was sweltering, stale brandy and jasmine simmering in the air, a woman's skin sticking like a branding iron to his naked back. Memories crept into his mind, fragments of images better forgotten. Last night had been like mating with a bobcat in heat; definitely something he didn't want to do again. With a little luck, he could get out of here without waking her.

He slid his legs across the sheets, cringing at the sound of skin on satin, beads of sweat breaking out on his brow. His gaze rested on an overturned glass on the table near the bed, a dark stain barely visible against the black marble top. There was more than brandy in that glass last night, he was sure of it. Never again. The next time Allan came up with the bright idea of . . .

The blow hit him with enough force to drive the air from his lungs. He glanced down to find two pale arms cinched around his waist. So much for luck.

"You weren't thinking about leaving, were you, Spence?"

He glanced over his shoulder at the woman who held him, her green eyes narrowed like a cat stalking prey, her bare breasts burning into his back. She looked hungry, and he had the uneasy feeling he was breakfast. "I have to meet someone this morning."

"This is San Francisco, Spence. No one does business before noon," Olivia said, her hands slithering down his belly. "Except for me, and my associates."

He grabbed her hands before she could get to anything vital. "The man I'm meeting rises with the sun."

Sunlight pierced the slit at the joining of the red velvet drapes, and Spence wondered just how late it was. He cringed as she slid her tongue upward, along the column of his spine, sparks of pain spiralling from what felt like gashes slashed across his skin.

"You're not going yet," she said, her lips brushing his shoulder.

"Olivia I . . . damn!" he muttered, as her teeth sank into the sensitive skin at the joining of his shoulder and neck.

She threw one arm around his neck and brought him down to the mattress, pouncing before he could move, her breasts swinging like melons in nets above his mouth. "I like the way you taste."

"Thanks." Jasmine oozed from her pores, choking his nostrils. "Olivia, I have to . . ."

"I want to try something," she said, rubbing the moist flesh at the joining of her thighs against his hard belly.

One dark brow rose as he looked up at her. "Try something?" He wondered if this *something* would have anything to do with the black bull whip he had noticed hanging in her closet. His muscles tensed as she pulled the black curls on his chest. "Olivia, I really have to leave."

"I knew you would be incredible when you walked in last night," she said, sliding a little lower. "I knew you were too good to waste on one of my girls."

He glanced up, groaning as he saw his image reflected in the mirror above her bed. "I appreciate the offer," he said, grasping her shoulders. "But I can't stay." He tossed her to the side and rolled to his feet, his head reeling with the motion.

"You're one gorgeous Texas stud," she said, grabbing for his morning arousal.

Spence jumped back. "Maybe some other time."

Olivia raised up on her knees to turn up the gas jet burning behind a cut crystal globe on the wall by the bed. Pouting, she tossed her coppery tresses over her shoulder and slid her hand over one plump breast, her fingers toying with the dusky tip. "You might say no, but I can see a part of you saying yes." Her right hand crawled across her belly to the triangle of bright curls at the joining of her thighs. "Come on, Spence. You know you want me."

Right now all he wanted was a hot bath in his own room. Olivia Fontaine's Pleasure Palace had been Allan's idea. Last night Spence had intended only to have a few drinks before going home, but Olivia had changed his mind. He still wasn't sure how.

"Olivia, I . . ." Spence paused as the door flew open, the sound of solid oak slamming against the wall vibrating against his throbbing temples.

"My word!" a woman said, her voice little more than a gasp.

Spence snatched a pillow from the bed and clutched it to his belly, black satin cool against his skin. Two people were standing in the doorway, and they looked as startled as he felt. A police officer stood with his mouth open, his gaze fixed on Olivia, who had failed to cover anything. A tall, stout woman, with white hair and wire-rimmed glasses stood next to the police officer, her expression changing from shock to disgust. Spence felt as though his grandmother had just caught him with his pants down.

"Just what is the meaning of this, Felix!" Olivia asked, lifting the sheet to her breasts.

Officer Felix Perkins cleared his throat before he spoke. "We got the wrong room, Miss Olivia."

"What the hell are you doing here, you and this self-righteous prig!" Olivia demanded, her white cheeks blazing red with anger.

"She said there's a girl . . ." Perkins began.

"We're thinkin' there's a girl bein' held here against her will," the old woman said, her gray eyes looking fierce behind her little wire-rimmed glasses. "And we're goin' to find her." She turned and marched out of the room.

"Sorry, Miss Fontaine. She's got a paper from Judge Nichols saying the chief was to help her," Perkins said, tipping his hat to Olivia, backing out of the room and closing the door behind him.

"Who was that?" Spence asked, tossing the pillow to the bed.

"Charlotte McKenzie," Olivia said, spitting out the words as though they left a bad taste in her mouth.

Spence found his trousers on the floor, under a black silk corset. "Just what were they talking about?" he asked, shoving his legs into his trousers, black wool scratching his bare skin. A door slammed against a wall nearby, followed by a high-pitched scream.

"That Irish bitch!" Olivia mumbled, getting out of the big, gold-plated bed. She snatched a black silk robe from the chest at the foot of the bed. Mumbling under her breath, she pulled the robe around her nude body, hurrying toward the door, looping the silver-tasseled sash as she walked.

Spence ran his hands through his tousled dark waves as he followed her out of the room. A short distance away, one of Olivia's men was standing with his hands pressed against the walls on either side of the hall, crushing white and yellow columbine in the wallpaper. Over the big man's shoulder, Spence could see Charlotte McKenzie.

Miss McKenzie faced the big man, glaring at him like a terrier meeting a bull. Officer Perkins was content to watch from a distance, standing near the windows at the back of the hall, stroking his big blond mustache, looking anxious to watch a battle.

"Stand aside, Moe," Olivia said, tapping the big man on his shoulder. "I'll take care of this."

When Moe stepped aside, Spence saw a young, fair-haired woman standing beside Charlotte McKenzie. The girl clutched a green blanket around her, staring at Olivia with wide, terrified brown eyes, eyes that were rimmed with dark, purplish circles.

"And just where do you think you're taking her?" Olivia demanded.

Charlotte's big chest heaved. "To the mission, where she'll have a chance to live again."

As the old woman spoke, the girl started to collapse. Spence moved quickly, reaching her before she slumped to the floor. As he swept her up into his arms, the blanket slipped, revealing her nude body and the dark bruises marring the pale skin of her arms and ribs. He tried to juggle her in his arms to pull the blanket back over her naked breasts, but the old woman was there before he could manage.

Charlotte slipped the blanket back into place, glaring at Spence as though he had dropped the blanket on purpose.

"This girl owes me money," Olivia said, pointing her finger in the girl's direction.

The night before, Spence had been treated to a hint of Olivia's penchant for torture. He hated to guess at what had been done to this girl. "How much?"

Olivia looked surprised at his question. "I'm not altogether sure."

"Owes ye fer what?" Charlotte demanded, facing the woman, hands planted on her bulky hips.

Olivia tossed her bright hair over her shoulders, her full breasts swinging beneath black silk. "For clothes, food, and lodging."

"From the looks of her that shouldn't amount to much," Spence said, looking at Olivia, seeing the ugliness beneath the bold beauty of her face. "I'll settle with you after the young lady is safely on her way."

"Officer, will ye come over here and earn yer pay," Charlotte said, laying her hand on Spence's arm. Her eyes narrowed as she stared up at him. "We won't be needin' yer help."

It was a surprisingly young-looking hand, Spence thought, glancing at the slender hand clutching his arm. "You have it just the same, ma'am."

Charlotte's hand tensed on his bare arm, her fingers digging into his skin. "I said we don't need yer help."

"I can take her," Officer Perkins said, moving to his side.

"No. I'll take her," Spence said, dismissing the officer with a glance.

"Yes, sir," Officer Perkins mumbled, stepping back.

The girl in his arms moaned softly. She stirred, her brown eyes growing wide as she stared up into his face. "Who are you?" she asked, her voice strained with fear.

"A friend. Someone who's going to help you get out of here," Spence said, his voice caressing, soothing, as though he spoke to a small child.

The girl choked back a sob and hid her face against his bare shoulder. She couldn't be much older than his sister. With the warm drizzle of the girl's tears against his skin, a paternal instinct swelled inside Spence. He looked up and found the old woman staring at him as though he were a viper about to strike. He smiled, trying to gain her trust, knowing he was failing miserably. "Lead the way, ma'am."

Charlotte's hands formed tight balls at her sides. She looked as though she intended to say something. Instead, she turned on her heel and started marching down the hall.

"Spence, just what are you doing?" Olivia asked, grabbing his arm.

"Carrying this little lady to her carriage, Olivia," he said, shaking off her hand.

"Do you want me to stop 'em, Miss Olivia?" Moe asked.

"I wouldn't try it, big man," Spence said, casting Moe a long look over his shoulder.

Moe shifted on his feet, a bull about to charge, but Olivia restrained him with a small hand on his huge forearm. "Later," she said, staring at Spence.

Spence followed Charlotte McKenzie down the stairs and out of the house, her back as straight and unyielding as an old hickory. The brisk, damp air blowing in from the bay sent shivers across his skin as he walked in bare feet down the granite stairs and across the sidewalk toward a shabby black carriage. He was surprised to see the old woman climb into the high carriage seat with the agility of a much younger woman.

Charlotte patted the worn leather seat. "She'll be sittin' here beside me."

Spence nodded and smiled down at the girl in his arms. "What's your name, little lady?"

"Claire," she whispered. "Claire Butterfield."

"I'm Spencer Kincaid, Miss Butterfield." He wondered if this woman-child would recover from the wounds that didn't show. Damn Olivia! He pushed aside the anger and disgust churning inside him and gave Claire a smile. "If you need any help, just let me know."

She swallowed hard, and he thought she might cry. "Easy," Spence said, his arms growing tighter around her. "Miss McKenzie is going to take care of you."

He lifted her to the seat beside Miss Charlotte McKenzie and stood back. Charlotte slipped one arm around the girl and glared down at him. He was about equal with a rattlesnake in that old woman's eyes, Spence thought.

"You're not coming?" Claire asked, looking down at him with adoring eyes.

"No, ma'am. But, I'll be round to see how you're doing."

Charlotte gave him one last glance, her gray glare freezing all in its path, before she flicked the ribbons over the horse's rump and started down the street.

Spence watched them for a moment, feeling a little like the snake the old woman thought him to be. He needed a hot bath, needed to scrub Olivia's scent from his skin.

"You made Miss Olivia pretty angry in there, sir," Officer Perkins said. "I'd watch my step."

Spence frowned as he glanced at the police officer. No doubt the man was on Olivia's payroll. "Thanks for the warning."

The scent of stale cigars and ripe perfume wrapped around Spence as he entered the house, like a damp, cloying cloth slapped against his face. He took the stairs two at a time. The sooner he got out of this place the better.

When he reached the second floor, Allan staggered out of one of the bedrooms near Olivia's room. He was naked, one arm slung around a blonde, the other around a brunette. Both women wore red ribbons around their necks and nothing more. Spence looked at the girls and wondered if either of them had started the way Claire had.

"What's all the noise?" Allan asked, as Spence drew near.

"An Irish whirlwind just whipped through."

"Ah, that McKenzie woman is at it again," Allan said, nuzzling the brunette's cheek. "She doesn't think anyone should have any fun."

Spence frowned. There were times when Allan was a little too wrapped up in his own pleasure. "The young girl she took out of here didn't look as though she was having much fun."

"How about you girls?" Allan asked, dropping his hands. The girls squealed as he grabbed their breasts. "How about the three of us go back inside and have some fun?"

Spence shook his head as Allan stepped back into the room, high-pitched laughter following in his wake. Allan hadn't changed since college. Sometimes it made Spence wonder just how his old friend could manage his inheritance.

Moe stood outside Olivia's room, like a hound guarding the gates of hell. Spence passed the big man and tossed open Olivia's door. His eyes narrowed against the light as he entered her room. Sunlight streaked through lace curtains, striking the gilt-trimmed mirror above the black marble mantel, reflecting on the red velvet chairs and sofa, each heavily plated with gold, igniting the room into a riot of red and gold, like flames in the middle of an inferno.

Olivia stood in front of the windows, framed by red velvet drapes, her hair flaming in the sunlight. He looked at her and wondered once again why he had taken the bait. She wasn't even the type of woman he normally found attractive. Although she was the ideal of fashion, he preferred his women less rounded, taller, more elegant, a lot less vicious.

The blood-red carpet swallowed his footsteps as he found his clothes. Three pearl studs remained in the button holes of his white linen shirt; the others were lost. He didn't intend to take the time to find them.

"How dare you side with those people!"

Ignoring her, he sat on the plush red velvet cushion of an ornately carved chair and began to pull on his shoes. He had no idea where his socks were. His underwear lay on the floor nearby, but he dismissed it. He wasn't about to pull off his trousers. Not around this little she-devil.

"I will not tolerate anyone interfering in my business."

Spence stood, meeting her angry glare with an even gaze. "Tell me, why did you torture that girl? Did she object to working for you?"

The expression on her face changed when she realized he wasn't going to beg for her forgiveness. As if a magician had snapped his fingers, the spitting cat turned into a soft purring kitten.

"Spence, darling, that girl owed me money," she said, starting to move toward him, swinging her broad hips seductively. "I never tortured her. She just had a hard time with one of her customers, that's all."

Spence had a feeling that poor girl hadn't seen anyone but Olivia and her henchmen for a long time. His muscles tensed as she laid her small hand on his chest.

"Let's forget about that silly girl," Olivia said, sliding her hand down the starched linen covering his ribs. "She doesn't have anything to do with us."

Spence turned away and lifted his coat from the back of the chair. "I never felt it was my business to tell people how to live," he said, shrugging into his black evening coat. "As long as they don't hurt anyone, I figure it's their right to do what they please. If a woman decides to go into business selling pleasure, well, I figure there's nothing wrong with that."

He stared down at her. "As long as it's her decision."

"You're not saying I forced that girl to join my house!" Olivia said, plucking nervously at the black lace that edged her robe.

"I'm saying you're a cold, sadistic little tyrant," Spence said, staring at her with naked disgust. "You derive pleasure from pain."

"Oh, you didn't seem to mind last night, Spencer Kincaid," Olivia said, her small nostrils flaring. She pulled open her robe and lifted her large breasts in her white hands. "Admit it. That self-righteous do-gooder has you feeling like a choirboy caught drinking the communion wine."

No doubt about it. There had been something besides brandy in his drink last night.

"But you're still hungry for more." Her hands slipped down across her rounded belly to the triangle of bright curls at the joining of her thighs. "I can see it in your eyes. You want me. You've never had a woman like me before."

That was true enough. And, if he were careful, he would never have one like her again.

"I should think a hundred should cover the girl's expenses," he said, pulling a money clip from the right-hand pocket of his trousers. He unfolded the stack of notes and slipped two fifties from the gold clip. On impulse, he withdrew another note. "And here's an extra ten for your services last night."

Olivia sucked in her breath. "Ten! You bastard! Other men have paid hundreds just to take me to dinner. I gave you the best time you'll ever have. Gave it to you!" She leaped for him, her hands curved, her fingers arched to spread her nails.

He grabbed her wrists and held her at arm's length, sidestepping her plump bare feet as she tried to kick him. "Careful, Olivia, you're going to hurt yourself."

She growled and sank her teeth into his wrist. Out of reflex, he jerked his arm. Olivia stumbled back, striking a chair with her hip, falling flat on her wide behind.

Spence glanced down at his wrist and saw her tooth marks etched in his skin. The little cat had drawn blood.

"Moe!" Olivia screamed.

The big man came rushing through the door an instant after her call, ducking his head to keep from hitting the lintel. Moe took one look at his mistress and charged Spence, head down, a raging bull. Spence drew back his fist and connected with the big man's jaw. Moe stumbled and went down like a felled redwood, his big body falling across Olivia's lap.

"Get off me you stupid oaf!" Olivia wailed, pushing at the big man. Moe was too big for her to move and too senseless to move on his own power.

Olivia looked half crazed sitting there on the floor, her bright red hair tangled around her face, her eyes so wide the whites shone all around the green irises. "You'll regret this," she said, glaring up at him.

"I already do," Spence said, pulling a handkerchief from his coat pocket. He regretted ever coming to Miss Olivia Fontaine's house of pleasure, he thought, wrapping his bloody wrist.

"You'll be back, Kincaid," Olivia said, as he walked toward the door. "Begging for me."

"And the South shall rise again," he said, glancing back at her. The look in her eyes made the tiny hairs on his neck tingle. This was a woman who could kill, with cunning, with pleasure. He left her room and closed the door behind him. If he never saw Miss Olivia Fontaine again, it would be too soon.

The rescue mission was one in a row of houses on Chestnut Street. From the outside it was indistinguishable from its neighbors; all had two stories with high-peaked attics, bay windows adorning the first and second stories, and gingerbread millwork adding Victorian charm. But the attic of this house served as nursery, dormitory, and schoolroom, and each of the five bedrooms in the house held three beds. Girls at the mission didn't have much room, but they had their freedom.

Charlotte McKenzie followed Dr. Wallace out of the room where Claire was sleeping. "Will she be all right?"

The doctor turned in the narrow hall and faced the old woman, sunlight from the window at the end of the hall bathing his face. "She should be fine," he said, slipping off his glasses. He pulled out his handkerchief and started to clean the lenses as he continued. "She needs rest and nourishment. Start with broth, and then give her something more substantial." He slipped on his glasses and sighed. "That poor child."

Charlotte's jaw clenched as she thought of the horrors that young woman had suffered. She had seen many girls like Claire, girls who had once lived with their parents on farms or in small towns, girls who once dreamed of marriage and children, girls whose dreams had been stolen by men who didn't deserve to draw breath. She led the way down the narrow steps to the front door.

"If you need me, just call," Dr. Wallace said, taking her hand.

"Ye can be sure. Thank ye, doctor."

He held her hand a moment, looking at her, a curious expression in his eyes. "You know, I think your father would be proud if he knew what you were doing."

Charlotte snatched her hand from his grasp. "And how are ye knowin' me poor departed father?"

"I've known for some time," he said, smiling down at her. "And don't worry. I won't tell him. You're old enough to make your own decisions."

"To be sure, I'm old enough to be yer mother."

Dr. Wallace chuckled and shook his head. "Just let me know how the girl is doing."

Charlotte leaned a moment against the door after she closed it, hoping the doctor would be as discreet as he promised.

"Are you all right, Charlotte?" a small gray-haired woman asked, coming out of the parlor.

"I'm fine, Mother Leigh," Charlotte said, pulling away from the door.

"You do nice work, Charlotte McKenzie," Mother Leigh said, taking her hand. "I don't know what Sister Flora and I would do without you." Her bony fingers tightened around Charlotte's hand as she continued. "Either of you. I'm not sure we could survive."

"I need to be goin'," Charlotte said, slipping her hand from Mother Leigh's grasp, feeling her cheeks grow warm from the other woman's praise. "Claire will be needin' some clothes when she's up and about."

"You're an angel, Charlotte."

Charlotte shook her head and hurried down the narrow hall that led to the back of the house, her heels clicking against bare wooden planks. A small room behind the kitchen served as her office and bedroom. Like Charlotte, the room was spartan, the white walls unadorned except for a crucifix above the narrow bed. Three spindly oak chairs, a small oak desk, and a walnut washstand filled the little room.

Once inside, safely behind a closed door, Charlotte pulled off her glasses and lifted the white wig from her light chestnut brown hair. Under her somber gray dress she wore an extra set of drawers and camisole, each padded with cotton to give her slender figure the appearance of bulk.

When she was dressed only in a pair of fine lawn drawers and camisole, she poured water from the pitcher into the basin on the washstand and began to scrub away the layers of makeup that gave Charlotte her lines and wrinkles.

She patted her face with a towel and looked at the young woman staring back at her from the mirror above the washstand. Dr. Wallace might be right—Quinton Granger might be proud of her; but if Lillian Granger ever discovered her daughter was doing more than just teaching children at the rescue mission, the explosion would be heard for miles around.

From a closet by the desk, she pulled out a linen petticoat trimmed with embroidered lace, a starched white linen shirtwaist, a gray merino skirt, and a matching jacket. As she fastened the last button on her shirtwaist, a knock sounded on the door.

"Come in."

Flora opened the door and stood for a moment, staring at the tall, slender young woman before her. "I guess Charlotte has gone home for the day."

Torrie Granger smiled at the plump, dark-haired woman standing just outside the room. Flora never entered without an invitation. "Come in, Flora. Is there anything I can do in Charlotte's place?" she asked, pulling on her jacket.

"There's a man to see Charlotte." Flora fluttered into the room, talking and waving her hands. "Oh, he's such a handsome man, with eyes to charm a beast, like gold they are. Never have I seen such eyes. I wonder, just what do you suppose he wants with Charlotte?"

Torrie's heart jumped into her throat. "Kincaid."

"Yes, that's his name," Flora said, bobbing her head. "Spencer Kincaid. Isn't that a nice name. And such nice manners. He sounds as though he might be from the South."

So, he really had meant to visit Claire. Torrie pressed her hand to her racing heart and began pacing the floor. "Tell him Charlotte isn't here."

Flora nodded and began to leave.

"No!" Torrie said, grabbing her arm. "Tell him Charlotte won't be back for a few days."

Flora turned, but Torrie stopped her. Flora glanced up at the younger woman with wide blue eyes, her mouth open.

"No, ah, tell him . . ." Torrie glanced at her reflection in the mirror. The sunlight streaming in through the window behind the desk couldn't find a trace of makeup left on her face, although her cheeks looked as though she had rouge high on her cheekbones. "No, I'll tell him. Where is he?"

"The parlor."

"Who is with him?"

"No one," Flora said, wringing her hands. "Mother Leigh went with Gretchan and Jane to the exchange, Maria is cleaning the kitchen, Jo is upstairs with the children, and Nellie and Blanche are doing the wash. I didn't think it was a good idea to bring him back here, so I left him in the parlor. Was that all right?"

"You did just fine, Flora." Torrie took one more glance in the mirror above the washstand, pushed another pin into her chignon, and rushed from the room with Flora following close behind.

Chapter Two

Torrie halted just outside the parlor, trying to catch her breath, intending to make a dignified entrance.

"Oh, gracious, I'm sorry," Flora said, as she collided with Torrie's back, propelling the younger woman into the parlor.

Kincaid was standing just inside the door. He turned as Torrie came hurtling at him, his arms opening as if by instinct, catching her, saving her from the fall.

The shock of bumping up against his blatant male body drove the air from Torrie's lungs. She looked up at the man who held her in his powerful arms. Sunlight sought him through the bay windows, painting his features with gold, highlighting the sharp planes and angles of a face that could have been carved by a master artist. The man even had a cleft in his chin. But this was no cold work of art. This man was vital, vibrant with energy and life. Torrie felt the pulse of that energy throbbing all the way down to her toes.

She felt suspended, caught like a moth in the lure of a flame, compelled by its beauty, frightened by the destruction it would bring. His smile grew as he looked down at her, tiny laugh lines spreading out from his incredible eyes; eyes fringed with thick black lashes; eyes the color of a mountain lion; eyes filled with entirely too much amusement at her expense.

"Let go of me," she said, trying to pull free of his arms, fighting the curious weakness sliding down her legs.

One dark brow rose at the sharp tone of her voice. "Why, Miss McKenzie, you have changed."

"You know perfectly well I am not Charlotte," Torrie said, wondering if there were any way he might be able to recognize her. "Now release me!"

"Not before I get a proper introduction," he said, grinning down at her. "I always like to know the name of any pretty woman I find in my arms."

His voice was a deep baritone, full of resonance and colored with a drawl that could only come from Texas. "Oh, I hadn't realized you were so particular, Mr. Kincaid."

He pulled her closer, easily quelling her struggles. "You have me at a disadvantage."

Wool and linen, petticoats and camisole, couldn't protect her from the heat of his body, from the hard thrust of his hips, from the solid imprint of his chest against her soft breasts. She felt a wild current of electricity race along her nerves. "You're the one holding me prisoner," she said, glaring up at him, trying to hide all the emotions inside of her except anger.

"You hold the key."

Her breath escaped in a hiss between her teeth.

"I'm Victoria Granger, and I'm not at all pleased to meet you, Spencer Kincaid."

He dropped his hands to his sides and stepped back, looking at her as though she had just slammed her fist into his belly. "Quinton Granger's daughter?"

"Yes," Torrie said, backing away, tugging at the bottom of her jacket. "You know my father?"

"We're old friends. In fact, I just left him."

"My father never was very particular about the company he kept."

One corner of his lips quirked upward as he held her gaze. "I can see Miss Charlotte has been spreading rumors about me."

"Just what are you doing here, Mr. Kincaid?" Torrie asked, grasping the top of a high-backed chair, her fingers sliding across the grapes carved into the smooth mahogany.

His brows raised as he met her silvery glare. "I was wondering the same thing about you."

"I help out here a few days a week." She was standing with her back to the big bay window. Although the sunshine spilling through the panes warmed her back, her knees were trembling as if she were freezing. "You look surprised."

"I suppose I am. I wouldn't have expected Quint's daughter to be working at a rescue mission."

"I assure you, Mr. Kincaid, I am quite capable of working here."

He held up his hands in a gesture of surrender. "I get the notion you can do just about anything you take a mind to do."

Of course he did, she thought, and he still believed in Santa Claus. The man thought he could charm her with a few compliments. He couldn't. "Now that we know why I am here, suppose you will do me the courtesy."

He nodded. "Miss Claire Butterfield was brought here today."

"That's right," Torrie said, fighting a curious breathlessness. "She's upstairs, resting. The doctor doesn't want her to be disturbed."

"I don't mean to disturb her. I just wanted to see how she was getting along."

"She will recover, with rest and care," she said, glancing away, finding it disturbing to hold his gaze. She had never seen eyes like his before, never such a clear, compelling shade of gold.

Flora was standing a few feet away, her head tilted to one side as she gazed at Kincaid. Another woman enchanted by the man, Torrie thought. Well, she would not, could not, allow herself to fall under this man's spell. She forced some air into her lungs and turned to face him as he began to speak.

"She'll be needing some clothes when she's well," Spence said, pulling out his money clip.

"She doesn't need your money, Mr. Kincaid."

"My goodness," Flora murmured, cupping her hands beneath her plump chin.

"Shouldn't she be the one to decide that, Miss Granger?" Spence asked.

"If you think you can buy this girl," Torrie said, taking a step toward him, "you are very much mistaken. In case you didn't notice, she was in that place against her will."

"I think Maria may need me in the kitchen," Flora said, rushing past the two young people, the green cotton drapes on either side of the door fluttering as she left the parlor.

"Do you believe every man who offers to help a woman wants to buy her?" Spence moved toward Torrie as he spoke, stopping a foot in front of her.

The scent of bayberry and spices and something else drifted from his skin, an intriguing male scent that made her pulse quicken. The dark brown coat he wore emphasized the richness of his hair, the silky waves just a whisper above black. He looked every inch a gentleman, but she knew better. "I'm not concerned with what other men may have in mind, Mr. Kincaid."

"I don't believe in slavery," Spence said, his voice deep and smooth as velvet, a sharp contrast to the glitter in his eyes.

"Oh, one wouldn't know that by the company you keep,"

"Is Olivia Fontaine the burr under your saddle?"

"Friends of Olivia Fontaine are not welcome in this house." She turned and walked toward the door, her footsteps tapping out a determined rhythm against the wooden floor. Near the door, she faced him and gestured with her arm to show him the way out.

He ignored her gesture, remaining where he was, planted like a giant oak in the little parlor, radiating power until the air vibrated around him, until she felt the pulse of him throb in her chest. The sunlight streaming in through the windows shimmered around him, conjuring an image of him standing as she had first seen him, naked in the morning light. The memory started queer quivers in her stomach. Torrie blinked, trying to erase the shameful image from her mind.

"I wouldn't exactly call Olivia Fontaine a friend of mine."

"No," Torrie said, clasping her hands at her waist in front of her. "I suppose you are much more than friends."

He shook his head and began to rub the back of his neck, as though his muscles ached. His lips curved into a smile, warm and boyish and completely unexpected. "Let's just say we all make mistakes sometimes."

She felt a tug at her heart as she looked into his smiling face. The man could definitely be dangerous. "I suppose that is what every criminal ever caught has said."

He ran his hand over his cheek as he looked at her. "I went there last night with no intention of getting that well acquainted with any of the women."

Torrie smiled. "I have heard most men just go to Olivia's for the stimulating conversation."

"I prefer my women to be willing companions."

Her only response was a delicate lifting of her brows.

"A friend of mine suggested we visit Olivia's."

"*He* did," Torrie said, as though trying to get all the facts straight.

"That's right, he did." Spence paused, studying her a moment, as though he were trying to see something beyond her face, something she was trying desperately to hide. "Miss Granger, if I didn't know better I'd say you sound like a jealous woman."

His barb hit far too close to the mark. "Jealous! Why you conceited, arrogant . . ."

"Don't protest too much, my lady."

"I am not your lady, thank goodness," Torrie said, shaking with what she would only accept as outrage.

"Do you know how bewitching you look when you blush?" he asked, moving toward her, a mountain lion stalking his prey. "Your cheeks put a scarlet rose to shame."

"I am not some silly schoolgirl," she said, taking a step back.

"No, you're a woman." He sent his gaze drifting from her flushed cheeks to her prim white shirtwaist, where he watched the rise and fall of her breasts before lifting his eyes once more to her face. "One of the prettiest I've ever seen."

Her skin tingled from that lazy perusal, as though he had stroked her breasts with his fingers. "Your shallow words have no effect on me," she said, taking another step back, wishing there were more truth in her words. She didn't seem to be able to think straight when he was near. "I suggest you save your charm for someone who doesn't know your vile nature."

"And you do," he said, advancing with steady purpose. "You know all about me. You know I'm a scoundrel, a lusty defiler of innocent women, a ravager."

Torrie took a step back; her heel hit the wall. "And should I think you are an innocent lad, a poor soul seduced by the charms of a scarlet woman?"

He smiled, and somehow that smile turned her knees into molasses. He invaded the protective cushion of air between them, stopping a few inches in front of her, close enough for her to see the individual lashes in the thick fringe framing his beautiful eyes. Too close. Far too close.

"When I was a boy I had the habit of reading the books my parents didn't want me to read, and not reading those they wanted me to."

"Somehow that doesn't surprise me." She sidestepped. He checked her move, resting his right hand on the wall above her left shoulder.

"One day, I found a book with a fast-sounding title in a stack of books in my father's library. So I shoved it into my shirt and ran to a hill near my house, somewhere I thought no one would find me."

Heat radiated from his big body. He was a flame, warming her, igniting an answering flame within her, drawing her toward the inferno, threatening to consume her.

"I expected gunslingers, and shootouts, and . . ." his grin grew into a devilish smile, "pretty girls."

"Mr. Kincaid," she said, giving him a chilly look, a look that had dropped many a presumptuous male in his tracks. Kincaid grinned.

"Well, I kept at it, reading that book, each night hiding it under my bed, enjoying it, even though there wasn't a single gunslinger in it."

His breath brushed her cheek as he spoke, soft, warm, smelling as sweet as a clover field after a spring rain. "I insist you . . ."

"Near the end, I discovered my father had put that fast-sounding cover over *The Odyssey*."

His eyes were warm and liquid, gold simmering in the sun. A woman could lose her soul in those eyes.

"I suppose the point I'm trying to make is, sometimes it takes a while to discover what lies beneath the cover."

She clutched at her anger, trying to banish the wayward emotions swirling inside her. "Mr. Kincaid, when my father handed me a classic, I knew it was a classic."

"And when you hear of a man spending time with the wrong type of woman, you know just what type of man he is."

"It isn't difficult to tell what kind of man you are," she said, her chin rising with defiance. "Just look at how you are behaving at this moment."

"Oh, and how am I behaving?" he asked, leaning until his lips brushed the tip of her pert nose. "Like a man? A man reacting to a beautiful woman?"

Her bones were melting, flowing downward, forming pools of liquid fire deep inside her. Her palms splayed against the wall like starfish as she fought to keep from touching him, from leaning against the beckoning heat of his powerful body. "You are a . . ."

"How about you, Miss Granger?" he asked, his

gaze reaching deep inside her, stroking her secrets.

She tried to move away from the wall, fighting to escape the compelling beauty of his eyes, the taunting heat of his body. His hands slid to her shoulders, his thumbs stroking heat across her neck just above her starched collar, just below her ears. His grip was as light as a ray of sunshine, but she couldn't break away, couldn't escape the warm web he was spinning around her. "You have no right . . ."

"Are you hiding behind a mask?"

He was consuming all the air. She couldn't breathe, couldn't think. If only she couldn't feel.

"You have lovely lips," he said, pressing his lips against her temple.

She felt her pulse throb beneath his touch. Her eyes fluttered closed.

"Lips just meant for a man's touch."

"Mr. Kincaid, I demand you step away!" Although she intended it to be a stern command, her voice was barely above a whisper.

"You smell good." He brushed his lips against the skin below her ear, breathing in her scent. "Like my mother's rose garden on a warm summer day."

His voice vibrated against her skin, his breath tickled her ear, warm, moist, raising gooseflesh along her shoulder, sending hundreds of shivers scampering down her spine. A soft moan filled the air, and she was horrified to discover it had come from her own lips.

"How long is your hair?" he asked, his lips grazing her cheek. "I bet it's past your waist. Do you ever wear it down, let it tumble around your shoulders?" He pressed his lips to her temple. "It's beautiful, soft, shining, filled with hidden fire, all gold and red in the sunlight."

"Mr. Kincaid!" she said, pushing against his broad chest. "I am not Olivia Fontaine!"

His hands slid along her shoulders, then dropped to his sides. He took a step back, allowing her room to escape, but her legs weren't taking orders. She pressed a trembling hand to her lips and sagged against the wall, her knees too shaky to support her, her eyes unable to look away from his.

"No, Miss Granger. You are definitely not Olivia Fontaine," he said, a frown digging into his brow. "But I wonder who you keep hidden beneath your icy mask. I have a feeling she's one hell of a woman."

"I don't have to wonder what lies beneath your cover. You are an arrogant, conceited, skirt-chasing buffoon!"

"And you are a woman afraid to be one. You need a man. A man who can show you what it's like to be a woman."

"How dare you! You think because I don't swoon at your feet I am less of a woman."

"No. As a matter of fact, I think you're more woman than most I've met."

"Oh, including your friend Miss Fontaine?"

"Definitely. She uses men. That's how she feels powerful. You run from them."

"Perhaps I prefer gentlemen."

He nodded, a crooked smile curving his lips. "As long as they don't get too close."

Torrie pressed her shoulder blades against the wall, fighting the urge to run, to hide. This man saw too much with his beautiful eyes.

He pulled five fifty-dollar-bills from his gold money clip and dropped them on the round black walnut table near the door. "You decide what you want to do with this. I trust your judgment."

With an exaggerated bow, he turned and walked away, pausing at the door, glancing over his shoulder, catching her watching him. "Until next time,

Miss Granger."

"That man," Torrie said, her voice a strangled whisper as Kincaid's heels echoed in the hall. He confused her, enraged her, touched her as no man had ever touched her. The door in the hall opened and closed. He was gone.

Torrie pressed her back firmly against the wall. The sofas and chairs in the parlor were a mix of black walnut and mahogany, one sofa covered in dark green brocade, the other in a yellow and blue floral pattern. Of the four chairs in the room, only two had matching fabric, and neither matched either sofa. Every piece was a relic of one of the houses on Nob Hill, and every piece was threadbare.

Yet, a moment ago, in his presence, the furniture had seemed fit for a palace. A moment ago the parlor had vibrated with life, had seemed the most exciting place on earth. Now, the room was drab, lifeless. Even the sunlight was less brilliant.

She took a deep breath and tried to shake off the strange feeling of loss gripping her. Spencer Kincaid was the type of man who could destroy a woman, especially a woman like her. She knew the type. They collected hearts the way some men collected butterflies, pinning them to boards, destroying life, leaving only an empty shell. She wouldn't let that happen to her. Not again.

Chapter Three

The Granger house stood on an acre of land facing fashionable Van Ness Avenue, near California Street. Steep granite steps rose from the street to a tall wrought-iron gate. Perched on pedestals along a granite walk, statues of Roman warriors stared down proud granite noses at anyone approaching the house. At the end of this gauntlet, three stories of wood soared in baroque grandeur, surrounded by lawns manicured by six Chinese gardeners.

Torrie glanced at the rosewood clock in the hall as she entered the house. It was close to six. It had taken hours to spend Mr. Kincaid's money, but it had all been put to good use. Now she had to rush to be ready for her mother's party.

Lillian Granger considered herself the Mrs. Astor of San Francisco. As ruling queen, she felt it her duty to entertain regularly and lavishly. Tonight

Lillian was holding court, and Torrie knew her mother expected her to be ready before the guests arrived.

"Victoria, I want to talk to you," Quinton Granger said, his deep voice rumbling like thunder in the hall. "In my study."

Torrie froze at the base of the stairs, her hand tensing on the oak banister. Her father only used her given name when he was angry, and right now he sounded angry enough to scare a rattlesnake. "When?" she asked, glancing over her shoulder.

"Now."

His eyes were silver, the same color they always were when he was angry, the same color hers were turning as she met his glare. The staccato of heels clicking against marble ricocheted off the oak wainscoting as they marched across the Great Hall and down a long corridor to the study. Quinton stood aside, drumming his fingernails against the door as his daughter passed into the room.

In no other room was her father reflected more than in this, his lair. Rows and rows of leather-bound books lined two walls, each an old friend. In here the furniture was big, overstuffed, the sofa covered in a moss-green velvet, all the chairs in brown leather. For many years Torrie had loved hiding in this room, curling up in one of the soft leather chairs, helping her father while he worked at his big desk. But this room had ceased being a sanctuary months ago.

He slammed the door, the lace at her neck fluttering as the rush of air hit her. The loud crash of oak hitting oak had barely died when Quinton Granger exploded.

"What in hell is wrong with you, girl!" he shouted, anger propelling him across the room. "Damn-foolish, stupid woman!"

Torrie's chin rose as she turned and met her father's angry stare. It took her a moment to answer, a moment to calm the words before they were spoken. "I assume this has something to do with Richard Hayward."

"Dammit!" Quinton said, slamming his fist on his desk, his gold-nugget paperweight jumping, rattling across the cigar burns that scarred the smooth mahogany surface. "Is there a brain in your head? What feeble reason could you possibly have for turning down his offer?"

"I don't love him, Father," she said, keeping her voice low and even, the effort bringing a tremble to her limbs.

"Don't love him," Quinton said, shaking his head. He rested his palms on his desk and leaned toward his daughter. "Victoria, you are going to be twenty-eight in two months. Do you honestly suppose a knight in shining armor is going to ride up on a big horse and carry you away? Women of your age should be happy to take what comes along."

"I see," Torrie said, trying to control the hurt and anger that threatened to betray her. A lady always remained calm, a lady never raised her voice. Isn't that what Miss Lamarr had always told her at Lamarr's School for Young Ladies? "I hadn't realized I was such a pitiful wretch, Father."

"Don't use that self-righteous tone with me, girl," Quinton said, tapping his knuckles against his desk. "You know exactly what I mean." He pressed taut fingers to his brow, then slammed both fists against the desk. "Damn! What's wrong with you? Plenty of men have asked you to marry them, but you, you keep turning them away."

"They want your money, Father, not me."

He studied her a moment, as though he were trying to read her mind. She stood her ground, refusing to look away, the muscles in her shoulders growing taut as she forced her features into a calm mask.

Torrie was proud of her father. When other men had been throwing money into the Comstock, Quinton had been investing in mining equipment. When other men had gone bankrupt in the depression of 1893, Quinton Granger had built a small empire. At times she just wished he hadn't been quite so successful. At times she wished she weren't the heiress to the Granger fortune.

Quinton drew his hand over his thick dark mustache. "You're not still pining over Charles Rutledge, are you?"

Torrie stiffened at the mention of that name. "Charles Rutledge has nothing to do with this."

"For God's sake! You're not the first woman to be left at the altar!"

"Father, that happened a very long time ago," Torrie said, trying to sound as though she were free of the memories, free of the pain and humiliation of that day.

"Seven years is long enough to find yourself another man."

"As you say, Father, I cannot hope to make a love match," she said, clasping her hands together. "All I can hope is for my father to allow me to live my life as I choose."

"As a dried-up old spinster?" Quinton asked, leaning across the desk. "Do you want to die without having children?"

Torrie swallowed hard. There was nothing she wanted more than to have children. There were times, when working with the children at the rescue mission, that the longing for her own child grew until her chest ached. Still, she had long ago realized some dreams did not come true. "Better an old maid than to marry a man paid for by my father."

Quinton straightened and stared across the desk at his daughter. "How did you know?"

"I had only a suspicion until just now," Torrie said, stepping back. Suspecting and knowing were different, horribly different. She hadn't expected it to hurt like this, hadn't expected to feel as though she had been slammed against a wall. "I hope he didn't cost you much, Father."

His mouth pulled into a tight line, his lips disappearing into his thick mustache as he glared at her. "I don't understand you, girl! What's wrong with Hayward? He's young. He's good-looking enough."

"Oh, he is good-looking," Torrie said, thinking of the tall, fair-haired man. A little too good-looking for her taste. With his smooth skin and fine-boned features, Hayward could be called pretty. "And no one is more sure of it than Mr. Hayward. He is also one of the biggest gamblers in town. I'm sure that was one reason he jumped at the chance to take your money."

"Dammit!" He stood a moment, pulling at the right edge of his mustache, staring at her, deep lines etched into his brow. "Hayward isn't the only man available, you know. There are plenty of men who would jump at the chance to join this family. I can arrange for you to meet others."

"What makes you think I would want any man you could buy?" she asked, the calm mask dropping away as anger and frustration surged within her.

"What the hell difference does it make!" Quinton said, storming out from behind his desk. He stopped in front of her, glaring. "Do you think half the people in this town married because they were in love?"

"I don't care what half the people in this town did!"

"I want a grandchild!" he shouted, leaning until his nose nearly touched her slim nose.

"I am not a brood mare!" Torrie shouted, forgetting all about Miss Lamarr's teachings.

"You are my daughter!"

"Should I take an ad out in the *Examiner*? 'Old Maid desires healthy stud to sire a grandchild for her loving father,' " Torrie said, lifting her hands to indicate the headline. "What do you think, Father?"

"I think you had better take me seriously, girl," he said, his deep voice sounding menacing in the big study.

They stood for a moment, hands on hips, chests heaving like two thoroughbreds after a hard race, the soft glow of gaslight catching highlights of gold and red in their light chestnut hair. They were as alike as father and daughter could be, sharing the same cast of high cheekbones and narrow nose, both tall and slender, both full of anger and pride.

"I'm your father," he said, his voice deep and gravelly from the tension tugging at his throat. "You should have respect, you should want to please me."

"And what about me?" she asked, fighting the hot tears biting at the back of her eyes. "What about what I want?"

"You're a beautiful woman, you should want a full life, a husband, a child. You should want to please your father."

"I should want to be a slave to some man? I should want to sit at my dinner table waiting for my husband as he follows his friends from one free lunch to another? Popping one bottle of champagne after another. Spending time with ladies who aren't quite ladies."

"Dammit, girl! It takes more to please a man than a pretty face. Get all the facts before you start judging people, little Miss Prim and Proper. I have good reason for seeking some warm companionship. If you knew your mother as I do, you'd . . ." He turned as a knock sounded on the door. "What is it!"

The door opened and Lillian Granger entered the room, short, blond, beautiful, looking like a plump porcelain doll in a gown of burgundy satin. With her came an icy air that froze both father and daughter where they stood.

"I would think you two could manage your tempers for one evening," Lillian said, looking at them as a queen addressing her subjects. She glared at her husband a moment before fixing a cold blue stare on her daughter. "Victoria, your father has always had a vile temper, but you have been taught to be a lady. I am very disappointed in you."

For as long as she could remember, Torrie had wanted to grow up to look like her mother, to be a perfect lady like her mother. Her looks she could do nothing about, but she had tried with every ounce of energy she possessed to become a lady. She had attended finishing schools in New York and Paris, had done the grand tour of Europe, had tried her best to control her fiery nature, but she never seemed to be able to please her mother.

"A lady never raises her voice, a lady never argues," Lillian said, raising her head to look at her daughter down the length of her narrow nose. "I don't know how many times I have to tell you these things."

"Sorry, Mother."

"If you were a beauty, people would overlook such flaws. But you have only your manners to speak for you."

Torrie glanced down to the intricate red rose in the Aubusson carpet below the tip of her shoe, feeling the heat rise in her cheeks.

"Mr. Granger, did you tell her she missed Richard Hayward this afternoon?"

Quinton nodded and turned to glare at his daughter, his eyes the color of polished steel.

"Richard is such a dear young man, and if you aren't careful, you shall chase him away with your hoydenish ways."

Hayward was working on her mother now. Torrie only wished she could chase him so far away she would never have to see the man again.

"Now, both of you put away those sulky looks and get ready for my party. Our guests will be here shortly," Lillian said, flicking open her burgundy silk fan. "I will not be pleased if you are late, Victoria." She lifted the skirt of her heavy burgundy gown and sauntered from the room.

Torrie started to follow her mother, but her father grabbed her arm. "This isn't over," he said, his voice barely above a whisper.

She nodded, realizing the arguments would only get worse, his tactics deadlier, as her father got more and more desperate to get what he wanted.

Torrie stood in front of the cheval glass in her bedroom, fidgeting with her gown, fluffing the cream-colored lace draped at the puffed sleeves, tugging at the bow pinned to the side of her tightly cinched waist as her maid fastened thirty-five silk-clad buttons running down her back. She glanced at the ormolu clock on the mantel and groaned. "Millie, please hurry."

"If you aren't still, miss, I'm not going to be able to fasten these little buggers."

"Sorry," Torrie said, growing stiff.

This was the first time she had worn the gown, and she wondered what flaws her mother might find with her selection. Turquoise silk floated over an underskirt of patterned moire in varying shades of blue and green. She touched the cluster of three small silk roses pinned at the center of the neckline, which fell a few inches below the hollow of her neck. The neckline was well within range of what her mother would deem respectable, she assured herself, remembering the last time she had worn a gown that had not passed her mother's inspection.

"You look lovely, miss," Millie said, smiling at Torrie in the mirror as she fastened the last button.

"Thank you," Torrie said, grabbing her gloves from the vanity before dashing from the room. She lifted her skirts above her ankles and ran down the hall, hoping no one would see her. *A lady didn't run.*

The clock in the hall below was striking the hour as she ran downstairs, the deep chimes marking nine o'clock. Her mother would be furious. Torrie paused in the hall just outside the ballroom, pulling on her elbow-length gloves, gathering her courage.

The ballroom was located on the first floor in the back of the Granger house. The room could hold four hundred people comfortably. Tonight her mother had it filled to overflowing. The doors to the two adjoining salons were open, as were several of the doors leading to the terrace for those guests wanting to escape the music and dancing. Torrie only wished she could escape.

Festoons of smilax fell from the ceiling to the four corners of the room, and draperies of pink silk ribbons adorned the doors and windows. Bouquets of pink roses and white calla lilies in tall gold vases graced the center of the two long refreshment tables against the walls at either end of the room. Pink was the fashion this year. Her mother was always in fashion.

Lillian Granger sat at one end of the big room, surrounded by her court. Torrie glanced at her mother and headed for the opposite end of the room. The music cascading from the second-floor minstrel's gallery churned with laughter and sparkling spirits as Torrie crossed the crowded room, the gaiety heightening her own feeling of gloom.

"Victoria, you are looking lovely tonight," Richard Hayward said, approaching Torrie at the refreshment table.

Torrie's hand clenched around the glass of lemonade she was lifting from a silver tray, the crystal feeling cold and brittle against her gloved fingers. "Mr. Hayward," she said, without looking at the man.

"I enjoyed a pleasant visit with your mother this afternoon."

"You have been busy today," she said, looking up to find him smiling at her in that snide, confident way he had.

"A man has to protect his investments."

"You are pretty sure of yourself, aren't you, Mr. Hayward?"

He ran his forefinger across his mustache as he looked at her, his gaze dipping to her pearl choker. "You might say I have hopes for our upcoming marriage."

"You have hopes for my father's money."

His smile twisted, the corners of his mouth dipping. "A sharp tongue and willful nature aren't attractive in a woman."

"Just think of how difficult it would be to live with such a woman."

"Marriage has a way of taking the sting out of a hornet."

"Not this one."

He stiffened, twin spots of red coloring his pale cheeks as he glared at her. "The stakes are high, Victoria. Don't expect me to fold."

"Maybe you should try another game, Mr. Hayward. I might be holding a better hand than you think."

"We'll see. I'm holding the king and queen of hearts. I doubt you can beat that."

She had to beat him. Somehow.

"Torrie, I've been looking for you," a pretty, dark-haired woman said, emerging from the crowd of people standing to Torrie's right. When she noticed Richard Hayward her smile faded. "Good evening, Mr. Hayward."

"Mrs. Morrison," Hayward said, nodding his head, his neck looking as though it might snap from the movement, a lock of straight blond hair falling over his brow. "Perhaps we can talk tomorrow, Miss Granger."

"I'm busy tomorrow."

"Then perhaps I will have to content myself with another visit to your charming mother." He pivoted on his heel and marched away, dissolving into the crowd.

"What was that all about?" Pam Morrison asked, looking up at her friend, her dark eyes filled with concern.

Torrie set her glass on the refreshment table. "It was about the glorious state of marriage."

"Were you right about him?"

Torrie nodded. "Father and I had another argument, the same one we have had a hundred times this year. But at least now I know the truth about Hayward."

"Come on," Pam said, linking her arm through Torrie's. "I could do with some fresh air."

The cool, damp air bathed Torrie's warm cheeks as they walked out onto the veranda. Fog drifted in from the bay to wind around the twisted oak, eucalyptus, and cypress in the garden, until they seemed to belong to another place and time. The sharp tang of damp wood carried Torrie back to a time of innocence.

"Sometimes when I get all dressed up in one of these fancy ball gowns," Pam said, fluffing a wide sleeve of her yellow satin gown, "I still feel like a little girl playing dress up."

"I was thinking the same thing," she said, smiling at Pam. There was a scar on Torrie's right forefinger, marking the day she and Pam had mingled their blood and had become the sisters neither girl had.

"Remember the time we got into my mother's closet?" Pam asked. "We got dressed in two of her best gowns and served high tea to our dolls."

"Your mother just smiled and told us how pretty we looked."

Pam laughed. "Thank goodness we had the good sense not to get into your mother's closet."

Torrie nodded, remembering how strict her mother had always been. "There were times, when I did something Mother didn't like, she would lock me in my room."

"I remember."

Torrie rested her hands on the wrought-iron balustrade and looked out at the dark trees and bushes rolling away from the house. "On those days, I would stare out at the garden and imagine I was a kidnapped princess, being held in a dismal castle, surrounded by a treacherous forest. In my dream, a handsome knight would fight his way through the thorns, slay all the dragons lurking in the forest, scale the wall, and rescue me."

She glanced down, her white gloves growing taut over her knuckles as her hands tightened on the balustrade. "Do you know what I hate, Pam? I hate knowing my knight is never going to come."

"Torrie, stop acting like an old maid," Pam said, tapping Torrie's shoulder with her fan. "You're still young, still pretty. Maybe you just have to realize all knights have a few chinks in their armor."

Torrie laughed, trying to shake off the feeling of gloom settling around her like a shroud. "You got the last one in shining armor."

Pam smiled and tilted her head. "Yes, well, Ned is pretty wonderful."

"Mine got lost," Torrie said, hiding her pain behind a smile.

Pam shook her head. "Not lost."

No. The truth was, her knight had found her so lacking, he hadn't stayed. "Perhaps you're right. Perhaps a dragon got him." A dragon named Annette.

"Don't talk like that. You don't know, you might meet him tomorrow."

"One thing I do know." Torrie leaned back, stretching her arms taut, her fingers squeezing the railing. "Kings cannot buy knights for their little girls."

"Why is your father being so persistent?" Pam frowned and shook her head. "You've always been his soft spot."

"I'm not sure. I do know he is getting more and more desperate. Hayward is proof of that."

"I know things will work out for you, I just feel it," Pam said, taking Torrie's hand. "You'll see."

"You're trembling," Torrie said, rubbing Pam's thinly gloved hand between hers. "We'd better go back in before you catch your death."

"Are you sure you're ready to face that crush of people?" Pam asked, shivering in the chilly night air.

Torrie nodded. Still, as they walked across the terrace, she wished she could just go to her room, wished she could slip away to the rescue mission and into her disguise as Charlotte, wished she could be almost anywhere but in that room full of people who thought of her as *Lillian's poor spinster daughter*.

"Amy loved the doll you brought yesterday. She wouldn't go to bed without it," Pam said as they entered the ballroom. "You know, Torrie, you spoil her."

"And what are godmothers for?"

"She's now got a collection that rivals . . . Oh my!"

The sudden change in her friend's expression ignited Torrie's curiosity. Pam was staring straight ahead, her lips parted, her eyes wide, as though something shocking had just happened. Torrie followed Pam's stare, her gaze colliding with a face she had hoped never to see again, her senses instantly becoming sharp, focused, captured by the man moving toward her, only that man.

The music, the laughter, the voices swirling around Torrie faded, becoming lost in the echo of her heart throbbing in her ears. Her vision narrowed, as if she stared through a tunnel, as if he commanded the light tumbling from overhead, leaving everything dim except his tall, broad-shouldered figure. Her skin tingled, as though she were caught in an approaching storm. Yet she couldn't move, couldn't escape the destruction sweeping toward her in long, loose-limbed strides.

"Miss Granger," Spencer Kincaid said, reaching for her hand, smiling, his eyes crinkling with amusement and something else, something Torrie couldn't define. "It's a pleasure to see you again."

Torrie stiffened, pressing her arms to her sides to keep from touching him. "What are you doing here?"

"Torrie! Is that any way to greet one of our guests?" Quinton asked, his voice a low growl.

For the first time Torrie noticed her father was standing beside Kincaid. The two men knew each other. Of course, Kincaid had mentioned that this afternoon, she thought, trying to pull together her scattered wits.

Like a hawk snatching its prey, realization sank talons into Torrie's heart. Her father's words swirled in her head: *I can arrange for you to meet others.* Other suitors. Other men low enough to take money to marry a woman they didn't love. So this was the reason Kincaid had met with her father today.

"Miss Granger is just surprised, Quint, that's all," Spence said, breaking the taut silence stretching between father and daughter. He turned toward Pam, shifting attention away from Torrie. "We haven't met."

Torrie clenched her hands into fists as her father introduced Kincaid to Pam. Her friend was fluttering, blushing as though John Drew had just stepped off the stage and into the ballroom. The man certainly had an effect on women.

"How have you been, Torrie?" Allan Thornhill asked, moving from behind Spence to stand at her side.

She hadn't even noticed Allan was standing there, Torrie thought, incensed by the way Kincaid could dominate her attention. "Fine, thank you."

Allan had lived down the street from her for as long as she could remember. He was seven years her senior, but that hadn't kept him from putting a frog down her back when she was six. Although he was tall—just over six feet—he was several inches shorter than Kincaid. Once she had considered his dark good looks attractive. Now, standing next to Kincaid, Allan faded into the wallpaper.

As the thought formed in her mind, Kincaid turned to face her, capturing her eyes, the impact knocking the breath from her lungs. What was wrong with her? The man had her acting like a girl at her first cotillion. No. She was acting like a jittery old maid. Which, unfortunately, was just what she was.

"Would you care to dance, Miss Granger?" Kincaid asked.

Torrie glanced up into his face, so handsome, a fairy-tale prince come to life, flawless in his male beauty, arrogant in his male dominion. No doubt the man thought she would swoon at the chance to dance with him, at the chance to become his wife. "I'm not interested.".

Torrie was sure she heard Pam groan. Her father merely stared at her as though she had escaped Bedlam.

"You're not fond of the mazurka, Miss Granger?" Kincaid asked.

"Of course she is," Quinton said, slapping Kincaid on the shoulder. "She's just a little shy at first. Aren't you, Torrie?"

Torrie met her father's angry stare. "I'm sure Mr. Kincaid can find any number of women who would enjoy being his partner. I suggest he find one if he would like to dance."

"Victoria, I . . ." Quinton began, his tone betraying his anger.

"Perhaps another time," Spence said, smiling down at Torrie, before turning his attention to Pam. "Mrs. Morrison, can I persuade you to dance with me? I promise not to step on your toes."

Pam glanced at Torrie, then smiled up at Kincaid. "I would love to, Mr. Kincaid."

Torrie watched as Pam walked away on Kincaid's arm, hoping Pam wouldn't fall under Kincaid's spell. That kind of man wouldn't care if a woman were married. Allan didn't waste any time before he drifted away, leaving Torrie alone with her father.

"Damn-foolish woman!" Quinton said, taking her arm. His voice barely made a ripple in the music and laughter that flowed in the big ballroom, but his fingers bit into her arm, pinching the muscles above her elbow, sending pointed sparks of pain along her nerves, conveying the anger he held inside.

Torrie tried to maintain her dignity as her father propelled her from the room, turquoise silk billowing in her wake. Quinton cursed under his breath as he dragged her down the corridor and into his study. She stumbled when he released her, flinching at the sound of the door slamming behind her.

Chapter Four

"Do you have any idea how long I've been trying to get Kincaid here?" Quinton shouted. "Years! Dammit, the man would be good for you."

"Did you pay him more than Richard Hayward?"

Quinton halted in front of the black marble hearth, turning to stare at her a moment before he spoke. "What are you talking about?"

"I know you paid Kincaid to take me off your hands."

"You think . . ." Quinton swore sharply. "No one buys Spencer Kincaid. The man owns hotels from New York to California, including the Hampton House here in San Francisco. He has silver in Colorado, gold in California, real estate, shipping, railroads! He could buy and sell me."

Torrie glanced down to the carpet. Perhaps she had been wrong about one little detail, but it didn't change anything. "The man is a scoundrel." At least where women were concerned.

"He's one of the most respected businessmen in the country. And you won't even dance with him."

"I think he will recover from the rejection."

"This man takes a fancy to you, and what do you do!" Quinton said, raising his hands to heaven. "You put on your little Miss Prim and Proper face and chase him away."

"Father, I am not interested in . . ."

"I'm tired Torrie, tired and getting old," he said, sinking to the leather chair behind his desk as though he weighed a thousand pounds. "I want a grandchild."

Longing swelled within her chest, crowding her lungs until she could barely breathe. "Father, if I could, I would give you a grandchild. There's nothing I would rather do."

"Do you know how I feel, knowing you will be alone when I die, knowing I will have left nothing behind after you are gone?" Quinton asked, staring into the flames on the hearth. "I've worked hard, Torrie, and I'm not about to leave this world knowing it will all go to some charity. I won't go the way Frank Carstairs went out."

His words confused her. Frank Carstairs had been one of her father's dearest friends. Last fall he had died suddenly. "What does Mr. Carstairs have to do with this?"

"You know, he was a year younger than me." Quinton pressed his palm on top of his desk. "What was his legacy? A woman who took his money and made some other man rich. No children, no grandchildren, just one greedy woman."

"Father, please try to understand." Her voice was barely above a whisper as she forced the words past the constriction in her throat. "I want to have children. I want to make you happy. But . . . I can't marry a man I don't love."

"Do you know they call you the Ice Princess?" Quinton asked, staring up at his daughter.

She knew. Oh yes, she knew the ugly title they had given her. More than once she had overheard men talking about the Ice Princess, laughing at her. It made her feel ugly, barren.

"My beautiful daughter, turned to ice. Lillian finished you when she sent you to those finishing schools, finished you with her twisted sense of morality." He paused a moment, staring at her as though she were a stranger. "You are carved from ice."

Torrie pressed a trembling hand to her lips. She wished she *were* made of ice, wished she couldn't feel the pain, the humiliation she was feeling right now. "Father, please don't say such things."

"Maybe your mother is right. Maybe I do spoil you." Quinton stared down at his hand, flexing his fingers against the wood. "She keeps telling me it's my fault you haven't been forced into marrying someone. Hurts her pride to have a spinster for a daughter."

"Please don't do something we'll both regret."

"I've never asked for anything, except this."

"I can't," she whispered.

"I'll give you until your birthday," he said, his deep voice holding a strident tone of finality. "Two months to find a husband. If you don't by that time, I'll consider myself without a daughter. You will leave this house, this city, and be left with only enough money to feed and clothe yourself."

Could he just abandon her? Would he never want to see her again? "You can't buy me," she said, pride forcing her back to go rigid.

"Oh, I know. You can do without my money," he

said, lifting a cigar from the rosewood humidor on his desk. After rolling the firm brown leaves between his fingers, he lit it, taking a deep drag, releasing a pungent cloud of blue-gray smoke.

Memories tugged at her heart. As a little girl she had often crawled up into her father's lap and helped him light his fragrant cigars. Yet the warmth of those memories vanished under his cold stare. This was not the face of her beloved father. This was the face many a man had met, the face of a man who would win at any price.

"Think, Torrie, think of all those poor souls who will go without because of your selfishness." He slipped the cigar from his lips and stared at the smoldering tip. "The women at the rescue mission, the children you are trying to save from a life on the streets. How will you support them without my money?"

His words hit her, a near physical blow that sent her reeling back a step.

"Why, some of the girls will probably return to their old ways, just to feed and clothe themselves." He took another long drag and exhaled, blue-gray smoke rising, gathering to form a wall between them. "It's a pity you can't convince your mother's friends to support your little charity, but your soiled doves are too dirty for their dainty hands, aren't they?"

Smoke engulfed her, singeing her nose, spreading an acrid taste across her tongue. "They contribute," she said, fighting to keep the tremble from her voice.

"Oh," Quinton said, flicking ash into a crystal tray. "And how long could the mission continue without my money?"

Torrie didn't answer; she couldn't, her voice was lost in the tight grip of her emotions.

"You always did have an expressive face, Torrie," Quinton said, with the confidence of a man who knows he has won. "The fact is, your girls are dirty linen to the other good ladies of this town. Without my money, the mission will go under in a year."

"Father, we are talking about slavery," Torrie said, leaning her hands on his desk. "People who thrive on pain, who think because a young woman is poor, or naive, or unprotected, she is fair game for their sick perversions."

Quinton leaned back and smiled at his daughter. "And you want to save the poor innocent girls from a life of debauchery."

"I want to give them a choice!"

"Then I suggest you make a choice, girl," Quinton said, his voice expressionless. "Choose a husband, give me a grandchild, or desert your cause."

She straightened and stared down at him. "Sell myself?"

"Or abandon your little angels."

Her father had the reputation of being a ruthless businessman, and she knew he meant everything he said. She felt like screaming, like crying, like being held and told everything would be all right. Only there was no one to hold her, and everything would not be all right. The one person she had counted on her entire life had just turned his back on her; betrayed again by a man she loved.

"How many of the women you know are in love with their husbands?" he asked, jabbing at the crystal ashtray with the tip of his cigar. "Love is for fairy tales. It's time you woke up from your dream."

Torrie turned to the windows. Her face was reflected in the glass; beyond her reflection stretched darkness. She knew there was no argument to change his mind, knew she was on the verge of tears, knew she would die before she let him see how much he had hurt her.

"Dammit Torrie! This is for your own good."

Marriage. Slavery. They were one in the same. She pulled a mantle of cool indifference around her and turned to leave her father's study. At the sound of his voice she paused, her hand on the brass door handle.

"Remember, Torrie, you have two months. Use them wisely."

Spence glanced around the ballroom, but Victoria and Quinton hadn't returned. He didn't like the way Quinton had dragged his daughter from the room, didn't like to think he had been the cause of Quinton's anger.

After checking the adjoining salons for Victoria, he headed for the terrace. He needed some air, needed to escape the crush of people, needed to make sure Victoria wasn't hiding in the shadows. The terrace was deserted.

Music from the ballroom drifted through the open terrace doors, spilling into the gardens beyond, swirling around the bushes and trees, mingling with wispy fingers of fog. It reminded him of a place he had read about as a young boy, an enchanted forest where knights in shining armor defeated dragons and rescued ladies fair. He wondered if Victoria Granger needed rescuing.

Spence turned, hearing heels rap against the stone terrace, half expecting to see Victoria, seeing instead a dark-haired maid. She sauntered toward him, swinging her full hips, thrusting out her plump bosom.

"Can I get you anything?" she asked, offering Spence the glasses of champagne on the silver tray she was holding.

"Thanks," he said, lifting a glass of champagne.

She took a step closer, jasmine assaulting his nostrils. He took a step back.

"Is there anything else I might be able to do for you?" she asked, smiling up at him, an invitation in her dark eyes. His gaze followed her fingers as they slid over her full bosom, her breasts straining against the modest white cotton of her shirtwaist. "Anything at all?"

At the moment he was too preoccupied with another woman to consider the invitation. "Maybe another time," Spence said, his smile softening his rejection.

"This is where you've been hiding," Allan said, stepping onto the terrace.

The maid glanced over her shoulder, then looked up at Spence. "My name is Ella," she said, pulling a folded piece of paper from her bodice. She slipped the paper into his silver waistcoat and brushed her fingers upward along his cheek. "If you change your mind, you know where I'll be."

"You always did have a way with women," Allan said, watching Ella walk away, her full hips swinging like a pendulum.

"Not all women," Spence said, glancing at the note before slipping it into his coat pocket.

Allan chuckled and slapped his friend across his shoulders. "Still a little tender from your brush with the Ice Princess?"

"Ice Princess?"

"That's what we call Victoria Granger," Allan said, pulling a gold case from his inside coat pocket. He lifted the lid and withdrew a cigar as he continued. "All of us who have tried and failed to melt the ice. With one wintry glance she can freeze a man's heart."

Spence shook his head as Allan offered him a cigar. He drew his finger down his glass, clearing a path in the moisture that had collected from the cold wine. There was fire beneath the icy facade of Miss Victoria Granger, he would bet his life on it. "I'll just have to see if I have better luck with a waltz."

"A waltz! In this house?" Allan shook his head and looked at Spence as though he had lost his mind.

Business was the main reason Spence visited the city. He seldom attended parties, and had never really paid attention to the dances at the few he had attended.

"Lillian Granger once said she would rather see her daughter dead than be dragged around some room, molested in the guise of a dance." Allan held a match to the end of his cigar and puffed until it came to life. "My friend, you will not find a waltz in this house, or in any of the other houses of the good ladies in Mrs. Granger's sanctimonious set."

A woman who thought the waltz was indecent had to have a strong effect on her daughter, one Spence suspected he wouldn't like. "Have you known Victoria Granger for very long?"

"I knew Torrie when she was a scrawny little girl with pigtails. She could ride a horse or climb a tree with the best of us. When Quinton realized he wasn't going to have a son, he raised Torrie to be one."

Allan chuckled to himself. "Of course, Lillian Granger had other ideas. My most vivid memory of Lillian is her marching Torrie into the house to practice piano every afternoon at three. She sent her away to finishing school when Torrie was sixteen. When she got back, Torrie could drop a man with one glance."

"I'm surprised she never married." At Allan's wide grin, Spence continued. "Some men are bound to find Quinton's money attractive, even if the lady does come with it."

"She almost got married." Allan continued at his friend's inquisitive look. "A few years ago she was engaged to marry Charles Rutledge. But old Charles eloped with Annette Marshal on the day of the wedding. Annette also happened to be one of Torrie's friends. Charles left our beauty with a house full of guests and wedding cake."

Spence released his breath in a long sigh. Well, that explained some things. A woman could develop a bitter streak a mile wide after something like that happened. He wondered if she were still carrying a torch for this Rutledge.

"I'll tell you one thing, the lady has courage. She's the one who faced the crowd of us gathered for the wedding in the ballroom. She stood in her white gown, with her little chin held high as she told us she was terribly sorry for the inconvenience, but the wedding wasn't going to take place."

His hand tightened on his glass as Spence thought of the humiliation that proud young woman had suffered. For some curious reason he was filled with a powerful surge of protectiveness whenever he thought about her. If Charles Rutledge were here tonight, Spence would have to fight the urge to plant a fist in the middle of the man's face.

"Since then, Torrie has turned down every single man in San Francisco, including me." Allan pulled his cigar out of his mouth and removed a small piece of tobacco from his tongue. "For a while it became a rite of passage, a game to see who could get the Ice Princess to the altar. Some men were even placing bets on who would win the lady's hand. She sure was angry when she found out about it."

"You're telling me someone told her half the men in town were betting to see who could marry her?"

Allan nodded. "Quinton caught wind of it. He was proud and thought Torrie would be pleased. She wasn't. She stopped seeing everyone, including me. That was four years ago."

Spence glanced at Allan and wondered if his friend had taken it all as lightly as he sounded.

"Don't worry, old chum, I'm over my madness." Allan clamped the cigar between his teeth. "In fact, I'm happy the lady was smart enough to turn me down. I would make a lousy husband."

Spence frowned and stared across the gardens rolling out from the Granger estate. He didn't like to think of Victoria Granger wasting herself over any idiot who had let what was in his pants dictate the course of his life.

"She really got to you, didn't she?" Allan asked, sounding more than a little amused.

"She's not my type." Spence glanced at his friend, a frown digging into his brow. "I've always preferred my women warm and soft. The only thing a man can get by snuggling up to that woman is frostbite."

"She's a challenge, all right." Allan smiled in a way that let Spence know he didn't believe a word he was saying.

"She's like a wild rose, pretty, but if you try to touch her, you're going to get a handful of thorns."

So why had the image of Victoria Granger haunted him all day, Spence wondered? More than once he had found himself thinking about her, imagining her hair spilled across his pillow, wondering if her silvery eyes were different when filled with passion. "She's as skinny and dry as a willow in a drought. If she ever tried to bend, she'd snap in two."

"She's no Lillian Russell, that's for sure," Allan said, shifting his cigar to the other side of his mouth, grinning at Spence. "But she is round in the right places."

"Her idea of having a good time is reading sonnets on a Saturday night. Anything masculine puts the fear of God into her." Still, there was something about Victoria Granger, something that made Spence want to strip away her prim mask of respectability, something that made him want to bury his face in her fragrant hair, taste her smooth white skin, toss her on her lovely backside and teach her all the pleasures that can be found between a man and a woman. He felt his muscles tighten, felt his blood surge, pumping in a painful rhythm deep in his groin.

Allan slapped Spence across the back, laughing, his cigar bobbing between his teeth. "Welcome to the club!"

"Thanks," Spence said, his voice revealing his feelings about the dubious honor. For some unholy reason, he had the awful suspicion he was destined to be with that little wildcat.

"You always did love a challenge," Allan said, shaking his head. "And, from the way she acted tonight, you've got your work cut out for you."

"I'm not sure if . . ." From the shadows at one corner of the terrace a figure emerged, skimming the ground like a swan on a smooth lake, pale turquoise silk floating around the slender figure of Victoria Granger.

"What do you suppose she's doing?"

"I don't know," Spence said, handing Allan his glass. "But I'm going to find out."

Spence vaulted over the balustrade and followed Victoria down a winding gravel path and through the wrought-iron gate at the back of the garden. He caught her on the street, a few feet from her father's property. She turned at the sound of his footsteps, her lovely face pulling into a frown when she recognized him.

"Did anyone ever tell you it isn't safe for a pretty woman to be prowling the streets alone at night?"

"She might be accosted by a scoundrel?" she asked, glaring at him.

"She might."

"Please go away," she said, walking away from him.

He followed her. "A man would be a scoundrel to leave a woman unprotected."

She tossed him a chilly glance and increased her pace, hugging her arms to her waist, shivering in the damp air.

He shrugged out of his coat and slipped it around her shoulders. "Do you want to talk about it?"

"I don't need your coat, or your company," she said, snatching his coat from her shoulders.

He grinned. "Afraid you've got both."

She mumbled something under her breath, and tossed his coat at his head.

Spence caught his coat and jogged a few steps to catch her. "Are you always this stubborn?"

"Me?" Her eyes caught the flickering lamplight, making them shine like polished silver. "You are the one who won't go away."

"Who says we don't have anything in common," he said, dropping his coat over her shoulders.

Her breath escaped in a hiss between her teeth. "Fine," she mumbled as she turned and once again resumed her steady march down the sloping street, mist swirling around her.

Gaslights flickering behind the grimy glass of the street lamps created grayish islands of light in the thickening fog. Their footsteps echoed against the buildings, and somewhere lost in the fog behind them a carriage rattled against the cobblestones.

Spence glanced at the girl who marched beside him, admiring the curve of her cheek, the rise and fall of her long lashes. "Are we going anywhere in particular?"

She came to an abrupt halt. "Mr. Kincaid, can't you see I do not want your company?"

"I can see you're upset. The way I figure it, Quint tanned your hide for not dancing with me. Right?"

"Just what do you know about it?"

There was something more, he could see it in her eyes, a haunting despair that touched his heart. She looked so young, so beautiful, so heartbreakingly vulnerable. He had to fight the urge to take her in his arms.

"I've known your father nearly three years. Every time I've been in San Francisco he's done his best to get me to your house to meet you. I have to confess, I thought you were probably some cross-eyed, spindly-legged little rabbit."

He brushed his fingers across her cheek, her skin chilled marble beneath his touch. She flinched as though he had slapped her. This wasn't going to be easy. "If I'd known you were so pretty, I would have been here years ago."

"I thought I made it clear this afternoon what I think of you, Mr. Kincaid."

Spence didn't consider himself an expert with women. He doubted any man was truly an expert where women were concerned. Yet he knew desire when he saw it in a woman's eyes. From the first moment Victoria Granger had tumbled into his arms, he had sensed a fierce attraction between them. Something primal simmered in the air, clutched at his vitals when she was near. And she wasn't immune. He could see it in her eyes, and at the same time he could see she was frightened of that attraction, frightened and confused.

"Sometimes it pays to take a second look, Miss Granger," he said, resting his hands on her shoulders, drawing her near. He wanted to hold her, protect her, slay all of her dragons.

Torrie twisted free of his grasp. "I've known men like you. I grew up with one. You are as arrogant and stubborn as a bull. You charge through this world pushing aside anything that gets in your way. You don't care about other people. You don't care about what they may want, their hopes, their dreams. You only care about one person. You!"

Spence studied her a moment, trying to see past the pain in her eyes, trying to understand her. "Do you always make snap judgments about people?"

"Some people we know the moment we meet them," she said, turning to leave.

He grabbed her arm. "What are you afraid of, Miss Granger?"

Her chin soared. "Certainly not you."

"Good. Because I don't want you to be afraid of me."

A carriage rumbled past them and slipped into the fog, disappearing except for the steady rattle of wheels against cobblestones. The noise seemed to come from all directions until it died suddenly.

"Go away," she said, twisting her arm, trying to break free. "Just go away and leave me alone."

Through the wool of his coat, her arm felt small and delicate in his grasp. He knew if he didn't release her, he would hurt her. "Would you leave me stranded in the fog?" he asked, dropping his hand. "It's getting worse. Why, I might wander for days without finding my way home."

She took a step back, staring at him a moment, biting her lower lip when it started to curve upward. "I suppose you are just a poor babe in the woods," she said, resuming her pace.

"In need of protection," he said, following her, a cool mist brushing his face, bathing his senses with the salty tang of the sea.

A carriage was parked beside the sidewalk near a

street lamp a short distance in front of them, gray tendrils of fog curving around the wheels and up the sides. A man stepped out of the carriage as Spence and Torrie approached, short and broad, lumbering like a bear. Spence felt the tiny hairs on the back of his neck rise as the man drew near. He moved closer to the girl who walked beside him, sensing a need to shield her.

"We've been waiting for you all night, Mr. Kincaid," the man said.

The man wore a slouch hat pulled low over his face, obscuring his features. "Miss Granger, I think you better get out of here," Spence whispered, before turning to face the man.

Torrie started to run, freezing as the man spoke.

"Stay where you are, miss," the short man said, his voice low and menacing.

She turned and faced the man, her eyes growing wide as she saw the pistol in his hand. "My word," she whispered.

"What do you want?" Spence asked, stepping so he was between Torrie and the gun. He felt her hand touch his back, her slender fingers curling against the white linen of his shirt. He wished he could take her into his arms, tell her all would be well, but he was having his own doubts.

"We just want you to take a little ride with us." The burly man gestured toward the carriage with the pistol as he spoke. "Do a little visiting."

"Let the girl go," Spence said, his voice bearing a strong note of command.

The short man shook his head. "Now get in, both of you."

Spence took a step forward, then lashed out with his foot, catching the man's hand and sending the pistol flying through the air.

"Run, Torrie!" Spence yelled, lunging forward. He

brought his right fist up under the man's chin before the pistol hit the ground. The big man slammed into the back of the carriage, grunting and cursing, grabbing his jaw.

"Behind you!" Torrie screamed.

Before Spence could turn, hands grabbed his arms, hands the size of hams and as strong as iron. Cursing loudly, the first man came hurtling at him. Spence reared back against the huge man behind him, planting both feet in the smaller man's chest, sending him sprawling to the ground, a loud groan marking his descent.

"Why you . . ." A deep voice vibrated next to Spence's ear.

Spence slammed his foot back, catching his captor in the knee. A loud snap, an ear-shattering cry, and the giant went down, taking Spence with him. Spence rolled and came to his feet, facing his first opponent. The man shifted his arm. A gun barrel flashed in the gaslight, the muzzle directed at his chest. A sharp metallic click slammed against his ears. One thought registered in Spence's mind: He was a dead man.

"Look out!"

Spence heard Torrie's warning, felt her slam into his side a heartbeat before the loud bark of the pistol shattered the air. His heart stopped as a shriek of pain ripped from her lips. Pain shot through his shoulder and hip as he hit the granite sidewalk, Torrie falling across him, pinning him to the ground.

"Why'd you do that?"

"He would've killed us!"

"The boss lady ain't gonna like this."

"Hell, Slattery's the one who ain't gonna like this."

Frantic voices overlapped, spun around in the fog as Spence shifted Torrie's dead weight. He came to a sitting position, cradling her in his arms.

"My leg! The bastard broke my leg!"

"We got to get out of here!" a man shouted. "That gunshot's going to bring somebody running. Help me with him."

Torrie's eyes were closed, her lips parted. In the dim light of the street lamp Spence could see the dark stain of blood spreading across her bodice from a gash under her right breast. "Torrie!"

A soft moan was her only reply. He lowered her to the ground and sprang to his feet, ready to kill with his bare hands, but the carriage was already vanishing into the fog. Cursing, he returned to the woman who lay bleeding on the ground.

"Are they gone?" she whispered.

"Don't try to talk," he said, brushing a wayward curl from her cheek. Her blood flowed warm and thick across his hand as he pressed his palm to the wound, trying to quell the bleeding.

"What are you doing?" she asked, slapping at his hands as he pulled up her gown.

"We've got to bind the wound, and I don't have anything else to use," he said, pressing her back against the ground. She was pale, her skin moist and cool against his palm as he cupped her cheek. "Damn! Why the hell did you jump in front of me?"

"You're welcome," she said, her long lashes brushing the crests of her cheeks. "I'm fine, Mr. Kincaid. It's nothing more than a scratch. I just had the breath knocked out of me."

His hands paused, holding her petticoat, the linen warm from her skin. "I sure as hell hope you're right."

"I would appreciate it if you would not use such foul language, Mr. Kincaid."

Spence couldn't help but smile. "Take long, slow breaths," he said, as he rolled a strip of cloth into a thick pad. People died if they lost too much blood. The realization sent a bolt of dread through him. He should be the one bleeding, not her. He pressed the pad to the wound and wrapped another piece of linen around her, a soft moan slipping from her lips to rip at his heart as he bound her wound. "It has to be tight."

"It is."

He lifted his coat from the ground a few feet away, and wrapped it around her. "You're going to be all right," he said, lifting her in his arms, hoping he sounded more confident than he felt.

"There is a doctor at the party. I'm sure he will be able to put your fears to rest."

Her blood was drying on his hand, and she was trying to reassure him. She sure was quite a lady. He just prayed she hadn't sacrificed her own life while saving his.

Chapter Five

"How is everything going in here?" Quinton asked, poking his head inside Torrie's bedroom.

"We're done," Dr. Wallace said, rinsing his hands in the basin on the bedside table.

Quinton came into the room, closing the door behind him. "Are you all right, baby?" he asked, cupping Torrie's cheek in his big hand.

"Father, I'm fine. It's just a scratch."

Quinton looked to Dr. Wallace for reassurance. "Joe?"

"She's lost some blood, but there's little damage done," Dr. Wallace said, rolling down his sleeves. He smiled down at Torrie. "You should be back on your feet in a few days, but take it easy. No strenuous activities."

She smiled, knowing exactly what he meant. Charlotte would have to rest a few days. "Thank you, doctor."

"You take care, young lady," Dr. Wallace said, giving her hand a squeeze before leaving her alone with her father.

"Dammit, Torrie!" Quinton shouted. "What were you doing roaming the streets at night?"

She closed her eyes and tried to figure out how to breathe without moving her side. "As I recall, it had something to do with an ultimatum."

"Don't try to put this on my back, young lady. You should have more sense than to run around the streets unprotected."

Torrie lifted innocent eyes to her father. "I had a protector."

Quinton shook his head. "Don't be sarcastic with me, girl. Kincaid wouldn't have been attacked if he hadn't been chasing you. Have you thought of that?"

She was having trouble thinking about anything except the hot coals pressed to her side.

"And don't think this little scare is going to change my mind," Quinton said, pacing back and forth beside the bed. "It only makes me more sure of my decision. I could have lost you, and with you . . ."

"Your chance for immortality," Torrie said, smiling up at him, hurt and anger rising inside her.

His back went rigid. "A man has a right to want to leave something behind."

She held him in a steady gaze. "A woman has a right to live her life as she chooses."

"Damn!" Quinton said, turning. He walked to the windows and took two handfuls of blue brocade. Brass scraped against brass as he threw open the drapes, allowing fog-tinged moonlight to enter the room.

For a long time he was quiet, staring out into the gardens. Torrie watched him, sensing the battle waging inside him, praying he might relent.

"Why do you have to fight me on this?" Quinton asked, his deep voice filled with pain. "You can't want to live your life alone."

"What kind of life would I have married to a man I don't love?" she asked, trying desperately to make him understand. "Can't you see, I don't want to be forced into marriage, forced to live with a man I don't love."

"Love." He spun on his heel and faced her. "Torrie, we don't all find love in this life."

Torrie stared at the blue roses rising in twisted columns in the white silk covering the wall behind her father. And sometimes, love is taken away when you do find it, she thought.

"Look, I don't care if you marry Hayward," Quinton said, returning to her side. "Pick someone. You like Kincaid."

She wasn't sure how she felt about Kincaid. It was far too disturbing to probe the emotions he evoked inside her. "Father, I just met the man."

"You threw yourself in front of a bullet to save his life. People don't usually do that for people they don't like."

"I acted out of instinct." Torrie felt heat rise in her cheeks. "And what makes you think he would want to marry me?"

"Why the hell wouldn't he? You're a beautiful woman, a bit headstrong, I'll admit. But you'd make him a grand wife."

Somehow she doubted Kincaid was looking for a wife. No doubt that man had hundreds, thousands of women tossing themselves at his feet. Why would he even think about marrying a woman past her prime?

"You know, he's feeling pretty bad about what happened." Quinton stroked his mustache as he spoke, watching her closely. "He figures you took that bullet instead of him. I expect he's feeling pretty beholden to you."

A sharp pain ripped through her side as her muscles tensed. "And you expect me to take advantage of the man?"

"Do as you please." Quinton straightened, his lips disappearing into his mustache as he glared down at her. "Just remember, you have two months."

It was seared into her memory. She closed her eyes and wished this was all some horrible nightmare, but the pain in her side reminded her it was all too real.

"Kincaid is waiting to see you. Right now he's downstairs suffering your mother's company."

She lifted a hand to her hair and wondered if she looked half as bad as she felt.

"You look fine, Torrie," he said, his voice softening. "I think seeing you would put his mind at ease."

But seeing Kincaid never put her at ease. Still, she didn't want him to think she was lying here half dead. "Please hand me my brush and my blue, no, turquoise bed jacket."

A smirk tugged at Quinton's lips as he retrieved the brush from her vanity and her bed jacket from the closet. After helping her into the bed jacket he left her alone.

She dragged the brush through her hair trying to tame the mass of chestnut waves, each movement of her right hand bringing fresh waves of pain rolling across her side. By the time a knock sounded on her door, her hair lay in a neat braid over her shoulder.

"Come in," she said, shoving the brush under the covers.

The door opened and Spence Kincaid filled the

threshold, hair tousled as if he had used his fingers as a comb, evening coat rumpled and stained, and looking handsome enough to add several beats to her already racing pulse. His golden gaze glided over her, warming her like the sun, bringing heat to her cheeks.

"Now they told me there was a sick lady in here," he said, moving toward her. "I didn't expect to see a pretty woman with rose blossoms in her cheeks."

Her cheeks grew warmer under his praise. "Are you feeling better, Mr. Kincaid?"

A crooked grin curved his lips, a deep dimple slashing his right cheek. "I'm feeling much better now that I know a certain young woman is going to be all right."

Torrie glanced down at her hands. "I told you it was only a scratch."

"So you did." He sat beside her on the bed and took her hand, his long fingers wrapping warmly around her skin. "How are you feeling?"

The man had no sense of propriety, but at the moment she had no will to chastise him; his big hand felt far too good wrapped around hers. "I'm fine. It's nothing. I suffered more from fright than from the bullet."

He glanced down to her hand, his thumb sliding back and forth across her slender fingers. "Miss Granger, that bullet probably would have killed me if you hadn't pushed me aside."

The friction of skin against skin kindled a delicious warmth in her blood. The man was far too disarming, she thought, looking up into his glorious eyes. "You shouldn't have followed me."

"Well, Miss Granger, you might find this hard to believe, but I was hoping to keep you out of trouble."

"You failed miserably," she said, feeling a smile tug at her mouth.

He laughed and lifted her hand to his lips. For an eternity, he held her in his gaze, tracing every curve of her face with his eyes, as though she were the most precious gem in the world. Under that warm gaze, she had trouble drawing a breath.

"I'm in your debt. If there is anything I can do to repay you, just let me know."

"I just reacted, that's all. You don't owe me anything."

"You have great instincts," he said, grinning down at her. "And, even if you don't want to take responsibility for it, I owe you my life."

She wished he would stop talking that way. Her need was too great, the temptation too strong. A child. How many nights had she dreamed of having a child of her own to hold, a child to take care of, a child to love?

"Are you all right?"

She swallowed hard, pushing back the pitiful words crawling up her throat. "Yes," she said, pulling her hand from his grasp. "I'm fine. It really was only a scratch. The doctor said I will be fine in a few days. Please, don't make it any more than it is."

"Are you sure you're all right?" he asked, brushing his fingertips down the curve of her cheek.

His touch was so warm, so tender. She remembered the way he had held her, his arms strong, protective. If only . . .no, she couldn't allow herself the luxury of dreams. "Yes, I'm sure." Unable to hold his gaze, she stared at the embroidered lace on the sheet folded across her lap. "Do you have any idea who was behind the attack? It seemed as though they might have been following you."

"I thought so too. Do you remember hearing them mention the 'boss lady'?"

Torrie shook her head. "I don't remember much after I was shot."

"Well, I have a feeling they were talking about Miss Olivia Fontaine." His lips curved into a crooked grin. "We didn't part on the best of terms."

Olivia Fontaine was the worst kind of person, the kind who could sell her fellow human beings into slavery, the kind who could kill without a second thought. "You'd better watch your back. Olivia Fontaine doesn't fight fair."

"I'll remember that next time."

It was inevitable that there would be a next time, Torrie thought, anxiety twisting her stomach into knots. She hated to think something horrible might happen to this man. He was special, in ways she didn't want to think about, in ways that haunted her despite her attempts to put him out of her mind.

"I better let you get some rest," Spence said, taking her hand. "If there is anything you need, please let me know. I like to repay my debts."

"Please don't mention it again."

"All right." He pressed his lips to the back of her hand, his breath warm and moist against her skin. "As long as you keep it in mind."

Keeping it in mind wasn't the problem. She watched him leave, admiring his long, lithe stride. A wayward part of her wondered what price he was really willing to pay. With a silent oath, she pushed the thought from her mind. She would get out of this mess without the help of Spencer Kincaid, or any other man.

Her side pinched as she turned down the lamp on the table by her bed and sought some peace. Tomorrow she would need a clear head to chart a course out of her father's web.

As sleep wrapped warm arms around her, Kincaid invaded her dreams. She was standing on a white sand beach, looking out across turquoise water, when she saw him. Like a prince from an underwater realm, he rose from the shimmering waves. Water dripped from his dark hair, slipped along the smooth curves of his shoulders, streamed in tiny rivulets down his broad chest, black curls glistening in the sun.

Torrie stood frozen at the water's edge, staring, unable to look away from the man wading through the water, moving toward her with each long stride.

Sunlight surrounded him, bathing his naked skin in a golden glow. He reached out to her, a red rose in his hand, a roguish grin tilting his lips. *Come to me,* he said, his deep voice little more than a sigh. *Let me show you my secrets. Let me hold you.*

She shook her head and said she couldn't, but her body moved toward him of its own will. He waved the rose, and her nightgown slipped from her shoulders, leaving her naked and vulnerable before him. Taking a step back, she crossed her arms in front of her naked breasts and told him this was wrong.

Nothing is wrong between us, he said. *Don't you see, I'm the one. I've always been the one.*

Her naked skin grew warm under the heat of his gaze. She stared at the broad expanse of his chest, thick muscles shaded with black curls, golden skin glowing in the sun. She wanted to touch him, to feel the warmth of his skin. Her gaze lowered, following the black curls that narrowed across his belly and widened again to form a nest for that forbidden, frightening, yet oh so intriguing part of him.

He lifted the rose to her cheek, brushed the velvety petals against her skin. *Come to me,* he whispered.

She lifted her hand to the rose, the petals soft against her palm. As she took it, a thorn bit into her finger, bringing her awake with a gasp.

Torrie stared into the dark canopy over her bed, a pulse throbbing low in her belly, her breath coming in uneven gasps. What was happening to her? She

pressed trembling fingers to her lips, her cheeks
growing hot with shame. Never in her life had she
felt this way, all twisted and restless. Kincaid made
her feel things no lady should ever feel.

For a long time she lay staring into the darkness,
afraid of what waited for her in the misty realm of
her dreams.

Torrie glanced from the volume of *Pride and Preju-
dice* she was reading to the roses perched on the
round walnut table beside the sofa. Sunlight filtered
through the lace curtains at the wide bay window
behind her to warm the two dozen blood-red blooms
until their fragrance filled the air of her sitting room.

"Roses for a Wild Rose," she whispered, leaning
back against the blue silk damask covering the sofa,
repeating the words of the note that had accom-
panied the flowers. Just what had Mr. Kincaid meant
by calling her a wild rose? she wondered.

Glancing from the blossoms, she forced her gaze
to lower to the printed page. She shouldn't be thinking of that man. Hadn't he caused her enough trouble? She was still tender from the lecture her mother
had given her first thing this morning.

Lillian had been furious that Torrie had left the
party, aghast at the trouble she had caused by being
shot. The roses had arrived during her mother's lecture, and Torrie learned that on top of her other
crimes, no respectable lady received red roses from
a gentleman.

Red roses had always been Torrie's favorite, but
the beautiful blossoms and the note had only added
fuel to her mother's inflamed emotions. Still, Torrie
hadn't been able to throw the blossoms away as her
mother had requested. They were too beautiful to
waste.

She lowered her book as her mother entered the

room. Lillian cast a disparaging glance at the roses rising from the cut crystal vase, then glared at her daughter. "Victoria, there is a police officer here to see you," she said, clipping each word as though she could barely bring herself to speak them.

Torrie glanced past her mother to the tall man standing just inside the door. He was slender, his cheekbones sharply defined, his nose thin and straight. His thick, straight hair looked black at first, but as he moved toward her into the sunlight, she realized it was dark brown, almost as dark as Kincaid's.

As he drew near, his dark gaze raked her from her head to her toes. Unconsciously Torrie lifted a hand to her starched white collar, making sure the buttons of her shirtwaist were all still fastened. He noticed the gesture and smiled, a slight twisting of his full lips.

"Miss Granger," he said, offering his hand. "I'm Police Inspector John Samuels."

Torrie took his proffered hand and tried not to feel intimidated. For some reason she thought that was what he wanted her to feel. He took a seat on the wing-backed chair across from her, his black clothes stark against the pale blue damask. As he began asking her questions concerning the previous evening, it became apparent he had already spoken to Mr. Kincaid. Torrie got the impression the police inspector wanted to make sure their accounts of the evening matched.

"Do you think you could identify the men if you saw them again, Miss Granger?" Samuels asked, crossing his long legs, looking at her with those dark, unreadable eyes.

"I'm not sure," Torrie said, forcing herself to hold his piercing gaze. "It was dark and everything happened so quickly. As I've told you, one of the men was huge, and I believe Mr. Kincaid broke his leg."

Samuels nodded and scribbled something in the black notebook he held. He glanced up at her, smiled, and continued asking her questions he had already asked her once before. Torrie was sure he was trying to see if she would change her story. The thought made it very difficult to hold her temper, especially when her mother was sitting on the chair across from her, looking at her as though Torrie had just committed an ax murder.

Lillian sat motionless several moments after the inspector left. Torrie felt her mother's displeasure, felt it surround her, coiling, constricting, draining the life from her.

"Well, I hope you realize your reputation is in shreds," Lillian said, staring at the roses behind Torrie.

"My reputation?"

"Such promiscuity is not tolerated in this town, young woman. You should know, Elizabeth Farnsworth and Margaret Salisbury, as well as several other ladies, were here earlier. I told them you were too fatigued to receive visitors."

Lillian stood, pacing the length of the room before turning to face her daughter. "Your behavior last night was not overlooked by our guests. It seems they couldn't understand why a young woman would be out alone with a man."

"I didn't invite Mr. Kincaid to . . ."

"And now the police in my home, asking all sorts of sordid questions. Half the population of this city is already talking about how you are carrying on with Mr. Kincaid."

"They couldn't really think such things of me."

"Elizabeth and Margaret saw the roses being delivered this morning." Lillian stared at her daughter.

"Elizabeth was so kind to mention that Sarah Bernhardt will accept only red roses from her lovers. Of course you realize the conclusion they have drawn from all of this."

"They have known me all my life." Torrie hesitated, the full impact of her mother's words hitting her, setting the room whirling. "How could they believe I would do something so . . . so . . . I am certainly not carrying on with Mr. Kincaid, or anyone."

"I don't know what you expect, running around town with a young man, a man that indecently handsome." She shook her head. "Mr. Hayward was not pleased about all of this."

Torrie glanced down at her hands, twisting the sapphire and diamond ring she wore on the right one. "I wasn't aware I needed to worry about what Richard Hayward might think."

"Well, you better start worrying, my girl," Lillian said. "You mustn't deceive yourself into believing a man like Spencer Kincaid would ever fall in love with you."

Torrie shrank a little farther into the sofa.

Lillian studied her daughter a moment, staring at her down the length of her nose. "Mr. Hayward said you were quite rude to him at the party."

So Hayward had gone running to her mother. "I hadn't realized I was being rude."

"You mustn't lose Mr. Hayward while chasing after a dream." Lillian spoke as though she were addressing a wayward child. "Mr. Kincaid might be more handsome, and he may be charming, but Mr. Hayward is interested in making you his bride."

"He told you that?"

"You know, Victoria, I had given up hope of you ever marrying."

Torrie clenched her hands together in her lap. "I didn't realize."

"Well, you aren't exactly a young girl any longer," Lillian said, taking a seat beside her daughter on the sofa. "And you were never a beauty."

The bright rays of the sun pouring in through the windows behind her couldn't touch the cold dread curling at the base of Torrie's spine. She didn't want to be here, listening to this. It seemed she had spent half her life being lectured.

"I thought we would have the wedding in July. That should give us ample time to plan."

"The wedding?" Torrie stared at her mother.

"Yes, dear. Your wedding." Torrie just stared at her, and Lillian shook her head. "Your wedding to Mr. Hayward."

"But I haven't agreed to marry Richard Hayward!" Torrie said, panic rising in her like a great hawk taking flight. Hearing her mother talk about planning this wedding made it all too real.

"Yes," Lillian said, a frown marring her smooth brow. "I know. But you will. He has agreed to overlook last night."

The tiny hairs on the back of her neck prickled as Torrie looked into her mother's dark blue eyes. "I don't want to marry Richard Hayward."

Lillian drew a deep breath. "I don't know what is wrong with you."

"I don't love Hayward," Torrie whispered.

"You can love anyone you put your mind to," Lillian said, thrusting out her large chest. "I assure you, being married does not mean you will need to spend a great deal of time with your husband."

Being married should mean wanting to spend time together, Torrie thought.

"Victoria, I know we have had this discussion before, but I feel we need to have it again. If you are worried about the physical nature of marriage, I must say again that no decent woman enjoys the marriage act."

"Pardon me?"

"If you fear your husband's bed, it is perfectly natural. No lady enjoys such things. Fortunately, no gentleman expects his wife to enjoy such base behavior. A lady submits to her husband for one reason and one reason alone— to produce a child."

Torrie's cheeks grew warm. Her mother had given her this lecture once before. Torrie hadn't found comfort in it then, and she couldn't now.

"After the first time there is very little pain. If the man is a gentleman, he will not tarry. I usually concentrated on the menu for my next dinner party, and before I reached the dessert it was all over. With good fortune, it will not take long for you to conceive, and Mr. Hayward will then be able to leave you alone."

Torrie felt her stomach grow sour. In her mind, she could see Hayward coming at her, his damp palms on her skin, his mouth . . . the thought made her shiver. "I can't marry Hayward."

Lillian stared at her daughter as though Torrie had just crawled out from under a rock. "Wasn't it enough to humiliate me by being left at the altar? Now you are throwing away your last chance to marry. How could you even think about refusing this man? I just don't know why you are like this. None of the women in my family are like this. Have you no feelings for me?"

Torrie felt confused, as though she were lost in a storm, the wind swirling around her, pushing her farther and farther away from home. "Mother, I love you."

"You love me, do you," Lillian said, pulling her handkerchief from her lace-edged cuff. "How can you hurt me this way? Who would ever believe I could give birth to an old maid, a spinster! Me, Lillian Augusta Claridge. Why, men from four counties wanted to marry me."

Torrie's throat tightened, tears burning the back of her eyes. "I never meant to hurt you."

"You will marry this man," Lillian said, rising to her feet. "You will not humiliate me again."

Torrie sat rooted to the sofa, staring at her mother's departing figure. A tear pricked her eye and she quickly blinked it aside. She felt alone, more alone than she had ever felt in her entire life, as though she had just been dumped in a desert, nothing but miles of sand surrounding her, and there was no hope of escape, no hope for survival.

Lillian turned at the door, staring at her daughter a moment before she spoke. "I have invited Mr. Hayward to visit this afternoon. You will receive him. I know you will not disappoint me."

She had always tried to be a worthy daughter. She had always failed. Now, if she married Richard Hayward . . .her stomach heaved at the thought. There had to be another way.

Chapter Six

Spence stepped out of the Western Union office, his eyes narrowing against the early afternoon sun as he headed for the carriage he had waiting. After giving the address to the hack driver, he climbed into the carriage, the Colt in his shoulder holster nestling against his side. Spending two hours with Inspector John Samuels this morning had convinced Spence he was going to have to take matters into his own hands. Today was a good day to start.

Spence's father Jason had always told his sons, "There isn't anything a man can't do if he puts his mind to it." Jason Kincaid was living proof of it. Son of a poor dirt farmer, Jason had carved an empire out of Texas and had married the only daughter of the Duke of Ashford. Spence smiled as he thought of his oldest brother, Alex, the former Marquess of Leicester. Once again Spence thanked his lucky stars he had not been the first-born male.

From the time he was a young boy, Spence had been filled with wanderlust, gripped with a powerful hunger to etch his mark on the world. He was lucky enough to have two brothers: Alex to take over his grandfather's title and lands, and Tyler. Ty was perfectly suited to take over the reins from their father, leaving Spence the freedom to make his own way.

At thirty-four Spence was a rich man. Yet, few people knew just how successful he was. He liked it that way; better to have people accept you for what you were, not what you had. Besides, the money had always been secondary. The game—figuring out what moves to make—that was the fun of it, that was the challenge, and he had always loved a good challenge. Now he had two: Victoria Granger and Madame Olivia Fontaine. He was fairly certain how he was going to deal with Olivia, but Victoria was another matter.

Women had always been attracted to Spence, the way bits of metal are attracted to a magnet. He had always been able to shake them off when the time was right, never pretending there could be anything more than a pleasant interlude, never getting involved with any innocent woman who might get hurt. He had learned that lesson the day his father had caught him with Nancy Connors in the hayloft.

At the time, Spence had been fifteen, Nancy eighteen. Spence had just discarded his trousers when Jason had appeared. Nancy had been allowed to get dressed and escape; Spence had not. His father's lecture had been short and to the point: "Don't mess around with any innocent girl you aren't planning to marry. If you've got an itch, stick to the women who can scratch it and not get hurt. If you ruin some girl, I'll be right behind you at the church making sure you don't trip over your vows."

That evening Jason had taken Spence to town and introduced him to Miss Amber Starr. In a room above the saloon, on lavender-scented pink satin sheets, the pretty blonde had given Spence his first lessons in how to please a woman. From that moment on, Nancy and all the other innocents had been safe. Until now. Until Victoria Granger. The thoughts he had about the silver-eyed beauty were anything but innocent.

Leather groaned beneath him as Spence shifted in the seat and stared out at Market Street, watching a cable car rumble past. Next to a man in a tall silk hat and dark gray frock coat sat a Chinese vegetable vendor dressed in blue cotton and wearing a bamboo hat, his long poled baskets bobbing along the side of the cable car.

The city had become his domain, with a flavor all its own. San Francisco was young and proud, built by adventurers. Some of the men Spence saw in their elegant clothes strolling the granite-lined streets had, in another time, roamed the gold fields in wool and denim, had trudged through muddy streets and across wooden sidewalks. Spence envied them for that adventure. They had built a city complex in its blend of nationalities, a city with a mix of rigid standards and loose morals.

Gathered on the corner of Market and Geary were at least fifteen men watching the girls walk by. The breezy corner had been named "Cape Horn" because of the way the wind ripped down the corridor of tall buildings. Spence smiled as two girls clutched in vain at their many-gored skirts and flounced petticoats, giving him and the other gentlemen a glimpse of pretty ankles. After meeting his wife, Spence understood why Quinton Granger was one of the men on that corner.

In this era of England's portly queen, Spence had heard that virtuous women bathed in their night-gowns. Fortunately, he had never been involved with any virtuous women. No doubt women like Lillian Granger hadn't been completely undressed since the day they were born. It was little wonder Olivia Fontaine did a thriving business. His smile slipped as he thought of the red-haired madame. He and Olivia had unfinished business to attend to.

The carriage rumbled down O'Farrell Street and came to a halt in front of Olivia's three-story house. "I should be out in a few minutes," Spence said, climbing down from the carriage. "If I'm not out in an hour, get the police."

The driver's gray brows lifted beneath his tall silk hat. "Yes, sir."

At his knock, a short, stocky man opened the door and stared up at Spence. The top of his head was bald, and with his thick sideburns, heavy jowls, and little brown eyes, the man looked like a bulldog. "What's your pleasure?"

"Tell the boss lady she has company," Spence said, pressing his hand against the door. "I'll wait in her office."

"Miss Olivia might not like it should I leave you in her office when she's not there."

"Miss Olivia would not like me to be waiting on the street."

"Maybe." The man's grizzled brow folded into a frown. "Maybe not. Who should I say is calling?"

"I'd like to surprise her." When the bulldog hesitated, Spence continued. "What's your name?"

The man glared up at Spence, suspicion lurking in his eyes. "Harry."

"Would you like me to tell Slattery you kept me waiting, Harry?"

Harry took a step back at the mention of Slattery's name. Inspector Samuels had also known Slattery; he had warned Spence to stay clear of the man. Before this was all over, Spence was going to meet this Slattery, this king of the underworld, face to face. Without another question, Harry showed Spence to an office on the first floor and went to fetch his mistress.

A gold and black Persian rug muffled his footsteps as Spence walked into the large room. Olivia definitely had a taste for gold, Spence thought, glancing around the room. The sofa and chairs were upholstered in black and gold silk brocade, the walnut arms and legs gold-plated. Gold and black brocade framed the bay window behind the gilt-trimmed desk, sunlight flooding in from the garden beyond. Etched in black silk, wigged gentlemen bowed to demure seventeenth-century ladies up and down the gold-silk-clad walls.

From a perch above the gold and black marble mantel, Olivia stared down at Spence with arrogant green eyes. Spence frowned up at the nude portrait of Olivia, the heavy scent of jasmine hanging in the air around him, bringing back memories of the first time he had looked up at this painting. No doubt about it: There had definitely been something in that snifter besides brandy the other night.

Spence sat in the leather chair behind the desk. There were no papers on the top of her desk; just a crystal paperweight in the shape of an apple and a gold stand with two pens and a pot of ink. He tried to open one of the drawers, wondering if he might find something incriminating about the lady, but the desk was locked. The sound of footsteps echoed in the hall. He leaned back in her chair and propped his feet up on the smooth rosewood desk.

"I'm not sure I like surprises," Olivia said, walking into the room. Her mouth dropped open as she stared at Spence. "You!"

"Why, Olivia, you don't look happy to see me," Spence said, lifting the crystal apple from the desktop.

"Harry!" Olivia screamed, backing toward the door.

"I don't think we need any company." Spence moved the crystal into the sunlight streaming in through the windows behind him, sparks of color shooting in all directions, striking Olivia's face, making her flinch. "Remember what happened the last time you tried to throw me out?"

"What do you want, Kincaid?" she asked, taking a step back, trying to get out of the sharp glare of the light.

Spence moved the apple, focusing the light once again on her face. "I want to show you just how nasty it is to have people shot. Sometimes they get very angry." A lazy smile curled his lips. "And sometimes they get even."

"You want me, Miss Olivia?" Harry asked, running into the room.

"Do you, Miss Olivia?" Spence asked, grinning at her.

The black satin above Olivia's heavy breasts rose and fell with each angry breath she took, her huge breasts threatening to spill beyond the tight bodice. Spence could see she was struggling with curiosity and the desire to boot him out on his tail.

"Wait in the hall, Harry," Olivia said, glaring at Kincaid. "And shut the door on your way out."

The bulldog gave Kincaid a dark look, then turned to follow Olivia's order.

"Look, Kincaid, I didn't have anything to do with the shooting."

"No?" Spence tossed the apple from one hand to the other as he continued. "One of the men looked like the two-legged bull who works for you, the one with the glass jaw. I would guess he came limping home with a broken leg last night. Is that why Harry is guarding your front door?"

Olivia lifted her necklace and began to roll one of the diamonds between her fingers.

"You know, I believe you didn't intend to have me shot," Spence said, glancing down at the paperweight he held. "Tell me, just what did you have planned for me?"

Olivia dropped her necklace and placed both hands on her plump hips. "You can't prove anything."

"I don't need to." He placed the apple on the middle of the desk and came to his feet. "I don't expect to rely on the law to extract my pound of flesh."

"Don't you touch me!" she said, backing away as he drew near.

"Not with a lightning rod," he said, walking past her. "I just wanted you to know, I'm going to ruin you."

Her nostrils flared. "Your talk is bold."

A pretty note of panic colored her anger, making him smile. "I'm just making a promise," Spence said, taking hold of the brass door handle. "You hurt a young lady last night. That made me angry."

"Just what are you going to do?"

He glanced over his shoulder and smiled. "I think I'll let you wonder for a while."

"I have friends, you know, powerful friends," she said, following him out of the room. "Some in very high positions in this state. They wouldn't like it if you hurt me."

"We'll see," Spence said, without a glance back at the woman who followed him down the hall.

"You'll be making a big mistake if you try to hurt me."

Spence pinned Harry to the wall with a look when the stocky man took a step toward him. "Stay, boy."

Harry growled under his breath but didn't move.

"Kincaid! Don't you walk out on me when I'm talking to you," Olivia said, as Spence walked out the front door.

"Enjoy yourself while you can, Olivia."

A string of curses followed Spence down the steps before he heard the slam of her front door. He took a deep breath of air to clear his nostrils of the heavy scent of her perfume and headed for his hack. He had two more stops to make this afternoon, and one very pretty young woman to see.

Chapter Seven

Spence had a feeling he wasn't going to like this, he thought, as he followed the butler toward Lillian Granger's double parlor. At the doorway, he paused as Bramby announced him. Every square inch of wall in the parlor was covered with art, each piece in an ornate gold frame, all chaste, most landscapes and still lifes. Some of the paintings were very good, but the way they were hung made them run together until they looked like so much wallpaper.

"Ah, Mr. Kincaid. I thought you might visit today. Please come in," Lillian said, waving her hand. She was sitting on a high-backed chair of carved black walnut, dressed in a starched white shirtwaist and a dove gray skirt, looking like a queen on her throne.

The furniture in the room was displayed just as were the paintings. All the pieces were expensive, but they were crammed together until most of the detail in the yellow and white Aubusson carpet was covered. Sunlight filtered through lace curtains, shimmered on black walnut tables that had been polished to a mirror finish with lemon oil and beeswax; the scents lingered. In one corner Spence noticed a piano covered with a white silk shawl. He smiled, thinking of a little girl sitting there every day at three.

"Please be seated," Lillian said, gesturing to a chair across from her.

Spence took a seat on the Brussels carpet back chair and rested the package he had been carrying on the floor by his feet. Lillian arched a brow at the package, as though the silver wrapping paper might dirty her carpet.

"Cream and sugar?" she asked, lifting a cup from the walnut tea caddy on her right.

"No thank you." He accepted the delicate cup and saucer and tried to settle a little more comfortably on the horsehair-stuffed chair. Apparently Lillian Granger didn't believe in progress.

"It would seem you are not aware of the fact that a lady does not accept presents from men to whom she is not engaged," Lillian said, casting a glance at the silver package.

Spence looked at her over the rim of his cup. "Even if the lady has saved the gentleman's life?"

Lillian waved her hand as if to dismiss his argument. "I prefer not to be reminded of the incident. Neither does my daughter need to be reminded. Also, I must tell you, it was most improper for you to send Victoria red roses."

Although Lillian kept her voice level, Spence could see the anger simmering behind her social mask. Why? he wondered. "Does Miss Granger not like red roses?"

"My daughter adores red roses. Despite her age,

she is entirely too naive at times," Lillian said, her voice revealing her displeasure. She cocked her head and stared at him as though he were a delinquent schoolboy. "Mr. Kincaid, are you aware Sarah Bernhardt will accept only red roses from her lovers?"

The woman was entirely serious. Spence coughed to cover the chuckle rising in his throat. "I'm not altogether sure what Sarah Bernhardt has to do with me sending red roses to Miss Granger." Especially since he knew Sarah liked pink roses.

"No, I suppose you don't." She smoothed her starched white collar. "That is part of the problem."

Lillian took a deep breath, as though she were reloading. No doubt about it, he wasn't going to like this, Spence thought.

"I've never been one to mince words, Mr. Kincaid."

"An admirable trait." He lifted the cup to his lips, tasting the weak tea, glancing at a stuffed owl under a glass dome on the table behind Lillian.

"Just exactly what are your intentions where Victoria is concerned?"

Spence nearly choked on his tea. "I thought this conversation was usually conducted by the father."

"Mr. Granger has not always been able to see straight when it comes to Victoria." She sipped her tea, her gaze remaining on Spence.

For a moment the steady click of the clock on the mantel was the only sound in the big room as Lillian waited and Spence recovered from his surprise.

"Well, young man?"

Spence managed a smile in spite of the way he felt. "My intention is to get to know your daughter."

"Mr. Kincaid, I was not happy to learn Victoria

had taken a walk with you last night. It was quite promiscuous on her part."

The way she talked about her daughter, as though Torrie were a woman of the streets, prickled his anger. "Miss Granger didn't invite my company."

"Regardless. Her conduct was not at all appropriate."

When he had brought Torrie home last night Lillian Granger had been more concerned about what the guests would think than about the severity of her daughter's wound. Here was not a mother filled with devotion, or even affection. He thought of his own mother, of his father and family, of the love he had always taken for granted, and wondered what he would be like if he had grown up in this house.

"She has always acted with proper decorum, Mrs. Granger." Spence rested his cup and saucer on the round black walnut table on his left. "I understand she was upset and just needed some time by herself. If I hadn't followed her, chances are she would have returned without a scratch. I must take full responsibility."

"Very gallant, Mr. Kincaid." Lillian took a sip of tea. "Perhaps you can understand why I am going to ask you not to see Victoria again."

Spence wasn't accustomed to mothers asking him to stay away from their daughters. Matchmaking mamas had always tried to toss a lasso around his neck. "And what does Quinton think of this?"

Lillian tilted her head so she might look down her nose at him. "As I said earlier, Mr. Granger does not always think clearly where Victoria is concerned."

"Perhaps he feels Victoria is old enough to make some of her own decisions."

"Mr. Kincaid, you are a man of the world, handsome and with a degree of charm that could easily turn a young woman's head."

Too bad his charm wasn't working at the moment, Spence thought.

"I will not have Victoria throwing away her chance for a proper marriage on a man who has no intention of marrying her."

"What makes you so certain I won't want to marry her?"

Lillian shook her head. "Mr. Kincaid, I am not blind. Victoria has never been a beauty. I cannot imagine a man such as you ever being interested in her."

"She may not be the fashion, Mrs. Granger, but your daughter is one of the most beautiful women I have ever met." Spence came to his feet, fighting to keep his anger in check. "She has more spirit than a room full of starchy, overfed debutantes, and courage enough to risk her life to save mine. Perhaps you should take another look."

Lillian's lips pursed as she glared up at him. "I will not be spoken to in such a tone, young man."

"Forgive me," he said, giving her an exaggerated bow. "Thank you for the tea." He lifted his package and started for the door.

"You will stay away from my daughter," Lillian called after him.

He paused in the doorway and turned to face her. "Have you ever thought you might not know what's best for her?"

"And you do?"

"Maybe," he said, turning to leave.

"Victoria has company, Mr. Kincaid."

"She's about to have more, Mrs. Granger."

He swore under his breath as he crossed the entry hall, his heels clicking against the marble, his anger growing with every step. He mounted the stairs, heading for Torrie's room. If Lillian Granger thought he was going to turn tail and run, she had another thought coming.

"I am not your property," Torrie said, coming to her feet.

Hayward sauntered to the round walnut table by the bay window in her sitting room, where two dozen red blooms rose gracefully from a crystal vase. "From him?" he asked, flicking a dark red rose with his finger.

Torrie couldn't answer; her anger wouldn't allow a single word to pass her taut throat.

"I wouldn't be pinning any hopes on Kincaid." Hayward picked a piece of lint from his light brown sleeve. "I hear the man has women scattered across the country."

"Get out!"

Hayward turned to face her, hatred carving his features into an ugly mask. "The sooner you get the message, the better off you're going to be. You and I are going to be married. So get used to the idea."

"Get the message, Hayward: Go away!"

"When we're married, you are going to regret this," he said, his hands forming fists at his sides. "I'll make damn sure you regret this the rest of your life."

"We are not going to be married," she said, enunciating each word clearly.

"Yes we are," he said, moving toward her.

There was a touch of madness in his eyes, a wild desperation that made her shiver. Torrie backed away as he approached her. "Get out of here."

"I've got debts, Victoria. And people anxious to collect. Nasty people who will break my legs if I don't give them their money."

"I'm sorry you got yourself in over your head, Mr. Hayward," she said, feeling the sofa against the back of her legs. "But I will not be sacrificed to pay for your folly."

"Bitch!"

Torrie gasped as his open palm hit her cheek, the blow knocking her back against the sofa. She fell across the cushions, her shoulder hitting the curved walnut arm. For a moment she lay stunned, clasping a trembling hand to her burning cheek, staring at him as he stood above her. It was the first time in her life anyone had ever slapped her.

She had never seen Hayward like this, his hazel eyes wide, wild, spots of color staining his pale cheeks, beads of sweat breaking out on his brow. He looked like a man gone mad. "How dare you! Get out of . . ." Her words ended in a cry as Hayward plummeted on top of her.

"I'm going to make sure you don't have a choice," he said, grabbing her hands and thrusting them above her head, stretching the torn skin of her side.

Torrie gasped with the sudden pain. She sucked in her breath and opened her mouth to scream, but his mouth cut off her shout. She bucked wildly beneath him, every move sending needles of pain shooting from her side.

"Think you're too good for me," Hayward said, grinding the words against her lips. "I'll teach you."

Bile rose in her throat as his damp mouth slanted across her lips, the taste of stale cigars and whiskey seeping into her mouth. A part of her couldn't believe he would have the nerve to do this, but another part realized he was crazy with desperation. He threw his right leg over both of hers, holding her pinned to the sofa.

She screamed, the sound muffled against his mouth. He slid his hand across her belly. She twisted wildly beneath him as he tugged at her skirt and petticoats, pushing the garments above her thighs. Dear lord, he couldn't mean to rape her, not here in her own sitting room. But she knew that was exactly his plan.

If he succeeded, she wouldn't have a choice but to marry the man. She moaned, fighting like a wild creature caught by a predator. Yet he held her, pushing against her thighs with his knees, trying to force her legs apart. She had to stop him! She had to . . . through the roar of blood in her ears, Torrie heard a savage growl.

One moment Hayward was pushing her against the cushions, the next he was suspended above her, looking dazed and frightened. Torrie looked past Hayward to where Spencer Kincaid stood, one hand in the back of Hayward's collar, the other holding the waistband of his trousers.

Torrie pressed a hand to her lips. Kincaid tossed Hayward across the room. Hayward flapped his arms like a giant bird, then crashed to the floor.

Torrie lay gasping for breath, staring at the scene before her as though she were watching the last act in a horrifying play. Kincaid grabbed the collar of Hayward's shirt and dragged him to his feet.

"Don't hurt me," Hayward muttered, before Kincaid's fist slammed into his jaw.

Hayward's head snapped back, and he would have fallen if it hadn't been for the grip Kincaid had on his shirt. Torrie cringed at the sound of flesh hitting flesh as Kincaid rammed his fist over and over into Hayward's bloody face. Hayward stumbled and fell, but Kincaid wasn't finished with him. Spence reached down, wrapped his hands around Hayward's neck, and dragged him to his feet.

Kincaid lifted Hayward until the blond man's toes barely brushed the carpet. Terrible gurgling sounds escaped Hayward's lips as Kincaid's powerful hands squeezed the life from him. Torrie couldn't let it happen. No matter how much she hated Hayward, she couldn't allow Mr. Kincaid to be responsible for the man's death.

"Mr. Kincaid, please stop. You'll kill him."

He didn't seem to hear her. She dragged herself off the sofa and stumbled to Kincaid's side. "Please stop. Please, you mustn't kill him. You mustn't! He isn't worth it."

Spence glanced at her, and for a moment she was afraid he was too far under the influence of rage to hear her. "Please, you mustn't kill him," she said again, her fingers tightening on his arm, his muscles bulging beneath her palm.

With an oath, Spence tossed his opponent to the floor. Hayward curled into a ball and lay gasping, chomping at the air like a hungry dog at food.

"Are you all right?" Spence asked, closing his hands around Torrie's trembling shoulders.

Torrie nodded, but her knees decided at that moment to buckle. If not for his strong arms, she would have fallen. Spence slipped one arm around her shoulders and the other under her knees. She sagged against him as he lifted her into his arms.

In his arms she felt safe, protected. A part of her—that needy, frightened part of her—wished she could stay in his arms forever. She pressed her cheek against his shoulder, the dark blue superfine wool soft and warm against her skin, his scent rushing past her nostrils to tug at her belly in some odd manner.

He carried her to the sofa and lowered her to the cushions. After arranging a pillow beneath her head he sat beside her and took her hand in his warm grasp, his gaze roaming over every feature of her face. "We should put some ice on that," he said, brushing his fingers across the red mark staining her pale cheek.

Torrie touched her cheek with trembling fingers. "Do you think I'll have a black eye?"

"Not as black as the one he's going to have," Spence said, grinning down at her.

"Good heavens!" Lillian Granger said, poised on the threshold of the room.

Torrie's hand closed reflexively around Kincaid's arm as her mother looked in her direction.

"Mr. Hayward, what on earth has happened to you?" Lillian asked, staring down at the man who was curled on the floor.

"Kincaid," Hayward mumbled.

Lillian turned a blazing blue glare on Kincaid. "I demand you leave this house at once."

"Mother, Mr. Kincaid was protecting me."

"Protecting you? From your fiancé!"

"Fiancé," Spence whispered, looking as though he had been kicked in the ribs by a mule. He glanced down at Torrie, his lips parted, his golden eyes reflecting his surprise.

Torrie shook her head. She wanted to explain, to tell him the mess she was in, but she had her mother to deal with first. "Hayward was trying to force his attentions on me."

Lillian went rigid. "Nonsense. I'm sure you misinterpreted his intentions. Is that not so, Mr. Hayward?"

"We were talking and Kincaid burst in." Hayward dragged himself to a sitting position and looked up at Lillian through thickening lids. "He's a madman."

Lillian lifted her head and stared at Kincaid. "Mr. Kincaid, you are not welcome in this house."

"Listen, lady," Spence said, taking a step forward, looking as though he wanted to take Lillian's neck between his hands. "When I came in here . . ."

Torrie grabbed the hem of Kincaid's coat and

tugged, stopping him, fearing he would only make things worse than they already were. "Mother, Mr. Kincaid only tried to help me."

"You stay out of this, Victoria," Lillian said.

"But, Mother . . ."

"Mr. Kincaid," Lillian said, ignoring her daughter. "Leave this house before I have you removed from the premises."

"Well of all the cock-eyed, stupid . . ." Spence mumbled an oath under his breath as he turned toward Torrie. "Do you want me to leave, Miss Granger?"

"Mr. Kincaid, my daughter does not make the decisions in this house," Lillian said, her voice grating on the still air.

Spence didn't flinch, didn't lift his gaze from Torrie. "Miss Granger?"

Torrie glanced from her mother's scowling face to Spencer Kincaid. He looked fierce, tall, broad-shouldered, ready to take on the nearest dragon bare-handed. Yet she had tasted his gentleness, and one taste had left her craving more. Oh my, she didn't want him to leave. She wanted to curl up in his strong arms and let him protect her, if just for a little while. But that was impossible. "It might be better if you left," she said softly, silently scolding that needy part of her. She could handle her own problems.

His shoulders rose on a deep sigh. After a moment Spence nodded and took Torrie's hand in his warm grasp. "Remember what I said the other night. If you need me, I'll be at Hampton House."

Lillian Granger moved back as Spence drew near, pulling her skirts aside as though she were afraid he might contaminate them. Spence glanced back at Torrie as he reached the door, then his gaze moved from her mother to Hayward, as though he expected them to strike the moment he left.

"I'll be all right," Torrie whispered.

Although he didn't look convinced, Spence nodded, then left her alone with her mother and Hayward. Torrie tried to explain, but her mother refused to listen. Somehow Torrie had managed to become the villain of this drama, a scarlet temptress who had set two men against each other. Her mother was blind to the bruise on Torrie's cheek, blind to everything but her own ambition.

It was clear—her mother was determined to see her wed to this man, clear Hayward would stop at nothing to get her father's money. Even if Torrie decided to turn her back on her family, Hayward would be there, waiting to force her to his will. Hayward had failed today, but she might not be so lucky next time.

As she sat half listening to her mother's lecture, wayward thoughts drifted into her mind like phantoms, Kincaid's words mingling with her father's ultimatum. Fragments of a plan pulled together to weave a compelling tapestry in her mind, coaxing her heart to a quicker rhythm.

There was a way to have a child and keep her independence, a way to appease her father and maintain the rescue mission. For a moment Torrie didn't move. She sat staring at her clenched hands, her breath hovering in her throat. It could work. But did she have the right to make it work?

Torrie glanced up at her mother. Lillian was pacing in front of her, her voice slicing the air, shredding Torrie's fragile confidence. Her mother would never forgive her if she went through with this plan. It was far too scandalous. She couldn't do it.

Still, did she have a choice? Her options seemed to be slipping away as quickly as ice on a warm August afternoon. Torrie's gaze fell on Richard Hayward, the triumphant look in his eyes deciding the issue. There was only one means of escape. She only prayed she was strong enough to take the last gamble.

Chapter Eight

The moon slid behind a cloud, cloaking the earth in darkness, sending fingers of night crawling along Olivia's spine. She moved closer to the lantern she had set on the steps of the mausoleum, the flickering light venturing a few feet into the darkness, reflecting off the white marble, casting shadows on the granite monuments at the edge of the light. Why did he want to meet here? she wondered, slapping her riding crop against the skirt of her black velvet habit.

A rustling nearby made her peer into the darkness. "Jack?" she asked, her voice barely above a whisper. She held her breath and waited, but there was no reply. He was late, again.

A soft creamy light flooded the cemetery as the moon peeked out from behind its veil of clouds, flooding the ground, reflecting on the gravestones, reminding her of the first time she had been in a cemetery at night. Funny, she hadn't thought about that first time in many years.

When she was fourteen she had sneaked away from the house to meet a boy in the cemetery behind the church where her father preached. It was there she had come to realize just how much power a woman could hold over a man. The fools would do almost anything for a little taste of honey. It was then she first realized a smart woman could make a fortune with that knowledge.

At sixteen she had left her father's house in that dreary little Kansas town and made her way to San Francisco. A woman could own property here, and there were plenty of men, men willing to pay a great deal of money for the pleasure of her company. San Francisco still remembered the days of the gold rush, the days when men worshipped the pretty whores who allowed them to snuggle next to their perfumed bodies. Here in San Francisco, the men still adored their fancy whores.

In six years Olivia had earned enough money to buy her own place. Now, at twenty-nine, she was rich enough to buy that little town in Kansas. It made her smile to think of her father's reaction if he knew what his darling little girl was doing.

An owl hooted to its mate. Olivia jumped at the sudden sound. "Damn him!"

"You're a little jumpy, Olivia," a deep voice vibrated on the evening breeze.

She whirled and stared up at the man who stood perched on the steps above her like a malevolent bird of prey. He smiled down at her, his black cape rippling in the breeze, his dark hair slicked back from his wide brow.

"Of course I am, left waiting in a place like this," Olivia said, trying to hide her fear behind annoyance. "Why did you insist on meeting here?"

He leaned his shoulder against the door of the mausoleum and smiled down at her. "I thought it might start you thinking, my dear." His words were clipped, spoken in an upper-class British accent. He wore a patch over his right eye; the other was dark and stared at her in a way that sent dread crawling across her skin.

"Thinking? About what?" Olivia asked, staring up at him.

"You've been making some serious decisions without consulting me, haven't you, Olivia?"

Beneath her black kid gloves, Olivia felt her palms grow moist. "I don't know what you mean."

"Don't you?" he asked, swooping down the steps, gliding toward her, his cape spreading out behind him. He stopped a foot in front of her. "Victoria Granger was shot last night. I'm not pleased, not pleased in the least."

Olivia took a step back. It was useless denying her involvement. Jack Slattery knew or she wouldn't be here. "The orders were to bring Spencer Kincaid to me. Alive. I hadn't planned for him or anyone else to be shot. I intended to take my time killing him."

"You might have killed the girl."

The tone in his voice made Olivia wonder if Slattery had an interest in the Granger woman. It suddenly occurred to her that the society lady might be having a fling with the king of the underworld. The thought jabbed her with jealousy. "What is Victoria Granger to you?"

"What is Spencer Kincaid to you?" he asked, avoiding her question, heightening her suspicions.

Slattery moved forward. Olivia retreated until her back was pressed against a tall granite monument, until he was leaning over her, his face inches from hers. "It would seem you have taken quite a liking to Mr. Kincaid."

His cape lifted on the breeze, brushing her skirt. "He needs to be taught a lesson. Jack, he came to my place today. He threatened me. I think he's going to try to put us both out of business. We have to get rid of him."

"I see," he said, brushing her cheek with his leather-clad hand.

Moonlight caught the icy glint in his eye, making her shiver. "We have to do something about him."

He smiled, a cold twisting of the lips between his full beard. "You have put me in an awkward position."

"Jack, I . . ." His hand dropped to her neck, squeezing her throat, cutting off her words.

"He can identify your men. Your men also work for me, Olivia. The police know this."

She clawed at his arm, her heart beating wildly against her ribs. "Jack," she whispered, forcing his name past her tight throat.

"Kincaid can hurt us," he said, his breath brushing her pale cheek.

With her eyes, she pleaded with him. His grip loosened enough for her to speak. "I'll take care of it, I promise."

He dropped his hand and turned away. "I have already made plans to take care of it."

A smile curved her lips as she stared at his sharp profile. "You're going to have Kincaid and that woman killed."

His laughter rumbled in the air, a deep unholy sound echoing from the solemn marble and granite. "You are a bloodthirsty little whore, aren't you? Did Kincaid bruise your ego so badly, my dear?"

"He helped those people from the mission take one of my girls." She didn't like to hear the truth, especially from Jack. "Something should be done about those people."

He shrugged his broad shoulders. "They are a nuisance, nothing more."

"Nuisance!" Olivia said, her hand growing taut around her riding crop. "They barged into my house and took my property, a virgin I already had sold."

"There are other girls. If the little bird was so anxious to fly away, we are better off without her. Some cannot be trained."

Slattery was the one man who could satisfy her in bed, or at least she had thought him to be the only man. Spence Kincaid had left her with a hunger in her belly and a heart full of vengeance. And she would need Jack's help if she were going to have her vengeance. "Darling, you aren't still angry with me, are you?"

"You have your uses," he said, raking her body with a heated stare.

"I wanted to tell you what I had planned." She tapped the tip of her riding crop against her chin as she spoke, stripping away the layers of his clothes with her eyes. He had a body like a cat, lean and sleek. "I tried to contact you at least a dozen times yesterday, but you were nowhere to be found. You know, darling, sometimes I think you live two lives."

He turned, his dark gaze sending fear slithering like a viper along the column of her spine. Three years ago Jack Slattery had suddenly appeared in San Francisco. No one knew where he was from or who he was. Some speculated that he was the second son of a nobleman who had come to America to make his fortune. Some said he came to escape the hangman's noose. No one knew for sure.

Jack Slattery was the king of an empire built on opium and the traffic of young girls. He was the man who had taught Olivia how to increase her profits and how to moan beneath a man with real passion. And he had secrets, secrets that might prove profitable, secrets that would be dangerous to explore. She wasn't feeling that brave tonight.

"When is the next shipment due?" she asked, leaning against a gravestone. "I have a customer who wants a small blonde, and he's willing to pay a fortune to break her in."

"I'll have the order sent tonight," he said, glancing at her. "You should have one by next Tuesday."

Olivia smiled and lowered the tip of the riding crop to her left breast. She could see him following the tip of the little stick with his gaze as she rubbed it around her nipple. "I've got an idea."

His tongue slipped out to moisten his lips and she smiled, knowing she had the bit in his mouth. Slowly she raised the skirt of her riding habit, sitting back on the granite stone, feeling a rush of heat between her thighs. She moved the tip of the riding crop lower over her belly, brushing her black silk drawers. "Are you hungry?"

He stood for a moment, watching her, a smile creeping across his face. She trembled as he moved toward her, his long fingers working the placket of his trousers. When he drew near she reached for him, freeing his swollen flesh from the wool of his trousers.

"Do you want it so badly, Olivia?" he asked, smiling down at her.

His scent filled her nostrils: fine cigars, leather, and man. Her blood heated. "Yes," she whispered, her voice naked with need.

He slid his hand along the black silk that covered her thigh as he took the riding crop from her hand. Olivia's eyes grew wider as he brushed her skin with the leather tip of the stick, finding the slit in her drawers. "Yes," she murmured, leaning back against the stone, pain jabbing through her body, mingling with a hot, throbbing pleasure.

She could control him. It might take time, but she was sure she could convince Jack they needed to kill Spence Kincaid.

Chapter Nine

Hampton House rose seven stories high and spread an entire city block, covering more than two and a half acres of prime San Francisco real estate. Every outside window in the hotel boasted a huge bay from the first floor to the top. Rainy gloom gave way to the light of hundreds of incandescent lights, dazzling behind polished crystal high overhead, as Torrie crossed the garnet and white marble floor and walked toward the long, polished mahogany reception desk.

Elegant shops and restaurants occupied the first story. Torrie had shopped here a hundred times, but she had never come here to see a man. In fact, she had never gone unescorted to meet any gentleman, except Charles. And she had certainly never in her life had the purpose she had today.

A bellboy dressed in red and gold livery led her

from the reception desk to a private elevator near the rear of the lobby. As the elevator rose, Torrie's courage fell. Silently she went over in her mind what she might say to Mr. Kincaid, clutching the silver package she held in her arms as the little iron cage carried her seven stories to his floor. With a clang of iron the elevator came to a halt, the wrought-iron door opened, and Torrie stared into the hall.

"This is it, miss," the elevator boy said. "Mr. Kincaid's private floor."

She nodded and forced her feet to move. Iron jangled behind her, and she turned to watch the elevator descend. Perhaps this wasn't such a good idea, she thought. At home it had seemed her only option. On the way she had kept reassuring herself that Mr. Kincaid would understand. Now, she was wondering how quickly the elevator would return if she tried to summon it and get out of here before Spence Kincaid knew she was there.

"May I help you, miss?"

Too late. Torrie swallowed hard and turned to face a short man dressed in a formal black coat and trousers. His thin dark hair was swept back from a high forehead. His dark brows were raised slightly as he stared at her, his lips a disapproving line beneath the thin line of his mustache. For a moment she couldn't find her voice.

"This is a private floor, miss," he said.

It surprised her to discover Spence Kincaid had an English butler. "I know. I've come to see Mr. Kincaid."

The man's head tilted slightly, his dark stare sliding over her charcoal-gray coat as though he were trying to decide if she were dressed well enough to meet his master. A smile curved his lips as his gaze rested on the silver package she held. "Please, allow me to take your coat, Miss Granger."

How did he know her name? she wondered. He took her package and rested it on a mahogany table that stood beneath a large gold-trimmed mirror. After taking her coat, hat, gloves, and umbrella, he turned and opened one of the white panels in the wall, revealing a closet.

Torrie glanced at her reflection as he stowed her things. She smoothed the collar of her light blue gown and touched her hair, trying to coax a wayward curl back into place. Mr. Kincaid will understand, she assured the frightened-looking woman in the mirror. The woman in the mirror didn't look convinced.

"Please, follow me," the butler said, lifting the package and leading the way down the hall.

Torrie stood behind the servant as he knocked on Mr. Kincaid's office door. She swallowed hard as she heard Kincaid's deep baritone rumble through the white paneled door. The servant opened the door, and Torrie clutched at her dissolving courage.

"What is it, Jasper?" Kincaid asked, without turning from the rain-splattered windows. He stood behind a large mahogany desk, his hands on his slim hips, moss green velvet trimmed in gold braid draping the windows on either side of him.

"There's a lady to see you, sir."

Spence turned, his gaze locking with hers. Several emotions swirled in his golden eyes as he looked at her, surprise the only one she could identify. He was coatless, his white linen shirt open at the neck, the sleeves rolled up to reveal strong, dark forearms. Even standing a room away, she felt stunned in his presence, as she had the first time she had fallen from a horse.

"Miss Granger," he said, moving from behind the desk. "This is an unexpected pleasure."

Torrie glanced down at his long, dark fingers as

his hands engulfed her own. "Mr. Kincaid, I came to apologize for yesterday."

"That will be all, Jasper," Spence said, glancing at his servant.

The little man nodded. "What would you like me to do with this, sir?"

Spence glanced at the silver package, then smiled down at Torrie. "Returning my present? Without even opening it?"

Torrie nodded. "I couldn't possibly accept it."

He shook his head and gave her hands a squeeze. "Just put it on the chair by the door, Jasper."

Jasper complied, placing the big package on the chair, leaving the room and closing the door behind him. Spence grinned at Torrie. "Aren't you even curious about what's in it?"

"A little," she said, giving him a weak smile. In truth, that package had tempted her more than once. "But I can't accept it."

"Your mother wouldn't like it, would she?"

She shook her head, her hands growing tense in his grasp. "I'm terribly sorry about what happened."

"There's no need for you to apologize for anything," he said, his deep voice filled with tender concern.

"Yesterday was . . ." She shook her head, trying to find the right words. "A disaster."

He brushed his fingers over the slight bruise on the crest of her left cheek. "Are you all right?"

Torrie shivered at the memory of Hayward's attack, at the realization of what she was about to do. Her throat tightened. She felt as though she were wrapped in flannel from her head to her toes, unable to move, unable to breathe. As if he sensed her distress, he slipped his arm around her shoulders and led her to the sofa near the hearth.

The rich smell of leather lifted from the sofa and

chairs, each one the color of creamy coffee. Electric light glowed on the polished mahogany wainscoting and the bookcases that were built into two of the walls. She glanced at the rows and rows of leather-bound books and wondered what titles she would find on his shelves. You could tell a great deal about a person by the books he read. She only wished she knew more about him. Would he agree to her plan? And what if he did?

Spence sat beside her on the sofa, his arm riding the curve of her shoulders, his fingers curled around her upper arm. It wasn't proper. She shouldn't let him touch her like this, but considering what she was about to ask, it seemed foolish to move away from him, especially when his light embrace felt so . . . pleasant.

She sat as still as a sculpture, her eyes lowered, her hands tightly clasped in her lap, absorbing the warmth of his nearness, the vitality and strength vibrating from his big body. Once again she felt that same strange surge of electricity coursing through her, the same odd sensation she felt whenever he was near. She took a deep breath, inhaling his scent, her pulse picking up speed.

After a few moments he broke the tense silence. "I've always loved the sound of rain against the windowpanes," he said, his deep voice a soft caress.

She knew he was trying to calm her, the way he had tried to calm Claire the first day they had met. She looked up at him, seeing a tenderness in his eyes, a warmth that chased away some of the anxiety nibbling at her heart. He would understand. He had to. "We have something in common."

He grinned. "Frightening, isn't it?"

She lowered her eyes. "I apologize for my behavior the other night. I realize you were only trying to help."

"I want to help now." He slid his open palm down her arm, holding her closer. "If there is anything I can do, anything at all, please let me know."

He was so strong, so capable, and she needed that strength, needed to feel she wasn't facing this all alone. "Mr. Kincaid, I am in a most difficult situation," she said to her folded hands.

"This has something to do with Hayward."

She nodded.

"Can I help?"

For a moment she couldn't speak, an inner battle raging within her—pride warring with self-preservation. "Yes. Yes, I think you can help. I'm just wondering if you will."

"Name it, it's yours."

Torrie swallowed the lump of pride in her throat and took a deep breath before plunging ahead. "Mr. Kincaid, will you marry me?" she asked, her voice barely lifting above the sound of the rain against the windows.

His arm stiffened on her shoulder, his fingers tensing. She raised her gaze to his face. He was staring at her, his lips parted, looking like a buck facing a hunter's shotgun.

"You needn't stay married to me," she said, her words tumbling one after the other. "In fact, I'm sure we would only need to stay married for a short while, and then you could be on your way." *My word, she was making a mess of this.*

He let out his breath in a long sigh. "I'm not sure I understand."

"Mr. Kincaid, my father has given me two months to find a husband or be disinherited. He wants . . . he wants a grandchild, and he doesn't care how . . . you see, he doesn't care how I provide him with one."

He withdrew his arm from her shoulder, staring

at her. "You want a stud," he said, sounding as if he didn't quite believe the words as he spoke them.

"Mr. Kincaid! I want a child."

He studied her a moment, probing her with his eyes. "Why me? Why not Hayward?"

"You don't need or want my father's money, so there would be no reason for you to want to stay married to me." She glanced down at her hands. "Hayward wants my father's money. He wants it desperately."

"I see. You want me to stay just long enough to plant a seed in your belly."

Her back stiffened. "Quite eloquently put, Mr. Kincaid."

"Call me old-fashioned, but I always thought people should marry only if they were in love."

She laced her fingers together, squeezing hard. "Love is for fairy tales," she said, somehow managing to keep her voice from cracking.

"I guess I always believed in fairy tales."

So had she. Dear Lord, so had she. "Mr. Kincaid, I'm not asking you to stay in a loveless marriage. Once I am with child, we can both resume our separate paths. I give you my word, I will not hesitate to give you a . . . divorce." Her voice faded to a whisper on the scandalous word.

He glanced away, mumbling an oath under his breath, his hands growing into fists on his knees. He looked hurt, and she realized she might have bruised his ego a little, but she wasn't sure how else to put it. She flinched as his gaze returned to her, his anger striking her like a sword.

"And what if I should decide to stay married to you?"

She shook her head, thinking how absurd the question really was. Spencer Kincaid would never want to stay married to her. "Since you are not in love with me, I cannot imagine why you would want to stay married to me."

A muscle worked in his jaw as he stared at her. "If I were in love with you?" he asked, his tone deceptively calm.

If he were in love with her, he would be the one proposing. If only he . . . she pushed the thought from her mind. She couldn't continue to hold on to a dream. Still, dreams died hard; she could feel them writhing in her chest, shuddering, fighting for life in her heart. "Well, in that case I wouldn't be asking, would I?"

"I see; you only ask men who are not in love with you to marry you."

Did he think she wanted to be doing this? "Mr. Kincaid, you said you would do anything to repay me. I only . . ."

"I will not be your stud!" he said, springing to his feet.

Torrie stared up at him a moment, seeing the stern set of his jaw, the anger burning in his eyes, and she realized her worst fears had just been fulfilled. Slowly she rose to her feet, fighting the trembling in her legs, forcing her back to remain straight. She felt like curling up and crying, but she would not allow herself to be further shamed in front of this man. "I should have known you would not be a man of honor."

"Honor has nothing to do with this," he said, turning to stare into the fire on the hearth, his hands curling into fists against the jade marble mantel.

"I see. I thought you were willing to help me. I guess I was mistaken."

With head held high she crossed the thick green and gold carpet, keeping her gaze fixed on the brass door handle. She didn't need Spencer Kincaid. She didn't! Somehow she would find a way out of this mess, she assured herself. *But how?* a small voice echoed in her brain. How was she going to escape her fate? Two months; she still had nearly two months. She would just have to think of something.

Spence stared down at the flickering gas jets behind the grate on the hearth, listening to the rustle of her skirts as she left the room. The door closed with a soft click, the sound a clap of lightning to his ears. He rested his brow on the cool marble and wondered how he could have been so wrong about that woman.

Maybe he was an arrogant, conceited buffoon. He had actually convinced himself she liked him, more than liked him. Hell, he had himself convinced Victoria Granger was falling in love with him. Maybe because he had the awful suspicion he was falling in love with her.

"Women! Trouble, that's all they are," he mumbled to himself, walking back to his desk. He sank to his chair, lifted a telegram, then lowered it to the desk, staring at the door.

Honor! The woman had the nerve to talk to him about honor when all she wanted from him was . . . "Damn!" He would go to hell before he acted as a stud for any woman.

Spence stood and stretched, trying to ease the muscles in his neck and shoulders. He looked once more at the stack of telegrams and letters on his desk, then turned to stare out the window. Rivulets of water coursed down the panes, and seven stories below him swirled a sea of gray and black; people clutching black umbrellas, strolling along gray, rain-swept streets.

For a long time he stared down at the rain-splattered street, realizing he was trying to pick out one slender young woman in the crowd. What was she going to do now? Would she marry Hayward?

His jaw clenched as he thought of her in another man's arms.

Why should I care?

Why the hell should I care?

Spence was still trying to plow his way through his correspondence when Allan came strolling into his office three hours later. The task normally took him an hour, but he couldn't concentrate on business today.

Spence tossed the letter he was holding on the desk and greeted his friend. Allan was dressed in black evening clothes, carrying a tall silk hat and smiling as though he hadn't a care on this green earth.

"Enough work for one day," Allan said, sinking to one of the two leather wing-back chairs in front of the desk. "There are champagne bottles all over this city just waiting to be popped, pretty girls just waiting for a squeeze."

The last thing Spence needed right now was a woman. "You go ahead. I'll catch up with you later."

"I sense something wrong here." Allan cocked his head and studied his friend a moment. "What's this I see? Could it be a tinge of frostbite around your ears?"

Spence frowned as he scrawled a few lines on a telegram, pointedly ignoring his friend.

"I talked to Quinton a few minutes ago and he said Torrie was doing well. So it must be you who aren't doing so well."

"I'm doing just fine," Spence said, tossing the telegram to the desk. Torrie wanted to use him. Well, maybe she had the right. She had saved his life, and all she was asking for was a life in return: his first-born child. His chest tightened at the thought.

"All right, we won't talk about the lady," Allan

said, propping his feet on Spence's big mahogany desk. "You have bigger problems anyway."

Spence glanced at Allan. Right now it was hard to think of a bigger problem than Victoria Granger.

"Word has it you intend to put Slattery out of business."

"Word travels fast. How did you find out?"

"There are no secrets in this town."

"What do you know about Slattery? The police weren't much help."

"It doesn't surprise me. Most of them are on Slattery's payroll." Allan lifted a gold letter opener from the desk as he spoke. "He's a pretty ruthless character. Maybe you should think about leaving him alone."

"He hurts people."

"Exactly," Allan said, pointing the letter opener at Spence. "I wouldn't like to see you tangle with him."

"Did you know Olivia Fontaine is involved with white slavery?" Spence asked, rubbing the stiff muscles at the back of his neck. Torrie had him tied into knots.

Allan shrugged. "I've heard. You're not falling for all that nonsense they preach at the rescue mission, are you? Those girls are right where they want to be."

Spence shook his head. "I don't think so."

Allan turned the letter opener in his hands, allowing light to play across the blade. "What do you have planned?" he asked, glancing at Spence.

"The first thing I'm going to do is find out where they are the most vulnerable."

"You're not going to back down from this, are you?"

"I'm not sure I can back down from this." Spence frowned as he studied Allan. His friend seldom showed any concern for anything, but right now Allan looked worried. "I appreciate your concern, but I can take care of myself."

"You're making a mistake." Allan came to his feet and looked down at Spence. "Slattery is a dangerous man, powerful, deadly. He controls this city's underworld."

Spence grinned and leaned back in his chair. "Another reason why I can't back down."

"You haven't changed." Allan dropped the letter opener onto the desk, the gold clanging against the smooth wood. He grinned, erasing all traces of worry from his face. "You're still fighting bullies, just like the time you went after Fitzwilliams for forcing underclassmen to do his papers."

"As I recall, you didn't think that was a good idea either."

Allan laughed. "I don't like trouble."

"Neither do I. But sometimes it can't be avoided."

Allan shrugged and lifted his hat to his head. "See you tonight at the Palace." He gave the tall hat a pat and left the office.

Spence swiveled his chair around to look out the windows behind his desk. On a clear day he could see the bay. But it wasn't clear. It was raining. His throat grew tight as he thought of Victoria Granger. He didn't need to close his eyes to see her image; those silver-blue eyes had haunted him from the first day he had met her. He rubbed his neck, listening to the steady tap of the rain, swearing under his breath. Would he ever be able to hear the rain without thinking of her?

Chapter Ten

Torrie came awake with a start, her body jerking against linen sheets, her breath rushing from her lungs in a startled gasp. What was it? The air stirred around her, brushing her face, alerting her every nerve. Something had penetrated her restless sleep, but what?

Staring into the dark canopy above her head, she held her breath, straining her ears to hear every sound in the big room. Beyond the sound of her own pulse, she heard a steady beat, low, ticking away the seconds in the shadows. It had to be the clock on the mantel. A rustling, like silk on satin . . . what was that? Her skin tingled as she sensed someone in the room, someone in the shadows, someone close.

She resisted the urge to slink under the covers, to hide her head and hope whatever lurked in the dark would go away. It was probably nothing more than her imagination, she assured herself. The past few days her nerves had been stretched to near breaking. The floorboard creaked nearby; she felt the hair on her arms prickle and rise.

She turned, glancing toward the French doors leading to her balcony. Panic surged in her blood as a dark shape loomed above her, huge and powerful. She opened her mouth to scream, the sound ripping from her throat, dying against the big hand the intruder clamped against her mouth. She grabbed his arm, twisting beneath him, trying to break free. Richard Hayward! He had sneaked into her room. He had come to force . . . Dear God, she couldn't let him!

"Relax. I'm not going to hurt you."

Torrie fell still at the sound of Kincaid's deep Texas drawl, her hands wrapped around his big arm, her lips pressed to his callused palm. With his forearm, he held her pinned to the bed like a butterfly under glass.

"Promise not to scream?" His breath stroked her cheek as he spoke, warming her skin.

The scent of his skin—spices and an intriguing fragrance that defied a label—swirled around her, soaking into her senses. Somewhere low, deep inside of her, her body responded to that scent, tightening, warming, frightening her with its raw, primitive need.

"Miss Granger, do you promise you won't scream?"

When she nodded he removed his hand from her lips. She lifted trembling fingers to her mouth, searching the shadows for a glimpse of his face. He moved, his hand reaching toward the table by her bed. A moment later the lamp on the table came to life, tossing golden light across his features.

Torrie stared, shocked by the deep lines etched into the sides of his mouth, the dark smudges beneath his beautiful eyes. Why, the man looked as though he hadn't slept in the three days since she last saw him. "What do you want? How did you get in here?"

"The balcony."

"The balcony?"

Her mind whirled. Was this a dream? Or was this man really standing beside her bed? His deep voice swirled in her head and she tried to concentrate on what he was saying.

"I've never gone back on my word in my life, and I'm not about to start now." His broad shoulders rose and fell as he took a deep breath. "Do you still want to marry me?"

It must be a dream. Things like this just didn't happen to people like her. "Marry you?"

His breath escaped in a long sigh. "Marriage, a child, disinheritance, divorce. Remember?"

"Yes." Of course she remembered.

His brows pulled together. "Yes, you remember, or yes, you still want to marry me?"

Her father had always told her it was important to be decisive. "Both," she said, still not quite believing this was actually happening.

He nodded. "All right, then, get out of bed, get dressed, and come with me."

Torrie blinked and stared at him. "Now?"

"I'm not going to go through any long engagement."

"But, my mother . . . she's planning a wedding."

A muscle in his cheek jerked at the mention of her mother. He moved toward her, his golden eyes burning into hers. "I don't give a damn what your mother has planned."

She sat up, clutching the covers to her breast,

meeting his angry stare with a defiant tilt of her head. "How dare you talk to me that way. I will not run away in the night like a criminal."

He looked fierce enough to scare a grizzly bear as he stared down at her, but Torrie refused to be cowed. "My mother would never forgive me if I eloped. What would she say to her friends?"

One corner of his lips curved upward. "I suppose she would be angry."

Torrie nodded. "Oh, my, yes, she would be furious."

His smile grew a little wider. "It would probably knock the legs right off her throne."

He understood the situation, she thought, allowing her muscles to relax. "She is a leader among her set, and she is very strict about standards. The other women would have a carnival if Lillian Granger's daughter eloped."

"She probably wouldn't be able to show her face in town for weeks."

"Months." Torrie smiled; he really did understand. "You don't know my mother."

"Yes, I do." He moved closer. "Probably better than you."

"I'm glad you . . ." Her words ended in a gasp as he snatched the covers from her hands. Before she could utter another sound, he scooped her up into his arms and started toward the balcony. "What are you doing?"

"Unless you want company, I suggest you keep your voice down," he said, his voice a husky whisper.

Torrie glanced at the door leading to the hall, pressing her hand to her lips. What would her mother think if she found her like this? "I demand you put me down!" she said, her voice barely above a whisper.

He ignored her and just kept walking. The hard muscles of his chest shifted against her breasts with every move he made. The heat of his body radiated through the thin cotton of her nightgown, drenching her skin. "Put me down!"

He carried her onto the balcony. Cleansed from three days of rain, the damp air bathed her face with the scents rising from the garden. A full moon dripped a creamy light over the garden, glittering on the moist grass, the shiny leaves of the eucalyptus, the pointed needles of the pine, transforming the gravel paths into silver, exposing her to Kincaid's gaze.

Torrie crossed her arms over her breasts. "I can't leave the house like this."

He grinned at her, his lips a scant inch from the tip of her nose. "Better hold on tight. I need one hand to get down."

Torrie glanced at the wooden ladder propped against the outside of the wrought-iron balustrade, then back at the man holding her in his arms. "You aren't serious."

He shrugged. "All right, we can do it this way."

Her breath escaped in a gasp as his hard shoulder rammed into her belly, her tender side crying out in pain. The balcony vanished from her sight, the ground looming in its place as he swung out over the railing onto the ladder. "Dear lord," she murmured, clutching his coat.

"Hold on."

She could hear the smile in his voice. The man was enjoying this. She mumbled an oath under her breath and closed her eyes, swaying with each step he took. His warm hand slid along her bare leg, grasping her thigh, sending shivers running along her skin. "Stop that," she said, trying to shake free.

"Easy," he said, squeezing her thigh. "I'm just

making sure you don't end up on your head, Miss Granger."

The man was stark-raving mad. And she was going to marry him. Dear lord, just what was she getting herself into?

"There, down without a hitch."

She peeked, breathing once again when she saw a dark cushion of grass beneath his feet. Her thick braid brushed his calves as he crossed the grass to a gravel path. "Let go of me," she said, pounding her fists against his back.

"Are you always this contrary?" he asked, ignoring her fists as though they were no more than butterflies flitting against his back. His feet crunched against the gravel as he carried her toward the back of the garden. "One minute you're proposing, the next you're trying to pound me to a pulp."

As if he felt anything, she thought. He opened the gate at the end of the garden and swung around to close it behind them, her braid flinging out to catch on a point of the wrought iron.

"Wait!" Her hair tugged against her scalp as he kept walking. "My hair . . . I'm caught!"

"Sorry," he said, turning to free her tangled tresses.

"I bet you are," she mumbled under her breath.

He tossed her like a sack of potatoes into his waiting carriage. She snatched her gown, covering her legs as he climbed up beside her. Torrie crossed her arms over her thinly clad breasts and glared at him. Her angry look had no effect on Kincaid; he flicked the reins and started the horses at a trot.

"I can't go anywhere dressed like this."

He glanced at her, his grin growing mischievous. "You're right."

"Well, I'm glad you've finally come to your senses."
He slipped off his coat as she spoke, moving the reins

from one hand to the other. "If you just turn at the next corner . . ."

"There," he said, slipping his coat around her shoulders.

Torrie fell back against the carriage seat. "I suppose this makes everything all right?"

His reply was a devilish grin.

"You're insane," she said, pulling his coat up around her chin, his scent clinging to the gray cashmere, swirling in her nostrils, making her dizzy with an emotion she didn't understand.

"I'm afraid you'll just have to take me as I am."

She was going to marry a complete stranger. An insane complete stranger. "My parents will be frantic."

"Your father knows. I talked to him at the Palace this evening."

"He knows." Torrie clutched his coat beneath her chin. "I suppose you told him how I coerced you into marrying me."

He glanced at her, a crooked smile curving his lips. "I told him we were so mad about each other, we couldn't wait another day to be married."

"And he believed you?"

Spence nodded, keeping his gaze fixed on the street in front of them. "He gave me some grief about wasting three years, told me he knew all along how right we were for one another, then gave me directions to your balcony."

Torrie sank back against the seat, smiling, wishing she could have seen her father's face when Spencer Kincaid asked him for her hand. "But he must have known an elopement would humiliate my mother."

Spence smiled as though he were enjoying a private joke. "I'm sure it never occurred to him."

The bright jingle of a bell caught her attention. She froze as the lamp of a cable car hit her face.

"Gracious!" she whispered, sinking into his coat like a turtle withdrawing into her shell.

The cable car rumbled past, iron wheels clattering against iron rails. When the sound echoed in the distance, she peeked to make sure it was out of sight. Huddled against the side of the carriage, she tried to make herself as small as possible. "I can't believe I am driving through the streets of the city dressed in my nightgown," she said, pulling her feet up under her gown.

"Relax; it's after midnight. No one you know is going to see you." He glanced at her, moonlight catching the glint of humor in his eyes. "And if they do, no one is going to believe it's really you."

She glared at him. "You are going to see me."

He lowered his eyes, his gaze sweeping her from her chin to where her toes peeked out from beneath her white cotton gown. There was a lusty sparkle in his eyes when they raised up to meet hers. "In a little while, I'm going to see all there is to see."

Feeling her cheeks grow hot, she dropped his gaze. Anticipation, sweet and thick, rose from deep within her, coursing like hot oil in her veins. Under his cashmere coat, beneath her prim cotton nightgown, her skin grew warm and tingling, the tips of her breasts puckering into tight buds. She sank lower in his coat, and tried to ignore the shameful reaction of her body, clutching at her mother's teachings: "A lady never reveals her emotions, a lady never . . ." What had her mother said?

She gripped the seat as they crested a hill, the street lamps shimmering in glowing ribbons down the slope toward the lights of Market Street and the dark bay. Kincaid handled the pair of matched bays on the hilly streets better than most men who had lived here all their lives.

She watched his hands on the reins, the flexing

of the muscles of his forearms beneath his shirt. A curious thrill crept up her spine as she realized in a short while she also would see all there was to see.

The horses' hooves pounded against the cobblestones and vibrated off the dark buildings they passed, the sound a pale reflection of the rhythm of her heart. "I suppose you don't intend to tell me where we are going," she said, tossing him a chilly glance; she hoped it would disguise the rising heat inside her.

"You'll see soon enough," he said, grinning at her.

He rested his wrists on his knees, holding the reins casually between his fingers, drawing her attention to the thigh resting so close to hers. Dark gray wool stretched tautly over the thick muscles. She imagined what it might be like to touch him, to trace the curve of his thigh, to feel the heat of his skin beneath her palm. She clasped her hands together and tried to control her runaway emotions.

What would he expect of her? Her imagination, always too active for her own good, took over. A pulse fluttered and throbbed somewhere low in her body, somewhere she couldn't even name. She wasn't sure she was ready for this. Still, a part of her had been waiting years for what would come.

Torrie glanced up at the sky, the stars looking like diamonds sprinkled on black velvet. In her mind, she could see a twenty-year-old girl sitting with a young man in a carriage under the same stars. The man was eager, too eager, groping the girl's bodice, finding her breast. The girl was confused and frightened, pulling back, slapping him hard across the cheek.

Torrie would never forget the look on his face, the face she had loved for so many years, the swift shift of emotions twisting his handsome features:

surprise, wounded pride, bitter hatred. Charles had wanted her to be a woman in his arms, and Torrie had failed.

Torrie had known Charles Rutledge all her life, and from the time she was twelve, she had known one day he would be her husband. She had loved him. Yet she hadn't been able to give him what he had wanted. Every time he had drawn near, she had turned cold and frightened, panic rising within her until she wanted to scream, to run, to escape him.

Strange, she never felt like running away when Kincaid touched her. Her gaze drifted to the man sitting beside her, moonlight painting the planes and angles of his face with creamy light. No, with Kincaid the danger was in feeling too much.

She knew the pain that came when you surrendered your dreams to a man. This time would be different. This time she knew he would be leaving. This time she knew she had to keep her dreams safely hidden, her heart well protected. This time she would not allow herself to be hurt. She couldn't. This time she wasn't sure she would survive.

Kincaid stopped the carriage by one of the many docks along the bay. The ship tethered to the dock was long and sleek, with three masts spiraling toward the starlit sky. It was a pleasure yacht the size of an old clipper ship.

"Why are we here?" Torrie asked, as Kincaid climbed down from the carriage, the springs creaking with his movement.

"We're taking a little trip," he said, without glancing at her.

"A trip?"

Her heart crawled up into her throat. Just what did she know of this man? Maybe he hadn't talked to her father. Maybe he didn't plan to elope. Maybe he had something entirely different in mind. Kincaid reached for her and she drew back. "I thought we were going to be married."

He rested his hands on the edge of the seat and looked up at her. "I'm getting the impression you don't trust me."

Torrie clutched his coat beneath her chin. "Mr. Kincaid, I don't know what you have planned, but if you think I am . . ."

"What's wrong, Miss Granger?" he asked, grinning up at her. "Afraid I'm going to shanghai you?"

"And just what are your intentions?"

"Entirely honorable."

She glanced around the dock. It was deserted, except for the three men leaning on the railing of the ship, staring down at them. No doubt they were in Kincaid's employ.

"One way or another, you are coming with me." He didn't move, the tone of his voice conveying his intention.

"I will not be treated in this manner."

He lifted his head, moonlight striking the gold in his eyes. "Over my shoulder, or in my arms. The choice is yours."

"Neither," she said, lifting her chin.

She scooted across the seat and climbed down the opposite side of the carriage. The first touch of her feet against the cold granite cobblestones made her gasp. She forced her back to straighten and tried to ignore the cold as she marched toward the gangplank.

"You are one stubborn little filly," Kincaid said, taking her arm.

The touch of respect in his voice made her smile. "You should see me when I really get determined," she said, looking up at him.

He grinned. "I have a feeling I will."

"Good evening, Mr. Kincaid," a stout, sandy-haired man said, as they stepped onto the deck. "And this must be Miss Granger."

Torrie clutched the coat to her chin, wishing she could hide in Kincaid's pocket.

"Captain Amos Hurley, may I present my fiancée, Miss Victoria Granger."

"Miss Granger," Hurley said, offering his hand. "We've been expecting you."

Torrie slipped her hand from beneath Kincaid's coat and accepted the captain's hearty handshake and warm welcome.

"Everything's all arranged, Mr. Kincaid," Captain Hurley said, pulling his gaze from Torrie. "If you would follow me."

The breeze tugged at the coat she clutched to her chin, tossing her nightgown against her legs, outlining their shape. Although the coat fell to her knees, she felt horribly exposed. Deep male laughter rumbled in the still night, and Torrie was grateful for the darkness that gave her some measure of relief from the roving stares cast in her direction.

"Why didn't you let me get dressed?" she asked, her voice a strident whisper as she walked beside Kincaid across the deck.

He smiled, a devilish grin that crinkled the corners of his eyes. "It would have been a waste of time."

Heat flared in her cheeks, and lower, she felt a shocking twin to that fire. She refused to acknowledge the wicked response as anything but anger. Anything else was simply too disturbing, too frightening to think about.

Captain Hurley bellowed orders, sending sailors scurrying as he walked toward the quarterdeck. Sails lowered above her head, the breeze snapping heavy canvas. They were reaching the point of no return.

"Mr. Kincaid," she said, following him up the stairs to the quarterdeck, "I am not going anywhere with you until we are married."

He paused as he reached the quarterdeck, turning to face her, a challenge in his eyes as he looked down at her. "All right, let's get married."

He stepped aside, allowing her to take the last step. Her toes curled against the cold oak planks beneath her bare feet as she glanced around the deck. Flowers in silver vases formed an aisle leading to the railing at the stern of the ship, white roses and gardenias filling the air with their heady fragrance. Captain Hurley stood at the end of a narrow white carpet, dressed in a dark blue uniform, surrounded by flowers, holding an open Bible.

"Shall we?" Kincaid asked, offering his arm.

Always, she had imagined being married in a flowing white gown, surrounded by friends and family. Never had she pictured being married in her nightgown with a man's coat wrapped around her shoulders.

"Miss Granger, you haven't changed your mind, have you?"

"I wish I could, Mr. Kincaid," she said, taking his arm. "I only wish I could."

Chapter Eleven

"You may kiss your bride."

Through a steady throb of blood in her ears, Torrie heard the distant murmur of Captain Hurley's words. It was over. It was just about to begin.

Kincaid's breath, warm and moist and flavored with a hint of mint, touched her cheek as his mouth descended toward her lips. His lips brushed hers as softly as the dew touches the petals of a rose, a kiss of breath, of flesh, a kiss to awaken the dreams that dwelt deep within her soul. By the time he lifted his head, her mind was in a shambles, her body trembling uncontrollably.

Congratulations came from the captain and the seamen who had acted as witnesses. Amid cheers from the dozen sailors perched in the rigging, Kincaid lifted his bride in his arms and carried her to a cabin beneath the quarterdeck. A wave of scent engulfed them as he carried her into the cabin, the spicy sweet fragrance of warm roses invading her every breath.

"The honeymoon suite, Mrs. Kincaid," Spence said, setting her on her feet.

Torrie turned slowly, scanning her surroundings. Roses, hundreds of them, stood in vases throughout the room, on the polished mahogany tables, kneeling at the foot of chairs, lining the base of every wall. Red screamed at her from all directions: blood-red roses, red plush sofa, red velvet chairs and drapes.

Torrie stared at the large bed built into one wall of the cabin, anger simmering inside of her. The dark red counterpane had been drawn back to reveal black satin sheets. So, the man intended to treat her like a harlot, she thought, turning to face him, watching as he tossed his cravat to a chair near the bed and began unfastening the studs lining the front of his shirt.

"Just what do you think you are doing?"

"You wanted a stud," he said, pulling his shirt from his trousers, revealing deep creases pressed into the linen by the heat of his body. "You have one. Texas bred." Giving her a wide grin he stripped the shirt from his back and tossed it to the chair by the bed.

For the second time in her life she was facing a man nude from the waist up, and from the way he was working the buttons of his trousers, very soon to be nude from the waist down. For a moment she could do nothing but stare at him.

Lamplight reflected on the smooth skin of his shoulders and arms; thick curves of muscle pulsing beneath sun-drenched skin. A lush pelt of soft-looking fur hugged the contours of his broad chest before tapering to a narrow line that plunged across taut bands of muscle and dipped into the waistband of his trousers . . . the trousers he was unfastening. Oh, my word, she wasn't ready for this.

"Wait," she said, holding up her hand to hold him at bay.

"Miss Granger?"

"We need to discuss a few things before we . . . before . . . please do not go any further."

He hooked his thumbs in his unbuttoned trousers and grinned at her. "What would you like to discuss?"

His trousers sank slightly with the pressure of his hands, revealing a glimpse of skin much lighter than his dark chest. Even through her anger, looking at him brought a fine trembling to her limbs. Knowing he possessed that power over her made her all the more angry.

"Mr. Kincaid, I assure you I do not want to be in this situation any more than you. Our marriage will be as brief as possible, I promise you."

"I know." His features grew tense, one corner of his lips dipping. "And I'm only trying to give you what you want."

He took a step toward her. She retreated behind a chair, grabbing the high back for support, her fingers sinking into the soft red velvet. "I doubt you have any idea of what I want." He kept moving, stalking her like a hungry mountain lion. "Please just stay where you are."

He paused, resting his hands on his hips. "Miss Granger, you might not realize this, but we'll never be able to make a baby if you keep hiding behind a chair."

She raised her chin at his mocking tone and stared straight into his glittering eyes. "If you think I want to be married to a man I barely know, to be brought to this floating brothel, to submit to the perverse rutting of some brutal barbarian, then you are very much mistaken. I do not expect to be treated like a . . . a . . . courtesan," she said, gesturing to the huge bouquet of roses at her feet.

He shrugged. "I thought you liked red roses."

"And you thought I would like being dragged around town in my nightgown, being pointed at and . . . and laughed at by those men on deck." She drew a deep breath, fighting the trembling inside her, trying to control her emotions. "You thought to humiliate me. Well, my father has already managed to do that."

Spence held her gaze, a muscle working in his jaw as he clenched and unclenched his jaw. "Like father, like daughter."

Although spoken softly, his words slapped her across the cheek as sharply as an open palm. Never had she imagined anything she might do would humiliate this self-assured male. "I apologize if I humiliated you, Mr. Kincaid," she said, glancing down at her hands. "It was not my intention. Please, believe me, if I had another choice, I would not have asked you to do this."

"Oh, I believe you. Marriage to me was the last thing you wanted," he said, staring past her to the portholes.

Torrie was astonished. She really had injured his pride; she could hear it in his voice, see it in the tensing of his muscles. This man, with his wealth, with his flawless male beauty, could be injured by one unattractive old maid. It was simply astonishing. What did one say on the occasion of bruising a finely crafted male ego?

"A life for a life." Spence brought his gaze back to her as he spoke. "I suppose it's only fair."

"No it isn't fair. I am afraid desperation sometimes makes people do things they aren't very proud of. Please believe me, I am deeply sorry for putting you in this situation."

He was quiet, studying her features, some of the anger draining from his own expression. "You told me what you don't want; what is it you do want?"

Courage. At the moment she was finding it a scarce commodity. "I expect to be treated with respect. The respect any husband should accord his wife. I would hope in public . . ." She hesitated, feeling the hard clutch of pride at her throat.

"What?"

She tried to draw a deep breath, yet her lungs were too taut to receive more than a wisp of rose-scented air. "If you could, I would ask you to allow people to think you are in love with me," she said softly. "I would like even my parents to think you wanted to marry me. At least for the time we are married."

He stood motionless, watching her, as though he could see inside her soul with those golden eyes. Perhaps he could. Unable to hold his penetrating gaze, she glanced down at her hands, staring at the stark white of her clenched knuckles against the plush red velvet, wishing she could hide from him, knowing there was nowhere to run.

"All right. I don't see why anyone should think either one of us was forced into this marriage."

She closed her eyes, releasing her breath and with it some of her tension. "Thank you."

"You've told me what you want. Now I'll tell you what I want."

Startled, she glanced up at him. "What do you mean?"

"You want a loving husband in public." His lips lifted into a boyish grin. "I want a loving wife in private."

A loving wife: it was a role she had dreamed of for too many years. Yet now the implications of those words sent tendrils of fear curling around her heart. "I intend to be a proper wife for as long as we are married."

"A proper wife by my standards, Miss Granger, not the standards you've been taught."

Looking at him, she wondered if she could possibly live up to his standards. And if she tried and failed, what then?

"Come here."

She couldn't move. Fear kept her planted behind the chair, fear of her own inadequacy, fear of losing more than her innocence.

"Come to me," he said, lifting his hand, his voice deep and compelling.

Torrie stared at that outstretched hand, his long fingers reaching for her, willing her to take the few steps separating them. But there was so much more keeping them apart. She was afraid of what he might be able to uncover hidden deep inside her, afraid of the emotions he evoked inside her whenever he was near, afraid of the cost of those emotions. Still, she couldn't hide behind a chair the rest of her life.

"I'm not going to bite."

The amusement in his tone pricked her pride. With head held high, she left her hiding place and moved toward him, forcing each foot in front of the other, ignoring his outstretched hand and all it implied. His fingers curled as he raised his hand to her cheek.

"What do you say, Miss Granger?" He brushed the back of his fingers upward across her cheek, stroking his warmth across her cool skin. "Do you think you can handle this barbarian?"

"Mr. Kincaid, I am not a backward schoolgirl,"

she said, taking a step back, knowing she was no more than a backward schoolgirl compared to this man. "I want a child, and I have some idea of what that will entail."

"Spoken like a true martyr," he said, taking her hands in his. "I'm sure your mother has told you how horrible it is for a lady to have to endure the primitive coupling of her husband."

Heat rose from her neck to burn Torrie's cheeks as her mother's words echoed in her brain. "Mr. Kincaid, my mother has done her best to teach me to behave in a proper manner, to live by strict standards, to be a lady."

"Oh, and she has succeeded, quite well."

He lifted her hand, his breath streaming warmth against her wrist as he pressed his lips to her palm. With the tip of his tongue he touched her skin. She jerked her hand back as though touched by a flame.

"Perhaps too well," he said, a gentle smile curving his lips as he captured her hands once more. "She has taught you to keep your emotions locked up inside you, to ignore every natural urge of your body." His thumbs slid back and forth across her knuckles as he spoke, as if he were trying to ease the blow of his words. "She has taught you to be a proper Ice Princess. Now, I intend to teach you a few things."

Had Allan told him about her? Had they pointed at her and laughed at the frigid old maid? Had they placed bets on Kincaid's ability to melt the Ice Princess?

Tears burned the back of her eyes, but she fought them, trying to hide the anxiety, the pain his words had dredged up within her. She would not humiliate herself in front of this man. He tugged on her hands, but she remained where she was, rigid with indignation, cold dread sliding down her legs to freeze her where she stood.

"I'll have no Ice Princess in my bed," he said, his voice a velvety caress. "Kiss me," he said, lifting her hands to his shoulders.

Traitors, her fingers curled against the smooth skin stretched tautly over solid oak, the heat of his skin branding her palms. "Mr. Kincaid, I expect to be treated with respect."

"It seems you expect a great deal from this arrangement." He rested his hands at her sides inside his coat, his long fingers riding her ribs just below her breasts. "You want my respect—earn it. Show me you can bend."

Silently, she cursed the man. He seemed intent on humiliating her. Didn't he know she had never felt more humiliated in her life? Didn't he know she realized he could never love her? She didn't need to be told she was unattractive. She knew.

He was waiting. She lifted on her tiptoes and pressed her lips to his, pulling back in a heartbeat.

"I think you can do better," he said, grinning at her. "Pretend you're a woman in love with her man. Let's see how good an actress you can be." He covered her hands with his and slid her hands along his bare shoulders. "Put your arms around my neck. A woman in love would want to get close to her man."

Torrie swallowed hard, tasting the bitterness of pride upon her tongue. "Just what do you want from me?"

"A kiss. Warm and loving, to seal our vows." His lips curved into a grin as his hand slid down the curve of her back. "The kiss of a new bride."

He was mocking her, hurting her in a way that was unspeakably cruel. "Must we play this game?

You and I both know the only reason for this farce."

His full lips pulled into a taut line. He pulled her against him, crushing her soft breasts against his rigid chest. "This farce, as you choose to call it, may go on for quite a while—until I've planted a seed in your belly, as I recall."

"As usual, your delicacy knows no bounds," she said, trying to ignore the fluttering of her heart against her ribs. In spite of his cruelty, she was drawn to this man, compelled by a perverse attraction that had nothing to do with honor or love.

She reveled in the heat of his naked chest against her breasts. She wanted to touch him. She wanted to kiss him. She wanted to absorb his power, his strength. Yet she knew he would consume her, destroy her, leave her empty inside. And he would revel in her destruction. It would be a testament to his blatant male power.

"Lady, I won't play the stud for any woman," he said, his eyes flashing golden fire. "If you're not interested in at least pretending to be a wife, I'm not interested in performing any marital obligations."

"Damn your black-hearted soul," she said, throwing her arms around his shoulders, his coat falling to the floor at her feet. She meant to give him a parody of a kiss, a twisting of her lips against his to show her contempt, but the first touch of his lips shattered that noble resolve.

He parted his lips to take her mouth in a smoldering kiss as he closed his arms around her, as he held her flush against the flame of his body. She pushed against his shoulders. He slid his hands over the curve of her hips, pulling her into his loins, forcing her to feel the heat of his arousal swelling against her belly.

She gasped against his lips, unwittingly allowing

him to plunge his tongue into her mouth. Despite her efforts to push him away, he continued kissing her, his mouth hard and insistent, his lips slanting across her lips, his breath scorching her cheek, charring her resistance like parchment tossed on a flame. His was a kiss like no other, a revelation that left her stunned and shaking in his arms.

Sweet yearning flowed in her veins at the intimate feel of his body pressed hard against her trembling flesh. Smoldering embers deep inside her came to life, igniting into flames, shooting upward, scorching all in their path. In the blaze, the icy shell surrounding her heart melted and drizzled downward like warm caramel, flowing between her thighs, shocking her sense of propriety, quenching the thirst of her long-suffering femininity.

He thrust his tongue in and out of her mouth, moving his hips to the same hypnotic rhythm, brushing the heat of his arousal against her belly, spreading his warmth up and down her back with the firm caress of his hands. Without thought, she began to return his kiss. She moved her lips against his, entwining her tongue with his, struggling to get closer and closer to the heat of his big body, her yielding curves melting against his ever-hardening muscles.

When her knees gave way he was there, slipping one arm around her shoulders, the other beneath her knees. She snuggled in his arms, resting her hand over his heart, marveling at the frantic rhythm beneath her palm, as he carried her to the bed. Lowering her to satin sheets, he stared into her face, his eyes glittering like molten gold. And then he was leaving her, taking away his warmth. She grabbed his arm, a drowning woman snatching a lifeline.

He smiled, a gentle curving of his lips, tenderness filling his eyes. "I want very much to lie with you," he said, coaxing her to release her death grip on his arm.

Torrie leaned back, watching him, trembling with anticipation. The things she was feeling no lady should ever feel, the thoughts running through her mind never flitted in the mind of any true lady.

"But I have a confession to make."

"Confession?" she tried, but couldn't look away as he peeled the dark gray wool from his hips. Beneath, silk drawers molded his skin, a white veil revealing a tempting glimpse of golden skin, dark hair, and the intriguing bulge that proclaimed his desire.

"I never wear anything to bed."

He stripped away the veil; her eyes grew wide. One glance on a misty morning could not prepare her for the sight of him. He was magnificent. Every inch of his naked flesh blazed with powerful masculinity and raw, sensual virility.

Overwhelmed by the force of her own desire, she turned away, heart pounding, skin tingling, a pulse throbbing in that mysterious part of her he would soon claim. She pressed her hand to her heart and fell back against the bed, looking up, startled at seeing her own reflection in a mirror suspended above the bed.

Torrie went rigid, staring at the woman who lay on black satin sheets, her eyes shining, her cheeks high with color. With icy malice, reality flooded her veins, cooling the fire in her blood. She was no better than Olivia Fontaine, lying on black satin sheets, lusting after some man who cared nothing for her.

Spence Kincaid did not love her. He wanted only to humiliate her, to shame her, to punish her for forcing him into this horrid bargain. And she did feel ashamed and dirty.

Now I want to teach you a few things, he had said. Well, humiliation was a lesson she had learned a long time ago.

They would fulfill this bargain, but she would not surrender what little self-respect she still possessed. She would behave with the proper decorum expected from any lady of good breeding. He would not turn her into a harlot to assuage his injured ego. Propriety would be her shield, her only protection against this man, her only hope for leaving this marriage with a shred of her dignity.

Kincaid lay beside her and touched her shoulder. She cringed, fighting the sudden stirring in her blood. "Have you no decency?" she asked, glaring up at him. He looked as though she had just poked him in the nose. "You could at least turn down the lamps before you . . . before you go ahead with this."

Spence rested on his elbow and searched her features, his eyes reflecting his confusion. "What's wrong?"

"Nothing," she said, hugging her arms to her breast.

"Talk to me," he whispered, brushing his warm fingers across her cheek. "Tell me what's wrong, sweetheart."

She flinched, trying to escape the feathery caress. "Please turn down the lamps. I prefer not to see what you intend to do."

He hesitated, looking at her as though he were trying to find the answer to a puzzle.

"If you were a gentleman, I wouldn't need to ask."

He mumbled something about virtuous women under his breath as he got out of bed. His feet were nearly soundless as he padded across the red and gold carpet, extinguishing the lamps one by one.

The room was smothered in shadows when he turned toward the bed, but she could see him clearly. Moonlight spilled in through the portholes, bathing him in a soft, creamy light, revealing every hard line and sharp angle of his beautiful body.

Torrie hid in the shadows and stared in fascination at that part of him so exclusively male, so intimidating, so alluring. The bed dipped as he slipped between the sheets, and she held her breath, her entire body tense, waiting. She would not allow herself to get involved with what he would do to her. She couldn't. She would think of something else, anything else.

"I understand this can all be done quickly and without much . . ." She stumbled, biting her lower lip, searching for the right words. "Without much . . . disturbance."

"Is that so? And tell me, how is it done?"

The sarcasm in his voice flooded her cheeks with heat. "Mr. Kincaid, I am sure you have done this before."

"Not the way you're suggesting. I think you're going to have to tell me just what you want."

She balled her hands into fists at her sides. "Just proceed!"

He didn't move. Each beat of her heart pounded against her eardrums as she waited. Seconds dragged into an eternity. Still, he didn't move. She turned and stared into the shadows, trying to see his features. He was lying on his back, staring into the mirror above their heads.

"Well, Mr. Kincaid? Are you going to get this over with?"

"This barbarian has never developed a taste for rape."

"Mr. Kincaid, we are married."

"Perhaps another time, Princess."

Torrie cringed at that name. "I prefer you didn't call me that."

"I prefer you didn't act like one."

So he found her so lacking he wouldn't even consummate their vows. "Fine," she said, rolling to her side.

Instead of feeling relieved, she felt like punching something, like screaming, like sobbing. She had to get control of her emotions. This man would not make a fool of her. He would have to take her as she was, or not at all. After all, he had some stake in all of this, she reasoned. If he wanted his freedom, he would carry through with his side of the bargain. He would soon grow tired of this game he was playing, she assured herself.

She huddled against the wall and willed herself to sleep. Just pretend he isn't there, she told herself. Yet she was aware of his every move, every sigh. The scent of his skin still clung to hers, teasing her. Her body ached in a way she had never known. She felt strained and so horribly restless. Fight; she had to fight against this destructive attraction. He threatened her dignity.

Worse. Far worse.

He threatened her heart. He threatened her soul. If she got out of this ordeal with her heart in one piece, she would be very, very lucky.

Spence stared into the mirror above the bed, watching her, wanting her. He ached for wanting her, the pain in his loins throbbing like an open wound. Never in his life had a woman evoked such a strong response in him with just a kiss. In dreams, Torrie had come to him night after night, but dreams couldn't compare to the feel of her warm and trembling in his arms. He wanted her, needed her, needed to bury himself in the honeyed core of her body.

What the hell had he done? She had melted in his arms, and then . . . What had he done to bring about the change? What had he done to turn the warm, sensual woman in his arms back into a statue of ice?

He only knew he had to find the woman he had held, find her under all the ice. He wasn't about to settle for a cold reflection of the dream he had held.

Chapter Twelve

Torrie drifted in a cozy place between waking and dreams, images of a white sand beach, of turquoise water sparkling in the sun, dissolving, giving way to reality. Someone was there with her on the beach, a man holding a red rose, smiling as he moved toward her. She didn't want to awaken. Not yet. Not until she felt his arms slide around her. Not until . . . until what, she wondered?

Resisting the persistent tug of morning, she buried her face in the pillow beneath her cheek. Something soft tickled her nose, a spicy scent teased her nostrils, a compelling warmth enveloped her. Curious, she opened sleep-filled eyes to a vast expanse of dark fur. For a moment she couldn't move, holding her breath, snatching at wisps of memory, nerves waking, sensing, emotions stirring.

"Good morning, Princess."

His chest rumbled beneath her cheek, his deep voice dragging her to full awareness. She lay snuggled against a man's side, her arm slung across his waist, her thigh across both of his. Her nightgown was tangled somewhere in the vicinity of her hips, exposing her smooth inner thigh to the lush cushion of warm male skin. She jerked upward, her heart slamming against her ribs as she looked down into golden eyes.

"Kincaid!" She scrambled off him, ramming his thigh with her knee, snatching the sheet to cover herself, revealing his nude body in her haste.

"Easy, Princess," he said, rubbing the top of his thigh. "You said you wanted children, remember."

His morning arousal stood tall and proud from a nest of black curls. She felt a tug inside her, somewhere low and forbidden. With a little cry, she tossed the sheet back over him, only to have him toss it aside. "Haven't you a shred of modesty?"

He grinned and scratched his chest. "As much as any self-respecting barbarian."

A low growl rose from deep in his chest as he stretched, his long body growing tense, muscles twisting, turning, growing sharply defined beneath golden skin. She sat on her heels, her back against the wall, and watched, mesmerized by the latent power of those muscles, stark virility filling the air, permeating her every breath with his intriguing essence. Her skin tingled from her scalp to her toes and everywhere in between, electricity suddenly coursing through her veins.

He got out of bed. For one reckless moment her hand lifted toward him, reaching for him like a beggar reaching for food. She gripped the sheet with both hands, praying she could grip her runaway emotions. Memories from last night rose to taunt her: his arms sliding around her, holding her to the

compelling heat of his powerful body, his lips . . .
Stop it! She had to gain some control, some small
shred of control.

Helpless to look away, she watched as he walked
across the cabin, her gaze lingering on his taut little
behind. "What are you going to do?"

"Bathe, shave, and have breakfast." He glanced
over his shoulder, his lips curving into a grin as he
rubbed his bristly chin.

She turned away, realizing he had caught her staring at him in a most disgraceful manner. And he
knew. Those eyes didn't spare her. He could read
her thoughts. He could see her desire. Desire! What
self-respecting lady felt desire for a man she didn't
love?

The man was casting spells, transforming her into
someone she didn't know, someone who was wanton. Worse—someone who was reckless. Someone
headed for a terrible fall. She wouldn't tumble under
his spell. She couldn't!

Her gaze drifted back to where he stood at the
washstand. Sunlight streamed through the portholes
to worship this masterpiece of God, to bathe his skin
in gold. She sat paralyzed, feasting on all the glorious skin displayed so freely to her ever-awakening
senses. Never had she realized looking at a man,
seeing him stripped of society's shackles, could be
so . . . so . . . pleasurable.

The thick muscles in his back flexed as he poured
water from a pitcher into the washbasin. He had a
beautiful back, full swells of muscle flanking a deep
valley, gliding down to that taut behind. She caught
herself staring once again and turned away. What
type of woman stared at a man's bare behind? She
didn't want the answer.

She glanced up at the mirror above her and
groaned at her reflection. Compared to this man,

she was a brown potato. Was it any wonder he
refused to touch her? She reached for her anger like
a shield. Anger was much more comfortable than
the emotions simmering inside her, much more safe.
"Mr. Kincaid, are your mistresses always anxious to
watch themselves in bed?"

He glanced over his shoulder. "I'm not sure what
you mean."

"The mirror," she said, gesturing toward the mirror above her head.

Spence frowned and turned back to the mirror
above the washstand. "This is Allan's yacht."

"Oh."

He drew a soapy sponge over his shoulder. Small
rivulets of water coursed down his shoulder and
along the swell of his back to the slight curve of
his hip. Her throat went dry. *Think of something
else. Hold on to your anger. Remain detached.* She
nearly laughed. Her heart was pounding too hard
to allow any pretense of being detached. "Is it too
much to ask our destination?"

"Mexico." He turned, scrubbing his chest. "Allan
has a place on the beach. I've been there a few times,
though it's been a while."

"I see." She followed that swirling sponge with
her eyes, something odd happening inside her at
the sight of dark curls caught in white lather.
He turned away. She smoothed the black satin
laying across her lap, her fingers oversensitive to
the smooth material. "And how long shall we be
there?"

"Just a few days," he said, glancing over his
shoulder. "I have some unfinished business in San
Francisco."

The sponge dipped lower and her imagination
wandered. Dear Lord, help her! She wanted to touch
him, to feel his lips against hers, to feel his arms

around her. If she didn't think of something else, she would make a fool of herself. Again. "It seems I find myself without clothes. Tell me, do you have any suggestions?"

He rinsed the sponge and mopped the soap from his shoulders and chest. "A few," he said, glancing over his shoulder. "But I doubt you're ready for any of them."

Her cheeks grew warm. "Do you expect me to spend the next few days in my nightgown?"

He turned, rubbing his chest with a towel, giving her a lusty smile. "It can come off anytime."

Torrie pulled the sheet to her chin. "Unlike you, I do not feel inclined to parade around in a disgraceful manner."

"I doubt there is anything disgraceful hiding under there."

"You are an impossible man," she said, tugging the sheet free from the mattress.

"Impossible? No. I've always believed anything is possible."

She wrapped the sheet around her shoulders and climbed out of bed, intending to search for something to wear. "I wonder if it is possible for you to behave as a gentleman."

"When the time is right."

The trunk at the foot of the bed was empty. She slammed the lid shut, threw open the door of a closet nearby and started rifling through the coats, shirts, and trousers hanging there. On the floor of the narrow closet sat shoes, boots, and a large package wrapped in silver paper. She stared at that package, curiosity curling around her ribs.

"I think it's all right for you to accept that now," Spence said, coming up behind her.

Torrie glared at him over her shoulder. "I'm more interested in finding something to wear."

"Here." Spence pulled a white shirt off a hanger. "This should do."

"Oh, yes. I should be able to attend the captain's table in this." Torrie took the shirt, then grabbed a pair of trousers from the closet. "Here. At least one of us can be properly dressed." She slapped the trousers against his belly, keeping her eyes focused on the silver package gleaming on the closet floor.

"And I thought I was properly dressed. For a honeymoon."

He kissed the nape of her neck, the soft touch a flame against her skin. She raised her shoulder in defense. "It's morning."

"I like the morning, the afternoon, the evening," he said, punctuating each phrase with a kiss, brushing his lips against her temple, her cheek, her shoulder.

"It isn't at all proper." She turned to face him, determined to show him she would not play his games; only to discover facing him was a grave tactical error. The warmth of his body reached out to her, all that glorious skin radiating a delicious heat that seeped inside of her to fan the burning embers deep in her flesh.

His lips curved into a mischievous grin. "I always thought anything was proper between a man and his bride."

Bayberry soap, and spices, and something else, a scent all his own, tingled her senses, tripping her heart. She wasn't prepared to defend against the dark, male beauty of his skin, the maddening magnetism drawing her near. She felt as though she had come to the battlefield as naked and vulnerable as a newborn child.

He grazed her cheek with his lips, tracing a fiery path to her right ear. Her breath hovered in her throat as he circled the curve of her ear with the tip of his tongue. A soft sigh escaped her lips before she could snatch it back as he rolled the soft lobe of her ear between his teeth, coaxing tingles to ripple across her skin, raising gooseflesh in their wake. Her hand moved of its own volition, finding his chest, his skin warm against her palm, her fingers curling into the crisp curls.

"Morning light adores you," he whispered, brushing his lips against her temple. "It takes a true beauty to shine in the full light of morning."

She was plummeting headlong into the darkness. Yet she knew what awaited her at the bottom of her fall: sharp, jagged rocks. She turned away from him, staring down at the shirt she clutched in her hand, trying to corral her scattered wits. "I suppose you have awakened with enough women to be an expert."

"A few." He trailed his fingers along the curve of her neck. "None more beautiful than you."

She trembled at his warm touch. How many women had believed that lie? It would be easy, so easy to believe any lie spoken in that rich, drawling baritone. She curled her shoulders away from him. "Please, Mr. Kincaid, save your flowery praise for your next conquest. I don't want it."

"Is that what you think this is?" He placed his hands on her shoulders and forced her to face him. A muscle flashed in his cheek as he clenched his jaw. "Seductive words to lure another innocent into my clutches?"

"This isn't a game, Mr. Kincaid."

His eyes sparkled, like fine brandy in cut crystal held over a flame. "I'm glad you realize that, Princess."

She watched his lips lower toward her mouth, memory sparking desire. His kisses made her forget who she was, made her forget why they were

together. She couldn't afford to forget. This was his
game, played by his rules, and she was going to lose.
The stakes were too high.

His breath brushed her cheek, warm with promise. She turned her head. "If you must do this now,
I won't stop you. But . . . I would rather you didn't
kiss me."

Spence tilted his head, his breath escaping in a
rush between his teeth. "Is that because you don't
like it?" His eyes penetrated hers, searching out
the truth she was desperately fighting to hide. "Or
because you like it too much?"

She hugged her arms to her waist. "Mr. Kincaid,
I just want to keep things in proper perspective."

"I see. You want to make sure I realize there's only
one reason why I'm here, one reason why you're
willing to spread your lily-white thighs for the likes
of me."

"Must you always be so vulgar?"

"Must you always be so damn proper?"

He turned and marched toward the washstand.
Torrie sagged back against the closet door, staring
at him, fighting the urge to punch him, to throw
her arms around him and bury her face against his
warm back. If things were different, she wouldn't
care about the time of day. If this were a real
marriage, if he loved her, if she loved him, if . . .
if dreams came true. Dreams didn't come true. She
had learned that lesson a long time ago.

She stared at him, watching as he swirled the soft
bristles of his shaving brush against the soap in a
light blue porcelain mug, muscles dancing beneath
his smooth skin. With a touch he inflamed her
senses, while she left him cold. It was all a game
to this man. He wanted to melt the Ice Princess,
add her to his long list of conquests, assuage his
bruised ego. She slammed the closet door and

marched to the open portholes, gripping his shirt in her hand.

"Something wrong, Princess?"

She took deep breaths, the cool breeze doing little to smother the fiery rage building inside her. "Besides being married to a man I despise, nothing at all."

"Such anger. Now what did I do?"

"You know perfectly well what you did," she said, glancing over her shoulder. "Don't try to look innocent; it doesn't suit you."

He grinned and began to lather his cheeks. "I thought I obeyed your wishes."

She spun on her heel and faced him. "My wishes indeed! You strut around here like Adam before the fall, without the decency to cover yourself, or bathe in private. You touch me as though . . . as though you want . . . and then you just walk away!"

His brows raised slightly. "Isn't that what you wanted?"

My word, just what did she want? She turned away, trying to hide, knowing he could see the confusion in her eyes, afraid of what it meant. "I don't want to play your games."

"What is it? Don't think you can manage to play the role of a wife?"

She hugged her arms to her waist. "I'm afraid you are confusing the word 'wife' with something else."

He was quiet a moment. She could feel his gaze on her—warm, compelling, coaxing her to meet his eyes, those eyes that saw too much. It took every ounce of control she possessed to keep from turning to him.

"Is that all that frightens you?"

She wished that was all. He evoked emotions in her she shouldn't feel. Not for this man. "I wish I had never met you," she said, her voice strangled with unshed tears.

"Take heart, Princess, I won't always be around."

No, one day he would leave, and if she weren't careful, very, very careful, he would take her heart with him. Dear lord, she had to keep her distance. "Your one saving grace, Mr. Kincaid," she said, staring out at the sea.

Sunlight struck each rolling wave, sending shards of light in all directions. Her eyes narrowed against the glare. She tried to ignore the man standing a few feet away, determined to show him how unaffected she could be. This man would not make a fool of her, he would not humiliate her, he would not destroy her. Unless she allowed him to.

Spence soaped his cheeks, frowning at his own reflection. So she didn't want his kisses, his flowery praise. When it came right down to it the little lady didn't want him. He only wished to hell he didn't want her.

She was his wife. He could do what he wanted. And right now he wanted to toss the little filly on her lovely backside and plunge into the soft, honeyed heat of her, over and over and over. . . . A sharp pain twisted in his belly. Damn! He couldn't. Not this way. Not like a hired stud.

He opened his razor and drew the blade across his cheek, cutting a path in the lather. Memories gathered inside him: of a woman awakening in his arms, discovering the heady wine of her own exquisite arousal; of surrender so sweet, so passionate it had stolen his breath. Last night he had glimpsed the lady without her icy mask. She might not love him, but she wanted him. She was just too damned stubborn to show it.

His gaze drifted back to her reflection. She was clutching that sheet to her chin as though her life depended on it. Swathed in black satin and white cotton from her chin to her toes, she was more seductive than any woman he had ever seen in the flimsiest wisps of silk. Yet at the same time she reminded him of a child lost in the woods: frightened, certain a hungry bear would devour her.

She was a thoroughbred filly who had been shown nothing but cruelty. It would take patience to win her trust, a steady hand to tame her.

What the hell was he thinking? Those were long-term thoughts. And it was clear he and Victoria Granger were not in this for the long term. Still, he didn't intend to play this game by her rules. He refused to be treated like an animal, to be tolerated as though his touch were something dirty and ugly.

She glanced in his direction, her gaze sliding over him, hot and liquid, making him burn, making his hand shake. The blade nicked his chin. With a silent oath, he lowered the razor and pressed the towel to his bloody chin.

Her words might push him away, but her eyes drew him near. The lady needed to learn the power of her own passion. She needed to realize she wanted him just as much as he wanted her. And he was going to teach her. He would have her warm and pliant and begging for him. He wouldn't settle for anything less than total surrender. He cleaned the blade and started on his other cheek. He just hoped he could survive the lesson.

Torrie pulled her gaze from his beautiful skin and stared out the porthole. She heard him move, felt the soft brush of air as he walked behind her, and pulled the sheet closer around her shoulders.

"Do you want breakfast first, or fresh water for your bath?" he asked, pulling on a pair of drawers.

"I would prefer a bath," she said, glancing at him. "In private."

He grinned. "Of course, Princess."

Her hands clenched into fists at the use of that ugly name. He dressed quickly and left her alone with her confusion. She prowled the cabin, restless, miserable, feeling like a caged tigress. Red roses shrieked at her from all directions. The man had done his best to humiliate her and had succeeded, with her help.

She snatched at the roses near her feet, thorns digging into her hand. Smiling, she tossed the roses out a porthole, satisfaction curling inside her as the blood-red blooms floated away on the rolling sea. Filled with delight, powered by determination, she roamed the room, gathering roses, tossing them to a watery grave.

She sat on the window seat and watched as the last blooms fought against the rolling sea, pain prickling her palm, regret twisting her heart. A heady scent lingered in the cabin long after the last bloom succumbed to the sea, a specter haunting her, reminding her she couldn't escape Spencer Hampton Kincaid.

She had loved Charles all her life, yet she had never felt the things for him she felt for Kincaid. He appealed to her senses—all of them, some she hadn't even known she possessed until she had met him. He filled her with disgraceful sensations, delighting her, making her delirious with some odd, throbbing need deep inside her. Even now, the memory of him made her crave his touch.

The danger was far greater with this man than it had ever been with Charles. With this man she could lose more than her pride, more than every hope and dream; she could lose every will and desire, every fiber that formed the woman she knew as Victoria

Granger. Kincaid was the type of man who infected a woman's blood, the type of man a woman could never forget, the type of man who didn't stay to witness the destruction he had caused.

Somehow she had to defend herself against him, against the compelling beauty of his eyes, against the warm rush of desire she felt whenever he was near. She would surrender her body but nothing more, and she would do it under her own terms.

"Not this time," she whispered. She would not allow herself to be broken into pieces this time. This time she was afraid she couldn't put all the pieces back together again.

She was still sitting on the window seat when he returned with a pitcher of warm water. He glanced around at the empty vases and smiled at her. "Why do I get the feeling my face was etched on every rose you tossed to a watery grave?"

"You are more perceptive than you appear, Mr. Kincaid."

He laughed. "Some books are easier to read than others."

"Oh, and you think you can read me like a book."

"Sometimes." He set the pitcher on the washstand and turned toward her. "And then, there are times when you are a mystery."

She had never thought of herself as a mystery before. It made her sound . . . intriguing. "I thought you were an expert where women were concerned."

"The only man who says he's an expert where women are concerned is a liar."

How many women had he known? With that face, that body, that smile, that treacherous charm, hundreds—perhaps thousands—of women must have succumbed to the madness, must have sacrificed themselves to this man. She wondered if any had touched his heart.

He swept his hand toward the washstand. "Your bath is ready, my lady."

He didn't look as though he had the slightest intention of leaving. "I said, I would like to bathe in private."

"So you did." He sank to a nearby armchair, settling comfortably against the red velvet, stretching his long legs out in front of him. "But I've decided to stay."

Torrie's back went rigid. "If you think I will bathe with you gawking, you are mistaken."

"I've heard some women bathe in their nightgowns." He gave her a wide-eyed look of pure innocence. "Is that true?"

She clutched her nightgown to her chin. Her mother had preached: "A lady never bares her flesh to anyone, including herself." Yet Torrie had never become adept at bathing under the cover of towels or in the folds of her nightgown. Still, she wasn't going to put on a show for this grinning rogue. "The way I bathe is of no concern to you."

"Unless I miss my guess, you could bathe without giving me more than a glimpse of what you're hiding beneath all that cotton and black satin." He rested his ankle on his knee, leaning back in a flagrant male pose. "Come on, Princess, satisfy your poor husband's curiosity."

Her chin soared. "No."

"Now what would a barbarian do in the face of such willful disobedience?" He smiled, holding her in his gaze. "Would he strip the nightgown from your back and bathe you with his callused hands?"

A curious thrill chased down her spine. "You wouldn't dare."

"I think you know better," he said, his eyes reflecting his intent. "Now, what's it going to be?"

Torrie mumbled an oath under her breath, one of her father's favorites, and tossed the sheet to the sofa.

"Did you say what I think I heard you say?" he asked, sounding far too amused.

Feeling no need to dignify his question with a response, she marched to the washstand, glaring at his grinning face, maintaining as much dignity as she could muster.

She opened five buttons at the center of her gown, then slipped her arms out of her full sleeves. Using the opening to gain access to the sponge and towel, she bathed under the concealing folds of her voluminous nightgown.

"Satisfied?" she asked, slipping her arms back into her sleeves.

"Bravo, Princess!" Spence said, clapping his hands. "Done without giving this mere mortal more than a hint of the loveliness hidden beneath your chaste gown."

Torrie felt fire rise across her breasts, her neck, until the humiliating stain of her blush heated her cheeks. "I am so glad I could entertain you, Mr. Kincaid."

He lowered his eyes, and she could feel each button fall open beneath his gaze, feel the cotton slip away from her skin. Heat simmered deep in her flesh, spreading across her skin, desire rising within her like steam, bringing a trembling to her limbs.

"The entertainment has yet to begin, Princess," he said, his voice deep and husky. He traced the full curve of her lips with his eyes and she tried to draw a deep breath.

"And I wonder what keeps the beast at bay."

"All the ice. I'm waiting for the thaw."

Charles had called her frigid. What if she couldn't please a man? Lord help her, she was both terrified and anxious to discover the truth. "Are you sure there will be one?"

"I have my hopes."

Her stomach chose that moment to make a plaintive plea for food. She grabbed her middle and glanced at him.

He laughed and came to his feet. "Seems it's time for breakfast."

She glared at his back as he left the cabin. So the man didn't find her attractive, she thought, lifting one corner of the black satin sheet from the sofa where she had discarded it. The Ice Princess, was she. Following an instinct she didn't pause to understand, she stripped off her nightgown.

The black satin felt terribly wicked, shameful, absolutely delicious against her naked skin as she wrapped it around her body, draping it over one shoulder, fashioning a gown from the soft fabric. From the closet, she took a white cravat and tied it around her waist. She pulled the ribbon from her hair and began to unplait her braid as she rushed across the cabin.

As she lifted his brush from the washstand she caught a glimpse of her reflection in the mirror. With her hair tumbling around her shoulders and the black satin clinging to her figure, she looked like a woman trying to entice a man to her bed. And what then?

By the time Kincaid returned to the cabin, she had one of his shirts over her makeshift gown, every button tightly fastened, and her hair in a neat braid. Although the white shirt dipped to her knees, hiding most of her daring makeshift gown, it was strangely intimate, wearing his clothes, feeling the brush of this linen, knowing it had once touched his skin.

One dark brow rose as he looked at her, his gaze sweeping her odd outfit. "Very becoming."

Her chin rose at his sarcasm. "If you had allowed me the time to collect some of my things . . ."

"You could be bound from head to foot in all that rigging ladies always wear," he said, grinning at her. He crossed the cabin and opened a door leading to the dining room, allowing the heady aroma of fresh rolls and coffee to drift into the room. "Breakfast is ready."

Torrie swallowed back a comment and followed him. An oval oak table and six chairs fit snugly into the small dining room. Sunlight streamed in through the open portholes, slanting across the silver, the dishes and platters covering the white linen tablecloth, glistening on roasted filets of steak, crisp fried potatoes, scrambled eggs, and juicy slices of melon and oranges. She felt hungry enough to eat everything. Sparring with Kincaid was stimulating to her appetite. She just wished that was all he stimulated.

"I have an idea how we might spend the rest of the day," he said, holding her chair.

His arm brushed hers as she took her place at the table, her composure fluttering at the slight touch. "You do?"

He nodded as he took his place at the head of the table, adjacent to hers. "After breakfast, if you open the package in the closet, I'll tell you what I have in mind."

Chapter Thirteen

Torrie toyed with the silver ribbons adorning the package sitting on the round mahogany table before her. She didn't want to look too anxious. Still, one could resist curiosity for just so long. She dove into the package like a little girl at Christmas, sending pieces of silver paper flying. Polished rosewood emerged as she pulled back the paper. Just what was inside, she wondered, unhooking a gold latch at the front of the case.

"A chess set," she whispered, spreading open the rosewood case to form a chess board of ebony and inlaid pearl.

"Quinton said you enjoyed chess." Spence opened twin drawers beneath the board as he spoke. He threw back black velvet and revealed porcelain chess pieces. "I thought you might like this," he said, sitting beside her on the sofa.

He was so close she could feel the heat of him against her side. If she moved her thigh just a little she could touch his. She remained frozen, her legs anchored to the sofa.

"They're beautiful," she said, lifting the white queen. Three round emeralds adorned a gold crown set atop her long yellow hair. In one slender hand she held the skirt of her pink gown, lifting it to reveal one crystal slipper.

"Do you recognize her?" he asked, his warm breath stirring the tiny curls above her ear.

"Cinderella," Torrie said, turning the figure in her hands, admiring the fine detail, hoping he wouldn't notice the way her hand was trembling.

"The black queen is Snow White."

"I've never seen anything like it," she said, lowering Cinderella to her bed of black velvet next to her fair-haired prince.

She lifted the black queen. A simple crown of blue and white flowers graced her long black hair, but she wore a necklace of gold and diamonds, the gems catching the sunlight streaming through the portholes behind Torrie, spinning a kaleidoscope of color. "It is far too expensive. I couldn't possibly accept."

Spence shook his head. "The rules are different now, Torrie. We're married. Remember?"

In name only, she thought.

"Quinton said you were pretty good. You'll have to be." He began to arrange the pieces on the board. "If you're going to beat me."

"Pretty sure of yourself," she said, placing the black queen on her throne.

He grinned at her. "Let's see you take me down a peg."

At the moment there was nothing she wanted to do more. He pulled two chairs up to the table and

held one for her. As she took her seat, his spicy scent
teased her nostrils, tugging at her vitals, sending her
heart pounding against her ribs. It was humiliating
to know she had no effect on him, while he turned
her into a swirling mass of feelings.

"We'll see if you are really as good as you think
you are," she said, needing some comeuppance for
the way he made her feel.

He settled into the chair across from her, smiling. "Your move," he said, resting his fingers on his
queen.

Her gaze tarried on his hand a moment, his
curving fingers reminding her of how it felt to be
touched by him, to be held in his arms. She tried
to dismiss those dangerous thoughts. "Tell me, why
did you call me a wild rose?" she asked, moving her
knight.

He glanced up from the board. "Pardon me?"

"The note you sent with the roses when I was ill.
You called me a wild rose."

He grinned and moved a pawn. "Because it suits
you."

She countered with one of her pawns. "I'm not
sure I understand."

He didn't hesitate, moving his bishop, capturing
her in his gaze. "Maybe one day I'll explain it to
you."

Her mouth went dry under his heated gaze. She
glanced down at the board, trying to concentrate,
strategy eluding her.

The warm essence of the man drifted across
the battlefield, potent masculinity stripping her
defenses. Unshielded, her army succumbed to his
advances, piece by piece marching to his side of the
battlefield, becoming his prisoners. Soon her queen
was in jeopardy, his loyal knight sitting outside her
castle walls.

Torrie gnawed her lower lip as she studied the board. The battle was lost. "Looks as though you have me."

"This game," Spence said, smiling at her across the battlefield. "I might not be as lucky the next one."

Her concentration was better as they started the second game. Shortly after lunch, she had him in check, but he eluded her. Two hours later, she took his queen.

"It would seem we're well matched," Spence said, replacing his pieces on the board. "How about making a wager on the next game?"

"What sort of wager?" Torrie asked, handing him one of his knights.

He closed his hand over hers, imprisoning his knight in her palm. "If I win, I want something from you."

She suddenly found it difficult to breathe. "Such as?"

He smiled. "A glimpse of the Ice Princess in all her glory. Naked, the way God made you."

She tugged free of his grip. "You want me to parade in front of you, like a slave on the block?"

"I want you to drop the veil. I want to see if you're as beautiful as I imagine you are."

"Why don't you just strip the clothes off my back?"

He shook his head, his grin growing wider. "Not much fun in that."

And not enough humiliation either. She slipped her tongue out to moisten her dry lips. "And if I win?"

Leaning back in his chair, he opened his arms. "What do you want?"

Torrie sat back, twisting her diamond and sapphire ring around her finger. Looking at him, she realized she wanted too many things, things she could never have. "I want you to stop calling me Princess."

Spence laughed. "It's a deal."

She was appalled to see her hands trembling as she positioned her pieces. This was one game she intended to win.

The breeze blowing in through the portholes turned warmer as afternoon faded into evening. Kincaid rolled up his sleeves and unfastened the first few buttons of his shirt. The intriguing triangle of dark curls and tawny skin he revealed whispered to her imagination until tremors trembled deep in her flesh. She caught herself staring and immediately focused her attention on the board.

Time and time again Torrie thought she had broken through his defenses, only to find herself in retreat. After a break for dinner, the two generals returned to do battle. As the sun set, Kincaid's forces attacked with renewed vigor.

"It's going to be a beautiful evening," Spence said, glancing out the portholes. "Want to go on deck and take a look at the stars?"

Torrie was more interested in defending her queen. "Dressed like this?"

He grinned, one corner of his lips lifting higher than the other. "Everything is covered."

At least for the moment. If she didn't protect her queen, it would be an entirely different situation. "I would rather not." She had to castle, hoping he wouldn't notice the vulnerable position of her bishop.

Her bishop fell.

"Did you know, you get a little crinkle between your eyes when you plot your next move."

Torrie glared at him over the battlefield. "Mr. Kincaid, I'm trying to concentrate."

"I know." He grinned at her. "Your crinkle is showing."

The man was impossible. She moved her queen. Kincaid glanced at the board and penetrated her defenses with his knight.

"You could at least look as though this is a challenge," she said, sitting back in her chair.

"No doubt about it," he said, rising to his feet. "You are a challenge." He stretched, his white shirt growing taut across his broad chest, betraying the sharp definition of broad muscles, the dark shadow of black fur.

Torrie forced her gaze back to the board. His strategy was flawless, his defenses well fortified. If she moved her king to . . .

"Sure you don't want to take a walk on deck?"

"Mr. Kincaid!"

He raised his hands in surrender. "Sorry."

She moved her king and he returned to the table. In five moves he had her queen in check. In three more, her kingdom was lost. Torrie sat back in her chair and looked at him from her fallen throne. "It seems you win."

He leaned back in his chair and met her gaze. "So it seems."

Time to pay the forfeit. No man had ever seen her naked. Even Dr. Wallace had treated her wound without seeing her nude body. *What will you think of me?* "Where did you learn to play chess like that?"

"My father taught me to play when I was six. I was lucky enough to play some real masters in college."

She twisted her ring, ashamed of her damp palms. Would he think she was homely? She knew she was too thin, much too thin.

"You're stalling."

She still couldn't move.

"You're not the type of person to go back on a bet, are you?"

An honest man always paid his debts, her father had told her. The same should hold true for an honest woman. She rose from the table, her legs far from steady. What would he think of her? she wondered, working the top button free of the linen. Why should she care? Yet, if he laughed . . . *please don't let him laugh*, she prayed.

Spence sat back and watched, frowning as he noticed her fingers trembling. "You look like Joan being led to the stake."

Her chin soared. Without hesitation, she unfastened the buttons running down the front of his shirt and pulled it from her shoulders. Black satin hugged the willowy curves of her figure, the firm globes of her breasts, the slight curve of her hips.

"Very nice," he said, imagining the feel of that warm black satin beneath his hands.

"You would like black satin," she said, tossing the makeshift belt to the sofa.

"You happen to look very nice in black satin."

As the sheet sagged away from her body, she snatched it to her breasts. Holding his breath, he waited for her to drop the sheet, but she stood frozen like an ice statue.

The look in her huge, silvery eyes told him she wanted to run, to hide. And he had to fight the urge to give in to her. It was time for her to stop hiding. "Princess?"

She mumbled something under her breath and dropped the sheet. The black satin fell like a rippling shadow to her feet, baring her flesh to his startled eyes. She was even more beautiful than he had imagined.

A dark blush rose to stain the white satin of her

breasts, her neck, her cheeks. Firm, round breasts rose and fell with each quick breath she took, the pink tips puckering like rosebuds beneath his gaze. He wanted to taste her breasts, to roll the little buds between his teeth, to feel their delicious weight fill his hands.

He lowered his eyes, his gaze sliding down the curve of her arm, past her tiny waist to where she held her hands tightly clasped in front of her. Still hiding from him. But, she couldn't hide the long, lovely curve of her legs. He imagined those long legs wrapping around his waist, imagined the feel of her tight, quivering flesh closing around him. A very real heat seared his loins, his muscles growing taut and throbbing with need.

She reached for the sheet and he raised his hand. "Not yet."

"Mr. Kincaid, haven't you seen enough?"

"A man never has enough of a beautiful woman," he said, his voice husky to his own ears.

"I think the bet has been paid." She pulled the sheet around her and turned away. "Pity you don't have one of your mistresses on board. I'm sure they would be happy to provide you with such sport as you are accustomed."

He studied the proud set of her shoulders a moment, longing to take her in his arms, knowing she would push him away. She was all tied up in knots, and somehow he had to find a way to free her. "You have nothing to be ashamed of."

"I'm not ashamed." She gathered the sheet around her, clutching it with both hands. "If you had your way, I would be turned into a harlot."

"If I have my way, you'll stop being afraid to be a woman."

"Thank you very much, Mr. Kincaid. But, I assure you, I am not afraid to be a woman, just not the type of woman you seem to crave."

"And Charles Rutledge, what did he crave?" he asked, deliberately probing the old wound.

She sank her teeth into her lower lip. He could see she was fighting for that icy control she so loved. "Just what do you know about Charles?"

"I know he left you on your wedding day. I know he got a little anxious and jumped the gun with a friend of yours." He glanced down to the pawn he was holding, then back up at the girl, weighing his words. "Maybe he was afraid the Ice Princess would never melt."

"Oh, you are so smug, so sure of yourself, so sure of everything."

Her control was slipping, he could sense it, and he pushed on, hoping to shatter it completely. "How do you plan to make a baby?"

"I'd rather not discuss such things."

"Do you think I'll just slip into bed and lift your nightgown? Do you think all you'll have to endure is a few quick thrusts and then it'll be over? Maybe you're hoping you can sleep through it."

She drew a ragged breath. "I wouldn't expect you to understand."

"When Charles touched you, did it feel right, Torrie? Did you want to feel his hands on your bare skin, did you want to feel him moving deep inside you?"

She twisted the sheet above her breasts. He could see her struggle, see the tears sparkling in her huge eyes. He knew she was going to have to face the past if there was any hope for a future. And, at that moment, he realized he wanted a chance to face the future with this woman.

His voice was low and calm as he spoke, masking the emotions churning inside him. "Did you ever think maybe he was the wrong man?"

"How can you say that? You don't know him. You don't know how I feel about him. Tell me, Kincaid, have you ever been in love, really in love?"

Never in the past had he imagined himself in love. But now? What did he feel now?

"No, you haven't. I can see it in your eyes. Well, I have. And it hurts."

He wished she would cry, wished she would wash away all the hurt she kept bottled up inside her. Maybe then she could let go of the past. Maybe then she could bury her feelings for Rutledge. "Torrie, you can't judge all men by what he did."

"Stop it! Just stop it!" Her voice was strangled with unshed tears as she forced the words from her lips. "You're a horrible man."

"You're right, I am a man. Not a boy who's going to run away to lick his wounded ego with some other woman. Not a monster who's going to rape your luscious body. Just a man, Torrie." Every word brought him closer, until he was a few inches from her. Yet a chasm separated them, a gulf littered with the sharp pieces of shattered dreams. "A man who finds himself married to a woman he barely knows, a woman for some reason he feels he has known all of his life."

Her shoulders shook with an effort to keep her emotions under a tight rein. "What do you want from me?"

"I want you to realize it's natural to feel desire, it's healthy to cry. I want you to know how good it feels to be alive. You gave me my life; let me help you find yours."

A single tear escaped, catching the lamplight as it slid down her cheek. She slashed at the glistening droplet and glared up at him. "I don't want what you have to offer, Kincaid."

"Have you ever thought there might be some ladies

who enjoy a man's kisses, who enjoy being held?" He brushed his fingers over her damp cheek, absorbing her tears. "Some women who believe it's their right to enjoy lovemaking as much as any man?"

She pulled away. "I doubt you have had many ladies as acquaintances, Mr. Kincaid."

"Dammit, woman!" he said, taking her shoulders. "Stop hiding from me!"

"Go away!" She broke free and stumbled back, hitting the side of a chair. "Go away and leave me alone!"

He moved toward her, driven by a deep aching need he didn't stop to understand. "Torrie, let me touch you."

She slapped his hand as he reached for her. "We have a bargain, Mr. Kincaid. Why don't you just get this bedding over with? Give me a child, and get out of my life."

He was quiet a moment, holding her in the warmth of his gaze. "Because I want to meet the woman you keep hidden beneath that prim mask of propriety. I think she's very warm, caring. I think she might be the woman I could love." The words were out before he even thought about what he was saying. Yet it didn't make them any less true.

Torrie looked stunned, then angry. "You would stoop to any depths to humiliate me, wouldn't you?"

"Torrie, I . . ."

"Look, Kincaid. I don't need or want your lies, or this game. All I want is a child." She lashed out with her words, aiming them like spears. "I certainly don't want you, or what you call love."

Her words struck his face with the strength of a prize-fighter's fist. It took a moment before he could find his voice. "That's going to make it difficult to have a child, Princess."

She hugged her arms to her breasts. "I wouldn't

think it would matter to you."

"Afraid you're wrong." He wanted more from her, more than he wanted to admit, even to himself. Did he want more than she could give? "When you're willing to be a wife, let me know."

Spence stepped onto the deck and took a deep breath, filling his chest with warm air. Why the hell did he keep trying? Why didn't he just toss her on her back and have done with it? The woman wanted a child, not a husband. So, why didn't he just plant the seed and get the hell away from her?

He gripped the smooth oak railing and stared at the water, the moon silvering each rolling crest, reminding him of her eyes. He felt bruised, as though he had just gone ten rounds and his opponent hadn't worn gloves. Well, he'd be damned before he let her get the best of him again. He would think twice the next time he got a notion to bare his soul to that woman.

"It's a nice night," Captain Hurley said, coming up behind Spence. "I hope you and Mrs. Kincaid have enjoyed the trip."

"It's one I doubt either one of us will soon forget." No matter how hard either of them tried.

Spence had hoped getting her away from the city, away from the strict standards she had lived with all her life would help melt the ice. Now, he wasn't sure this trip would help. He wasn't sure what would help. He only knew he had to find a way to break down the walls, a way to heal her wounds. He couldn't just walk away from her. Not yet. Not without trying.

Hurley leaned against the railing. "We should be at the *hacienda* late tomorrow morning."

An image blossomed in Spence's mind, of a white sand beach and turquoise water, of a woman dressed in a soft skirt and clinging white blouse. He glanced at the captain. "I'd like to get Mrs. Kincaid some clothes before we reach Allan's. Is there somewhere we can stop?"

Captain Hurley shook his head. "There are several villages, but I doubt you'll find any clothes for a lady like Mrs. Kincaid."

"That's all right." Spence grinned as he thought of Torrie's reaction to what he had planned. "I'm not looking for anything she's used to. I want clothes a pretty village miss might wear."

Captain Hurley smiled as though he understood. "I think we can find what you are looking for, Mr. Kincaid."

Spence had an uneasy feeling he had already found what he had been looking for all his life. He just had to find a way to keep her.

Chapter Fourteen

Allan's *hacienda* was nestled in palm trees at the base of a rocky cliff. Low and white, the house looked like a huge sea gull with its wings spread. Supplied with its own well for water and carbide for gas, the house was fitted with all the luxury one would find on Nob Hill. Torrie wasn't sure what she had expected. Perhaps a small cottage, not a six-bedroom, sprawling one-story house set against the mountains.

The caretakers accepted them with wide smiles and set about making them comfortable. At Kincaid's request, two bedrooms were made ready.

Torrie stood alone in her room, staring out the double doors leading to the gardens, wondering why Kincaid had requested separate bedrooms. A length of brick patio separated the two rooms. Torrie thought it might as well be a brick wall.

The room was cool despite the heat she had felt on the beach. A breeze flowed in from the garden, ruffling the white gauze curtains, bringing the scent of lemons and the sea into the room. Several bronze carvings adorned the white walls, the most impressive being that of a blazing sun rising over the mountains.

Torrie turned as a knock sounded on her open bedroom door. A dark-haired woman, plump and smiling, stood on the threshold, holding a silver tray laden with a tall crystal pitcher and glasses. "Come in, Rosita."

"I brought you some lemonade, *señora*."

"Thank you."

Rosita's heels tapped against the red tile floor as she carried the tray to the table near the double doors. She filled a glass and handed it to Torrie. "You look so pretty, *señora*. All the women *Señor* Allan bring here wear lots of fancy clothes. They look like peacocks strutting. But you, you are smart to know the days are hot here."

Torrie smoothed the ruffle edging the neckline of her white blouse. She had argued with Kincaid when he had presented her with the clothes this morning. There was nothing beneath the cotton blouse and moss green skirt except a thin cotton shift. She had refused to put them on, until he threatened to carry her off the ship in her nightgown. It seemed indecent to roam around without stockings, without drawers, corset cover, corset, chemise, and petticoats, but, Torrie had to admit, it was also cool.

Torrie took a sip, the tart liquid puckering her taste buds. "This is delicious."

Rosita smiled. "Thank you, *señora*."

"Have you lived here long?"

"Many, many years. My mother and father took care of the *hacienda* for *Señor* Allan's father when he first built it. After I marry Fernando, we stay here and help. But, it is not the same since *Señor* Warren died." Rosita clasped her hands below her chin and shook her head. "More than three years now, and I still look for him to come each January."

Warren Thornhill had been a close friend of Torrie's father. He had died in an accident: his gun had discharged while he was cleaning it. Mr. Thornhill had always been serious about his business and his family. He had been devoted to his wife, mourning her passing for years. Somehow, Allan had managed to grow up the direct opposite of his father. Allan was a womanizer, dedicated to his own pleasure. And Kincaid had a great deal in common with his friend.

"Ah, it is good to see you and *Señor* Spence married. It is not good the way *Señor* Allan live."

"Does Allan spend much time here?"

"He come maybe three or four times a year. But each time it is with a different *señorita*." Rosita shook her dark head. "He needs to settle with one and have babies."

Torrie stared down into her glass, slices of lemon swirling with her agitation. No doubt Kincaid had brought a woman here on those occasions when he had visited. A woman who knew how to please a man.

"Are you all right, *señora*?"

"Yes, I'm fine." Except, of course, she was married to a man who would like to be rid of her, a man who would stoop to any level to humiliate her, even words of love. Had he really expected her to swoon at his tender declaration last night? She wasn't that foolish.

"Ah, *Señor* Spence is a very handsome man. He'll make fine babies."

Torrie felt her cheeks grow warm. "Does Mr.

Kincaid visit here often?" She really wanted to know how many women he had brought here.

Rosita shook her head. "He come two, maybe three times. But not since Mr. Warren die. I always say . . ." Rosita paused, looking past Torrie as though an angel had just descended from heaven.

Torrie turned and saw Kincaid standing in the doorway, his dark head nearly brushing the top of the door frame. He was wearing a pair of blue denim trousers and a light blue shirt. Torrie turned and set her glass on the tray, trying not to notice the way the faded denim molded his long legs.

Rosita fluttered over to Kincaid. "*Señor* Spence, I just brought your lovely *señora* some lemonade. Now, I go. If you need anything, just call."

"Thank you, Rosita," Spence said, smiling down at her.

Rosita left the room, her girlish giggle trailing behind her. Spence leaned his shoulder against the door and grinned at Torrie. "All settled in?"

The first four buttons of his shirt were open, and his sleeves were rolled up to his elbows, revealing tanned skin and dark hair. Torrie turned and focused her attention on the lemon tree just outside her door. "Yes. The room is lovely." And private, very private. Too private.

Her back grew stiff as she heard his footsteps on the tile, each step bringing him closer, until she felt his warmth brush her side. Heat radiated from his big body to seep into her pores, warming her blood.

"Is something wrong, Princess?"

She stiffened at his form of address. "Wrong? Now what could possibly be wrong?"

"Let's see, for starters you're married to a man you detest, a brutal barbarian."

His scent tingled her senses, tugging at her until

she felt a growing tightness in her most intimate regions. All he had to do was come near her and she turned into a person she didn't recognize, someone ruled by her emotions. And he was completely unaffected by her. She turned and speared him with her eyes. "Mr. Kincaid, I realize you and I did not choose one another for tender reasons, but I would hope we could treat one another with some measure of respect."

His broad shoulders rose as he took a deep breath. "Now what's my crime?"

A single drop of perspiration slipped down his neck, glistening, mingling with the dark curls on his chest. She turned and stared at one bright lemon hanging from the bough outside the room. "As if you didn't know."

She heard him swear under his breath and her chin rose.

"Princess, it doesn't do any good to be angry with someone without letting him know why you're angry. Did anyone ever tell you it's better to talk about it?"

A lady never revealed her anger. A lady never discussed her problems. Sometimes it was just too hard to be a lady. She turned and met his even gaze. "Just why did you ask for a separate bedroom? Am I so hideous you can't stand to be in the same room with me?"

He looked as though she had just kicked him in the ribs. "I thought you'd want a separate room."

Her mother had always had a separate bedroom. In fact, Torrie had always took for granted all married couples had separate bedrooms, but for some reason it infuriated her to know Kincaid wanted a separate bedroom. "Well, I do want a separate room."

"Pardon me if I look a little confused."

She knew she was being unreasonable. She knew it, yet could do nothing about it. "I'm sure you never requested separate rooms for your mistresses."

"My . . . damn! If I try to make love to you I'm a barbarian, if I leave you alone I'm a negligent husband." He grabbed her shoulders and forced her to face him. "Just tell me what the hell you want."

"Stop swearing in my face!"

"You're the most confounded woman I've ever met!"

"And you're the most disagreeable man *I've* ever met!" She struggled to break free of his grasp. "You're hurting me."

"Damn!" He dropped his hands and took a step back. "We seem to be good at hurting each other, don't we?"

She turned away, hugging her arms to her waist, staring at the big brass bed that dominated the room. What did she want? Something was happening to her, something she didn't understand, something she couldn't seem to control. He rested his warm hand on her shoulder, long fingers curling near her neck.

"I don't know about you, but I'm ready for a truce. What do you say? Will you take a walk with me on the beach?"

The urge to rest her cheek on his big hand was almost too tempting to resist. She glanced over her shoulder and looked into his handsome face, doubting there was a woman alive who would not want to go for a walk on the beach with this man. "I would like a truce, and a walk on the beach."

He smiled and offered her his arm. "Shall we go?"

She slipped her arm through his, resting her hand on his bare forearm, the dark hair crisp against her palm. He had forearms like a prize-fighter. She pulled her gaze away from the hard muscles beneath her palm, but she couldn't keep her fingers from curling against his warm skin.

Soft cotton swirled around her naked legs, brushing her skin, arousing her every nerve, as she walked beside him out the double doors of her bedroom. Her skin tingled. He was too near, much too near for her to keep a cool head. A short distance into the garden she dropped his arm and put a foot of air between them.

"It's warm," she said, answering the question in his eyes. And it had little to do with the sun.

She kept her distance as they followed a stone path through the gardens of citrus and palm trees to steep stone steps leading down to the beach. On the top step she paused, gazing out at the wide stretch of turquoise water. "Where's the ship?"

"Captain Hurley took it up to the village. They'll be back in a few days."

The muscles in his back rippled beneath taut blue cotton as he moved down the stairs, pulling her gaze to the dark stain running down the middle of his back. Something stirred inside her, earthy and forbidden. She clenched her hands to keep from touching him.

At the base of the stairs he removed his shoes and socks and rolled his trousers up above his ankles. "You might want to tuck that skirt up," he said, dropping his shoes on the bottom step.

"What?"

"Just take the back hem, bring it through your knees and tuck the end in your waistband."

Her mouth dropped open at his suggestion. "Mr. Kincaid, if you think I am going to walk around with my skirt tucked into my waistband, you . . ."

"I know." He raised his hands in surrender. "I must have been in the sun too long." He gave her a wide boyish grin and turned to walk toward the water.

Sand trickled into her sandals as she trudged across the beach, following him to the hard-packed sand near the water. She shook her feet, trying to get rid of the sand, tempted to remove her shoes, but some distant rule kept them firmly attached to her feet.

Each wave that rolled in sent her scrambling for higher ground, where the deep sand and hard going sent her back. Walking through the roiling surf, Kincaid was wet to the knees, but he didn't seem to care.

"As I remember, there's a cove just past those rocks up ahead, very private, very beautiful."

Torrie looked around the beach. There was nothing in sight, no other people, no houses, just sand and water, gulls and palm trees. It seemed to her the entire beach was private, but she didn't mind walking with him to the cove. Being honest with herself, she admitted she liked being with him. At least, when he wasn't trying to provoke her.

She glanced at the man walking beside her. The afternoon sun touched the planes of his cheek, the thin line of his nose, the tips of his lashes, gilding all, making him seem carved from gold. A curious warmth spread across her belly; she looked away, glancing down to the sand beneath her feet. My word, she was obsessed with the man. *Think of something else, anything else,* she told herself. "How long have you known Allan?"

"We met in college."

"But he went to Cambridge!"

He laughed, deep and full, the sound of a man who was used to laughter. "It's a shame the riff-raff they're allowing in Cambridge these days."

Torrie felt the heat rise in her cheeks. "I didn't mean that."

One dark brow quirked upward as he looked at her. "Didn't you?"

"Well, perhaps I did," she said, smiling. "You just don't sound as though you went to Cambridge."

"You can take the boy out of Texas, but you can't take Texas out of the boy," he said, deliberately deepening his drawl. "Cambridge was my grandfather's idea. He was real anxious to make sure my mother's sons had the opportunity to be proper English gentlemen. Since I never planned to be a rancher, I was happy for the chance to go to Cambridge."

Strange, she could imagine this man on a ranch, dressed in those tight-fitting blue denim trousers, wearing a dark Stetson pulled low over his brow, sitting atop a big chestnut stallion. Her gaze drifted down the length of that tight-fitting blue denim, thick muscles straining beneath, flexing with each step he took, conjuring images in her mind.

Would he come to her tonight? Would she learn the feel of those muscles beneath her hand? She pulled her gaze away from those tight-fitting trousers and tried to pull her thoughts from the night ahead. "Your mother is English?"

He nodded. "If you're wondering how a very proper British lady ends up married to a rowdy Texan, I can tell you her family had the same question."

If he looked anything like his son, she could imagine a queen giving up her throne. A woman could look into those golden eyes every day of her life and never tire of their beauty. "I bet they had fun with you at Cambridge. Because of your accent, I mean."

"Accent?" He tilted his head, gazing down at her with an inquisitive look in his eyes. "And what accent would you be referring to, milady?" His words were spoken in a crisp British accent.

"You do that very well."

"It's easy. Especially when you've been around people who have that distinct British upper-class accent. And most of the people in Cambridge have it, not to mention my mother and grandfather."

He took her hand and helped her climb a low wall of rocks. They paused at the top, and Torrie cupped her hand to her brow, shielding her eyes against the sun as she stared at the cove. Rocks flowed into the water from the cliffs to form a dark gray horseshoe in the turquoise water. Thick clusters of palms at the base of the cliffs curved their heads toward the water, shielding the white sand from the bright rays of the sun. At the base of the trees, orchids lifted their heads, splashing violet, pink, and white against the dark green and gray background.

"It's beautiful."

Spence glanced over his shoulder, smiling as he started to descend to the beach. "I'm glad you like it."

Here, it would be easy to believe they were the only man and woman on the face of the earth. Only she had a nagging suspicion she wasn't the first woman he had brought to this little paradise. "How did you find this place?"

Spence slipped his hands around her waist and lowered her to the sand. "I went exploring the last time I was here."

He held her, smiling in a way that started her knees trembling. She stepped out of the circle of his arms and moved to the edge of the trees. Wild orchids beckoned her, violet petals brushing her cheek as she inhaled the fragrance of a delicate bloom. "Did you go exploring alone?" she asked, glancing up at him.

He rested his hand on the trunk of the palm and

studied her a moment. "If you want to know if I've ever been here with another woman, the answer is no."

She dropped the orchid. "It certainly doesn't make any difference to me."

"It shouldn't. The past is just that. What's important is the present, because that's what shapes our future."

The future. She wasn't at all sure she wanted to think about the future she would have as a divorced woman.

He unbuttoned the rest of his shirt and tugged it from his trousers. Desire nipped at her belly as Torrie stared at his wide, furry chest, admiring each curve and line of muscle beneath warm-looking skin. He dropped his shirt to the sand and started to unfasten the placket in his trousers, each felled button revealing more black hair and golden skin. With a sense of panic, it occurred to her that he wasn't wearing anything beneath those tight blue denim trousers. "What are you doing?"

He peeled the denim from his naked hips. "I'm going swimming."

"Like that?"

He tugged the trousers from his legs, hopping on one, then the other foot as he freed himself from the tight denim. "What's wrong with swimming like this?" he asked, tossing the trousers to the sand.

Naked and unashamed, he stood with his hands on his slim hips, grinning down at her. She stared, helpless to look away, mesmerized by golden skin, fascinated by the black curls shading finely etched muscles.

"We're miles from civilization, Torrie. No one is going to know what happens here except you and me." He lifted the ribbon at the top of her blouse. "Come with me."

She stepped back, the ribbon coming undone. "I couldn't possibly go swimming."

"Can't swim?"

She tried to keep her eyes focused above his chin, tried to forget about all that beautiful skin. "Of course I can swim. I just don't have anything to wear."

"You have what God gave you." He moved toward her, smiling, his eyes filled with a devilish sparkle. "And, it's a particularly beautiful costume."

"Just stay right where you are." She held up her hand, hoping to keep him at bay, hoping to keep her own emotions under control.

He pressed his chest against her outstretched hand. "Come swimming with me, Princess."

So much for the truce. "You just won't stop, will you?" She pulled her hand from his flesh and backed away. "You keep hacking away, hoping you can strip every shred of dignity from me, trying to turn me into a harlot."

The smile slipped from his face. "I keep hacking away trying to find the woman under all the ice."

"What gives you the right to try to change me?"

"I'm your husband."

Her hands balled into fists at her sides. "I don't want a husband!"

His muscles tensed, his expression turned fierce. "Sorry, Princess. You want a child and I come in the bargain."

"Damn you!" She turned on her heel and started running down the beach, kicking up sand behind her.

He caught her before she reached the wall of rocks, grabbing her arm. "You can't keep running!"

She twisted, trying to break free. "Let go of me!"

He pulled her against his chest, wrapping strong arms around her. "Why are you afraid of me?"

"Don't be ridiculous." Golden eyes probed hers and she prayed he wouldn't see the truth. She *was* afraid, afraid of what he might think of her, afraid she could never be good enough to please him, afraid of something even more terrifying, something she wouldn't admit to herself.

She tried to break free, but his arms tightened, pinning her arms to her sides, holding her so close she could feel his heart beating against her breast. His flesh burned her through her clothes, his long, naked body touching her everywhere. "Let go of me, you arrogant, conceited . . ."

He plastered his mouth over hers, swallowing her words, quelling her struggles. He slid the tip of his tongue over the seam of her lips and she went rigid, glaring at him. His eyes were closed, thick lashes laying on the crests of his cheeks, ignoring her silent protest. The man had no right to treat her this way, mauling her as though she were his property.

He tugged on her lower lip, flicking the tip of his tongue against her teeth, tempting her. She resisted, anger and indignation overlapping inside her, fighting the intimidating excitement awakening deep within her.

He slid his right hand down, over her rounded behind, grabbing her, pulling her up into the throbbing heat of his rising arousal. Torrie gasped, the sudden parting of her lips letting him slip inside. A low moan escaped her lips as he explored the dark secrets of her mouth, brushing light strokes against her tongue, teasing her.

She felt her defenses crumble. One last spark of sanity shot outward, bringing her hands to his waist, intending to push him away. She felt the smooth heat of his flesh against her palms and her fingers curled, grasping his lean waist. Her knee slid upward, slipping between his thighs, as she tried to get closer, closer to his tantalizing heat.

A growl rose from deep in his chest, low and primitive, gentling her fear. Desire surged from a well deep inside her, cascading over carefully built walls, flowing freely, nourishing femininity that lay parched for too many years.

Her eyes fluttered closed. She felt his breath quicken against her cheek, felt his heart pounding against her breasts, rushing, meeting her own frantic rhythm. Every rule, every nagging fear vanished under the intoxicating influence of his kiss. The image of Charles she carried in her heart blurred, his features dissolving into time. Her blood, hot with desire, pulsed low in her belly, bringing a delightful ache, a warm rush between her thighs.

His grip slackened, his right arm sliding around her waist. Now free, her left arm flowed upward, her fingers trailing along his powerful arm, exploring the warm satin of his shoulders, sinking into the cool silk at the nape of his neck. She wanted to wrap herself in his skin, absorb his heat, his strength.

"I want you, Torrie." He whispered against her lips. He brushed his lips across her cheek. "I want to make love to you."

She could scarcely believe his words. "Here?"

He lowered his mouth, drawing warm kisses down her neck. "People should make love in a place like this."

"People do such things?" She felt him smile against her neck.

"They do." He stepped back, releasing her, holding her with his eyes.

Torrie swayed, staring at him, pleading without words for him to return. His skin glistened in the sunlight, beckoning her to the warm haven of his arms.

"Come to me," he said, offering her his hand. "Let me."

Reality mingled with dreams, filling Torrie with a compelling sense that this had all happened before. It was as if destiny had ordained them to come together in this place. She looked at his outstretched hand, his long fingers reaching for her. She shouldn't. Not here, not now. She was far too vulnerable. She glanced up, met his eyes, and slipped her hand into his warm palm.

Chapter Fifteen

"Torrie," he whispered, drawing her close, filling his arms with more than a dream. He pressed his cheek against her soft hair, breathing her fragrance into his lungs. They had stood like this before, on this beach, under the sun, in his dreams; the same dream that had haunted him since the first day he had met this woman. Only this was real. And reality was better than any wisp of his imagination.

She trembled in his arms, her breasts nestling against his chest, her hips snuggling closer to his, as though she were melting into him: an ice sculpture melting in the rays of the sun, a woman awakening to her man. His own body grew hard against her softness.

He drew a deep breath, his hands flexing where they rested on her waist, on the curve of her back. Somehow he had to keep his own desire in check.

She needed a gentle hand. She needed to be shown how beautiful, how bewitching she was. For she had bewitched him.

"Will you kiss me, Mr. Kincaid?" she asked, her lips brushing his bare shoulder.

Her words barely rose above the sound of the palms rustling in the breeze, a soft whisper melding with the rush of waves to the nearby shore. Yet he heard her, and the impact of her words stole his breath.

He cradled her face in his hands, stroking the crests of her cheeks with his thumbs, coaxing her chin to rise. She clenched her eyes closed, as though she were frightened to see what was in his eyes.

"I want to kiss you, Torrie," he whispered, kissing the tip of her nose.

Her lashes fluttered against her cheeks. Yet she still wouldn't open her eyes. He wanted her to look at him, to know him, to see the future in his eyes.

"I've dreamed of kissing you." He pressed his lips to one corner of her mouth. "Of holding you."

She lifted her eyes, looking straight into his. "You have?"

She was so unsure of herself, this beguiling woman who could twist him into knots with one glance from those big silvery eyes. "Since the first day we met."

She smiled, brushing his upper arms with her damp palms. "Then . . . why don't you, Mr. Kincaid?"

"Spence, my name is Spence," he whispered, lowering his lips until he could feel the warm pulse of her breath against his cheek. "I'd like to hear you say it." And it was just one in a long list of things he wanted to hear her say.

She rose on her toes to close the distance. "Spence," she murmured against his lips.

It was a beginning, he thought, closing his eyes. She slipped her arms around his neck, holding him close as she kissed him, startling him with her hunger. Her lips moved eagerly against his, her small tongue darted across his lips before dipping inside his mouth to tease the tip of his tongue.

The heat of her in his arms humbled the warmth of the sun on his back. He held her closer. He couldn't get close enough, not nearly close enough to this woman. Soft cotton scraped his skin. He needed to feel the smooth slide of her skin against his. He needed to feel the petal soft peaks of her breasts pucker and press into his skin. He needed to feel the soft brush of damp curls against the heated length of his pulsing flesh.

He slipped his hand down the thick coils of her braid, his fingers finding a white satin ribbon at the base. He explored the neat bow, sliding the ribbon between his fingers before tugging it free and allowing the wisp of satin to drift away on the breeze. From the bottom, he worked his fingers into her braid, freeing her hair, smoothing his fingers through the wavy tresses— silk warmed by the sun, warmed by the heat of her body.

Four small buttons at the back of her waist gave him no resistance. With the palms of his hands he slipped the skirt from her hips, green cotton brushing against his legs as it drifted to the sand. Slowly, he slid his hands over the thin shift covering her rounded behind, molding his palms to her shape, lifting her into the flesh she had forged into hot steel.

She gasped against his lips, and for one heart-stopping moment he thought she would pull away. Yet she didn't. Instead, she settled against him, pressing her belly into his heat, wrenching a growl from his throat. Never in his life had he wanted a woman more.

Yearning opened like a chasm inside Torrie, a gnawing emptiness longing to be filled. She wouldn't think about the dangers that lay in his arms. Not now. Not when it all felt so right. For now, she would believe his lovely lies, the words that whispered to the doubts deep within her. She wanted to believe, believe she was more than an object of ridicule, believe she was more than a frigid piece of ice in a man's arms, at least in this man's arms.

The heat of his palm seeped through her blouse as he slid his hand between them. Anticipation shivered across her skin, puckering the tips of her breasts, as his hand crept up her ribs . . . slowly . . . slowly . . . his fingers brushing the soft underside of her breast . . . rising . . . contouring to her shape . . . circling . . . squeezing the sensitive tip, sending sharp sensations shooting outward, shocking her. She jumped and grabbed his wrist, realizing too late how foolish her action must seem to this man.

"I'm sorry." She stared at his chin and hoped he wouldn't laugh at her, or start shouting his anger. "I didn't mean to do that. I just . . . wasn't prepared . . . I'm . . ."

"Hush," he whispered, pressing the tip of his finger to her lips. "You're doing just fine, sweetheart."

She looked up into his eyes, afraid she might see some trace of mockery behind the kind words, seeing only tenderness, and more, so much more. The look in his eyes filled her with a confidence she had never known. He made her feel the way she had always dreamed of feeling: beautiful, cherished, desired.

Could it be possible for this beautiful man to actually want her, desire her as a woman? For now she chose to believe him, to believe the feelings building inside her. For now, she would try to cast aside her doubts.

She wrapped her fingers around his wrist and led him back to her breast, sighing as his palm slid over her aching flesh. "Teach me, Mr. Kincaid."

"It's Spence." He kissed the tip of her nose. "Remember?"

"Spence," she whispered, lifting, craving his kiss.

"Torrie," he sighed, lowering his smiling lips to hers.

At the first touch of his lips, she threw her arms around his neck, clinging to him, anxious to learn all the secrets he held. He was every kiss, every caress she had been denied through all the wasted years. She wanted to banish the fear; the fear of never being good enough. She sighed as his fingers moved against her breast, stroking, stoking fires that lay too long smoldering with desire.

His hand left her breast and she whimpered for its return, aware of the shameful craving inside her, embracing desire for the first time in her life. She felt him loosen the lacing of her blouse, felt his palms warming her skin as he slid the cotton from her shoulders. She lowered her arms, allowing him to strip away her blouse.

Fingers of propriety reached for her, but desire slapped them aside. Soon she would be naked before him, she would feel his skin against hers. Nothing else mattered. He kissed her jaw, then lowered his lips, blazing a fiery path down her neck, his hands drifting down her body, following her blouse. Warm palms brushed her arms, her wrists, her hips.

Adrift in wonder, she lifted her chin, allowing him free access to the vulnerable column of her neck. The man conjured magic with his lips, with one

touch of his hand. With the tip of his tongue, he
drew intricate patterns against her skin, lingering
at the throbbing pulse at the hollow of her throat,
as if he knew the damp heat was stroking her all the
way down to her toes.

Soft sobs filled the air, and Torrie was amazed to
realize they came from her lips. She was alive for the
first time in an eternity. He moved back and forth
across her collar bone, nibbling, tasting, making her
feel as though her skin were spun from sugar and
cream.

She gripped his shoulders as he flowed downward, every nerve in her body sparking with life.
He breathed against her breasts, hot and moist; her
nipples strained against the thin cotton shift, seeking his touch. And he was there to give her what
she craved. A moan tore from her throat as his
mouth closed over the crest of her breast. Sensation
after sensation spiraled outward as he rolled the bud
between his teeth, as he laved her skin through the
thin cloth.

She sank her hands into the dark waves at his
nape and held him closer, cries of pleasure tumbling from her lips, quiver chasing quiver along her
spine. An instinct older than time made her arch
against him, made her seek something she didn't
yet understand, something she sought to make her
own, something he could give her.

Spence smiled against her breasts. She was heav-
en in his arms, guileless, responding to his touch
with an innocent passion, sending shafts of desire
shooting through his loins. His body responded to
hers like brandy touched by a flame. Somehow he
had known from that first day he had met her it
would be like this between them.

He moved lower, running his lips down the center of her body, touching her intimately, pressing

his lips to white cotton, feeling the warmth, the shape of the woman beneath. Her hair lifted on the breeze, brushing the smooth silk across his face, his shoulders.

He fell to his knees before her. He wanted her more than he had ever imagined possible, wanted to please her more than he wanted his own pleasure. And still, he wondered if she might pull away from him when the time came.

Torrie watched him, following his dark fingers as he removed her sandals. The breeze drifted across the damp patches above her breasts, cooling her skin, making her long to be warm again. The heat of his hand around her ankle, the touch of his fingers against her skin as he unfastened her buckles and removed first one then the other sandal, sent silent promises sparking along her nerves, promises he would soon fulfill. For a long moment he remained on one knee, looking up at her, a knight awaiting his lady's favor.

"Show me, let me see your beauty," he said, his voice adding deep notes to the steady sound of the rising surf.

Drugged with desire, she pulled the ribbon at the top of her shift and slipped the cotton from her shoulders, baring her flesh to the sultry breeze and the warmer heat of his gaze. More than anything in the world, she wanted to please him. The look in his golden eyes gave her hope.

Spence stared, as Adam must have stared upon first sight of Eve. Sunlight worshipped her, igniting gold and red streaks of fire in her chestnut hair, shimmering against ivory skin. If he were an artist he would paint her. If he were a poet he would write sonnets of her beauty. But he was neither of these. He was a man, who would adore her with all he possessed.

"Beautiful, so very beautiful," he whispered, brushing his lips against the soft skin above her knees, rubbing his hands along her thighs.

She was fashioned for pleasure, fashioned for him alone. Desire tugged at his loins, pulling, drawing his flesh until he felt an almost uncontrollable urge to throw her on the sand and plunge into her, bury himself in her warmth. But it had to be right, had to be sweet and slow and tender. He wanted to pleasure her, to free her, to give her the world and more.

Torrie felt beyond herself. It was as if a part of her recognized him from a distant time and place, recognized him as lover and mate. She slipped her hands through his thick, dark waves, knowing in some way she had met her destiny. He slid his hands upward as he rose, callused palms stroking every nerve in her body, gliding along the curves of her legs, the full swell of her hips, exploring the resilience of her rounded bottom.

"Torrie," he said, his voice a satisfied sigh as he plucked her from the sand and lifted her into his arms.

He cradled her to his chest as though she were the most precious gem in the world, as though he intended to keep her, protect her, all the days of her life. She snuggled against him, pressing her lips to his neck. She tasted his damp skin, inhaled his scent, nourishing the need deep inside her.

Warm water splashed her ankles and her eyes snapped open. He was carrying her into the water, away from the sheltering palms, the white sand, away from what she thought would be her first taste of paradise.

"I thought we were going to . . ." She hesitated, her cheeks growing warm at the humiliating candor of her thoughts.

He smiled and dropped a kiss on her nose. "We are."

"In the water?"

He grinned. "There to start."

To start! Oh my, did people really do such things? Such wicked, wanton, wondrous things as make love under the sun, with the warm caress of water surrounding them. Water lapped at her thighs and she smiled against his neck. "I think you are shameless."

His chuckle vibrated against her breast before the deep rumble filled the air. "I am."

He slipped his arm from under her knees and let her slide down the heated length of his body, letting her sink into the warm water, her soft skin rubbing against him, introducing her to the feel of his body.

"I'm shameless, and near bursting for want of you."

Since that first day she had caught a glimpse of him standing as naked as Adam before the fall, she had dreamed of this, imagined the feel of his skin against hers, warm and resilient, smooth and rough, inflaming her senses.

Nothing, not the finest silks or satins, could compare to the feel of his skin against hers. She moved her legs, her hips, trying to feel him everywhere. Water as smooth as satin oiled their bodies. Heat as pure as the sun rose inside her. He kissed her, hungry and wild, as though he were going to devour her, and she responded, offering her lips, her mouth, her tongue.

"Do you have any idea how much I want you?" he asked, running his hands down her sides.

Even in her innocence, she could recognize the heat of his desire pulsing against her belly. He was heavy, lush and full against her. It seemed a dream. It once had been. Now he was making the dream come true.

"I wanted to do this the first time I saw you," he whispered against her skin, his hands curving on her buttock as he lifted her against him, sliding her soft curves against his hard lines.

She smiled, slipping her arms around his neck, brushing her breasts against the curls on his chest. Was there some truth in his words? He bent his head and licked the water from her breasts, his tongue drawing lazy circles, tension building inside her as he drew closer and closer to the peak. When at last he captured the summit, she cried out, sinking her hands into his hair, holding him as though she were afraid he might disappear.

"Relax, sweetheart," he whispered, his lips sliding down the slope of her breast.

The man had to be joking. How could she relax when he was doing such wonderful, wicked things to her? He lingered a moment in the valley between her breasts before creeping up the slope of her other breast. Sunlight tingled across her skin, a mere shadow of the heat building inside her. She was on fire, flames licking upward from a blazing inferno, and she was sure steam would soon rise from the water.

He leaned against the smooth rocks and slid her against his hardened length. Dark curls tickled her skin as he slipped his thigh between her legs and pressed against her, her flesh pulsing with need. She gasped at the sudden stab of pleasure, grasping his upper arms. Warm waves rolled across her skin, lapping at her breasts as he rocked her gently against his thigh, desire rippling with each fluid movement.

She was more exquisitely responsive than Spence could ever have imagined. Each movement tore soft, pleasured cries from her throat. Each soft cry made him crave the feel of the heat he knew throbbed inside her. He lifted her, cradling her against his arm, letting her thighs drape across his bent leg. Her lips parted as he slid his hand upward along the smooth skin of her inner thigh.

She wanted him. He could see it, feel it. Yet, a tutored response made her clench her legs, blocking him from touching her. "Open to me, Torrie," he whispered, brushing his fingers across the top of her clenched thighs. "Don't hide from me."

Torrie turned her cheek into his shoulder and did as he asked, relaxing her muscles enough to allow him to touch her. He brushed her brow with his lips as his fingers brushed the curls crowning her thighs. He slid his fingers over the feminine folds of her body, seeking, finding, claiming her as he knew no man had ever done, drawing a shocked gasp of pleasure from her lips.

Like fiery arrows, the joy of her yielding plunged into the heart of his desire. Water licked at her breasts, circling the firm mounds, beading like tears on the rosy tips, taunting him. He fought the desperate urging in his groin, determined to give her pleasure, intent on assuring that she reached completion, even if it drove him to madness.

She arched her neck and lifted her hips to meet him. He saw the wonder in her eyes as he stroked the slick, damp petals of rosy flesh. With each stroke she gave him more of her trust, spreading her legs, arching against his hand with the sweetest moans he had ever heard. With her complete surrender, he grew bolder, more intimate.

Excitement coupled with trepidation in his heart as he slipped one finger inside her. She was small, so incredibly small. Lord, he didn't want to hurt her, but he knew he would.

Sobs tumbled from her lips, one after another, as his fingers played against her, probing, plying, preparing her for his tumescent flesh. He pushed, stretching delicate flesh until he saw the shock of pain on her face, then he withdrew, stroking wet fingers over contours he had learned long ago would bring intense pleasure. Retreat and plunge, retreat and plunge, deeper and deeper, each time stretching farther and farther.

He watched her passion rise, his finger sliding against the swollen heat of her, feeling the flow of warm honey, knowing she was ready for him, as ready as her virginal sheath would allow. Feeling she was ready, knowing he was more than ready, he carried her to the shore and laid her upon her discarded clothes.

She slipped her arms around his neck, and opened in welcome as he lowered himself between her silken thighs. He hesitated at her entrance, pressing against her softness, looking down into her lovely face. A virgin. She was beyond his experience. He was loath to give her pain, ravenous to feel her flesh close around his.

Torrie felt the first touch of his hardened flesh and trembled, her desire mounting to raw hunger. There was a restraint in him she couldn't understand, a restraint she wouldn't allow. Following her instincts, she wrapped her legs around his waist and arched her hips, capturing him.

Sharp pain ripped through her flesh as he slid inside her, joining their bodies for the first time. She fell back against the soft cushion of cotton and sand, burying her face against his arm, stunned, as ecstasy dissolved into misery. He didn't move, his chest pressed against hers, his flesh throbbing deep inside her.

"Are you all right?" he asked, his lips brushing her ear.

His deep voice, thick with concern, drew out some of the sting. Her first impulse was to break free, but she had wanted this, and she wasn't about to stop in the middle, leaving him in a state of frustration, no matter how much it hurt. She swallowed back the pain and found her voice. "I'm fine."

"I didn't want to hurt you, but . . . God, I knew I would." He shifted, brushing his lips against her cheek, coaxing her to meet his eyes. "It'll get better, Torrie." His gaze locked with hers as he moved his hips, withdrawing until all that remained inside of her was the tip of his invasion. "I promise."

She bit her lower lip and held her breath as he moved, sliding against her torn flesh, his hips falling and rising, her flesh screaming for him to stop. He lowered his lips to hers, his tongue slipping between her lips, dipping in and out, stroking her tongue, his hips moving to the same haunting rhythm, a part of him stroking her deep inside, healing her, quickening her.

Under his patient ministering, pleasure chased away the pain. Her arms tightened around his shoulders, holding him closer as a sweet ache replaced the ragged pain of a moment before.

Torrie opened her eyes and watched him as she explored this new terrain, amazed at the look of pain on his beautiful face. Had she hurt him in some way? Yet, she knew instinctively it was something else—he was keeping his own desire under close rein. And it was costing him.

Gripping his shoulders, she lifted, making tiny circles with her hips, slipping down, sliding back up, as he remained steady above her. The breeze ruffled his dark hair. She slipped her hand into the thick waves, sliding the silky strands through her fingers.

"Torrie," he whispered, the husky moan of a man being tortured.

She felt the trembling in his arms. He was holding back, allowing her to find her rhythm, allowing time to absorb each new sensation. It was then she discovered something else about this man, something frightening . . . he was gentle . . . and kind . . . infinitely kind.

"Tight, so tight," he murmured, burying his face against her neck.

Just like a hand in a wet kid glove, she thought, thrusting with her hips, reaching for the secrets he held. "I won't break," she said, smiling up at him.

He sucked air between his teeth. "I might if I don't move."

"I wouldn't want you to break," she whispered, tempting him by lifting her hips.

She ran her hands down his back as he started to move; slow, steady thrusts, long and deep, that quickened inside her when she rose to meet him. Time and time again he changed his rhythm, rotating his hips, circling inside of her, then dipping deeper and deeper, until she was rising and falling with him, meeting the ebb and flow of him, until her hips played in perfect harmony to his. And all the while he watched her, as if he wanted to press each moment into the pages of his memory, just as she was.

Each long, slick stroke sent her closer to the edge, closer to the unknown she sought to possess, something she knew only he could surrender. She gripped his shoulders and tried to draw him closer and closer, wrapping her long legs around his lean waist, gripping him, increasing her tempo, seeking more and more friction.

"That's it, sweetheart, that's it," he whispered against her neck, his voice husky and ragged. "Let it take you."

It remained just out of her reach, that mystery she had long pondered, that mystery she was frightened to discover. "I can't," she said, frustration sharpening her voice.

"Yes, you can." He rocked forward. "Just let go," he whispered against her lips. "Just let go."

Let go of doubts. Let go of fear. She couldn't!

"Come with me, Torrie," he said, threading his hands into her hair, cradling her head. "Soar with me."

He kissed her, letting her taste his need. Everything faded and sharpened at once. There was nothing but this man and the feelings he was summoning within her.

Swirling passion rose to a fierce vortex, ripping her from her maiden's nest like a fledgling in first flight, falling, catching the wind soaring upward, ever upward toward the sun. Torrie screamed, every muscle in her body growing rigid, gripping him with her arms, her legs, with muscles never before used.

Through a thick haze of rapture, she felt him thrust once more, felt his big body pulse and surge, heard her name burst from his lips as he, too, surrendered to the pulsing pleasure. Tears of joy burned her eyes, and she knew this was how it was meant to be. Until this moment she hadn't realized what was missing from her life, what had been missing with Charles.

Kincaid was the missing half of her soul.

He sagged above her, clutching her to him, and she loved the feel of him, big and bold, and throbbing deep inside her as she possessed him fully. She closed her eyes and tried to absorb the moment, wishing she could hold him forever.

He ran his hands up her sides, his fingers brushing her breasts. She opened her eyes to see him gazing down at her, the sun casting a golden nimbus around his head. He was smiling, a deeply satisfied smile, like a cat who had just finished a pint of cream. Or a man who had just made another conquest.

Reality crept across her soul like chilling tendrils of fog, gathering slowly to block out the rays of the sun. Spencer Kincaid had melted the Ice Princess. He had seduced her into tossing aside every shred of her dignity, seduced her into believing his lies.

This wasn't love. This was lust, nothing more. This man didn't really want to be with her. He wanted to prove a point, to humiliate her. And he had. Dear Lord, he had.

Now, she was ashamed of all the noise she had made, all the sobbing and crying and whatever else she had done. Fool! She was such a simpering idiot. She wiggled to free herself, unaware of what she was doing to him.

Spence sucked in his breath as her soft body brushed his skin. His blood surged, pulsating in that part of him still nestled deep inside her. He wanted her. Again. Already. It had never been like this before. A joining of flesh had never touched him deeper than the simple pleasure of sated lust. This was different. He wasn't sure how or why, yet he knew this joining had been more than the elemental coupling of man and woman.

He pressed his smile against her neck, breathing in the heady fragrance of her skin. "I knew it would feel this good."

She stiffened, a sound escaping her lips, a twisted sob of anger and pain. "Mr. Kincaid, let go of me."

Spence stiffened. Something was wrong. Very wrong. He rose above her, searching her face for the reason for this sudden change. "I thought you were going to call me Spence," he said softly.

"I prefer to call you Mr. Kincaid. It helps to keep matters in a proper perspective."

He grabbed her as she tried to break free, his hands around her shoulders. Her pale skin held the blush of his lovemaking, her breasts still taut with desire, but her eyes were shards of ice glittering in the sun. Anxiety twisted like a knife in his belly as he stared into those silvery eyes. "Just what is the proper perspective?" he asked, not sure he wanted to know the answer.

She twisted, trying to break free, as though she couldn't tolerate being touched by him. "You know very well what I mean."

Perhaps he did, and then perhaps he didn't. Right now he wasn't sure of anything. "Tell me."

"You wanted to prove I was human. Well, your little seduction proved successful on that point."

"My seduction?"

"That's right. You wanted to see me doing this . . . coupling like . . . an animal." She clenched her eyes shut, blocking out his image. "I congratulate you, Mr. Kincaid. Your worldly ways proved to be too much for my sensibilities."

Anger, red and glaring as the sun overhead, surged inside him. "So, I'm still the barbarian," he said, releasing her.

"Gentlemen don't do this sort of thing," she said, scrambling to her feet.

"Neither do proper ladies," he said, staring up at her, her figure blotting out the sun.

"I shall strive to maintain my composure in the future." She crossed her arms over her naked breasts, shielding them from his gaze. "Please get off my clothes."

He issued a curse under his breath as he rolled to his feet. "Look, Princess," he said, grabbing her arm, forcing her to face him. "You wanted this as much as I did, so don't start wailing about how the nasty barbarian raped your innocent body."

"Must you always resort to violence?" she asked, twisting to free her arm.

"Must you always hide behind that mask of yours? Tell me what happened just now meant nothing to you."

She closed her eyes, sucking in her breath. When she looked at him, the raw hatred in her eyes pierced his chest like a steel spike. "Mr. Kincaid, you and I both know the reason for this marriage. Let's not delude ourselves into thinking it's any more than it is."

"I see." He dropped his hand. "So what just happened was . . ."

"Indecent."

"Indecent?" How could she say what just happened was indecent? How could she remain cold after what they had shared? Had it really meant nothing? Could she reduce their joining to basic lust, like the crude coupling of a stallion and a mare? Yet she could. She did. Looking at her, the truth was clear; it settled on his heart like ashes settling after a blaze, the ashes of a dream. He felt . . . used.

She lifted her shift and shook it, the breeze slamming sand against his chest and face. Blinking the grit out of his eyes, he swore under his breath. If the woman thought she could just use him and toss him aside, she had another thought coming.

"You want a baby, you'll get one. The price is my lovemaking," he said, raising his voice, shouting over the crash of the waves.

She didn't spare him a glance. "Everything worth having has a price."

Spence watched her tug her shift over her head, the cotton sticking to her damp skin, outlining the shape of her breasts. His blood quickened. God help him, he still wanted her. "I think it's time you started living up to your side of the bargain."

"And just what is that?"

"A wife in private."

"Do you call this private?" Torrie asked, gesturing toward the water.

"Yes."

She groaned and bent to retrieve her blouse. "It might be private, but it's hardly proper. If you had any decency, you would never have done what you did."

"Would it have been better in the dark, on a bed?"

She ignored him.

"Look at me."

She tugged her blouse over her head.

"Dammit!" he shouted, grabbing her arm, forcing her to face him. "Tell me you didn't like the feel of me moving inside you. Tell me you didn't feel the heat. Tell me!"

He could see the doubt in her eyes, the quick rush of desire she couldn't hide. She might not love him, but she couldn't deny he lit a fire between her lovely legs. "What's so wrong with making love in a place as beautiful as this?" he asked, releasing her. "Tell me, Torrie. I don't understand your rules."

"Lord, I wish we had never come here." She turned her back to him and snatched her skirt from the sand. "I want to go back."

"Fine, just fine with me. I'll send a messenger to the village and we'll leave tomorrow."

"That's fine with me."

Spence trudged across the sand and grabbed his trousers. How could something that felt so right be so wrong? he wondered. He was tired of being cast as the villain. The next time they made love—and he knew there would be a next time—she would have to do the asking. He would be damned if he would be treated like a hired stud. If the lady wanted a baby, she would have to take him in the bargain, at least as long as they were married.

Which, with any luck, wouldn't be too long.

* * *

If the trip to Mexico could be described as uncomfortable, the trip back was torture. Kincaid had no modesty, not a shred. Before, Torrie's imagination had been taxed; now her memories haunted her. She knew the texture of his skin, knew the play of the muscles beneath, knew the rapture of their joining. He flaunted his body with ease, bathing when he knew she would see, sleeping naked beside her, teasing her until she thought her nerves would split.

On their second night at sea, Torrie found sleep an elusive creature. She lay staring up into the mirror above them, looking at his image. As usual, he had no use for covers, sleeping on his side facing away from her, with the sheet tossed to his side. Moonlight poured over him, silvering his long, muscular legs, the smooth curve of his hip, his arm, the side of his face. She lay with her side pressed against the wall, but she couldn't get far enough away to escape his compelling heat.

He hadn't touched her since that day on the beach. The simple truth was, he didn't have the slightest urge to touch her, while he was all she thought about; the sleek feel of his skin sliding against hers, the spicy taste of his mouth, the gentle touch of his callused palms. And there were other, more potent memories, memories that haunted her day and night.

Their encounter on the beach had left her sunburned everywhere, a scarlet stain reminding her of her guilt. It had been painful, but not as painful as the lesson he had taught her: Lust could be just as powerful as love. Yet, was it lust she felt for him, or something else, something far more fearful?

What did he want of her? But she knew. Oh yes, she knew. The bargain. He wasn't a man to settle for anything less than all she could give. Still, she had the horrible feeling she couldn't give her body freely without giving her heart. And giving her heart to this man would mean losing it forever.

He moved, turning, his leg brushing hers, sending sparks shooting along her nerves. A sigh escaped his lips as he slid his arm around her waist and cuddled close to her side, his breath warm and moist against her neck. Beneath the thin cotton of her nightgown her sunburned skin prickled. Yet a burn simmered deeper than her skin. She felt a stirring of embers deep in that part of her she barely knew, that part of her with a woman's needs, that part of her only he had ever touched. Lord help her, she wanted him.

This was a war between them. A war she felt destined to lose.

Chapter Sixteen

Spence dashed up the seven flights of stairs leading to his rooms at Hampton House. He was anxious to get back to business, anxious to work out some of the frustration gnawing at his belly.

"Jasper," he shouted as he reached the top floor.

The hall was much the same as the others in the hotel: the walls paneled in oak painted white, trimmed in gold, potted palms and mirrors adding a quiet elegance. In the past he had taken pride in his hotels, each providing the luxury wealth demanded when away from home, but today he wasn't proud of anything.

Spence glanced into his office as he passed the open door, frowning at the stack of telegrams on the desk. They could wait. "Jasper!"

The short, dark-haired servant appeared in the entrance of the parlor. "We weren't expecting you until Monday, sir," he said, his dark eyes filled with unasked questions.

Spence tossed his hat to Jasper. "Mexico didn't agree with the lady." And neither did her husband, he thought. "Did Ben arrive?"

"Yes, sir. Mr. Campbell is in the blue guest room."

His frown deepened. "Still in bed?"

Jasper's thin lips pulled into a smile. "The gentleman was out very late last night."

"Have a pot of coffee sent to my office."

"Yes sir."

Spence marched down the gold and white carpet and threw open a door near the end of the hall. In the light cast through one of the hall skylights, he could see a long lump under the covers, a dark blond head nestled against a plump pillow. Spence crossed to the windows and threw open the ice blue drapes, allowing afternoon sunlight to flood the room.

"What the hell," Ben croaked, squinting at the intruder. "Spence. What are you doing here?"

"I live here."

Ben sat up and ran a hand through his crumpled hair. "I know, but you're supposed to be away. On a honeymoon." His face split into a wide grin. "Did you really get married?"

Spence rubbed the taut muscles at the back of his neck. "Yes, I really got married."

"Well, I'll be damned. I would've laid odds . . ."

Spence wasn't in any mood to discuss his marriage. "What did you find out about Slattery?"

Ben studied his friend a moment, deep lines creasing his brow. "Some reason you're acting like a bear with a thorn in his paw?"

"I'm anxious to know about Slattery, that's all." Spence wished that was all that was eating at his belly. Sleeping beside a beautiful woman without being able to take her in his arms had him itchy, real itchy. "What did you find out?"

"Slattery's got a casino on the Barbary Coast, the Golden Hind. That's where I was last night. Working."

Spence sank into the upholstered armchair by the windows. "I never had a doubt."

Ben stacked another pillow behind his back. "Most people get real quiet when you mention this Slattery. But there's this gal, Ruby, who works as a barmaid there." He grinned and rubbed a hand through the hair on his chest. "Real friendly little gal."

Spence couldn't suppress a grin. Ben had a way of getting friendly with bar gals.

Ben yawned and stretched. "You suppose a fella can get some coffee in this palace?"

"I'm having some sent up. What about Slattery?"

"According to Ruby, Slattery stays out of sight most of the time, shows up in his casino once or twice a week. No one knows where he lives, or what he does when he isn't in the casino."

Spence leaned forward, resting his forearms on his knees. "That's all?"

"I just got into town day before yesterday."

Spence leaned back, trying to corral his emotions. He *was* acting like a bear with a sore paw.

"Oh, yeah. There was something else. Ruby said there's a couple of guys who come in from Chicago once or twice a month."

Spence nodded. "Three of the girls at the rescue mission were brought in through Chicago. Davidson is checking out the connection. Did you pull together a crew?"

"Five of my best," Ben said, scratching his head. "Police Inspector Samuels was here yesterday. He left some photographs for you to look at."

"Photographs?"

Ben nodded. "Of three guys who were found at the back entrance of your hotel, with bullets in their skulls. One of them was the size of a gorilla, and he had a broken leg."

"Moe," Spence said, under his breath. So, maybe Slattery didn't approve of Olivia's plan to kill him, he thought.

"What's up with this guy Slattery?"

"He runs a syndicate dealing in girls. Kidnaps them, then sells them to brothels."

Ben released his breath through his lips in a low whistle. "Ugly business."

"One of his partners tried to have me killed. The three men in the photographs are probably the ones who attacked me."

"Why did he try to have you killed?"

"She." Spence grimaced at the thought of Olivia Fontaine. "Let's say we didn't part on the best of terms."

"Ah." Ben leaned back against the pillows and grinned at Spence. "Does your lady know about this?"

"She knows." Spence wondered if Torrie would think he was any less a barbarian if she didn't know. "I want someone following my wife."

"Are you afraid she's tired of your ugly face already?"

"I'm afraid she might be a target."

Ben nodded. "If she's as pretty as I figure she is, I'll watch her."

A dull ache throbbed in his chest when Spence thought of Torrie. And the problem was, he never stopped thinking of her. "She's beautiful."

"I figured any gal who could get you to the altar had to be real special. Where is the little lady?"

"At home. She needed a few things." Spence grinned, imagining Torrie dressed in her simple skirt and blouse, facing her mother. If he opened the windows, he could probably hear Lillian howling all the way from Van Ness Avenue.

"I'll give you a chance to get dressed," Spence said, rising to his feet. "Then we need to talk strategy. I want to put this Slattery and his friends out of business."

Ben ran a hand across his bristly chin. "Sounds like war."

Spence turned at the doorway and met his friend's inquisitive gaze. "It is."

"I cannot believe you would drive through the streets of San Francisco dressed like some peasant," Lillian said, following Torrie into her daughter's bedroom.

Torrie glanced over her shoulder at her mother. "It was this or my nightgown."

"Good heavens!" Lillian pressed her hand to her heart.

"Mother, I didn't have anything else with me."

"An elopement!" Lillian shook her head, turning as her daughter passed her. "How could you do this? How could you hold me up for ridicule in this shameful fashion?"

Torrie threw open the door of her closet. "I didn't have a choice in the matter. Once Mr. Kincaid makes up his mind to do something, very little can change it."

"You should have insisted on a proper wedding."

Torrie withdrew a walking dress of ivory merino wool trimmed in black braid. "I tried."

Lillian sniffed. "Not well enough."

Torrie crossed the room and laid the dress on the light blue counterpane covering her bed. The truth was, the thought of going through another engagement, of planning another wedding had left her chilled inside. Mr. Kincaid had hoped to humiliate her with an elopement, but he had done her a service without realizing it.

"You don't know what I've been through," Lillian said, pacing back and forth in front of the open windows. A cool breeze lifted the lace curtains, brushing her celery green skirt as she moved. "Gossip is cheap, Victoria, very cheap. I don't have to tell you the sort of things people are saying."

Torrie didn't want to think about what anyone might be saying. She had enough to think about already. She tugged the embroidered bell cord beside her bed to summon Millie, anxious to get out of this house. "I'm sorry if I've caused you any discomfort."

"Discomfort! If you call being humiliated a mere discomfort! And your father—good heavens, the man hasn't any sense. He's delirious over this marriage."

Torrie's gaze fell on the golden-haired doll sitting as it had for twenty years on the small cabinet beside her bed. She still remembered the day her father had given it to her, the day she had taken her first tumble from the back of a horse. Today, he had grabbed her in the hall and hugged her until Torrie thought she might break in two. Poor man, he would be devastated when he learned the truth about her marriage.

"Father wants me to be happy."

"Happy indeed. You know what people think." Lillian moved around the foot of the heavily carved black walnut bed to face her daughter. "They think you had to get married. They think you and Mr. Kincaid were lovers."

Torrie felt heat flare in her cheeks. "Your friends actually believe I would do something so . . . so . . . how could they!"

"Quite easily. You opened up the door to that kind of thought." Taking a deep breath, Lillian folded her hands at her waist. "Now, I've thought about this, and I've decided the best way to rectify the situation is to hold a reception, to invite everyone and show them we have nothing to be ashamed of."

"No."

"No?"

"Anyone who would doubt my honor is not my friend."

Lillian stared at her daughter as though Torrie had just confessed to murder. "Victoria, this gossip must be put to an end."

"I have no wish to appease the gossip-eaters. If they can count to nine, they will discover I was not consorting with Mr. Kincaid before our marriage."

"And how do you intend to live in this city? As an outcast?"

"In a way, I've been an outcast since the day Charles left me standing at the altar. I see no reason to change."

Lillian shook her head. "Victoria, you must give this more consideration. Have you no care for your reputation?"

Her reputation would be irreparably damaged once she was divorced. She saw no need to slither on her belly, hoping these little women with their nasty little minds would see fit to welcome her into their fold. "I'm sorry, Mother, but I don't intend to give those women a second thought."

Spence laid three photographs on his desk. Sunlight spilled through the open windows behind him, streaking across the images of three dead men. "I guess I need to stop by the police station this afternoon," Spence said, rubbing the back of his neck. "Though I doubt anything will come of it."

"Are they the three who attacked you?" Ben asked.

"I can't be sure. I didn't get a look at their faces."
Spence tapped the photo of Moe. "This one I would
bet was one of them. He worked for Slattery's partner, and I think I'm the one who broke his leg."

Ben leaned back in the leather chair. "You think
Slattery had them killed?"

Spence nodded. "It looks as though Slattery didn't
approve of Olivia's tactics. I think this might be his
way of trying to appease me."

Ben rested his chin on the tips of his fingers.
"Has he?"

Spence looked across the desk at his friend. "No.
I've had a glimpse of the grief he brings to young
girls, and I don't like it."

Ben's face split into a wide grin. "Good. It's been
a while since I've been in a knock-down, drag-out
fight."

Spence returned his smile. "You're in one now,"
he said, handing Ben a telegram.

Ben read the telegram and glanced up at Spence.
"It doesn't sound as though the law is going to be
of much good."

Spence shook his head. "The penalty for stealing
a young woman's life is a fine, small enough to be
little less than a nuisance to Slattery."

Ben leaned back in his chair. "I guess I just don't
understand that kind of thinking."

Spence wadded the telegram into a ball and tossed
it into the basket by his desk. A distant rumble of
traffic drifted on a cool breeze though the open windows, the clatter of streetcars, the rattle of carriage
wheels on cobblestones, the sounds pulsing against
his throbbing temples. What he needed was a good
night's sleep; that among other things. "Too many
people believe a woman stays in a brothel because
she wants to be there."

Ben shook his head. "What are we going to do?"

"Put them out of business." He handed a letter to Ben and leaned back in his chair. "This should help."

Ben unfolded the white parchment and scanned the letter. When he was done he looked up at Spence, a smile curving his lips. "How did you manage this?"

"The governor is an old friend of my father." Spence took the letter from Ben and slipped it into his coat. "This should keep us out of jail."

"Where do we start?"

"Tonight I want to get all the men together and . . ." Spence glanced up as Torrie walked into the room.

"Oh, excuse me," she said, taking a step back. "I didn't mean to interrupt."

"You're not interrupting." Spence came to his feet, devouring her with his eyes. Dressed in an elegant gown, she was once again the lady, but now he knew the feel of the curves hidden by the demure cut of her gown. "Come in, there's someone I'd like you to meet."

Ben came to his feet and took her hand as Spence introduced them. "Spence said you were a beauty. But you're even prettier than that."

"You're very kind." She glanced at Spence, her cheeks deepening to a dusky rose. "They're delivering my things, and I'm not sure where to put them."

He was tempted to force her into his room, but he realized it wouldn't get him what he wanted. "I have the room next door. Jasper can show you the empty rooms. Take your choice."

She nodded and glanced away from him. "It was nice meeting you, Mr. Campbell."

"A pleasure." Ben followed her with his eyes until she disappeared around the corner. "Now there's a lady."

Spence sank into his chair. "Yes, she is."

"Don't worry, buddy, I'll stick real close to her."

Spence frowned. "Not too close."

Ben grinned at his friend. "Afraid she'll take a fancy to my handsome face?"

Maybe he was. Damn, he hated jealousy. It was a senseless, useless emotion, and he had a feeling one he was going to get to know well. "I just don't want her to feel smothered."

"I'll take care of her."

Spence had known Ben for twelve years and he trusted him with his life. He just wasn't sure he trusted him with his wife. He sat back and rubbed the taut muscles in his shoulders. Somehow he had to find a way to end this farce, one way or another.

Chapter Seventeen

Torrie lifted her golden-haired doll from one of the six trunks littering the floor of her room at Hampton House. She had worried Kincaid would expect her to share his room, share his bed. It seemed she was foolish to have been concerned. Kincaid didn't want her in his bed unless she was willing . . . to toss aside her pride . . . to expose herself . . . to risk falling in love with the man.

"What would you like me to do with this, miss?" Millie asked.

Torrie glanced across the forest of trunks to where Millie was holding up a gown. Her hands tightened on the doll as she stared at the yards and yards of white silk, her gaze gliding over hundreds of tiny seed pearls sewn upon exquisite embroidered lace. "Who packed that?"

Millie lowered the gown, shaking her head as she

looked at Torrie. "Must have been Ella, miss."

Torrie moved through the maze of trunks, drawn to the gown as though in a trance. She lifted a sleeve of the wedding gown and slid her thumb over the smooth silk. "I had almost forgotten how beautiful it was."

"Yes, miss, and you looked so pretty in it," Millie said, her blue eyes filled with pity. "Oh, I could have shot that Mr. Rutledge."

Charles. Torrie slid her thumb over the pearls at the cuff of the gown, exploring her feelings. In her mind she could see a twenty-year-old girl standing in this gown on a warm June morning, a note from her fiancé dangling from her fingers. She poked and prodded the old wound, but she couldn't feel any pain. After all this time, she was numb. It was as if some other girl had stood in this dress, had read the few lines that had changed her life forever.

"Are you getting settled?"

Kincaid's deep voice brushed Torrie's back like warm velvet. She pivoted on her heel and found him leaning against the doorpost. Just looking at him sent her heart careening into her ribs. He had one hand on his hip, his dark brown coat hitched back to reveal the gold-and-brown-striped waistcoat molding his broad chest and narrow waist. "The last of my things was delivered an hour ago."

He lowered his gaze to the gown Millie held, a frown etching lines into his brow. Torrie dropped the sleeve and turned to her maid. "Have the dress sent to the woman's exchange, Millie. There might be some young lady who can put this to use."

Millie's eyes grew wide. "The exchange, miss?"

"That's right," Torrie said, smiling as she banished the ghost. She was tired of living in the past.

The shock on Millie's face faded into a wide smile. "Yes, miss. I'll do that. I'll do that right away." Her brown curls bobbed on her shoulders, white silk billowing in her wake as Millie rushed from the room.

Alone with Kincaid, Torrie felt as if her tongue had been tied into a knot. There were things she needed to say to him. They couldn't go on this way. But at the moment everything was a jumble. Just how could they go on? She set her doll on the table by the bed and absently fluffed the blue silk dress.

His footsteps were muffled against the thick rose-colored carpet, but she sensed his approach. Instinctively, her nostrils flared, like a mare trying to catch a whiff of a stallion's scent. She glanced over her shoulder, watching him.

He leaned his shoulder against one of the cherry wood posts at the foot of her canopied bed. "How did it go at home?"

The amusement in his tone teased her anger. "How do you suppose it went?"

"I have a pretty good idea of what Quinton would do." He grinned at her. "Your mother was no doubt concerned you had made the right choice. I'm sure she believes there is no one good enough for her daughter."

Torrie turned to the window, trying to hide her feelings. These days her emotions seemed to skim the surface of her skin. "Does making fun of me give you much enjoyment?"

"I wasn't making fun of you."

The sincerity in his voice brought her gaze back to his. She expected to see him smiling that mocking little half smile. He wasn't. Instead he was looking at her with a curious blend of tenderness and something else, something that made her feel flushed from her cheeks to her toes.

"I just figure that's the reaction my mother would have if my sister had run off with a man she had known less than a week."

The rose-colored damask drapes had been pulled, allowing a breeze to flow in through the open windows. She stroked the white lace curtains that shielded the room against the sun, a breeze fluttering the delicate fabric beneath her touch. "I never know when you are teasing me and when you are serious."

"I guess there's a lot we don't know about each other."

His voice reached inside her, dipping into the deep well of longing she tried to keep hidden. She hugged her arms to her breasts, remembering the tug of his mouth upon her nipples, his hands gliding across her naked skin. Images of him haunted her . . . golden skin, smooth as satin . . .muscles hard and sinewy, flexing beneath her hands. A bittersweet ache began to throb between her legs, and she tried to banish the images. She had to stop torturing herself this way.

"I asked my maid to come work for me. I hope you don't mind."

"It'll save us the trouble of hiring one for you."

Odd, how his casual linking of the two of them made her blood race. But then, all she had to do was think of him and her blood quickened.

"Are you happy with the room?"

"Yes, it's lovely." And lonely, very lonely. If she wanted a baby, she would have to submit to this man. She nearly laughed at her own choice of words. *Submit* was hardly appropriate. Especially when there were times when she wanted to strip the clothes from his back, when she wanted to grab him, kiss him, consume him.

Her skin tingled.

She bit her lower lip, glancing at the bed. She stared at the white lace counterpane, thinking of a white sand beach. How long would it be before she held him in her arms again? Her gaze lifted to his, and she wondered if he could see the yearning in her eyes, the longing she could no longer hide.

He held her gaze a moment, his eyes dark, intense. He took a step toward her, then stopped, as though he had hit a brick wall. He stood a moment, staring at her, and she held her breath. Just a few more feet and she could touch him. If he would only move.

He took a step back. "When you're ready for dinner just let Jasper know. He'll bring you a menu." He turned and started to leave.

"You're not going to be here?"

He hesitated near the door. "No." After a moment, he turned to face her, as though looking at her was the last thing in the world he wanted to do. "Ben and I have some work to do."

"I see," she said, painfully aware of the disappointment she couldn't hide.

Spence frowned as he looked at her. "Knowing how little you enjoy my company, I didn't think you'd mind."

Torrie stiffened. "I don't."

He nodded. "Good night, Princess."

She turned and stared at the big bed, knowing he didn't plan to join her tonight, wondering if he ever planned to touch her again. Did he really expect her to go to him? Did he really expect her to ask him to make love to her? How could he expect her to expose herself that way?

He could go straight to blazes!

She kicked the lid of the nearest trunk. If he thought she would sit idly at home while he went out carousing with his friends, he was mistaken.

Spence drew up the reins and eased the horses to a halt in front of Olivia's townhouse. The click of a gun chamber being snapped into place brought his gaze to the man who sat beside him in the carriage. Moonlight glittered on the polished silver of the Colt Ben held. "Let's hope you won't need that."

Ben pulled back his coat and slipped the Colt into the holster slung around his hips. "Are you armed?"

Spence nodded and patted the gun he wore in the trim leather holster strapped to his shoulder. This afternoon Inspector Samuels had done his best to persuade Spence to leave this business to the police. Somehow he had the feeling the inspector was on Olivia's side.

A carriage stopped behind them and five men climbed out. Spence grinned at them as they gathered beside his carriage. "Let's get this started."

Spence led the way across the granite sidewalk, followed by Ben and the other men. The door opened as Spence reached the stairs. He paused on the bottom step, hand on the wrought-iron railing, staring up at the drama unfolding above him.

"Let go of me, ye big brute!" Charlotte McKenzie shouted, struggling in the grip of a bulldog of a man. She kicked the man's shin and he howled.

"Why you . . ." Harry said, tossing her toward the stairs. "Stay out!" He turned and slammed the door behind him.

Charlotte screamed as she lost her balance and went face first down the granite steps. Spence dashed up two steps and caught the old woman, the impact making him stumble. His foot caught on the edge of the step and he tumbled back, cradling Charlotte and colliding into Ben, who in turn fell back into another man. Like dominos, they went down to the ground, in a whirl of arms and legs and Charlotte's black skirt. She fell across Spence's chest, the top of her head colliding with his jaw, jarring him so sharply his teeth rattled.

A groan escaped Spence's lips as Charlotte shifted, her knee ramming into the top of his thigh as she came up for air. She knelt on top of him, her knees straddling his thigh, staring down at him from behind her little glasses.

Spence smiled up at her, rubbing his jaw. "I should have realized it would be you, Miss McKenzie."

"Should ye now." Charlotte struggled to her feet. "If it isn't Mr. Spencer Kincaid himself," she said, straightening her gown.

"Miss McKenzie." Spence rolled to his feet and offered Ben his hand. "Is everyone all right?"

"I'm fine." Ben came to his feet and grinned down at the man still lying on the sidewalk. "Thanks for breaking my fall, Cal."

Cal rubbed the back of his shaggy brown head and frowned. "You're welcome."

"And what is a newly married man doin' coming here, I wonder?" Charlotte asked.

Spence turned to find Charlotte glaring at him, her hands planted on her ample hips. "Does Miss Victoria know where ye spend yer evenin's?"

"Ah, Charlotte. It's good to see you haven't lost your high opinion of me."

Charlotte sniffed loudly. "It's Miss McKenzie to ye. Any man who'd be off consorting with jaded women after marryin' . . ."

"Charlotte, me darlin'," Spence said, taking her hand, "I think you should accompany us back into Miss Fontaine's parlor. You might enjoy this."

"I told ye, it's Miss McKenzie to ye. And I'm not at all sure I'm wantin' t'go anywhere with ye." Charlotte resisted as Kincaid tugged on her arm. "And just what are ye plannin'?"

"A little surprise for our friend, Miss Olivia." He grinned and pulled her arm through his. "Afraid?"

Charlotte's chin soared. "Not in this lifetime."

"Good."

Spence climbed the stairs, with Charlotte by his side. "Better stay back, Miss McKenzie," he said, leaving her standing on the second step.

"Be careful lad," she said, staring up at him, light from the gas lamp beside the door reflecting in the lenses of her glasses. "The Fontaine woman has men spread out throughout her house."

"Why, Charlotte, you do care."

Her response was a loud huff.

Spence smiled and grabbed the brass door knocker. At his knock, Harry answered the door. His dark eyes seemed to shrink into his skull as he looked up at Kincaid. "You're not welcome here."

Spence pushed against the door when Harry tried to close it. "I'm sure the boss lady wouldn't like to have trouble at her front door. My companions and I are coming in, Harry."

Harry reached inside his pocket and Spence hit the door with his shoulder, sending the door and Harry flying. He surged forward, using the door to pin Harry's right arm to the wall. "Now, Harry, is that any way to treat your guests?"

Harry moaned, his face contorting with pain as Spence leaned against the door. "My arm! You're breaking it!"

Spence stepped back and grabbed Harry's shirt-front. He dug his hand into the man's yellow plaid coat pocket and withdrew a Derringer. "Here," he said, tossing the gun to Ben.

"Nasty little toy," Ben said, tucking the gun into his coat pocket.

"Take care of our friend," Spence said, tossing Harry to Cal. He tugged on his cuff to straighten his sleeve before offering Charlotte his arm. "Shall we?"

With Charlotte on his arm, Spence walked down the hall and through a double door that was draped with red velvet, golden tassels brushing his head as he entered the room. A thick rug of gold and red stretched from the entrance to all four corners of the big parlor.

Olivia stood talking to Allan by the walnut sideboard on the far side of the room, her bright hair swept back into a nest of curls, a black feather curving above one ear. The woman definitely liked gold, Spence thought. The mirror above the black marble mantel, the lavish frames of the paintings—which were all of nudes—the two sofas and half a dozen chairs, as well as the rococo tables, were all trimmed with gilt. Even the upholstery was gold, with scarlet threads running through the silk brocade.

Heads turned as their little group moved into the parlor. Eight women, all dressed in the finest silks and satins, their gowns having the stamp of Paris, decorated the room. Six men buzzed around the women, and Spence recognized a few of them. Two men stood aside, watching, arms crossed, each dressed in black evening attire, each looking as though they had once worked in the boxing ring. Olivia's henchmen. His own men dispersed into the room, taking positions to cover Olivia's men.

"Stay close, Miss Charlotte." Spence glanced down at her. "If there's any trouble, you duck behind me."

She nodded, her gray eyes wide behind the round lenses of her glasses. Just then Olivia turned and caught sight of Spence. He smiled. Her cheeks flared into color as she marched across the room to face him, gaslight glittering on the diamonds dripping from her ears and neck, shimmering on the starburst of diamonds that started at her belly and rose across her black satin gown, lifting her heavy breasts, sending color sparking in all directions. Allan followed close behind her.

"What the hell are you doing here?" Aware of her customers, Olivia kept her voice just above a whisper. She glared at Charlotte. "I thought Harry showed you out."

Charlotte smiled. "I came back."

"Spence," Allan said, coming up beside Olivia. "I thought you were going to stay a week in Mexico. What are you doing back so soon?"

"Mexico didn't agree with my wife." Spence felt Charlotte's hand grow tight on his arm and glanced down to find her staring at him, a frown etched between her brows. No doubt she wanted to get on with this. So did he.

Olivia slapped her black lace fan against her open palm and took a deep breath, her bosom nearly popping from the tight bodice of her gown. "How did you get in here?"

"Through your front door," Spence replied.

"Go out the same way!"

"Can't do that, at least not yet."

Allan took his friend's arm and tried to steer him toward the door. "Maybe you should leave, Spence. Olivia's got some pretty rough fellows working for her."

Spence grinned. "So do I. Excuse me, Allan." He moved past his friend, putting his back to the wall, facing the center of the room. "Ladies, gentlemen. If I might have your attention for a moment."

Curious gazes turned in his direction and the room fell silent. "My name is Spencer Kincaid, and this is Miss Charlotte McKenzie."

"What is it, Spence?" Senator Woodley asked, stroking his full beard.

"Good evening, Senator." Spence smiled, speculating on how the senator was going to take what he had to say. "I'm sure the gentlemen here tonight might not be aware that some of these ladies have been forced to work in this establishment."

High-pitched gasps and a low rumble of voices rippled in the gilded room.

"That's a lie!" Olivia spat the words like a hissing cat.

Spence ignored her. "I've been asked by the governor to act as escort for any young lady who would like to leave." He glanced around the room as he spoke, looking from one painted face to another, his gaze resting on a small brunette standing by the mantel. Her fingers were curled against her pink satin gown just below her breasts, her stare fixed on Olivia.

"The governor?" Senator Woodley asked.

Spence nodded. "It's come to his attention that there's a ring of white slavers in San Francisco."

Senator Woodley turned to stare at Olivia. "White slavers?"

Olivia looked across the room and motioned at one of her men. "I'll have you thrown out of here," she said, glaring at Spence.

"I don't think so," Spence said, a smile curving his lips. "Take a look."

Olivia turned to see her man frozen to the opposite wall. Kincaid's man was standing beside him, pressing the muzzle of a pistol to his side. A short distance away, near the fireplace, another of her men shared the same fate.

"Ladies, I can assure you a safe escort to the Chestnut Street Mission," Spence said, glancing at the small brunette. "There, Miss McKenzie and the other ladies will help you take control of your own life."

The little brunette took a hesitant step forward, then stopped, glancing at Olivia.

"We'll provide passage back home and see to it no one troubles you," Spence said, coaxing the little brunette with his eyes.

"Please," the brunette said, her voice barely audible in the crowded room.

Charlotte dropped Kincaid's arm and went to the girl. "It's all right, deary," she said, slipping her arm around the girl's trembling shoulders.

The girl looked up with frightened brown eyes. "There's a girl upstairs, ma'am. Please help her."

Charlotte nodded and looked at Kincaid. "There's a girl upstairs."

Spence sent Ben and one of the other men to search the upstairs, wondering in what kind of shape they would find her. No doubt about it, he was going to enjoy putting this establishment out of business.

"Gentlemen, I realize none of you want to be a part of this." Spence looked from one man to the next, meeting their eyes. "So I think you should know, the *Examiner* will start publishing all the names of the men attending this establishment."

"What!" the senator said, puffing up his big chest, the diamond studs in his shirt catching the gaslight. "Now see here, Kincaid, a man has a right to privacy."

"Senator, I'm sure you don't condone white slavery."

Woodley's cheeks grew red above his gray beard. "No, of course not. But . . ." He glanced over his shoulder, as if he weren't sure who might be standing there. "Some people might not understand if they read about me visiting here."

Spence nodded. "That's why the *Examiner* won't start until tomorrow. You might want to tell your friends."

Screams from above echoed in the hall and drifted into the parlor. "Yes, yes, indeed," the senator mumbled, walking toward the door. He was quickly followed by the other men.

"Damn you!" Olivia shouted, pulling a Derringer from a fold of her skirt. "I'll kill you for this."

"Look out!" Charlotte shouted, rushing forward.

The warning sounded oddly familiar, though Spence didn't have time to think about the reason why. He stepped forward, grabbing Olivia's wrist and thrusting it upward. The gun discharged into the ceiling, dislodging bits of plaster to dribble over their heads.

"Seems you tried this once before," Spence said, twisting the gun from her hand.

"Damn you!" Olivia lunged for him with clenched fists. He ducked, slamming his shoulder into her belly, lifting her off the floor.

"Bastard!" Olivia shouted, slamming her fists against his back. "I'll kill you. I'll . . ."

"Mac, take care of this cat, will you?"

Mac smiled and nodded his dark head. Spence tossed Olivia back into Mac's arms, her skirt billowing to reveal black silk stockings. She shrieked as the big man threw her over his shoulder.

"You won't get away with this!" Olivia shouted, pounding her fists into Mac's back, kicking to free herself. Mac just kept walking toward the door.

"I have friends!" Red velvet and gold tassels fluttered as Mac carted Olivia from the room. "Slattery will kill you for this, Kincaid!" Her shouts and curses grew more distant as Mac carried her up the stairs.

Allan whistled, staring at the swaying drapes. "That is one angry female."

Spence nodded, dusting plaster from his hair. Olivia was emotional, unpredictable. The worst type of enemy. He would have to keep his back covered.

He looked at the women who were still standing in the parlor, eyeing him warily. "Ladies, you're free to go about your business. If you want to leave, you're welcome to come with us."

One by one they slipped past him and disappeared into the hallway. Spence shook his head. He had a feeling there were still a few young women too afraid to leave, at least for now.

"I'm thinkin' ye've made an enemy for life in Miss Fontaine."

Spence glanced down at Charlotte. "And how about you, Miss Charlotte? Have I at last redeemed myself?"

Charlotte tilted her head and studied him a moment. "I guess yer not as bad as I thought ye were."

"What are you going to do now?" Allan asked, swirling the brandy in his crystal snifter.

"Escort the ladies to the mission. And then visit Mr. Jack Slattery."

"Slattery!" Charlotte stared up at Spence. "On the coast?"

Spence nodded, a slow smile curving his lips. "I think it's time we met."

Charlotte shook her head. "He's a dangerous man, Spencer Kincaid."

"It warms my heart to think you're worried about me, Miss Charlotte."

She dismissed him with a huff. "I'd hate t'see Miss Victoria a widow, that's all."

"I appreciate the concern." Too bad his wife's only concern would be the loss of one stallion for breeding.

"Spence, you're not really going to the coast, are you?" Allan asked.

Spence was intrigued by this man Slattery. Just the mention of his name terrified people. "Care to come along to watch the show?"

Allan waved his hand to push away the idea. "Sorry, pal. The Barbary Coast is a hellhole."

Spence grinned. "Where else would you find the devil?"

Allan glanced down at his glass. "Be careful, my friend. Men have been known to disappear on the coast."

Chapter Eighteen

At the mission, Spence found most of the women in the parlor. Despite the shabby furniture and the bare floor, the room glowed with warmth. Gas jets behind the grate on the hearth stole the chill from the air. The brass gaselier overhead flickered a warm, golden light on the seven ladies who sat in the room.

Except for Flora and Mother Leigh, Spence guessed most of the girls were under twenty. Faces lifted from books and knitting needles as Charlotte led Spence and the two girls they had rescued from Olivia's into the parlor. One girl caught Spence's attention. She was small and dark and, in profile, very pretty. As she looked in his direction, he was stunned by the destruction that had been wreaked on her pretty face. The girl wore a patch over her left eye. Deep scars sank into her smooth olive skin above and below the patch, horribly disfiguring her face.

The two girls recently rescued from Olivia's clung to Spence as Charlotte introduced them to the group. Mother Leigh rose and came toward them with outstretched hands. Within minutes the two girls from Olivia's were sitting among the other girls, their satin dresses standing out brightly among muslin and linen.

"Mr. Kincaid, it's very nice to see you again," Claire said as she moved toward him.

For a moment, Spence didn't recognize the young woman. Her yellow hair was pinned back in a soft roll, her cheeks full of color and her figure swathed in blue muslin. The little waif he had helped rescue from Olivia's looked as healthy as a farm girl. "You're looking lovely, Miss Butterfield."

"Thanks to you," she said, smiling up at him. She glanced to where Charlotte stood next to Mr. Kincaid. "And, of course, Charlotte."

"Charlotte didn't need my help," Spence said, glancing down at the woman by his side.

"Congratulations on your marriage," Claire said. "Miss Victoria is a lovely lady."

Spence noticed Charlotte stiffen, cocking her head at a defensive angle, staring at him as though she were waiting for him to say something unflattering about his wife. Charlotte certainly didn't trust him. He wondered if she knew about the bargain Torrie and he had made.

Spence smiled at Claire. "Yes, she is. I'm a very lucky man."

He stayed a few moments longer before he bid the ladies good evening. Charlotte was quiet as she led him out of the house, yet he could sense her tension. Without saying it, he knew she was worried about him. Strange; having that old woman's approval was important to him.

"Charlotte, that young girl, the one with the patch," Spence said, as they stepped onto the porch. "What happened to her?"

"She came from Italy." Charlotte glanced down at a puddle of moonlight streaming across the wooden planks below her feet. "One of Slattery's scouts found her and shipped her here with the promise of a job. When Maria discovered what they wanted, she tried to escape. One of Slattery's men took a razor to her face. They slit her eyelid, so now her eye won't close. When they saw she wouldn't bring a price, they let her go."

Spence felt his stomach tighten.

"Slattery has to be put away," Ben said, stepping away from one of the posts supporting the roof of the small porch.

Spence nodded. "We'll leave a couple of men with you tonight," he said, turning to Charlotte. "Just in case Olivia has any ideas of making trouble."

Charlotte shook her head. "Ye'll need all the men ye've got if ye're goin' to the coast."

Spence grinned and chucked her under the chin. "Why Miss Charlotte, you really are worried about me."

Charlotte sniffed. "I worry about mongrels in the street as well."

Spence laughed. "Ah, Miss Charlotte, you're a woman after my own heart."

"Ye be careful, lad," Charlotte called as Spence and Ben walked down the stairs. "Watch yer back."

"You can depend on it," Spence called over his shoulder. He didn't intend to make his bride a widow. He didn't like leaving any fight unfinished.

The ripe smell of an open sewer assaulted their senses as Spence and Ben passed an alley opening on Pacific Street. Women called to them, their voices rising on the foul air like howling cats. Spence glanced down the alley, his nostrils pinching against the smell, his brow furrowing at the sight.

A dozen or more women leaned out of windows, red lamps glowing above them. Some of the women were naked from the waist up; others wore scraps of what might have once been a chemise or nightgown. In their shrill voices, each detailed their charms, trying to entice them to enter the alley.

Ben shook his head and released a low whistle. "I've been to a few places in my time, but I've never seen the likes of this Barbary Coast before."

"Up on Nob Hill they consider the waltz indecent." And taught young women to be afraid of men. Spence flicked the reins. "Hard to believe it's the same city."

Dance halls, wine cellars, and gaming halls crammed shoulder to shoulder for three solid blocks, spewing noise into the chilly night air. People jammed the wooden sidewalks, drunken sailors, soldiers from the Presidio, women in garish outfits, Chinese men with long black queues wrapped around shaved heads. Here a man could drop through a trap door and never be heard of again, sold into slavery on the sea for a few dollars.

Ben pointed to a two-story wooden building just ahead. "That's the place."

As Spence pulled the carriage alongside the Golden Hind, a man dressed in uniform came hurtling through the doorway to land face-first on the wooden sidewalk. An ape of a man followed him out of the gaming hall, cutting a thick shadow in the light spilling through the doorway.

The giant folded his arms over his broad chest and glared down at the boy. "Don't be coming back."

The young soldier came to a sitting position, swiping at the blood streaming from his nose, staring up at the ape. "They cheated me."

The ape's arms bulged beneath his green plaid coat. "Best leave while you still got your life, boy."

The young man stared a moment, seemingly weighing his chances. "Damn cheats," he mumbled, struggling to his feet. With one last look of disdain, he crossed the street and put some distance between himself and the Golden Hind.

The giant turned and ambled through the double doors leading to the gaming hall, music and laughter spilling into the street. The doors closed with a thump behind him.

Ben glanced at the carriage pulling up on the opposite side of the street, nodding at his three friends. "Maybe we shouldn't have left Frank and Ed at the mission."

Spence grinned and dropped the reins. "That old boy doesn't have you worried, does he?"

Ben shook his head. "It's the twenty more inside that bother me."

"Four-to-one odds. You had me worried for a minute. I thought we might be in trouble."

Ben let out his breath on a sigh. "Lead the way, boss man."

Spence threw open the doors of the Golden Hind. Tobacco smoke, so thick it burned his eyes, heavy with the stench of stale beer and unwashed bodies, enveloped him. The tinny sound of a piano cut through the smoke, drawing his attention to the stage running along one side of the room.

On stage, six energetic young women were dancing, arms slung around each other's shoulders, kicking until their dark unbound hair brushed the floor. Beneath their hip-length yellow skirts the girls wore black silk stockings, yellow garters, and nothing else. Shouts went up from the men standing in front of the stage each time the skirts flared.

With the instincts of a panther, Spence scanned the room, noting the doors and windows, searching the crowd for Slattery's men. They were scattered around the room, keeping their gaze on each of the four long gaming tables, leaning against the bar, positioned in the shadows on the gallery overlooking the hall.

"How many do you count?" Ben asked, as they walked toward the bank at the back of the room.

"Eighteen." Spence withdrew bank notes from his money clip. He glanced up at the gallery. "Slattery stays up there?"

Ben nodded. "He has a suite of rooms in the back."

"I'll take three hundred," Spence said, passing his notes to the banker who sat behind iron bars. The banker pushed a stack of chips at him. Spence shuffled the wooden chips between his fingers as he and Ben walked toward the nearest roulette table.

"There's that handsome Texan."

Ben and Spence both turned as a yellow-haired woman approached them. Her white shirtwaist was open, baring a deep valley, her full breasts swinging beneath the cotton with unrestrained charm. The yellow satin of her pleated skirt barely grazed the top of her black silk-clad thighs as she sauntered up to Ben.

"Good evening, Ruby," Ben said, giving her a wide grin.

"Glad to see you back, cowboy," she said, brushing the front placket of his trousers with her fingers. "And you brought a friend." She looked Spence over from the top of his dark head to the tip of his boots. "They do know how to grow them in Texas."

Under all the paint, Spence suspected Ruby was a pretty woman in her early twenties. He smiled as she moved between them, her hand snaking across his buttock. No doubt about it, Ruby was a friendly gal.

"Can I get you men anything?"

Spence dug into his pocket and pulled out a twenty-dollar gold piece. "A couple of beers, darlin'." He tossed her the coin. "Keep the change."

Ruby bit the coin, then smiled up at Spence. "Yes, sir. Coming right up."

Ben chuckled under his breath. "Real friendly little gal."

"No doubt." If only his wife were half as friendly, Spence thought.

With Ben following, Spence shouldered his way to a roulette table and stood beside a big blond man. Dressed in a red-and-white-plaid flannel shirt and blue denim trousers, the man looked as though he had just crawled down from the mountains.

"Hope you have better luck than me," the man said, stroking his thick yellow beard.

Spence shifted his chips, allowing one to drop to the floor. As he retrieved the chip, he glanced under the table at the croupier's foot. A smile curved his lips as he straightened. "I'll bet two hundred on twelve black."

A low rumble passed around the table. As he suspected, others followed his bet, hoping the reckless stranger's luck was better than their own. Piles of chips were heaped on black twelve until the croupier declared the betting closed.

With a flick of his wrist, the croupier started the wheel spinning. All stares were fixed on the small white ball as it dashed across the surface of the smooth wheel, the spinning sound drowning out the music and voices for those crucial few seconds.

Out of what looked like nerves, Spence dropped another chip and bent to retrieve it. He came up in time to watch the small white ball slow and slip into the zero slot with a clatter. A groan passed through the crowd gathered around the table, dark glances shooting at the impetuous stranger whom they had followed into ruin.

"Looks like you're about as lucky as me," the big blond man said, a good-natured grin splitting his beard.

Spence shrugged and moved away from the table, shuffling his chips, glancing around the room, making sure his men were in place.

"Is it rigged?" Ben asked, his voice barely above a whisper.

Spence nodded. "You know what to do. Wait for my signal."

"What are you . . ." Ben paused as he noticed Ruby pushing through the crowd a short distance in front of them, carrying two mugs of beer.

"Here's your beers." She handed one to Ben, then the other to Spence. Her tongue slipped out to moisten her lips as she looked up at Spence, fear naked in her eyes. "I got a message for you. Mr. Slattery wants to talk to you." As she spoke she directed her gaze to the gallery.

Spence turned and glanced up at the gallery. A man was standing in the shadows cast by swags of yellow velvet. As Spence watched, the man turned and walked down the hall, disappearing from sight.

"I imagine he does." Spence grinned at Ruby. "Lead the way, little darlin'."

Spence followed Ruby through the crowd and up the stairs at the back of the room. Two men stood guard at the top of the stairs, both the size of brahma bulls, each eyeing Spence as though he were invading their turf. He was.

"That's his office." Ruby turned as they neared a door at the end of a short, dark hall. "Be careful," she said softly, before rushing back the way they had come.

Apprehension nibbled at the base of his spine as Spence grasped the cold brass door handle. A little apprehension was healthy, he decided; it kept you on your toes. Without knocking, he threw open the door and entered Slattery's lair. A single gas jet burned by the door, casting flickering shadows on the man who sat behind the desk against the far wall.

"I've been expecting you, Mr. Kincaid." Slattery gestured with his hand to one of the two chairs in front of his desk. "Please have a seat."

"Mr. Slattery." Spence closed the door behind him, his gaze darting around the room as he moved toward the chair; one window, closed and draped with yellow velvet, two doors in addition to the one by which he had entered, each leading to another room, where more of Slattery's men could be waiting.

"It seems you paid a visit to one of my acquaintances tonight," Slattery said, leaning back in his chair.

So, he was English, upper crust by the sound of his accent. Spence sat on one of the oak armchairs in front of the desk, trying to pierce the shadows and get a good look at Slattery. "Word travels quickly," he said, setting his mug of beer on the man's desk.

Slattery slid a glance at the damp mug. "I find it wise to keep abreast of everything of any importance that happens in this city." He lifted the lid of a humidor to his right. "Cigar? I have them shipped in from Cuba."

Spence waved his hand and watched as the other man struck a match and lit his cigar. For a moment the flame illuminated Slattery's features. Spence caught a glimpse of a thin nose, a patch over his right eye, a scar running from that patch into his thick beard. Slattery blew out the flame, and once again his face fell into shadow.

"Mr. Kincaid, it would seem you are intent on running Olivia out of business."

"I am."

Slattery tapped the end of his cigar against a gold ashtray. "And I suppose you would also like to put me out of business as well."

"I intend to." In the dim light, he could see Slattery shift in his chair.

"You and I are both businessmen, so I don't have to tell you how important it is to seize the right opportunities when they come along. There's a great deal of money to be made in the business both Olivia and I have chosen."

"What are you suggesting?"

Slattery twisted his cigar against the side of the ashtray. "You may find it to your benefit to join us, rather than to take on the precarious task of trying to put us out of business."

Spence smiled, but he felt a hot tide of rage growing inside him. "I prefer my money without bloodstains."

"I've spent a good deal of time putting together this business. I own half the police in the city. The mayor is in my pocket; the boss of Chinatown reports to me." He paused a moment, as though he were waiting for Spence to absorb all he had said. "I control San Francisco."

"There's an election this year." Spence crossed his legs and draped one wrist over his knee in a casual pose that belied the tension in his body. "Your man is on his way out, just as you are."

Slattery sat back. "You can't touch me. I've done nothing illegal."

"I think your customers will disagree." Spence

rose and smiled down at Slattery. "There's something I think you might like to watch." He turned and walked toward the door, feeling Slattery's stare burn into his back. "Come take a look."

"What game is this?"

"See for yourself."

Spence passed Slattery's two watchdogs and paused by the railing of the gallery. Slattery stayed just behind him, keeping to the shadows.

"What do you have in mind, Kincaid?"

"You sound as though you think this is an ambush."

"Maybe it is."

Spence smiled. "I don't care much for back-stabbing." He glanced to where Ben was waiting. Ben nodded as he saw Spence and moved to one side of the roulette table. A few seconds later Cal and Mac joined Ben.

"All right," Slattery said, his voice filled with impatience and something else, a trace of fear. "What is this thing you want me to see?"

Spence glanced back to Slattery and smiled. "Watch." He turned back in time to see Ben and the other men send the eighteen-foot table toppling to the floor. The carpet beneath the croupier's feet ripped, exposing a metal plate with three buttons. A hiss of compressed air shot through the room, followed by a loud twang, as wire ripped and sprang from one leg of the table.

"My God!" Slattery gasped.

Every man in the place came running to see what had happened. For a moment they just stared at the wire as it raised and writhed like a cobra about to strike.

"An old trick, Slattery," Spence said, turning to face him. "A little compressed air, a few springs, and your croupier could tilt that wheel anytime he wanted with just a press of a button. Zero or double zero and the game belongs to the house."

"Cheat!" The shout seemed to come from all directions.

The big blond mountain man was the first to move, grabbing the croupier and tossing him into the nearest roulette table. The ape dressed in the green plaid suit grabbed the big blond's shoulder. The mountain man turned and smashed his fist into the ape's jaw, sending him reeling into the bar. Shouts went up, coupled with screams from the women as the hall was transformed into a mass of flying fists and careening bodies.

"You're a dead man, Kincaid." Slattery gestured for his two watchdogs. "Take care of him."

They stalked Spence, brass knuckles gleaming in the gaslight spilling beneath velvet swags, smiling as though they took pleasure in beating a man to death. Spence smiled, his hands forming fists at his sides. *Just don't let one of them get to your back,* he thought.

A fist came flying at his face. Spence blocked the punch with his forearm, coming up into the man's belly with his left fist. Groaning, the man stumbled back. The second one surged forward, leading with his right hand. Spence sidestepped, the brass-clad fist grazing his shoulder, leaving a trail of blazing flesh.

A hand grabbed his forearm. Spence spun away and landed a blow to the nearest jaw, sending one of his assailants slamming into the wall, a low grunt joining the noises rising from below . . . shouts . . . shattering glass . . .splintering wood.

Like a battering ram, a man slammed his head into Spence's chest, knocking the air from his lungs in a sharp gasp, bringing them both crashing to the floor. Spence rolled, dragging the man with him.

From the corner of his eye, Spence saw Slattery step out of range.

Spence grabbed the big man's head and brought it down against the floor, again and again, wishing it were Slattery, clenching his jaw against the sound of the man's skull connecting with oak, each thud coupled by a whimper . . .pain splintered along the nerves of his back, ripping a moan from Spence's lips. Before he could catch his breath, a foot slammed into his ribs, knocking Spence into the railing.

As Spence staggered to his feet, one of them grabbed his legs, trying to lift him, trying to toss him over the railing. The velvet drapes brushed his face. Spence clenched the wooden railing, feeling it shudder beneath his weight. The man pushed. Spence slid farther over the railing, his belt hitting the slender oak.

With a curse, Spence rammed his feet into the man's huge chest. Slattery's man stumbled back. Spence dropped his feet to the floor. The man surged forward, throwing a right. Spence took the blow on his left arm and countered with his right, hitting him under the chin, snapping back his head. The breath parted from the man's body in a slow groan as he slumped to the floor, his body crumpling over his unconscious compatriot.

Spence leaned back against the railing, sucking air into his lungs, pain rippling along his left side with every breath. He looked into the shadows to where Slattery stood, trying to find the man's eyes, seeing only the indistinct shape of his face. "You're lucky they didn't kill me, Slattery. Something happens to me or mine and you'll hang."

"Do you think the police will protect you?"

Spence shook his head. "I'm not talking about your police, I'm talking about a different kind of justice, one that won't quit until you're dead. On one hand you'll have the governor and his men, on the other you'll have my men. Both will make your life hell."

Slattery's hands clenched at his sides. "I have protection."

"Not enough. You better hope I live a charmed life."

"Accidents do happen."

"You better hope they don't happen to me. You better hope they don't happen to my family or my friends. Because I'll figure you were behind it. And I'll make sure you pay." He smiled, seeing Slattery stiffen in the shadows. "Now excuse me. I can't let everyone else have all the fun."

Spence turned his back on Slattery, showing his contempt, hoping his threat hit home. As he neared the bottom of the stairs, he caught a glimpse of something hurtling toward him. He ducked; a chair flew over his head to smash against the wall, a wooden leg bouncing back to hit his raised arm. Keeping his head low, Spence glanced over the railing, looking for Ben and the others. He spotted Ben near the bar, rearranging the face of one of Slattery's men.

Spence made his way through the fray, dodging flying bottles and chairs, pushing past flaying arms and legs. A man came stumbling past him with Ruby attached to his back.

"That'll teach you not to mess with a lady," Ruby yelled, hitting the man over the head with the leg of a chair.

Spence tapped Ben on the shoulder when he reached the bar. Ben spun round, leading with his fist. Spence ducked. "Easy; I'm on your side."

Ben gave Spence a big grin and let the man he was holding slump to the floor. "How did we do?"

"Look out!" Spence grabbed Ben's shirt and pulled

him down as a table sailed above their heads, crashing into the mirror behind the bar. "We did fine, real fine."

Ben rubbed his bruised chin and grinned. "I'll help you round up the boys."

One by one Spence and Ben found their men and steered them toward the door. An hour later, they entered Hampton House.

"Ben, tomorrow I want you to stay close to Torrie. It's hard telling what Slattery will try."

Ben nodded and opened the door to his room. "I'll stick to her like a tick to a spaniel."

Spence turned and walked down the hall toward his room. He glanced at Torrie's door as he passed, wondering if she were sleeping, wondering what she would do if she should wake to find him beside her. God, he ached to hold her again. With a sigh he pushed the thought aside and continued down the hall to his own room. He opened the door and paused on the threshold, stunned by what he saw.

Chapter Nineteen

Torrie rose from the sofa near the marble hearth as Spence entered the room. Dressed in a white satin robe, she looked like an angel as she moved toward him, an avenging angel.

"You've been in a fight, a brawl by the looks of you," she said, touching his brow near the cut above his right eye. "How badly are you hurt?"

The fragrance of roses warmed by her skin teased his senses, threatening his balance. He felt his blood quicken and throb, pounding with a steady pulse in his groin. One look at this woman and he was tumbling out of control. "What are you doing here?"

She lifted her chin defensively. "Waiting to see if Mr. Slattery had made me a widow."

"Slattery?" He felt a swift clutch of fear in his gut. "Did you go to the mission tonight?"

Torrie stared at his chin, refusing to look him in the eye. "And if I did?"

An image of Torrie in Slattery's hands flashed in his mind. "Dammit, woman!" he said, grabbing her upper arms, fear for her constricting his muscles. "You can't just go roaming the streets alone at night."

She twisted in his grasp, trying to break free. "It seems you gave me that advice once before."

He held her easily, his hands tightening on her arms. "This is serious. We're dealing with people who aren't afraid to kill."

"If you must know, Charlotte came here," she said, still refusing to meet his eyes. "She was worried about you and thought I should know what you were up to."

He had the feeling she was hiding something. "Charlotte was worried about me?"

A smile slipped along her lips. "I think she has taken quite a liking to you. I had to talk her out of following you to Slattery's."

Spence released his breath in a long sigh. "She's got a lot of courage, but she needs to stay clear of Slattery. I don't want to be worried about keeping her safe."

Torrie stared at his chin. "She has been taking care of herself for a long time."

"This is different. We're not just rescuing a few girls. We're going after Slattery and his whole organization." He shook her until her eyes snapped up to meet his. "Do you understand me, Torrie? The man is going to get real angry. I don't want you or any of the other women taking chances."

She tried to pull free. "You're hurting me."

He held her. "Do you understand me?"

"Yes, of course I understand. I have been speaking English since I was a child." She drew a deep breath before she continued. "I will tell Charlotte to stay clear of whatever it is you are doing."

He believed her, for now. "I swear, little lady, if you give me any reason to believe you're taking chances with your life, I'll toss you in your room, lock the door, and keep you there until this war with Slattery is over."

"I'm not a child," she said, her chin rising. "Please, do not treat me as though I were."

No, she wasn't a child. He knew far too well just how much of a woman she was. He only wished she were his woman. He opened his hands, sliding his palms over the satin covering her arms, trying to ease any pain he had caused, the smooth cloth warm from her skin. Yet warm satin couldn't compare to the heat, to the texture of her skin. God, it had been a lifetime since he had held her.

She didn't pull away from him, standing within his reach, her head bowed, her hands clasped in front of her, like a little girl. The lamp on the wall behind him reflected on the ivory contours of her cheek, slipped light into her shining hair, seeking the fire hidden in the chestnut tresses.

He could see the shape of her breasts outlined by white satin. In his mind he saw her standing beneath the golden arc of the sun, her unbound hair tossed back from her pale shoulders, her naked breasts rising and falling with each quick breath, the rosy buds tempting him.

Heat flowed in his veins, a slow burn of desire searing his every muscle, every nerve, until he was pulsing with the need to hold her.

What would she do if he slipped his arms around her, he wondered, sliding his open palms upward over the curve of her shoulders? What would she do if he tipped back her head, if he pressed his lips against hers, if he . . . pain twisted low in his belly. He dropped his hands and took a step back.

Not this time. He wasn't going to make a fool of himself again. This time he would be damned if he allowed her to treat him like a cheap whore.

She peeked up at him, keeping her chin down, her huge eyes wary, like a dove who found herself alone with a hungry hawk. No doubt she was thinking the big bad barbarian intended to toss her to the floor and slack his lust on her perfect little body. He had to admit, the idea had appeal.

"Well, you can see Slattery hasn't made you a widow. So, I guess there's nothing more . . ."

"Your brow, it should be . . . do you have anything to . . ." She bit her lower lip. "Perhaps some cold water would help."

He stared at her as she hurried toward the door leading to his bathroom, watching the sway of her braid against the small of her back, feeling the painful pulse of his blood low in his belly. Cold water might help. But he doubted it.

She disappeared into his bathroom, and a moment later he saw the light flicker to life. He heard water running, heard her rummage through the bathroom cabinet. When she returned she was carrying a wet washcloth and a bottle of alcohol in her hands. He took a deep breath and tried to calm the beast stirring in his loins.

Torrie glanced surreptitiously at the bed as she entered the room. The blue velvet counterpane had been turned down, allowing the soft glow of incandescent light to pulse against plump pillows, to slide across white silk sheets. It looked . . . inviting.

She glanced at the man standing near the door. The lamp on the wall behind him cast a golden glow around his dark head, drew shadows across his face. He was watching her every move, his eyes narrowed by thick black lashes, his posture oddly strained, one knee cocked at an angle, both hands planted on his hips, his dark brown coat hitched back at his wrists. He looked . . . intimidating.

"If you'll sit down," she said, glancing toward an armchair near the bed, "I'll see to that wound."

"It's just a scratch. You don't need . . ."

"Let me help you with your coat," she said, setting the cloth and bottle on the cabinet beside the bed. She didn't want to be sent away, sentenced to spend the night alone with her doubts.

His eyes never left her as she moved toward him. When she reached for his coat, he stepped back, as though he couldn't stand to let her touch him. He might as well have slapped her. He didn't want her in any way, not even in this simple gesture of rendering help.

Foolish woman, she thought, lowering her eyes. *Foolish, stupid* . . . her gaze grazed the front of his trousers and the distinct ridge that strained against the brown wool of his trousers. She bit her lower lip, but she couldn't stop her smile. Perhaps he did find her attractive, just a little.

He shifted his weight. As she met his eyes, she sensed something foreign in him: a strange, elusive vulnerability. "It's time you went to bed, Princess."

Perhaps it was. Only she didn't want to sleep in that big, empty bed in the next room. Still, she wasn't sure how to alter the arrangements. "After I've seen to that cut," she said, slipping her hands inside his coat, sweeping the brown wool from his shoulders.

Spence stepped back, hitting the closed door with his heel. Torrie came away with his coat; one minor victory, she thought. She tossed the coat over her shoulder and plunged ahead. "You won't need this tonight," she said, slipping the slim brown straps of his holster from his shoulders.

"Wait," he said, raising his arms, catching the holster around his elbows.

"I'm not armed, Mr. Kincaid," she said, tugging on the brown leather.

Although he looked doubtful, he lowered his arms, allowing her to sweep the holster down the length of his arms, the weight of the revolver swinging in her hand. "Where should I put it?" She wanted to know where everything belonged.

He looked as though she had robbed him of more than the revolver. "The closet. Top shelf."

She turned, hiding her smile. In the shelter of the deep closet, she lifted his coat, brushing the smooth brown wool against her nose and her lips, inhaling his scent deeply into her lungs. Strange how the scent of a man could be so appealing.

It seemed right, she thought, hanging his coat with the many others in the closet, helping him prepare for bed. *Wifely.* On the top shelf of the closet she found another holster, this one black, filled with a Colt and made to fit around his hips. A single shiver crawled along her spine as she stared at that revolver. She only prayed he wouldn't have to use it.

Spence hadn't moved. He stood in front of the door, watching her as she walked toward him. The man looked as though she intended to stretch him out on a rack. "It would be easier for me to reach your brow if you sat. And I'm sure you would find it more comfortable."

He didn't move.

She smiled. "I won't bite."

He looked utterly defenseless. "Why are you doing this?"

She didn't want to explore the reasons. She only knew she wanted to be here, with him. "I want to help."

He drew a deep breath. He was going to ask her to leave. She could see it in his eyes.

"Please, let me help." *Give me a little more time to find the words . . . to find my courage.*

He sighed, lowering his head as though accepting the inevitable. Like a man walking to the gallows, he moved to the chair by the bed.

She soaked the washcloth with alcohol, set the bottle on the table by the bed, then pressed the cloth to the broken skin above his right eye. He sucked in his breath as the liquid seeped into the open wound.

"Sorry," she said, smiling down at him.

"It's all right."

He moistened his lips with the tip of his tongue. The gesture was done quickly, nothing more than a man wetting his dry lips. Yet with that simple gesture came a tide of memories for Torrie. She traced the curve of those moist lips, remembering the shape of them against hers, the taste, the heat.

"Why are you going after Slattery?" she asked, resoaking the cloth in alcohol.

"Maybe I don't like the way everyone keeps telling me the man is untouchable. Maybe I don't like to see pretty girls with their faces slashed open." He was quiet a moment, frowning as he stared at the windows behind her, blue velvet drawn to close out the night. "He hurts people. Someone has to stop him."

She pressed the cloth lightly to his cut brow. "You surprise me."

He held her gaze for a moment, his eyes revealing nothing, as though he were trying to make sure she couldn't see the emotions inside him. "Because I don't fit the mold you had cast for me?"

She glanced down to the bloodstained cloth. She didn't know him well. She wasn't sure she wanted to know him better. If she did, she might discover she cared too much. She might discover she didn't have enough honor to let him walk out of her life.

She heard him draw a deep breath, heard him release it in a steady stream of warmth that brushed her arm. "How did you become interested in the mission?" he asked.

Torrie lifted his left hand and pressed the cloth to his torn knuckles, his sharp intake of breath telling her she was causing him pain. But she couldn't help it.

"When I was sixteen a young woman came to work for us as a kitchen maid. She wasn't much older than I." Torrie hesitated, keeping her gaze fixed on his hand, dabbing gently with the cloth. "One day I found her crying in the garden, sobbing as though her heart were breaking."

"What was wrong?"

"She was with child." She kept her eyes lowered, tending his wounds as though her own life depended on it. "When she was sixteen, some man had lured her away from her parents' farm in Kansas with a fake elopement. He was a white slaver. She was what they call 'broken in,' and sent to San Francisco. Mother Leigh rescued her and helped her get a job with my father."

"What happened to her?"

She rested the cloth against his bloodstained hand. "She slit her wrists and bled to death one August morning. She did it in one of the bathrooms, in the tub, so she wouldn't make a mess." Images flickered in her mind, images she had long ago tried to bury. "But . . . there was . . . so much blood."

"You found her."

Torrie nodded, fighting the tears crawling up her throat.

"I'm sorry," he said, wrapping his hand around

hers, her skin cold against the heat of his.

"So am I." She wiggled free of his grasp and took his right hand. "I decided that day I would do anything I could to stop them."

"We'll stop Slattery. I promise you."

Torrie looked down at him, taking in every detail of his face, the lock of dark hair tumbling over his brow, the swelling above his eye, the dark shadow of his beard roughening his cheeks, darkening the cleft in his chin. In a short period of time she had grown fond of this face. Perhaps too fond. She realized if it meant Slattery going free or something happening to Spence, she would choose the former. "Just be careful. He could have killed you tonight."

His eyes lowered, his gaze sliding along the curve of her lips, before returning to her eyes. "Your concern touches me."

From the quiet tone of his voice, she couldn't tell if he were making fun of her or if he were serious. Giving him a glimpse of her feelings made her feel exposed. "How am I going to have a baby if you are dead?"

He was quiet a moment, staring up at her, probing her with his eyes until she was sure he could tell what she was feeling. Even though she wasn't sure what she was feeling.

"How are you going to have a baby if you can't stand to be touched by me?"

Torrie stared down at his hand, spreading his long fingers to see if any were broken. He had beautiful hands, long, slender, shaded with dark hair. Strong hands. Gentle hands. There were times when she found herself daydreaming about his hands, his fingers, remembering them touching her skin, stroking her as he had done once so long ago. Had it only been a few days? It seemed a lifetime since he had touched her.

She needed to feel something more than anger, much more. She needed to pretend she was a beautiful woman loved by this man. If just for a little while. If just for tonight. "I never said I couldn't stand to be touched," she whispered, releasing his hand.

"I got the impression you thought making love was shameful and degrading."

Now was the time. There was no honor in being a coward, no glory, no reward. A brave woman went after what she wanted, and Torrie knew what she wanted: Spencer Kincaid. For the moment, he was within her reach. She just wished she had some idea of how to start. She felt as awkward as she had at her first cotillion.

"I thought so," he said, coming to his feet. He brushed past her as he walked toward the door. "I think you better go hide behind your castle walls, Princess. You never know when a dragon will awaken and devour you."

She stayed where she was, staring at his broad back. "I've been thinking."

He paused, his hand poised on the brass door handle. "About what?" he asked, glancing over his shoulder.

She took a deep breath and an even bigger step. "I've realized it's time to stop acting like a frightened schoolgirl. My mother always said I was my father's daughter. My father always lives up to his bargains." She tugged the sash at her waist and pushed the robe from her shoulders. "It's time to live up to my part of this bargain."

Spence followed the white satin with his eyes as it fell to her feet, his gaze gliding over her, peeling away the yards of white cotton shielding her secrets. Secrets he had shared. He noticed the trembling of her fingers as she unfastened the twenty pearl buttons running down the front of her white night-gown. But she didn't stop. *God, don't let her stop.*

She ran her fingers inside the open gown, sepa-rating it just enough to give him a glimpse of her pale breasts. She was teasing him, deliberately; a woman learning the power she held over a man. His Ice Princess was melting before his eyes. She trusted him. She wanted him. She humbled him with her surrender.

She moved toward him, slowly closing the chasm yawning between them. "I shall do my best to act the loving wife for as long as we are married."

With a trembling smile tugging at her lips, she ran the tip of her finger along the curve of his lower lip, then slipped her tongue between her lips and licked the tip of her finger, tasting the essence of his lips. The gesture wiped the inside of his mouth dry.

"Of course, I will need more training."

Without looking away from his face, she unfas-tened the buttons of his gold and brown waistcoat, smiling up at him. She slipped his cravat from his neck, folded it, then—finding nowhere to lay it—tossed the scrap of silk to the floor. Pearl studs fell beneath her fingers, exposing his chest to her wandering fingers. She tugged his shirt from his trousers before sliding her hands inside the warm linen.

She caressed him, sliding her hands over his chest, across his shoulders, as though she were absorbing the heat of his skin, as though she enjoyed touching him. By the time she peeled his shirt and waist-coat from his shoulders, Spence was having trouble breathing.

Her smile slipped when she glanced down at his naked chest. "What did they do to you?" she whis-pered, running her fingers over his ribs.

He followed her stare, glancing down at his side.

Blue and purple feathered outward from a series of small red marks shading the left side of his rib cage from just below his arm to his waist.

"Is it painful?"

Right now the only pain he felt was lower, much lower. "No. It looks worse than it is."

She kissed the dark stains, brushing her lips across his skin, painting feathery strokes across his back with her fingertips. He closed his eyes, absorbing her soft touch, inhaling her fragrance, hoping he wouldn't awaken and find this was all another dream.

"If you aren't too bruised, I thought we might work on the rest of my education tonight." She stroked the springy black curls covering his chest. "Are you?"

He glanced down at her. "What?"

"Too bruised?"

He chuckled low in his throat. "Honey, I'd have to be in my grave to be too bruised."

She smiled, looking pleased with herself. "I wonder," she whispered, lowering her lips to his chest. "Does this feel good?"

He dropped back his head as she pressed her lips to one dusky male nipple, the nub growing taut and tingling beneath her swirling tongue. "Good, very good."

"Tell me, what would a loving wife do now?" Torrie asked, sliding her hands over his hips. Spence resisted the urge to move under her touch, to thrust his hips, to press against her belly. He wanted to give her a chance to explore, to allow her to lead.

She glanced up at him as she trailed her fingers over the front placket of his trousers, as though she were gauging his response. "Would she perhaps unfasten these?"

Reflex brought his hips forward, sliding his swollen flesh across her hand. "Yes," he whispered, his voice husky with need.

A pulse came to life deep inside her as Torrie slipped one button after another through the wool warmed by his skin, his trousers taut from the pressure of his flesh straining from within. She slid the trousers down to his feet, then ran her hands upward, over the silk drawers covering his hips. "Oh my, I guess I should have removed your shoes first."

His hands clenched into fists at his sides as she flowed down the front of him, mimicking the motions he had made days ago on a white sand beach. A low growl escaped his lips as she brushed her cheek against the ridge of his arousal hidden beneath smooth white silk, the heat of him pulsing against her skin. Perhaps she didn't need much training after all, she thought. This all seemed as natural as breathing.

She knelt before him, allowing her nightgown to sag open to reveal the curves of her breasts. She lifted his left foot and pulled off the soft brown leather boot, then slid off the sock. After pressing a kiss to his instep, she removed the left boot and sock, then sat back on her heels and smiled up at him. "Now what should I do?"

Spence grinned. "Anything you want."

"Anything?" Torrie stared up at him, passion rising, breaking chains that had bound her.

"Anything at all, sweetheart."

She felt a delicious sense of freedom, an escape for the woman hidden too long beneath rules and standards and doubts.

He offered his hand. "Tell me what you want."

She put her hand in his warm palm and came to her feet. How odd to ever have resisted this man. "I want you to touch me, like you did before."

She stepped back and slipped her fingers inside

the edge of her nightgown. The cotton slipped from her shoulders and swept down her skin, falling with a sigh to the floor. His gaze followed, warm and fluid, evoking sensations to simmer inside her, to rise and shimmer across her skin.

She pulled the white satin ribbon from the base of her braid, shaking her head, letting her hair fall in thick waves over her shoulders, the heavy tresses tumbling past her waist. He had once asked if she ever let her hair fall free. This was her answer.

He opened his arms. "Come to me, Princess."

The name once spoken in anger, spoken now in desire, drew her to him. She felt a Princess, at last rescued from dark dungeon walls. As if in a dream, she floated into his arms, rising on her toes to receive his kiss.

His lips. How she had missed the taste, the feel, the joy of his lips. At the first touch of his tongue sliding along the seam of her lips, she opened to receive him. His arms tightened around her and she pressed against him, wanting his hard chest against her aching breasts, the thrust of his desire throbbing against her belly, needing to feel him deep inside her.

"Beautiful," he murmured against her lips, his fingers sliding through her long, soft hair.

Torrie sighed as he lifted her in his arms and carried her to the bed. This was enough for now. To have his arms around her, to feel his skin next to hers, to know soon she would feel his power deep inside her, that was enough for now. She wouldn't think of tomorrow. Not tonight.

Cool silk slid against her back as he lowered her to the bed. She watched as he stripped away his drawers, desire twisting low in her flesh as she absorbed the towering strength of unbridled masculinity. Anxious for the feel of his skin, she moved her legs against the white silk sheets, waiting, as he stood looking at her, scorching her skin with his heated gaze.

The bed dipped, and at last he was lying beside her. She rolled toward him, craving the touch of his skin against hers. He ran the tip of his finger from her collarbone down to her navel and back, sending sparks skittering along her nerves. "It won't hurt this time."

She brushed her hand down his chest, black fur teasing her palm. "It was worth the pain, last time." She paused at his waist, wanting to learn the feel of his hardened flesh. Yet, for all the distance she had traveled, there still remained a trace of uncertainty.

"Anything you want, Princess," he said, encouraging her to explore.

Her hand hovered at his waist.

Spence licked the tip of his finger and pressed it to the rosy tip of one pale breast. She cried out in a gasp of pleasure and pain, arching toward him. How could he manage such wonderful things with a single touch?

He slid his fingers across her skin, over her ribs. She stretched, feeling lithe and supple, sensual, like a cat in the rays of the sun.

"Heaven," he whispered, lowering his lips to taste one rosy bud of her breast. He pulled her breast into his mouth, making her moan, sucking, nibbling until she writhed against him.

Like warm summer rain, he flowed down her body, running his lips and tongue across her skin, dipping into the cup of her navel, nipping at the skin beneath, making her feel wonderful. Yet, at the first touch of his lips against the curls at the joining of her thighs, she stiffened. "You mustn't," she whispered, tugging at his shoulders, shocked he would even want to touch her *there.*

He looked up at her, his eyes dark burnished gold. "Let me taste you, Torrie. I want to taste all of you."

The gentle words entwined with husky passion grabbed at her vitals, making her tremble all over. "You do?"

"God, yes."

She felt his hands, firm and sure, slide upward over the curve of her hips, her resistance crumbling beneath his gentle touch. Femininity flowed warm and sweet between her thighs, weeping for him, pleading for surrender.

"Let me," he whispered, brushing his cheek across her damp curls.

Long-starved passion could no longer be denied. As though in a trance, she drew his dark head to her, opening to receive him, closing her eyes at the soft touch of his lips against her flesh.

Such pleasure! It was nearly unbearable in intensity. She arched her hips as his tongue delved and probed that part of her she couldn't even name, as he learned her better than she knew herself. He lifted her legs, draping them over his shoulders, pulling her closer.

Beneath his touch, soft folds of flesh opened, like a rosebud opening to the sun. She thrashed from side to side, stab after stab of pleasure knifing outward, upward, as he sucked and licked and drove her wild.

He lifted one hand, stroking her ribs, brushing her breasts, soothing and at the same time inflaming her senses. "Sweet, so sweet," he murmured against her flesh.

She heard the distant sound of sobs, and realized they were tumbling from her lips, one after another, as his mouth and fingers played against her. As he brought her to a final crisis, his name escaped her lips, her body erupting with pleasure, spasm upon spasm shaking her, heat pulsing, rising from deep inside, flooding every pore.

He covered her as the last seizure gripped her body and she reached for him, her hips lifting to receive him, her body aching to possess him once again. With one thrust, he joined their bodies, filling her with throbbing heat, jolting a cry of pure pleasure from her lips.

She moved against him, rising, falling, meeting him stroke for stroke, pleasure scintillating through her body. The muscles of his back danced beneath her hands, bunching, stretching, smooth and powerful. Nothing in her life had ever felt so right, so exquisite as feeling him move inside her. All of the waiting, the humiliation of betrayal, the long lonely years, were all worth this one moment in his arms.

"Let it come, Princess," he whispered, lowering his lips to hers.

Torrie had no choice, no will but to surrender to the power surging within her. She slanted her mouth across his, sucking at his lips, his tongue, aching with pleasure until she could contain it no longer. Sensation flashed through her body, pure and stark, a single streak of lightning illuminating a black velvet sky. Her body arched and convulsed, gripping him as he poured his essence deep inside her.

He clutched her to the heat of his body. She possessed him. Their hearts beat to the same dizzying rhythm, breaths mingling, skin searing skin, fusing two into one fluttering flame.

For an eternity they lay entwined, breathing as one, joined in a bond more intimate than any on earth. In time, he lifted and she looked up into his beautiful eyes, seeing a hint of wariness in their golden depths. She smiled and stroked his cheek, feeling the rasp of his beard beneath her palm, so foreign, so intensely masculine.

Not this time. She wasn't going to spoil it this time. Not when she knew they might have so little time together. She wanted each precious moment to be perfect. "How are your ribs?"

He covered her hand with his and moved to press his lips against her palm, his breath a hot stream against her wrist. "What ribs?"

Joy bubbled up inside her to tumble forth in bright sparkling notes. She watched as he pressed his lips to the tips of her fingers. "I think I'm going to enjoy living up to my side of this bargain," she said, smiling up at him.

Spence paused, his lips against her fingers, her words slamming into his belly with the force of a well-thrown fist. For a moment he had forgotten the real reason why she was in his bed. For a moment he had let himself believe she was in love with him. Her eyes were still a smoky blue from his lovemaking. But who did she see with those eyes?

He slipped from her body, breaking their union, the cool air chilling his moist skin. How easily he had fallen into the trap. How easily he had let himself believe in this farce of a marriage.

He fell back against the sheet and stared at the scrolls carved into the plaster over his head, fighting to corral his runaway emotions. His pride was hurting, but that wasn't all. No, he suspected what he was feeling went beyond wounded pride.

Torrie raised up on her elbow and looked at him. "Are you all right?"

Her breasts grazed his side, and he felt a knife rip into his loins. God, he wanted her again. He couldn't remember the last time he had wanted a woman with such a fierce passion. Perhaps because he never had.

And Torrie, what did she feel when they made love? Had she imagined it was Charles touching her, kissing her breasts, burying himself deep within her? His chest tightened, his heart squeezing painfully at those stark thoughts. Is this what love was all about? he wondered. A pain, a sharp killing pain that couldn't be healed?

"Spence, are you all right?"

Her hair spilled across his chest as she leaned over him, strands of silk brushing his skin. "I'm fine. Just a little sore."

She ran her fingers over his bruised ribs as though she wanted to heal them. "Is there anything I can get you?"

Heat flared in his loins. Did she have any idea what she was doing to him? Did she realize each gentle stroke of her fingers sent sparks sizzling across his skin, like fire sparking along a trail of gunpowder, growing ever closer to the powder keg?

Looking up into her beautiful face, he knew she hadn't a clue. She was as innocent as the day he had met her. He slipped his arm around her waist and pulled her down to his chest, needing to possess her. Her eyes grew wide as he pressed his hardened flesh into her belly.

"Are you sure you are up to this?" she asked, her voice soft and breathy.

"You should be able to feel that for yourself, Princess." He took her hips and lowered her until he felt the brush of damp curls, until he felt her moist softness against the tip of his turgid flesh.

"Do you want me, Torrie?" He moved his hips to help her decide, rubbing against the wet folds of her body, trying to pull together the shattered pieces of his pride.

A smile curved her lips as she answered with her body, sliding lower, guiding him with her hands. He groaned as she took him deep inside, wrapping around his body, her flesh hot and quivering and so incredibly tight.

She moved against him with a blazing sensuality he had never found before in a woman. He wanted to bury himself so deep inside her he could touch her soul, erase every thought of another man.

Hot velvet throbbed, surrounding him, drawing on his flesh, raising his blood to a fever pitch. He arched his hips, matching her rhythm, refusing to think about the day when she would turn him from her bed. For now she was his, and he intended to do everything in his power to keep her.

Chapter Twenty

Torrie stretched and reached for Spence, her hand sliding across his empty pillow. Clutching the sheet to her naked bosom, she sat up and glanced around the big room. Light crept into the room through the partially open blue velvet drapes, illuminating the rosewood clock on the mantel. It was barely past sunrise.

She sank back against the pillows, smiling. She wasn't dreaming. She was really in his bed, and what a bed it was. Wheat rose in intricate carvings along the four mahogany posts that staked the boundaries of one of the largest beds she had ever seen. It was long and wide, big enough to accommodate the length and breadth of Mr. Spencer Kincaid. And it seemed horribly empty without him.

His room. She had never been in a man's room before. Thin ribbons the color of cornflowers flowed down cream-colored silk from the ceiling to the mahogany wainscoting. The same shade of blue covered the sofa and wing chair near the white marble hearth. A low cabinet sat near the highboy on the wall between the closet and the bathroom, and Torrie wondered what it housed. Like the man, the room held a quiet elegance, a rich masculinity.

On the wall just across from the bed, a large painting of a slender woman standing on the brow of a hill, surrounded by wildflowers hung in a gilt-edged frame. Muted sunlight streamed across the impressionistic painting, making the flowers sparkle as if with dew. Torrie could almost feel the breeze that ruffled the young woman's unbound chestnut hair and lifted the hem of her gauzy white gown. She was looking out across a shimmering sea as though she were waiting for someone. A lover? And where was her own lover this morning? Torrie wondered.

A soft sound of lapping water drifted from the adjoining bath. Perhaps he wasn't far away, she thought, a curious thrill singing in her veins. Wrapping the sheet around her, she ran across the room and into his bathroom.

Spence was lying in a tub of steaming water, his arms draped along the edges, his head lolling against the rim. Sunlight poured in on him from the window above the white marble tub, baring every line and curve of his naked body.

For a moment, she stood in the doorway, admiring him, following the curve of his broad shoulders, his wet skin glistening in the sunlight. With each breath his wide chest rose, dark curls swaying in the water, making her palms itch to touch him.

"Good morning," he said, opening his eyes, smiling at her.

"That's a mighty big tub, Mr. Kincaid." She affected his drawl as she moved toward him. "I reckon they used tubs just like these in ancient Rome." She trailed her fingers in the warm water, moving along the tub, feasting on his long, muscular form.

"And what would they be doing with tubs like these?" he asked, innocence shining in his golden eyes.

She ran her fingers along his damp arm. She knew exactly what she wanted to do in this one. "Why, I wouldn't be surprised if they had orgies in them. I reckon you could put ten or twelve people in one of these."

He laughed and ran his finger up her arm, leaving a damp trail of gooseflesh. "In a bathtub? Sounds indecent."

She let the sheet slip, smiling as his gaze dipped to where the sheet bared the first swell of her breasts. "Oh, and here I thought it sounded intriguing." She let the sheet drop to the floor. "But if you think . . ." Her words dissolved in a shriek as he grabbed her arm and pulled her down on top of him, water cascading over the edges of the tub.

He wrapped his arms around her and held her against him, spreading kisses across her collarbone. "I think I might have unleashed a monster," he whispered, his lips brushing her skin.

"You have." She slipped her fingers into the damp waves at his nape and forced his head back so she could look into his beautiful eyes. A lifetime wasn't long enough to enjoy their beauty, and she would have far less. She slid her legs against his, dark curls rasping her smooth skin, making her shiver. "I can feel a monster waking against my thigh. Feels like a dragon. A fire-breathing dragon."

He laughed, the sound deep and husky in the quiet room. "Afraid, Princess?"

"Depends." She watched as he lifted a cake of soap from the gold holder on the wall. "Do you suppose there might be a knight around here? One with a mighty sword to save me?"

A devilish smile curved his lips as he rubbed the soap between his hands, bayberry filling the air. "Ah, Princess, this is a friendly dragon." He dropped the soap and reached for her.

Torrie sighed as he rubbed his soapy hands over her breasts, sliding the pliant tips between his fingers, sending sensation chasing sensation across her skin. He cupped the full white mounds and passed his thumbs back and forth over the frothy peaks, sparks shooting into the core of her body until she whimpered.

"Easy, Princess," he said, his voice a husky whisper as he slid his hands down her sides and gripped her hips.

Her eyes opened as he lifted her hips and started to turn her in the water. "What are you doing? I thought the dragon was ready."

"Oh, he's ready." As if to prove his point he moved his hips and let her feel the full extent of his arousal pressing against her inner thigh.

"Then what are you doing to me, my friendly dragon?"

Spence lifted her hair and dropped it over his shoulder. "I thought you wanted a bath, Princess," he said, his lips brushing her cheek. "Isn't that why you came in?"

"You know why I came in here." She leaned back against his chest as his hands slid over her breasts and slipped under the water. Her lips parted as she felt his hands roam over her belly, felt him pull her against the heat of his hardened flesh. "My word," she whispered, feeling the heated length of him nestled between the full swells of her buttock.

He rocked forward, sliding against the soft folds shielding her feminine secrets, finding the sensitive bud hidden beneath with his fingers. "You feel so damn good."

"So do you." She ran her hands along his hair-roughened thighs, drinking in the texture of his skin, the scrape of his hair, the heat of his body. He surrounded her with vibrant masculinity, impressing his hot muscled body against her back, her legs, around her waist, branding her as his.

His hands performed miracles as they roamed up and down her body, his fingers making feathery strokes, an artist completing his masterpiece. She laid her head back against his shoulder, her breath coming in thready gasps, desire licking at her senses, until she couldn't stand the emptiness another heartbeat. She needed to feel him inside her, she needed to possess his power and strength.

"Spence, please," she moaned, trying to capture him.

"Now, Princess?" he asked, smiling against her shoulder.

"Now, please." She tried to take him, crying out in frustration as her body refused to sheathe his huge sword.

"It's all right," he said, brushing his lips against her neck. He took her hips and lifted her, turning her until she faced him.

She felt the first touch of his hot flesh against her swollen need, and opened to receive him, a soft moan of welcome slipping from her lips as he became a part of her. No one ever told her it would be like this. No one told her it would get better and better, more exciting each time they came together. She craved him as one craved air to breathe, craved him as woman craves her mate.

Water lapped against her skin, flowing with the same rhythm of his hips, sliding like satin ribbons, splashing over the edge of the tub as they made love. His hands slid over her wet breasts, her back, her hips. He devoured her with his lips and tongue and teeth, making her feel delicious and restless and mindless with need. Her soft moans echoed off white marble walls as they moved together, sliding sinuously, seeking, finding the maddening friction, each drowning in the glory of the other.

Sunlight caressed her, warming her skin, as Spence stoked the fire in her blood. Tiny tremors rippled outward from the core of her body, growing in intensity, expanding until her body trembled with the force of an earthquake.

She threw her arms around his neck and buried her face against his wet shoulder, clutching him as her body surrendered to the irresistible power of pleasure. His deep moan joined her cry as he shuddered and held her close, surging inside her, his lips pressed against her neck.

Deep waves quieted to ripples, the ripples growing still around them. Ragged gasps calmed to deep, sated breaths as the now tepid water cooled the fire in their heated flesh.

Spence stroked her back beneath her hair and pressed his lips to her shoulder. The woman cradled to his loins had come a long way from the one who had bathed beneath her nightgown. Torrie was more than he had ever dreamed, sensual, wild with unbridled desire. He had awakened her passion. Could he touch her heart?

"I can't remember ever having a nicer bath," he said, before taking a nip at her shoulder. "I wonder if I could talk you into scrubbing my back."

She laughed, keeping her cheek against his shoulder. "Maybe."

Under the floating strands of her hair, he ran his hands up and down her back and over the curve of her rounded buttock. God, he wanted to absorb her into his skin, keep her all the days of his life. But could he? Dear God, could he?

Brass sang out against brass. Bright sunlight hit her face, prodding Torrie to open her eyes. She groaned and burrowed under her feather pillow.

"Oh no, you don't." Someone grabbed the pillow and tossed it to the side. "Wake up, it's nearly noon, and I'm nearly dead with curiosity."

Torrie blinked against the light and tried to focus on the face suspended above hers. "Pam, what are you doing here?"

Pam sank to the edge of the bed. "I should be angry with you, planning an elopement and not even telling me."

Torrie rubbed the sleep from her eyes and sat up, the sheet falling from her naked breasts. "Oh my!"

Pam laughed and tugged a lock of Torrie's unbound hair. "Oh my, indeed. The first time I awoke this way I was shocked. Now, I smile. No doubt you have a robe nearby." She got up and started searching the room.

"Where is Mr. Kincaid? Did you see him this morning?"

Pam lifted a white satin robe from the armchair near the windows. "No, I didn't. He was gone by the time I got here, but I have a feeling that note might let you know."

Torrie followed the direction of Pam's pointing finger to find a note resting on his pillow below a single blood-red rose. Each thorn had been carefully removed from the long slender stem, taming the rose as he had tamed her. A sweet, spicy scent filled her senses as she brushed the velvety petals across her cheek.

Pam stood by the windows, framed by blue velvet drapes, smiling at Torrie like a mother whose child has just learned to walk. "Mr. Kincaid has a pen-chant for red roses."

"So do I." Torrie unfolded the white paper and scanned the few lines, sighing when she realized she wouldn't see him until later that afternoon. "He's got a business meeting with my father this morning."

"If I had only come a few hours earlier, I might have caught him in bed." Pam shrugged and grinned at Torrie. "Maybe tomorrow."

"Pam!"

Pam tossed the robe at Torrie. "I'm teasing. Al-though . . ." She rolled her eyes. "Is he as beautiful beneath his clothes as I wager he is?"

Torrie slipped into her robe, smiling at the thought of Kincaid. His scent lingered on her skin, in her hair, evoking memories from the night before, from early this morning. "He's the most beautiful man I've ever met. And it has little to do with the way he looks."

"Thank goodness." Pam sagged against a mahogany post at the foot of the bed. "You are in love with him. I was afraid you might have married him only to satisfy your father's demands."

Torrie's spirits dropped. For a little while she had forgotten the bargain. For just a little while she had allowed herself to believe Spence wanted her. How convenient memory could be.

"Torrie, is something wrong?"

Torrie glanced away, afraid her friend would see the truth in her eyes. "No, everything is fine." She threw back the covers and got out of bed, her feet sinking into the thick blue and white wool carpet. She tied the belt of her robe as she walked to the windows.

"Since when do we lie to one another?" Pam asked, following her.

Torrie glanced through the lace curtains to the

courtyard below. Her gaze rested on a couple sitting on one of the stone benches nestled among the yew, her heart tugging at the sight. They sat talking, hands entwined, heads close together, each absorbed in the other. She felt a light touch on her shoulder and turned to find Pam by her side.

"Torrie, what is it?"

Sunlight filtering through the lace cast tangled patterns on Pam's face. For as long as she could remember, Pam had always been there, to share her dreams, her joys, and her sorrows. And right now, Torrie needed to share the turmoil in her heart. "You were right. I married Mr. Kincaid to avoid marrying Hayward."

Pam stepped back, pressing a hand to her neck. "Torrie, no."

Torrie nodded, and glanced out the window. "I used Mr. Kincaid's gratitude and his sense of honor to force him to marry me." She heard Pam gasp; she kept her gaze fixed on the couple below. "Oh, I was very clever. I even had Mr. Kincaid agree to give me a divorce after he gave me a baby."

"A divorce!"

Torrie turned and looked down at her friend's stricken face. "Pam, you won't desert me after I'm divorced, will you?"

"Of course not," Pam said, grabbing Torrie's hands. "But, Torrie, a divorce! Don't you think you might persuade him to stay married, to just live apart?"

Torrie felt tears singe her eyes. She shook her head, not trusting her voice, trying to fight the onslaught of emotions raging inside her.

Pam studied her a moment. "You are in love with him, aren't you?"

"In love with him?" Torrie slipped her hands from Pam's grasp. "I barely know him."

"How do you feel about him?"

"I'm not sure." Torrie stared down at her hands, at the plain gold band on her left hand. "When I first met him I thought he was arrogant, conceited, completely self-possessed. Yet I was attracted to him, in a way I've never been attracted to anyone. The man fills a room with his presence. He is so full of life."

Torrie hugged her arms to her waist. "For such a long time I thought I was in love with Charles, but it was different. I'm not sure I can explain the difference. But I wonder now if I ever really was in love with him."

"And Kincaid?"

"Kincaid." Torrie leaned her head back against the window casement, her gaze resting on the tumbled sheets of his big bed. "Sometimes I would like to strangle him. There are times when I don't recognize myself, when I shout at him like a shrew. He provokes me in ways I had never dreamed possible, challenges me and everything I have ever known. He grabs me and turns me upside down until I don't know what's right or what's wrong. He is . . . infuriating."

Torrie thought of last night, of this morning in his arms, of the things he made her feel. "And yet there is something about him." She took a deep steadying breath. "He can be infinitely gentle, and very, very kind. He cares about people. And when he touches me everything else fades into haze. It's as if we are the first man and woman on earth, the last, the only."

"It would seem you are in love with him."

Was she? Torrie released her breath on a long sigh. "It doesn't matter how I feel. We made a bargain. When it comes time I will give him a divorce without trying to hold him. It's only fair."

"But why be fair?"

Torrie's gaze snapped to Pam. "I do have some honor."

"Of course you do. I didn't mean to say you didn't." Pam plucked at the lace at her neck. "I just meant, make him fall in love with you."

Torrie laughed, but the sound was sad and brittle. "Just how do I do that?"

Pam smiled. "You could start by doing more of what you did last night."

Torrie felt her cheeks grow warm at the thought. "Making love to me is his way to escape the bargain."

"You're a beautiful woman, Torrie, and what's more you're smart. Use your charm. Make him crave the sight of you."

Torrie sank to the armchair by the window. "Sounds easy enough. Just make a man who could have any woman he wants fall in love with me." She stared down at her hands, twisting her wedding band around her finger. How could she ever hope to coax Spencer Kincaid into loving her?

Pam knelt beside her chair, crinkling her mint green walking dress. "Torrie, divorces are messy. It would be easier for him to stay married to you, especially if you have his child. He won't want to abandon his child."

Torrie shook her head. "I don't want him to stay just because of the child. He can have his freedom and see the child whenever he likes." Even though seeing him after their divorce would tear her into shreds.

Pam patted her friend's hand. "You love him very much."

She didn't want to love him, and yet . . . "It doesn't matter what I feel, what I want. What he wants is all that matters."

"Tell him; let him know how you feel."

Torrie tossed her hair over her shoulder. "I won't have his pity."

"Torrie, you need . . ."

"Tell me, would you have asked Ned to marry you if he hadn't asked you?"

Pam sat back on her heels. "No, of course not."

Torrie's chin rose. "And I do not intend to be the one who asks Mr. Kincaid to remain married to me. If he wants me, I'm sure he will do the asking." She would not stoop to begging. She would not be a clinging, needy woman.

"I understand." Pam smiled, trying very hard to look hopeful. "I'm sure by the time the baby arrives, he will be so in love with you, nothing could make him go through with a divorce."

Torrie drew her teeth across her lower lip. "I hope you're right. But I'm afraid Mr. Kincaid will only be too happy to hear the bargain has been satisfied."

"Torrie, I'm sure you'll have lots of time to convince him. It took us years to have Amy."

Torrie smiled at Pam's valiant attempt to ease her pain. "As I recall, you had Amy the year after you were married."

"I guess it only seemed like years," Pam said, smiling sheepishly. "But we haven't had any luck since then, and it's been five years. And, believe me, it isn't for lack of trying."

"That's true," Torrie said, allowing a seed of hope to take root. "It might take a year or two."

"Or three." Pam came to her feet and tried to shake the wrinkles from her gown. "I'm sure he'll . . ." She paused as a knock sounded on the door. "Do you suppose he's come back?"

"I doubt he would knock." But just in case, Torrie ran her hands through her thick waves.

Pam opened the door and Millie entered the room. "This message came for you, miss," the little maid said, handing Torrie a small white envelope.

After breaking the seal, Torrie withdrew a single sheet of paper. She read the few lines scrawled in black, then read them again.

"Torrie, you're as white as that paper," Pam said. "What is it? Has something happened?"

Torrie handed the note to Pam.

Pam's eyes grew wide as she read it. "What do you suppose he wants?"

"I don't know." Torrie came to her feet and tugged at her belt. "Millie, please lay out my blue suit, the one with the gray trim."

"Yes, miss."

Pam grabbed Torrie's arm as Millie left the room. "You're not going, are you?"

"Yes. I think I must."

"Torrie, he only wants to make trouble."

"You don't know that."

"I've heard rumors about him." Pam's fingers tightened on Torrie's arm. "He is gone every night, sometimes for days. And no one seems to know where he goes. Some say they have seen him on the coast, night after night."

Torrie shook her head. "Rumors are just that. I need to find out what he wants."

Pam stepped back and plucked at her lace jabot. "I'll go with you."

"I think it would be better if I met him alone." She forced a smile and tried to look confident. "Don't worry, I'll be careful."

Torrie got off the cable car and entered Golden Gate Park through the Haight Street entrance. The rumble of the city faded as the park wrapped cool, green arms around her.

"Get your balloons here," a short blond-haired man shouted.

"Three for five," chanted several men, each holding cones of sugared peanuts.

Torrie's stomach grumbled, reminding her that she had missed breakfast and lunch. She bought a cone and started munching the sweet nuts, the taste transporting her back seven years. No trip to the park had ever been called complete without a cone of sugared peanuts.

At the children's playground she paused, listening to the high-pitched laughter, her gaze resting on one dark-haired little boy as he rode the merry-go-round and waved to his mother and father. In another lifetime she had stood here with Charles and watched and talked about the children they would have. Torrie turned and walked deeper into the park, remembering days and evenings spent with him in this lush oasis, holding hands, whispering of the future, of dreams that never came true.

A bell jingled behind her, and she stepped aside as a couple riding a tandem bicycle passed her. She had always wanted to try riding one of those. Perhaps she could talk Spence into coming to the park next Sunday. She smiled, thinking how nice it was to have someone to plan things with, at least for a little while.

She paused at the summit of Strawberry Hill, wondering once more if she were making a mistake. It had been a long time since she had been to this part of the park—years, many wasted years. Inside her blue kid gloves her palms were damp, but she needed to see him again. She needed to be sure.

She passed the observatory and left the path, making her way across thick grass to a stone bench half hidden by trees. He was standing in front of the bench, by the rushing water, staring out across the waterfall. This had been their favorite spot in the park. Here you could see the waves break against the distant shore, or watch couples stroll sinuous paths through the park.

Charles turned as she drew near. "Torrie," he said, rushing toward her, reaching for her hand.

She stood for a moment with his hand wrapped around hers, staring up into his face, feeling the years slip away. As much as she had tried to avoid him, they had met at various social functions in the past seven years, passing civilities, sharing a wayward glance and nothing more.

He smiled, his lips curving in his dark beard. "You look wonderful, more beautiful than ever."

"Thank you, Charles." Torrie pried her hand from his grasp and stepped back. "You are looking well."

"I guess you won't want these," he said, pulling a cone of peanuts from his coat pocket.

Why did he have to buy those? Why did he have to make her remember? "I bought my own this time."

He nodded and jammed the peanuts back into his pocket. "I was afraid you wouldn't come."

"I'm curious." She turned away and glanced at the water, watching as it tumbled over the rocks and down the slope to the lake below. "What do we have to talk about after all this time?"

"I heard about your marriage."

"And you wanted to congratulate me?" she asked, her smile a little wider than it should be.

"I needed to see you." He ran his hand down his bearded cheek. "I know about Hayward. I know your father tried to make you marry him."

"Do you?" She moved around the edge of the bench and sat facing the water, her back to Charles. A cool breeze swept in from the bay, brushing her warm cheeks. "And who told you that?"

"Hayward was drunk one night at . . . well, at a place where I was. He started spouting off about how he was going to come into millions, about how old man Granger was begging him to take you off his hands."

Torrie set the peanuts on the bench beside her, wondering how many other people had heard about her disgrace. Just one more thing to amuse the people of this town at her expense.

Charles sat beside her. "I don't like the idea of you being forced into marriage with anyone. Even Kincaid."

She didn't want his pity. She wasn't sure she wanted anything from this man. "I stopped being a concern of yours a long time ago."

"Don't you know?" He turned, his dark gaze roaming over her face as though he were memorizing every line and curve. "I've never stopped loving you, Torrie."

How many times had she dreamed of this, dreamed of him taking her hand and asking for her forgiveness, dreamed of him telling her he would go to his grave still loving her? But now she wished he had never spoken those awful, frightening words. "Charles, you shouldn't say such things."

"Why? It's the truth." His shoulders rose and fell beneath his dark gray coat as he took a deep breath. "The only reason I married Annette was because of the child."

"You must have had some feelings for Annette, or Lisa wouldn't have been born."

Charles shook his head. "It happened only once, the night after the governor's ball."

Torrie remembered that night, remembered how angry Charles had been when she refused to allow him to make love to her.

"After I took you home I went back to the party, and Annette was there." He shrugged his broad shoulders and kept his gaze cast down at the rushing water, sunlight piercing the branches overhead to sparkle in the stream. "I didn't want to marry her. I swear I didn't want to leave you that way."

After all these years, to finally know the truth. It left a hollow feeling where there should have been more. "She must have loved you very much."

"She loved my father's money." He took her hand and pressed his lips to the back of her gloved fingers. "I tried to make it work, I did, but I couldn't stop thinking about you. Still, I knew my chance was over. Even if Annette had agreed to a divorce, you were too good, too fine to waste yourself on a divorced man."

Torrie looked away, the pain she saw in his eyes too much a reminder of her own pain; the pain she had lived with every day for seven long years.

"But when you didn't marry, year after year, I started to think you might still care for me."

She had cared. Or had she? His voice blended with the swish of the water as she listened. She felt detached, as though some other girl had once been in love with this man.

"Four years ago I asked Annette for a divorce, and I've been asking every year since then. Every year she's denied me, and every year I've grown more and more bitter. I started to hate her, hate you, hate all women. I got involved in things I never should have."

So, she hadn't been alone in her prison. Strange, there was no comfort in that knowledge.

He fell silent, staring into the water, holding her hand as though he were afraid she might run away. She studied him, this man she had once thought she was destined to marry, noting the deep lines running from the edges of his nose to disappear into his dark mustache, the lines fanning out from his brown eyes, the gray streaks in his dark brown hair. The years had not been kind to Charles.

"I come here sometimes, to think, to remember." He looked up, holding her in his dark gaze. "Do you ever come here, Torrie?"

"No. I spent most of my time trying to forget."

A smile curved his lips. "You still love me; I can see it in your eyes." He slipped his arms around her.

"I don't think so, Charles."

"Prove it."

She didn't hesitate as he pulled her closer, needing to know the truth as much as he. His beard scraped her chin as his lips slanted against hers. She gave the kiss her best, holding him close, parting her lips beneath his, but he couldn't summon a single shiver inside her. He lifted his head to look down into her eyes, and she smiled up at him, free at last of all the ghosts of her past.

"You never used to kiss like that." He sounded breathless, holding her closer.

His kiss was exactly as she remembered. She pulled away, pushing on his chest. He held her.

"You still love me, Torrie. We can be together. There's no danger now." He brushed his lips against her brow. "I wanted to come to you before, but I was afraid of what might happen should you find yourself with child."

For a moment she couldn't believe what he was suggesting. "I see," she said, her back growing stiff. "Pity you didn't put your plan forth earlier. I could have married some man and perhaps convinced him I should go with you on the honeymoon."

He tried to hold her, but she broke free. "Torrie, I didn't mean it the way it sounded."

She stood and straightened her jacket. "Oh, and just what is it you did mean?"

"I don't know what I mean." He looked at her, his

eyes filled with pain. "I've been half mad for seven years."

He had suffered. She could see that now. But it didn't change anything. "I'm sorry, Charles. Perhaps there was a reason for what happened seven years ago. Perhaps we were never meant to be married."

He grabbed her hand as she turned to leave. "Torrie, please. Say we can see each other."

"I'm sorry, Charles. I don't think it would be wise to meet again."

He opened his mouth to speak and she pressed her fingertips to his lips. "Let's part as friends."

He grabbed her hand and pressed his lips to her wrist. "One day, one day you'll see the truth. I'll make you see the truth. You still love me. You do! And we will be together. I know it."

Torrie swallowed hard, wishing there were something she could say to ease his pain. "I have to go." She tried to pull away, but he held her.

"See me again."

Torrie shook her head. "Good-bye, Charles." She turned and started walking back to the main path, feeling his gaze upon her.

Ben ducked back against a tall pine as Torrie passed, needles pricking his back. At first he had tried to convince himself this man she was meeting was only a friend, but that had not been a kiss between a man and a woman who were just old friends.

Was this the real reason Spence had asked him to follow his wife? Ben didn't like this, not anything about it. He watched her as she walked back to the main path, his jaw growing tight. How the hell did you tell your best friend his wife was seeing another man?

Chapter Twenty-one

Torrie was surprised to see Millie waiting for her in her bedroom when she returned to the hotel. The little maid rose from the sofa near the hearth, wringing her hands, looking as though the world was about to end. "What's wrong, Millie?"

"Mr. Kincaid is back, miss," Millie said, her voice trembling with apprehension. "And he asked about you. I didn't know what to say."

Torrie pulled off her gloves. "What did you say?"

"I told him you went for a walk in the park."

Torrie smiled, feeling a curious freedom. "And so I did," she said, unbuttoning her blue cutaway coat.

Millie nodded and glanced down to the floor. "Yes, miss."

Torrie draped her coat over the back of the chair near the vanity. "You needn't look so upset."

"No, miss," Millie said, keeping her gaze fixed on the carpet.

Torrie pulled the pin from her hat. "Everything is all right, Millie."

Millie lifted questioning blue eyes. "Is it, miss?"

"The ghost is finally buried." Torrie tossed her hat to Millie, who caught it and stared at her with wide eyes.

"Millie, please come and help me with this hair." She was going to need all the help she could get in this battle of hearts. Maybe Pam was right; maybe she could win Spencer Kincaid's love. She knew one thing for sure: She had to try.

Fifteen minutes later, Torrie left her room to find her husband. He was in his office, standing in front of the windows, one hand braced against the casement, the other on his hip. Green velvet framed him; the sun painted his image, shimmering around him, transforming his white shirt into shining armor—a portrait of a knight searching for something in the distance. What was his quest? she wondered.

She stood for a moment on the threshold, looking at him, making a memory for the future. At least memories were hers to keep. She recognized the moment he sensed her presence, his shoulders tensed with awareness, his fingers flexed on his hip.

"So you're back," he said, turning his head slightly, sunlight sliding across the curve of his cheek. "Come in, Torrie. Close the door behind you."

Something was wrong; the tone in his voice was cold, devoid of emotion, as if he were addressing a stranger. Her hand lingered on the handle after she closed the door. Without looking, she knew he had turned, knew he was staring at her. She could feel the burning of his gaze between her shoulder blades.

"You and I have some things to discuss."

There was emotion this time as he spoke, a chilling note of anger in his deep baritone. She turned to face him, searching his features, only confirming her frightening suspicions. He was staring at her, thick lashes lowered, narrowing eyes, the corners of his lips drawn down into a frown. "Is something wrong?"

"You bet there's something wrong," he said, moving toward her, stalking her like a mountain lion about to pounce.

Torrie pressed her hand to her heart, feeling each pump of her heart beneath the smooth white linen of her shirtwaist. "What?" she asked, taking a step back as he drew near, finding the door solid against her back.

Spence pressed his open palms against the door on either side of her head, leaning until his nose nearly touched hers. His breath fell against her lips, soft, warm, tinged with an elusive scent, a spice she wanted to draw into her lungs, an essence that started a tremor deep inside her. The man could make her tremble with need even when he was angry. *Why was he angry?* "Have I done something to displease you?"

He nodded. "There are still a few things you need to learn, Princess."

Tension balled her hands into fists at her sides. What had she done wrong? What did he find lacking? Had she been too bold this morning? Not bold enough? "Such as?" she asked, fighting to keep the tremor from her voice.

"Never neglect your husband." One corner of his lips lifted. With the tip of his finger he traced the curve of her jaw, drawing a warm line to her ear. "It's been six hours and forty-three minutes since I last kissed you, Princess. Too long for any man to go without nourishment."

Torrie felt the tension drain from her limbs, her muscles trembling in its wake. "I thought I had . . . you were teasing me."

"I really did upset you," he said, a frown chasing away his smile.

"It doesn't matter," she whispered, sagging back against the door.

"Yes, it does." Spence slipped both hands into the intricate coil of hair at the nape of her neck. "I'm sorry, Princess," he said, lowering his lips to the tip of her nose. "I didn't mean to upset you."

He wasn't angry with her. He wasn't going to tell her he found her clumsy, unattractive. That's all that mattered. Torrie closed her eyes as he kissed her cheeks, as he pulled pins from her hair, dropping them to the carpet, allowing her hair to tumble in one thick coil down her back.

"Just how am I going to make it up to you?" he asked, nuzzling the downy curve of her neck.

His husky voice sent shivers scampering down her neck and across her shoulder, raising gooseflesh. He brushed his hands over her shoulders, down her arms, grazing the sides of her breasts with his fingers, spreading heat across her skin.

"Spence," Ben said, knocking on the door.

Torrie bolted forward, ramming Spence with her shoulder. "Sorry," she said, stepping away from him, cringing as he rubbed his jaw.

"It's all right," Spence said, smiling at her. "No damage done."

"Spence," Ben said, opening the door. He frowned, looking from Torrie to Spence and back again. "I'll come back."

Ben's disapproval hit Torrie like a stone. The look in his cold blue eyes dredged up all the old rules by which she had lived all her life. A few more minutes in his arms and she would have been rolling around the floor with Spence. "No, that's all right," she said, sidling toward the door, hairpins crunching beneath her shoes.

Spence grabbed her hand. "Running away so soon?"

Her cheeks felt as though they were on fire. She smoothed her free hand through her hair, knowing she looked as shameful as she felt. "You have business and I just came in to tell you we've been invited to Pam's for dinner tonight. Would you like to go?"

"Anything you want, Princess." Spence lifted her hand and kissed her palm.

Shivers shimmered across her skin at his warm touch. Lord help her, but Spence was all she wanted. "They eat early because of Amy. We should leave by five."

He smiled, a smile she wished she could capture and press between the pages of a book, keep for all the days of her life. "I'll be ready."

She stood for just a moment, looking at him, allowing hope to form a tight bud in her heart. Maybe, just maybe he was beginning to care for her. It was a start. "Excuse me."

Ben stepped aside, bumping his shoulder against the doorpost in his haste to allow her clearance to pass. Spence watched her leave, his gaze traveling over her, a poor substitute for the things he wanted to be doing. The blood rushed in his veins. That woman had him as hard as a fence post. Again.

"Bad timing?"

"Maybe not." Spence grinned at his friend. "It would have been worse if you'd come along a few minutes later." A little later and he would have taken her right here, on the floor, in a chair, on the desk, he didn't give a damn where. He wanted her . . . day . . . night . . . in between . . .forever.

Ben nodded, deep lines digging into his brow. "I don't guess I've ever seen you like this about any woman before."

Spence turned away, hiding the evidence of Torrie's power over him, the evidence that nearly popped the buttons off his trousers. "I don't guess I've felt this way about a woman before," he said, stepping behind his desk.

"Yeah, well, she's a real pretty woman," Ben said, staring down at the tip of his boot. "Real pretty. The type of gal who can turn a man inside out."

The scent of roses clung to his cheek, to the sleeve of his shirt, teasing Spence, tugging at his groin. All she had to do was look at him and he was ready. God, he could be in for one hell of a fall. "What was it you wanted?" he asked, sinking to his chair, the leather sighing beneath his weight.

Ben turned, his gaze grazing Spence before skittering to the windows. "I was just wondering if you heard any news about Slattery."

Spence frowned as he studied his friend. "Is anything wrong?"

Ben shoved his hands into his back pockets and shrugged. "No, nothing's wrong. Did we put Slattery out of business last night?"

"We gave Slattery a black eye, but the casino is only a small part of his empire. Our people in Chicago think they may have a lead to the main clearing house for the girls. Once we break that, we break his back."

"Good." Ben stared down at his boot, frowning. "Well, I guess you'll be wanting a couple of men close by tonight."

Spence studied his friend a moment, wondering what was eating at him. "I think it would be a good idea."

"I'll tell Cal and Mac. You have a good time." Ben

turned and walked from the room, as though he didn't want to be around Spence another minute.

Spence clasped his hands and rested his chin on his knuckles. He wished he didn't have the uneasy feeling Ben's restlessness had something to do with Torrie. For a moment he thought about assigning someone else to the task of guarding his wife, then pushed it aside. *Jealousy.* It sure could grab hold of your imagination.

He glanced down at the stack of telegrams on his desk. Instead of the words formed in black against the yellow paper, all he saw was Torrie's smile, the curve of her cheek, her eyes darkened to a smoky blue. Releasing his breath through his teeth, he pushed away from the desk. Work could wait. He and his wife had some unfinished pleasure to attend to.

Torrie glanced across the dinner table, looking at her husband, pride swelling in her heart. Spence was charming, at ease with her friends, as though he had known them all his life.

Torrie couldn't count the number of nights she had sat at this table with Pam's family and wished she might look across at her husband, wished she might one day have a child like Amy. She hadn't realized how much alone she had felt until now, until she looked across at Spence Kincaid and knew he was hers. At least for a little while. She cherished this warm feeling of contentment, and knew these brief moments might need to last her the rest of her days.

Torrie smiled as Amy tugged on Spence's sleeve, demanding his attention as she told him about the toad she had seen in the garden this afternoon. The auburn-haired five-year-old had taken one look and fallen in love with Spence, but then, so had Torrie.

"Amy, stop bothering Mr. Kincaid," Ned said, failing to look severe as he scolded the little girl who was his image.

Spence smiled at his host. "A gentleman is never bothered by a pretty lady."

Amy lifted her big blue eyes to Spence, giving him her devotion. After dinner she took his hand and led him to a big wing-back chair in the parlor. "You ever seen a elephant, Uncle Spence?" she asked, crawling up on his lap, splashing pink linen and white lace across his black trousers, dragging a stereopticon with her.

"Once or twice," Spence said, slipping his arm around the child.

Torrie sat beside Pam on the sofa across from him and watched as Amy showed Spence one picture after the next, telling him a story attached to each. Once, Spence looked up and winked at Torrie, making her heart surge against her ribs.

"He is very good with children," Pam whispered.

"Yes, he is." Torrie prayed that one day she might be allowed to see him sitting each night with their child. Dreams could come true. Couldn't they?

Torrie barely felt the floor beneath her feet as they left the Morrisons' house. It was so nice to have someone by her side, someone to tease when she beat him at whist, someone to rest her head against as they drove home. Each sway of the carriage brushed Torrie's hip against his, a gentle reminder that the evening was far from over.

"When I was a little girl I used to imagine that house was Sleeping Beauty's castle," Torrie said, pointing to a four-story house across the street. The manse spread majestic gray arms in the moonlight, looking out at the unkempt lawn like a faded Renaissance palace. "I could imagine the princess, the king and queen, and all their subjects fast asleep behind those walls, waiting for the spell to be broken."

"It looks as though it's been empty for years," Spence said, glancing down at her.

"For nearly twenty years." She liked the way the moonlight stroked his skin, turning the smooth plains into white marble, like a sculpture. Only Spence was so much more than male beauty carved for the ages. "Mrs. Chamberlain left town and went to live with her daughter in New York City. Father said she refuses to sell the house because she hasn't met anyone she wants living there. It's a shame . . ." She paused, feeling Spence stiffen beside her.

Approaching them, on the opposite side of the street, a large black coach lumbered along the cobblestones, the driver cloaked in black, his tall hat pulled low over his eyes, hiding his features. Spence slipped his hand into his coat. Moonlight glittered on polished steel as he withdrew a pistol. She didn't like the way he shifted on the seat, shielding her body with his. She didn't like to think there might be a chance of anything happening to him.

Torrie held her breath, watching the coach approach, listening, waiting. The blackness of the coach was broken by a thin yellow slit at one of the windows. As the coach passed, the curtain snapped into place, veiling the occupant, but not before she caught a glimpse of his face and the patch he wore over one eye.

"You were saying?" Spence asked, slipping the pistol back into his holster.

Torrie had no idea what she had been saying. "Do

you think that was Slattery?"

Spence smiled. "Let's just say I've learned my lesson where coaches in the night are concerned."

Torrie jumped at a sudden noise. A deep rumbling sliced through the night air, a throaty, wheezing cry, like some great hulking beast. A light flickered in the intersection at the base of the hill, followed by a rattle against the cobblestones. The horses reared and strained in their harnesses, shying from the noisy monster, as an automobile crossed the intersection.

Spence held the team with a firm hand, calming them with a soft word, controlling their panic. More than one team had bolted at the sight of one of those smelly, noisy contraptions, Torrie thought, sinking back against the seat, pressing her hand to her pounding heart. Yet her fear had little to do with the threat of a runaway carriage.

"I've been thinking about buying one of those," Spence said. "In a few years you're going to see more of them than horses."

Torrie suspected Spence was deliberately trying to distract her from the threat they both knew Slattery held over their heads. "Do you really think so?" she asked, glancing over her shoulder, wondering if anyone was following them. She saw two men on horseback. Her husband's men. "They haven't nearly the charm and they couldn't possibly climb this hill."

"Not yet." Spence grinned at her. "But I think they will. I invested some money with a man in Michigan. I'm betting he makes them practical."

Torrie drew a shaky breath, trying to quiet her jangled nerves. "My guess, Mr. Kincaid, is that you have just thrown away your money."

Spence laughed. "Maybe. Maybe not. But what's

life without a little risk?"

A little risk took a lot of courage. She glanced down at her wedding band, the gold burning with silvery moonlight. What would he say if she asked to spend the night with him? she wondered.

Chapter Twenty-two

Spence glanced into his bedroom as he walked beside Torrie down the hall at Hampton House; the lamp on the wall by the bed was lit and the covers of the bed turned down, waiting for him. Torrie's room was next door. He wondered what she would say if he asked her to spend the evening with him. A wrong word, a wrong move might send him back to a prison of frustration. Yet he didn't want to spend another night without her in his arms.

He was about to put the question to her when she paused in the middle of the hall, staring down at the urn of flowers stitched into the carpet below her feet.

"I'm wondering...if you wouldn't mind, I might..." she said to the stitched yellow flowers. She drew a deep breath before she continued. "I thought I might stay with you tonight." She glanced up at him, smiling, a shy curving of her lips that held a wealth of promise.

He felt as though he could soar to the nearest star and pluck it out of the sky for her. "Well, I don't know. You like to hog the bed." He rubbed his chin as he smiled down at her. "You know, this morning I woke up and had about this much bed keeping me from falling flat on my behind," he said, pinching his fingers together.

"I'm sorry." She glanced down to the floor, biting her lower lip. "I'll just . . ."

He dropped his hands to her shoulders and held her when she tried to break free. "Princess, I wouldn't mind if you use that room of yours for a closet from now on. I like the feel of you all snuggled up against me."

"You do?" she asked, looking up at him.

"I do." Before she could say another word, he lifted her in his arms and turned to walk back to his room. Once inside, he closed the door with his foot and carried her to the bed, where he withdrew his arm from under her knees and allowed her to slip to the floor.

He pressed his lips to hers before her feet touched the floor, holding her against him, feeling her smile against his mouth. He smoothed his hand over the curve of her back, absorbing the texture of silk warmed by her skin, before opening the tiny silk-clad buttons running along her spine. She leaned against him, pressing her firm breasts against his chest, searing him with her heat.

He slipped the silk from her shoulders and moved back, allowing her gown to fall, burgundy silk billowing as it floated to the floor. One tug on the ribbon at the top of her petticoat sent it to the floor to join her gown.

"Take down your hair for me, Torrie," he said, moving away from her, wanting to paint her image across his memory. There might come a time when memories were all he would have.

The light on the wall behind her shimmered on her hair as she released the tresses to fall in thick waves to her hips, gathering the pins and combs in her hands. Her tightly cinched corset pushed her breasts upward, creamy flesh rising above the white lace edging her chemise. Dressed in her chaste white linen, she looked confident and so seductive he had trouble breathing.

She bent to set the combs and pins on the cabinet by the bed, then turned to face him, her lips curving into a lovely smile. The woman standing before him bore little resemblance to the frightened girl who had once clutched a black satin sheet to her neck. She was a woman fully awakened, and with her awakening had come one of his own; he was in love for the first time in his life.

He stepped back, watching her as he removed his clothes, slipping off his shoes, dropping his coat to a nearby chair, resting his revolver on the coat, then his shirt. She stared, following every movement, as he worked the buttons of his trousers. When he stripped them away, when he stood before her in nothing but his drawers, her gaze lowered to the part of him that couldn't hide his desire for her. He didn't want to hide from her.

"You owe me something, something I intend to collect tonight," he said, deliberately sounding severe.

"What?" Torrie knew she would gladly pay, whatever the price.

He turned and walked to the cabinet near the Chippendale highboy. Her gaze went with him, devouring his broad shoulders, the beautiful lines of his back, the taut curves of his behind. Muscles twisted beneath his golden skin as he lifted the cabinet lid and exposed a Graphophone. He adjusted the big brass horn, slipped a cylinder into place, and turned the crank. The strains of a Strauss waltz floated on the air as he moved toward her.

"You owe me a dance."

Torrie looked up at him, feeling awkward as he offered his hand. "I don't know how."

He grinned, and pulled her into his arms. "I can take care of that."

She smiled and snuggled against him. "Another lesson?"

"As I recall, you're a pretty good student."

She felt her cheeks grow warm. "As I recall, you are a pretty good instructor."

His grin grew wider. "Put your hand on my shoulder. And just follow me."

Anywhere, she thought.

He counted the rhythm and emphasized each step as he started to lead her across the floor. Torrie took two steps, the second landing on his toe. "I'm sorry," she whispered, flinching at the grimace of pain twisting his handsome features.

"I should have slipped off your shoes," he said, rubbing his toes.

She giggled and lifted one foot. "Please do."

He knelt and took her foot, resting it high against his thigh, near the tempting bulge veiled by white silk. She stared, her mouth going dry as he pulled he ribbon and slipped the shoe from her foot, his fingers brushing her skin through her cotton stocking. He dropped the shoe on the floor and slid her foot against his silk-clad thigh, higher and higher until he brushed her toes against his hardened flesh.

Torrie swallowed hard. "I think you might be teaching another lesson."

He smiled as he removed her other shoe. "And what's that?" he asked, sounding as innocent as a schoolboy.

"The pleasure of seduction, I think."

"That art comes to you naturally, I think."

She smiled, feeling playfully wicked, wiggling her toes against his flesh. "Do you?"

"Last night proves it." He laughed and came to his feet, pulling her back into his arms. "Let's try again."

She followed him, tentative at first, until her own natural grace took command. When he sensed she was ready, he increased their pace, sweeping her around the room, leading her in a series of dizzying dips and turns, her hair flowing, her laughter trailing behind them, joining the violins.

His movements were bold and sweeping, filled with the same powerful grace that seemed as much a part of him as his glittering golden eyes. His large hand held hers gently, long slender fingers wrapped warmly around hers. In his arms, she felt small and delicate, beautiful in a way she had never before felt.

With each swirling movement his scent teased her; spices, bayberry, and a hint of something else, something that made her blood race, her heart pound to a quicker beat. The way he looked at her made her a Princess in his arms, special, as though she were the only woman who could hold his attention, the only woman who mattered.

She leaned back in his arms, feasting on his face, loving every bold line and curve, her fingers curling against his bare shoulder. He held her closer, slowing their rhythm, until they were merely swaying to the music, his bare chest brushing her thinly clad breasts, his legs sliding against hers, silk against linen, man against woman, the friction igniting her need, like a flame to kindling.

This was the way it was meant to be. Today, she should have thanked Charles for leaving her at the altar. If he hadn't, she would never have known the truth, never have known the joy of being with the right man.

She leaned against him, wanting to get closer, needing to feel him inside her, soothing the throbbing ache deep in her flesh. Her lips parted as his mouth descended toward hers. At the first touch of his lips, she surged upward, wrapping her arms around his neck, opening her heart, offering him all the love she had stored away for too many years.

His hands moved between them, stripping away her corset cover, tugging on the laces of her corset, freeing her breasts. A growl issued from deep in his chest. He turned and fell back against the bed, taking her with him. Their laughter mingled as they rolled on the cool silk sheets, arms and legs entwining, pieces of clothing tearing, scattering, until they lay bare against each other.

Spence paid homage to every inch of her, running his lips and tongue up and down her curves, lingering on sensitive buds, exploring soft, moist folds, tasting her until she moaned and writhed beneath him.

"Your skin, Torrie," he whispered against her inner thigh. "I've never felt such skin."

"Never?" she asked, running her hands back and forth across his shoulders as he inched upward.

"Never." As if to prove his words, he lowered his lips to taste her right breast. "You're warm satin, and you taste good. God, you taste good."

Inspiration gripped her. If he could drive her wild with his lips and tongue, why couldn't she? Why couldn't she give him the same gift he had given her?

"And how do you taste?" she asked, pushing, rolling, until she was on top of him, her hair tumbling across his shoulders and arms. Love filled her, leaving no room for shame.

She sensed he held his breath, his eyes molten gold as he watched her. "You tell me."

She licked one dark male nipple. "Hmm, can't really tell." Her gaze never left his eyes as she drifted lower, flicking her tongue against his skin, nipping at his navel, mimicking what he had done to her. "You're smooth and rough, and just a little salty."

His hands clenched at his sides, grabbing hunks of sheet as she pressed her lips for the first time to his hardened flesh. "Smooth, very smooth," she whispered, her lips brushing the velvety tip of his arousal.

She watched his face as she explored him with her lips and tongue, amazed at the expression of mingled pain and pleasure on his handsome face. In a voice husky with passion, he told her how to please him, and she discovered her own pleasure heightened more than she imagined as she followed his guidance, as she added twists with her own instincts.

She heard him growl, felt his muscles stiffen beneath her and in the next instant she was flat on her back. "Did I do something wrong?" she asked, staring up into his face.

A muscle flashed in his cheek as he clenched his jaw. "Any more of that and you'll have me spilling myself all over you."

"Really?" she asked, amazed she could bring him to the same compelling precipice he always brought her.

"Really."

Hair-roughened thighs brushed smooth skin as he moved between her legs, joining their bodies with one graceful thrust of his slim hips. He took her with a savage hunger, jolting the breath from her lungs. Torrie wrapped her legs around his waist and rose to meet him, matching his hunger, the fierce fury of his passion. Soft growls escaped her lips as she thrust upward, meeting him stroke for stroke, primitive instincts seizing control.

He covered her mouth with his, drinking the pleasured sounds from her lips, plunging his tongue deep inside of her mouth, withdrawing, then plunging again, with the same maddening rhythm as his body moving inside her.

Pleasure rose from deep wells, building, swelling, like a spring in a summer storm, bubbling, swirling, racing toward the precipice. She gripped him, moving in a fury against him, feeling pleasure lift her toward the summit, needing to take him with her. He lunged, driving hard, pushing her over the edge, tumbling headlong with her, dissolving into light and heat and pure sensation. Soft, joyous sounds tumbled from pleasured throats and they clung, each to the other, finding their own piece of heaven.

In time, when her senses returned, Torrie moved her lips against his damp neck, tasting his skin, breathing in his scent. She opened her eyes, following the curve of a dark curl as it peeked out above his ear. She reached up to touch that curl, but before she could he stirred and rolled to his back, taking her with him, careful not to break their most intimate union.

"That was nice," she said, running her hand across the damp curls on his chest.

His laughter rumbled against her breasts before it filled the air. "You have a flair for understatement."

She folded her arms on his chest and rested her chin on the back of her hand, looking at him. He was smiling at her, looking contented, his golden eyes drowsy, like a mountain lion resting in the sunshine.

She ran her hand over his cheek, his skin smooth against her palm. Yet she could see the dark pin-points of his beard slumbering beneath the surface. In the morning his cheeks would be rough; they would rub against her skin in a delicious rasp of texture. She loved it all, smooth and bristly, each having its own special rewards.

She wished she had known him when he was a boy, wished she could have watched him grow into a man. Those years had been denied her. And the years to come—would they also be denied her? The thought threatened her lush feeling of contentment. She wouldn't think of that now. Not when she could look at him, not when she could touch him. "Tell me about you."

He sank his hand into her hair just below her left ear and threaded the silky strands through his fingers. "What do you want to know?"

"Everything there is to know."

He groaned. "Ask me questions. I'll answer."

Do you care for me? Will you want me after this bargain is satisfied? Could you ever love me? "How many brothers and sisters do you have?"

"Two brothers, Alex and Tyler, who are both older. And I have one sister, Amanda, who will be twenty-three this December."

"I'll bet she's pretty."

"Too pretty for her own good."

He began to massage her scalp just behind her ear, and she felt an urge to purr. "Why didn't you want to be a rancher?"

He was quiet, staring at the ceiling a long while before he spoke. "I wanted to build something of my own."

He ran his hand over her shoulder and down her back, spreading a delicious warmth where there had been a chill. She could feel him slipping away as he grew more relaxed, and her muscles tightened, trying to keep him as long as possible. She lifted her head to look down into his eyes when his breath escaped in a ragged sigh. "What's wrong?"

He swallowed hard. "Some women would kill to be able to do that."

She frowned. "I'm not sure I understand."

He pressed her cheek against his chest. "You grab me just as tightly as a hand clasping my flesh."

She smiled. "That's good?"

"That's very good."

So, maybe she wasn't just like every other woman who ever shared his bed. "What were you like as a boy?"

"What do you think I was like?"

Torrie stared at the curve of his shoulder, trying to imagine a time when his muscles had not been so well defined, a time when there hadn't been a luxurious pelt of hair on his chest. "I'll bet you were full of mischief, the type of boy who came home with snakes and put them in your brothers' beds."

Spence laughed. "Not me. I don't like snakes."

She raised herself to look down into his golden eyes. "You're not afraid of them, are you?"

Spence lifted one dark brow as he looked up into her eyes. "Let's just say, I'd prefer not to meet one face to face."

Torrie laughed. "I can't imagine you afraid of anything."

"Oh, there're one or two things," he said, his arms tightening around her.

She snuggled against his chest. "It occurs to me, I don't even know the names of your parents."

"Jason and Samantha."

"Do you look like your father?"

"My mother always told me I was my father's image."

"That explains it."

"Explains what?"

She tilted her head and smiled down at him. It explained why a queen would leave her throne, or a proper English lady would fall in love with a rowdy Texan, she thought. "Maybe someday I'll tell you."

"Being mysterious?" he asked, his fingers moving against her skin, tracing patterns just below her left ear, lulling her, making her eyelids droop.

"One must keep some secrets."

He laughed and kissed her brow. She was a mystery, but it was no mystery to him why he wanted to give her the world and more. He adored this woman. "I opened an account in your name today at First National."

Torrie lifted her head to meet his gaze. She looked tousled, beautiful. But there was a stiffness in her expression, a slight tensing of her muscles along the length of his body that made Spence suddenly wary.

"I appreciate what you did, but I have my own money."

Anger stirred inside him, and he fought to keep it under rein. "I doubt Quint is going to keep depositing money in an account for you now." He would be damned before he allowed his wife to live off another man's money.

"I don't need much. What I have in my account will be sufficient until . . ." She hesitated, staring at her hand, which had formed a fist on his chest, directly over his heart.

The unspoken words drove into his chest like a knife. "Until after the divorce," he said, finishing her thought.

322   **Debra Dier**

Torrie nodded, keeping her eyes averted from his, her gaze fixed on his chest.

Spence felt as though she had just pushed him from the edge of a cliff. He was plummeting with nothing to keep him from smashing against the sharp, ragged rocks below. The woman was willing to take his child, but not his money. Anger writhed inside him, frustration coiling around his heart. He shifted, sliding away from her.

"What's wrong? Think I'm trying to buy a woman again?" he asked, throwing his legs over the edge of the mattress.

Torrie drew the sheet up to her breasts. "No. It's just . . .well, I don't want you to feel obligated to give me money."

"I see." He stared at the fire burning behind the grate on the hearth, the logs nearly consumed, flames of red and gold licking over the charred remains. "It wasn't part of the bargain."

"No, it wasn't."

The bargain. It was still there, hanging like a veil between them. He could touch her, yet he couldn't. There was always that part of her hidden, kept safe from his touch, he thought, leaving the bed.

She was so beautiful, so damn alluring sitting there with the sheet pressed to her breasts, her hair tumbling over one pale shoulder, soft light glowing on the naked curve of her smooth back. The woman couldn't go a day without reminding him there was only one thing she wanted from him.

He had been fooling himself to think she cared. The truth was, she didn't give a damn about him. He was a substitute for her lost love, a means to an end. She was using him.

He could take her in his arms, this woman he had dreamed of all his life. He could bury himself inside her sweet, quivering flesh. Yet she was as far out of his reach as she had been that first day he had met her. He turned his back to her and snatched his trousers from the chair.

"What are you doing?"

"I need some air." He felt her gaze on him as he dressed, warm, compelling, a witch casting her spell. But he refused to look at her. Because if he looked at her, if he met those silvery eyes, he would be right back in that bed, playing the part of hired stud.

Not tonight.

He hurt too much tonight.

Chapter Twenty-three

Smoke filled the air, hanging in blue-gray clouds around the brass gaseliers in the Bella Union. In one corner a man sat at a piano, pounding the keys, trying valiantly to sing *Daisy Bell* above the low roar of voices and laughter. Spence stood at the bar, alone in the crowded room, his hand wrapped around a full glass of bourbon, staring into the amber liquid as though it held the secret of the ages.

Doubts about women had never plagued him in the past. Women had always been available, had always been willing, had always wanted him to stay. Torrie was different. One minute he could read her like an open book and the next she slammed the cover shut and became a mystery.

Was there nothing more between them than a bargain? Was this all a well-acted play, a role she had mastered? His instincts told him there was more.

There had to be more. Was it only his ego, his own need trying to convince him she felt something for him?

"You're Spencer Kincaid."

Spence glanced up, meeting the stare of the dark-haired stranger. His eyes were dark brown, red-rimmed, watery, as though the smoke bothered them, or he had been crying. The look in the stranger's eyes as they stared at him prickled the hairs at the back of Spence's neck; he saw nothing short of total loathing in this man's eyes. He was his enemy. Spence knew it without knowing the man's name.

Spence straightened away from the bar, surpassing the other man in height by less than three inches. "It would seem you have the advantage," he said, trying to place this angry stranger.

The man laughed, a bitter, mournful sound in the swirl of voices and music. "Torrie was going to marry me, you know that? She loved me from the time she was a little girl."

A pristine bolt of hatred ripped through Spence. "Charles Rutledge," he said, his hands clenching into fists at his sides.

Rutledge drained his glass of whiskey and slammed it on the bar. He dragged the back of his hand across his lips before he spoke. "Why are you here tonight? Why aren't you home with Torrie?"

"I think you'd better go home and sleep it off, Rutledge," Spence said, brushing past the other man, knowing if he stayed another second he would lose what little control he had over his emotions.

Rutledge grabbed his arm. "She still loves me. The only reason she married you was because of her father. Do you know that?"

Spence grabbed Rutledge's wrist. Slowly he pried the man's hand from his arm, squeezing so hard

Rutledge's bones dug into his palm. "You're drunk," he said, shoving the man against the bar as he started for the door.

"She still loves me, Kincaid. She told me so this afternoon."

Spence froze. *This afternoon?* She had gone to see this man today? Slowly, he turned to face Rutledge, anger sluicing through his veins. The men standing nearby scattered, sensing danger, clearing a wide space between the two men, spreading in an arc around them.

"You look surprised. Then I suppose she didn't tell you about our little rendezvous in the park," Rutledge said, smiling at Spence. "She kisses like a woman now."

Spectators gathered behind Spence. Through the roar of blood in his ears, he could hear them placing bets on the outcome of the coming confrontation.

"She's going to come to me, Kincaid. She loves me, not you. You see, now we won't have to worry about any accidents," Rutledge said. "You won't know which are yours and which are my bastards. I should thank Quint for . . ."

The force of the blow sent Rutledge reeling back across the bar. Spence grabbed his shirt and hauled him upright. Rutledge's head lolled, blood spurting from his nose onto Spence's shirt. Unconscious after one blow. The man wouldn't even give Spence the satisfaction of a decent fight.

With an oath, Spence tossed Rutledge to the floor, where he sagged against the brass foot rail at the base of the bar. The small crowd of spectators parted like the Red Sea before Moses as Spence stormed from the bar.

Outside, Spence paused on the sidewalk, pulling cool, damp air into his lungs. After making love with him this morning, Torrie had gone to Rutledge.

Spence didn't want to believe it. But he did. Oh God, he did. What the hell did she see in the man?

He sank his hands into his hair, raking the tousled waves back from his face, pulling until his scalp screamed. There was a queer twisting in his chest, foreign, painful, as though his heart had been ripped from it.

He was tired. Tired of being a fool for that beautiful silver-eyed temptress.

Sunlight streamed through the windows behind Spence, warming his back. Yet he felt cold inside. Dead. He turned his letter opener in his hand, staring down at the blade, frowning at his reflection in the gold. Just how big a fool had he been to believe he could win the lady's heart? He thought of the way she had responded to him the night before, the way she had touched him. And all the while she had imagined Rutledge holding her, Rutledge plunging deep inside her.

"What do you think?" Ben asked.

Spence had returned from the Bella Union early this morning, planning to tell the lady to get out of his bed. But she had already gone, leaving behind an intoxicating fragrance on his pillow.

"Spence? Are you with me?"

He glanced across his desk to where Ben sat. "I'm sorry. What did you say?"

Ben frowned. "You look as though you didn't get any sleep last night. I guess the honeymoon isn't over."

Spence met Ben's eyes. Ben glanced down at his hands, which were clasped into fists on his knees. He knew. Of course Ben knew. Ben had followed Torrie to the park yesterday. His best friend had seen his wife in another man's arms. That's what Ben had wanted to tell him the day before.

Spence pressed the tip of the letter opener to his palm. He never thought he'd be an object of pity, a man who . . .pain flared in his palm. He glanced down, staring at the small circle of blood forming around the golden tip of the letter opener. Out of control. Dangerous. He had to rein in his emotions. "I want to know what other houses Slattery supplies," he said, smoothing the tip of the letter opener between his fingers, wiping away his blood.

"I've got Frank working on it."

Spence tossed the letter opener to the top of his desk. "When Olivia is out of business . . ." He paused as someone knocked softly on the door. No doubt Torrie was finally up. He clenched his bloody hand, hiding the wound. "Come in."

Millie opened the door, pausing on the threshold, wringing her hands, her eyes wide and frightened. "Oh, sir."

Spence straightened in his chair, a swift blade of anxiety slicing into his ribs. "What is it, Millie?"

"Miss Torrie's gone."

The air froze in Spence's lungs. "What do you mean *gone*?"

"I thought she was in your room, sir. But she isn't. And her bed hasn't been slept in. She's nowhere to be found. It's not like her." Millie pressed her fingers to her lips. "I'm afraid—oh, sir, I'm afraid something's happened to her."

Spence came to his feet, his heart pounding at the base of his throat. "Get the men together. Check the mission, her father's house, the Morrisons. I want her found."

"Do you think Slattery somehow got to her?" Ben asked, following Spence from the office.

"I don't know," Spence whispered, a vice closing on his chest. He would kill the man with his bare hands if Slattery had touched her.

* * *

Torrie took a deep breath of the moist sea air, the breeze coaxing wisps of hair from her neat chignon to curl around her face. Dark, rugged rocks flowed from the cliff where she stood to the sand that lay two hundred feet below her. There, the ocean rushed to the shore, its deep booming voice lifting upward, mingling with the bellows of sea lions and the cries of gulls.

She had always loved this place, from the first time her father had brought her here when she was a little girl. There was something about the sea, something that could reach inside and calm a troubled spirit. But nothing could ease the ache inside her heart.

What had she done? What had she said to chase Spence away? Was it just too hard for him to pretend he cared for her? Was he tired of the game?

Clouds flirted with the sun, embracing the brilliant golden radiance, then flitting away, allowing shimmering rays to touch the ocean, setting it ablaze with gold and scarlet. In the distance, a three-masted schooner skimmed across the waves, white sails billowing in the wind, filling her with memories. She had been a fool to believe she could ever resist Spencer Kincaid. Had she been a fool to believe he could ever love her?

A rumble of hoofs against rocks brought her around in time to see Spence dismount from his black stallion, leaping from the saddle before the horse had halted. Standing beneath a silvery eucalyptus, her chestnut mare tossed her head and nickered softly upon seeing the stallion. The stallion whinnied sharply in response, tossing his head, his black mane lifting in the breeze.

Torrie pressed a hand to her neck as Spence

marched toward her, his breath coming in ragged gasps, his hands clenched into fists at his sides. He looked fierce enough to kill. Good lord, he was going to push her over the cliff! Get rid of her and end the bargain.

"Don't!" she screamed, throwing out her hands to ward off his attack.

He stopped a foot from her, his sides heaving as though he had been running a race. "What the bloody hell are you doing here?"

It took a moment for Torrie to find enough breath to form any words. "How did you find me?"

"Your father said you might have come here."

"You came looking for me," she whispered, absorbing the sudden pleasure that realization delivered.

"Dammit, Torrie! Haven't you a brain in that pretty head of yours?"

Her back went rigid. "How dare you talk to me in that manner."

"I'll talk to you in any manner I damn well please," he said, grabbing her arm.

"Let go of me!" she said, trying to break free as he dragged her toward the horses. His fingers tightened, sending sparks of pain shooting along her arm. "How dare . . ." Her foot turned on a rock. She lost her balance, plowing into his side.

Spence wrapped one arm around her waist and pulled her against the solid wall of his chest. She threw her head back, looking up at him. Sunlight peeked through the spindly branches of a cypress overhead to dapple him with light and shadow. His eyes flashed with the desire she had come to know, then darkened, anger filling the golden depths. Cursing, he pushed her away so quickly she nearly fell.

Where was the gentle man who had charmed her, beguiled her, taught her to believe in her dreams again? Who was this angry stranger who seemed to despise her? "What is wrong?" she asked, feeling lost at the sudden change in him.

Spence rested his clenched fist on the stallion's shoulder, the horse sidling, sensing his anger. "Did you ever think Slattery might have taken the opportunity to grab you?"

Hope soared within her. "Is that why you're so upset? Because you were worried Slattery had kidnapped me?"

He exhaled sharply. "He could use you for leverage."

Her hopes plummeted as quickly as they had risen. For a moment she had thought he cared.

"From now on, you don't go anywhere without Ben," he said, without glancing at her.

She knew this time he wasn't teasing. He couldn't stand the sight of her. "What's wrong with you this morning? Why are you so angry with me?"

His hand relaxed, then clenched into a fist once more on the stallion's shoulder.

"It's more than Slattery. Isn't it?"

For a moment she thought he wouldn't answer. When he turned to face her she was shocked at the rage etched into his handsome face.

"I met an old friend of yours last night. Charles Rutledge told me about your meeting in the park."

Torrie frowned, her mind snatching for some reason for this horrible anger. "And you're angry because I didn't tell you I saw him?"

I'm angry because you left my bed to go to him. I'm angry because . . . you still love him.

A cool breeze stirred his dark waves. His lips pulled into a taut line; his eyes snapped golden fire.

Torrie stared at him a moment, trying to solve the mystery of this man. Suddenly, an idea occurred to her, a silly, foolish, wonderful idea. "Are you jealous of Charles?" she asked, her voice barely rising above the distant roar of the sea.

He made a sound in his throat, somewhere between a strangled laugh and a growl. "Lady, I won't be made a fool by you or any woman. As you are so fond of reminding me, this isn't a real marriage." He moved toward her, clenching his hands into fists at his sides.

The raw fury in his eyes, the rage emanating from his big body, spurred her sense of survival. She fought the urge to run, choosing instead to face him with a defiant tilt of her chin, hoping he wouldn't see her fear. He stopped less than a foot away from her, bending until the tip of his nose nearly touched hers, his breath coming hot and fast against her lips.

"As long as you bear my name, as long as we are trapped in this tender union, you will behave like a respectable wife. I will not have my wife tumbled by some other man."

Torrie gasped. After what they had shared, after she had bared her heart to this man, shared her soul, he could stand there and accuse her of . . . of . . . "How dare you believe I would consort with another man!" She slammed her fist into his shoulder. "How dare you!"

He grabbed her wrist when she tried to strike him once more. "Love can play tricks with a person, Torrie. It can turn you into someone you don't recognize in the mirror."

Sunshine and shadow played across his face; his eyes glittered, stared into hers, probing, searching for what seemed an eternity. Below, waves crashed against the shore, the steady rumble lifting on the salt-tinged air.

"And we both know how you feel about Rutledge," he said, his voice strained as he forced every word past his tight throat. "Right?" *Tell me I'm wrong, Torrie. Tell me the man lives only in your past. Tell me I'm your future.*

Torrie stood captive in his gaze, confused, lost in the swirling sea of emotions she saw in his golden eyes, her own emotions crowding her chest. He had believed she would let another man touch her. How could he believe she would do such a dishonorable thing? She wanted to weep, to scream, to punch him, to hold him to her breast. Did he really think so little of her? "I would never do something so foul. No matter what my feelings."

No matter what my feelings. His hand tightened on her wrist a moment before releasing her. He took a step back, staring toward the sprawling emptiness of the sky behind her, feeling his life drain into the void.

After a moment his deep voice joined the steady roar of the sea. "I just want us both to keep things in proper perspective," he said, echoing her words from a lifetime ago, his voice flat, emotionless. *I should have listened, Torrie. I should have kept the bargain in mind. Falling in love has never been part of the deal.*

Torrie stared at the dark hair curling over his white collar, remembering the feel of those waves brushing her skin as he kissed her in places no lady would allow any man to ever kiss her. Too late. It was far too late to keep things in proper perspective.

Her wrist throbbed with heat, the brand of his touch, a brand that refused to cool in the chill of the breeze. She had trusted. Again. She had given away her heart. Again. She was a fool. Again!

When he glanced at her she forced her back to straighten, her chin to lift. She would not show her pain, she would not parade her emotion. "I have every intention of living up to my part of this bargain, Mr. Kincaid." And every intention of shielding what was left of her shattered pride.

Chapter Twenty-four

Morning light, filtered by fog, drifted through the windows of the attic dormitory in the mission. Torrie glanced around at the children sitting cross-legged on the braided rug, seven innocent faces beaming up at her to brighten the gloom of her morning.

Before her marriage she had spent every Tuesday and Thursday morning entertaining the children while their mothers worked. In the past two weeks she had visited the children almost every day. There was little else she could do with Mr. Ben Campbell following so closely she thought he might trip over her skirts, and Mr. Spencer Kincaid nothing more than a shadow.

Was there anything more honest than a child's face? Torrie wondered as she read to them the story of Alice and her trip through the looking glass. She loved to tell them stories, assuming the role of each character as she read their parts. With a sense of wonder, she realized one day she would be telling stories to her own child. With the thought came the pain of knowing Spence would not be by her side.

Spence hadn't touched her in two weeks, ever since the night he had taught her to dance the waltz. She missed him, and not just his lovemaking. He had withdrawn completely. Most of the time he was gone, and when she did see him he looked straight through her as though she didn't exist.

Each day she tried to be indifferent. Each day she failed. She felt shaken, abandoned, lost. She would survive. Yet there were days when she wasn't sure she wanted to survive without Spencer Kincaid. He had taught her to live, not merely survive. And now . . .

A movement in the doorway caught Torrie's attention. She paused, looking past the children to the tall, dark, shadowy form standing on the threshold of the room. Her heart picked up speed, pounding against her ribs, fear sliding down her spine. "Who is it?" she asked, coming to her feet.

The man stepped into the room, light spilling through the windows behind Torrie illuminating the features of Inspector John Samuels. Torrie pressed her hand to the base of her throat, relieved to know the intruder, and at the same time unnerved by the way his gaze roamed down the length of her green linen gown.

"Good morning, Mrs. Kincaid," Samuels said, his dark gaze lifting from her bodice to her eyes. "I apologize for the intrusion."

"Inspector," Torrie said, her back growing stiff. She glanced down as a dark-haired girl tugged on her hand.

"Who is that man?" Janey asked, staring up at Torrie.

"He is a police officer," Torrie said, smiling down at the girl.

"Are you in trouble, Torrie?" Janey asked, her blue eyes growing wide with concern.

"No," Torrie said, giving the girl's little hand a comforting squeeze.

Torrie looked across the room to where Claire sat staring at the tall dark-haired man, a curious expression in her brown eyes. "Claire, will you please take care of the children for a few minutes? I believe Inspector Samuels would like to talk to me." Torrie turned and looked up at the police officer. "Is that right, Inspector?"

Samuels smiled and nodded his head. "If you don't mind."

Torrie did mind. There was something about Inspector Samuels that made the hair tingle at the nape of her neck, but she wasn't going to let him know that. She led him to the opposite end of the attic.

The roof was slanted and the only place the inspector could walk erect was in the center of the room. She felt him walking close behind her, closer than propriety allowed. But, Torrie had the feeling the inspector wasn't one who followed the dictates of propriety.

"I was enjoying your reading. You have a lovely voice."

"Thank you," Torrie said, sitting on the window seat built into the dormer window at the front of the house. "Please be seated."

Samuels looked around, but the only chairs he saw were those built for a child. "I think I'll stand."

Torrie smiled, imagining the inspector's tall frame folded into one of those little chairs. "What is it, Inspector?"

He studied her a moment before he spoke. "Mrs.

Kincaid, I'm afraid it's about your husband."

Torrie's heart froze. "Has something happened to him?"

Samuels shook his head. "Not yet. But I'm afraid something will if he doesn't stop his war against Jack Slattery."

She released the breath that had turned to frost in her lungs. "Inspector, my husband knows what he is doing," she said, managing to sound calm when her emotions were churning into a tidal wave inside her. Slattery was a killer. He could kill Spence. She lived with that fear every day. "Jack Slattery should have been put out of business a long time ago."

Samuels frowned as he stared down at her. "Jack Slattery just might put your husband out of business, permanently. Have you thought of that?"

She only wished she could stop thinking of that. "And just what do you think I can do about the situation?"

"I think you can convince your husband to stop what he has started."

Torrie shook her head. She had no influence over her husband. "Even if I wanted to, I doubt I could convince Mr. Kincaid to give up this fight."

His eyes narrowed, the light from the window catching the dark pools, turning them to slits of polished ebony as he stared down at her. "I suggest you try, Mrs. Kincaid."

There was a whisper of a threat behind his words, and her back stiffened. "I suggest you do your job, Inspector, and help put Slattery behind bars."

He smiled, his gaze dipping to her bodice, lingering a moment before raising to her eyes. "Think of what I've said, Mrs. Kincaid. Although I'm sure you would look quite beautiful, I wouldn't like to see you dressed in black."

Torrie stared after him as he left the room, his

words spinning around in her brain. She hugged her arms to her waist and closed her eyes, trying to chase away her fear. Spence would be all right. He had to be. She opened her eyes as she heard someone approach.

"There's something very familiar about that man," Claire said, wringing her hands in front of her waist. "I think I've seen him at Olivia's."

Torrie frowned and glanced out the window behind her. Below, in a shallow, swirling sea of fog, Inspector Samuels climbed into a black carriage. "I suppose it's possible the inspector was there on police business," she said, watching as the team of bays pulled the carriage down the street, until it disappeared behind a wispy veil of gray.

"I suppose it is," Claire said, looking over Torrie's shoulder. "He's attractive in a dark, forbidding way."

Torrie nodded, but her thoughts were on another dark- haired man.

Torrie hesitated a moment in front of the door to Spence's office. She had changed for dinner, choosing a gown of striped geranium red silk. A thin band of black lace trimmed the neckline, which plunged in a shallow vee several inches below the hollow of her neck. The puffed sleeves were gathered just above her elbows where red silk joined wide bands of black lace. It was new, more daring than anything she owned, something she thought Spence might like. Nervously she smoothed the black moire bow at her tightly cinched waist before knocking on his door.

"Come in."

She took a deep breath and opened the door. He glanced up from the telegram he held, frowning when he saw her.

"What do you want?" he asked, returning his attention to the telegram.

Anger mingled with pain in her heart. She closed the door behind her and moved to his desk. She was tired of being treated like a servant. Worse than a servant: he at least spoke to them.

She waited, daring him to acknowledge her again, tracing the full curve of his lips with her eyes, remembering the feel of those firm lips against hers. It had been so long, so very long since he had kissed her, since he had touched her. He had opened a world of sensation to her, a world she longed to enter once more. At night she dreamed of him, of his lips, his arms, his body. If only he would take her in his arms. If only . . .

"Did you want something?" he asked, glancing up at her. "Or did you just come here to watch me work?"

She felt like punching him. "Inspector Samuels came to see me this morning."

Spence leaned back in his chair. "And?"

"And he wants you to stop this war against Slattery."

Spence tilted his head and began to rub the back of his neck. "Sometimes I think the good police inspector is on Slattery's payroll."

Torrie watched the play of muscles against the white linen of his shirt. His sleeves were rolled to his elbows, exposing tanned skin and dark curls. The first few buttons of his shirt were open; looking at that dark triangle of warm skin and dark curls started a flutter low in her belly. She wanted to touch him. She wanted to . . .

"Is that all?"

He was dismissing her. Just like that. Just as he had dismissed her for days. But she couldn't go. Not yet. "Are you coming in to dinner?"

"I've already eaten."

Finality; she heard it in his voice, a sharp knife piercing her dreams, shattering her hope. He was tired of her, tired of the game. "I see." She turned to leave, fighting the tears rising in her throat. She wouldn't cry. She wouldn't make a complete fool of herself in front of this man.

Spence watched her walk toward the door, resisting the urge to take her into his arms. More than once he had gone to her room, only to stop before opening her door. He couldn't do it any longer. He couldn't make love to her knowing he was a substitute for another man, knowing his seed was the only thing she wanted from him. His love for her wouldn't let him. It was his fate to love a woman who had given her heart to another man long ago.

Every day it was harder to keep his distance. Each night sleeping in the bed he had once shared with her, knowing she lay in the next room, knowing she would spread those lovely thighs for him, was turning him into a monster. He was curt with everyone. He needed time away from her. He needed to think. When he was around Torrie, all he could do was feel. "Torrie."

She paused with her hand on the door handle. "What?" she asked, keeping her back to him.

"I'm going out of town. I have a train waiting. I'm leaving tonight."

She turned. "Where are you going?"

"Chicago. New York after that."

Her eyes grew wide, like a frightened child. "Why are you going?"

"Business." He glanced down at his desk, unable to look at her. He would not go to her. He would not take her into his arms. He would not play the fool for this woman. He couldn't.

"How long will you be gone?"

Her soft voice curled around him, coaxing him, tempting him to go to her. He clenched his hands into fists on the desk, looking up at her. "I'm not sure." Long enough to figure out what he was going to do with his beguiling bride, with his life.

She glanced down at her hands, lacing her fingers, her shoulders slumping ever so slightly. For a long moment she didn't speak, and when she did her words were soft, barely rising above the clatter of the rain pounding against the windows behind him. "If you want a divorce now, I won't try to stop you."

His stomach cinched at her words. "What, and leave before the job is finished?"

"The job." She stared at him, her lips parted, color rising to stain her cheeks. "The job!" Her voice shook, her anger rising as she marched toward him.

She rested her hands on his desk, staring at him, dismembering him with her eyes, her nostrils flaring with each ragged breath. "Well, it seems to me you haven't been living up to your side of this bargain, Mr. Kincaid. How are we ever going to make a baby if you won't touch me?"

"Got some complaints about the service?" His emotions snapped their shackles. He stood, his chair rolling back from the desk, hitting the window casement with a crash. "Your stud not performing to your liking?"

"That's right. I guess I'm not very good at choosing good breeding stock."

She turned and marched toward the door. By the time she reached it, Spence was right behind her. As she pulled open the door, he hit it with his open palm, slamming the door shut.

She whirled on him, slamming her fist into his shoulder. "Damn you!"

Spence sank one hand into the coil of hair at her nape, cupping her skull, jerking her head back. At the same time he wrapped his other arm around her waist, locking her against his chest. "You want a stud, you've got one."

He slammed his mouth against hers with a brutal passion, grinding across her soft lips with all the pain and frustration that had been building in him over the past few weeks. With his mouth still locked to hers, he slipped his arm behind her knees and lifted her. She struggled against him, pounding his back with her small fists as he lowered her to the thick carpet.

He covered her body with his, pressing her into the emerald and gold wool, grinding his hips against her as he raped her mouth, taking what she had once given with sweet abandon. She pressed her palms against his shoulders, trying to push him away, her rejection throwing oil on the towering flames of hate and love and need raging inside him.

She was heaven, hell, his salvation, his ruin. He pushed her skirt and petticoats above her waist, intricate feminine barriers no match for his ravaged male pride. She wiggled beneath him, trying to escape him. With his knee he forced her legs apart and settled between her thighs.

"Is this what you want, Torrie?" he asked, cupping her face in his hands, feeling her hands clench into fists on his arms. He thrust forward with his hips, pressing the forged length of his sword against the warm linen shielding her sheath. "Just a few quick thrusts. Deposit my seed and go about my business."

She fell still beneath him, looking up at him as though he had slapped her, tears glittering in her silvery eyes. The rain marked the seconds that drew into an eternity as she stared into his eyes. Trapped in the silver prison of her gaze, he felt his anger fade.

Her hands opened on his arms before they fell away from him. "I'm sorry," she whispered, turning her head, as though she wanted to hide the tears trembling on her lashes.

Spence felt her soft words pierce his heart.

"I never meant this to happen." She hesitated a moment, drawing a deep, shuddering breath before she continued. "I never . . . I should never have asked you to marry me."

He lifted himself away from her, sitting back on his heels. She looked for all the world a defiled angel, laying against swirls of gold and emerald, her hands palm up on the carpet, her pretty red dress twisted around her waist, revealing outrageously innocent white linen drawers. Her lips were red and swollen from his brutal kiss. And she was crying, her breath escaping in uneven gasps, tears spilling across her pale cheeks as her body shook in silent sobs.

As he stared, she bit her lower lip, as though she were trying to stop the sobs. But her pain went too deep. And he was the cause. Pain and longing flooded his chest until he could scarcely breathe.

"Torrie," he whispered, brushing his fingers across her cheek, her tears searing his flesh. He had to do something. But what?

He smoothed her dress down over her legs and lifted her in his arms. Except for the trembling deep within her, she didn't move, neither accepting nor rejecting his embrace. He would have preferred her to shout at him, to fight him, anything but this quiet defeat. He had stripped his wild rose of her thorns, melted his Ice Princess, stolen her regal control. And he would do anything to give them back to her.

He carried her to her room and laid her on the

crisp white linen sheets. Words eluded him. He wanted to apologize, but words weren't enough to ease the pain he saw in her eyes.

Light glowed behind crystal on the wall beside her bed, casting golden light across her face, glistening on her tear-streaked cheeks. She looked shattered, like a porcelain doll thrown by a careless hand. His hand.

There was a train waiting for him. Business. Escape. Yet he couldn't escape her. No matter how far he traveled, she would be there, living in his heart. And he couldn't leave her this way, not with the memory of his rage, not with her tears falling like acid upon his heart.

He sat beside her on the bed and lifted her in his arms. She didn't resist him. For long minutes he held her cradled on his lap, rocking her, absorbing her tears, feeling her body shake with the pain he had brought her, the rain beating against the window-panes echoing the pain throbbing in his heart.

He wanted to pull together all the pieces. He wanted to heal her, heal his own heart. He wanted . . . God help him, he wanted more than she could give him. He wanted her love. Yet love was in the giving, wasn't it? And there was something he could give her.

"I'm sorry," he whispered against her temple. "I'm not sure how that happened."

"I understand." She had trapped him, coerced him into marriage with a woman he didn't love. What could she expect of this man?

He brushed his lips against her cheek while he drew the palm of his hand down her back. "Let me make love to you."

The tenderness in his voice, his soft touch, drew some of the venom from her wounds. It had been so long since she had felt the warm caress of his hands,

the sweetness of his lips. She wanted to hold him.
She wanted to kiss him. She wanted to pretend . . .
if just once more.

"Will you let me?" he whispered against her temple. "I promise, I won't hurt you. Dear God, I never
wanted to hurt you." He released a long sigh against
her skin. "Let me show you how I feel."

He was a gentle man by nature; an honorable man
trapped into a dishonorable bargain. She knew he
was only trying to ease her pain. But she didn't
care. Pride turned to dust in his arms. "Yes," she
whispered.

"Torrie," he whispered, pulling away from her.

She watched as he discarded his clothes, slipping
off his shoes, slowly shedding his shirt. The light
played across his golden skin, thick muscles twisting
beneath, tormenting her with the need to touch him.
When he was bare, he came to her, lying beside her,
taking her in his arms and holding her as though
he intended to etch his mark on her forever. He
already had.

Torrie nestled in his arms, her cheek against his
smooth shoulder, breathing in his spicy scent. She
slipped her thigh between his, the silk of her dress
sliding against his skin.

"You're more beautiful than my dreams," he whispered, brushing his lips against her neck. "Warmer
than summer, more precious than any jewel."

She felt beautiful, cherished, loved. It didn't matter that it was only an illusion. She wouldn't think of
it tonight. She wouldn't think about the train waiting for him at the station, the train that would carry
him away from her. Not while she could hold him.

Torrie felt his hands roam up and down her back,
his warm palms sliding across her shoulders, as he
undressed her with exquisite tenderness. Soon silk
and linen were replaced by the warm velvet of his

lips, the smooth satin of his skin.

She ran her hands up and down his back as he spread warm kisses across her shoulder and neck, welcoming the hot brand of his skin against her flesh. She knew this might be the last time she would ever hold him, the last time she would ever feel the exquisite beauty of having him move inside her. Tears gathered in her throat and she fought to banish them. Nothing must spoil this moment.

"You are the sun, my light, my warmth. Without you I'm lost in darkness, cold and empty," he whispered, before he lowered his lips to hers.

Lovely words, she thought, absorbing each into her heart. If only they were true.

He covered her with his body. He wanted to erase the image of violence he had etched on her soul. He wanted to give her so much pleasure she would never turn him from her side, so much love she would forget the bargain hanging over his head like a blade.

With his mouth and hands he adored her, her soft cries of pleasure sending stabs of longing shooting through his loins. When she tried to pleasure him, he stopped her, knowing he was on the brink, wanting to prolong her pleasure for as long as he could fight his own maddening need.

She opened to him as he lowered himself between her thighs, her skin gliding against his like warm silk. He sighed, his breath mingling with hers as he sank into her honeyed softness, filling her with the throbbing heat of his love.

They moved together, pouring out the love in their hearts, in their souls, each so absorbed in the giving neither saw what was theirs for the taking.

He brought her to climax time after time, punishing his own body to bring her pleasure, until he thought he would die from the pressure building inside him. His name escaped her lips on long shuddering sighs, over and over and over again, her body shimmering around him, tugging on him, tempting him to follow her higher. Yet he held back.

"Now you," she whispered, stroking his hip with her open palm.

Spence tossed back his head, fighting the pain in his groin. "Not yet."

"Please," she said, her lips brushing his shoulder. "Let me give something back to you."

She moved beneath him and he felt his restraint dissolving into her heat. And then it was shaking him, a force she directed deep inside him, spiraling outward, upward, until she controlled his will. Feeling her pulse around him, he erupted, clutching her to his body, pouring his essence inside her, surrendering his soul to this woman.

When their breathing grew quiet he shifted to his side, holding her in his arms, still locked inside the warm haven of her body. He slipped his hand into her hair and stroked the back of her neck, tracing serpentine patterns against her skin. She lay warm and drowsy against him, pliant, as if she were content to be with him. He heard her breathing ease to a low, steady rhythm, each soft exhalation warming his neck as she fell asleep in his arms.

He felt the press of time against his heart as he held her, knowing these few minutes with her were as fleeting as mist on a warm summer day. She didn't belong to him. Yet he would belong to her for the rest of his life.

Chapter Twenty-five

The big bay window on the first floor of the rescue mission glowed like a lantern in the gathering dusk. Ben looped the reins of his gelding through the hitching post in front of the house. Torrie had escaped him. Somehow she had managed to slip out of the hotel without him seeing her.

He clenched his jaw as he climbed the few stairs leading to the front door. Spence wasn't out of town a day and the woman was sneaking off. He just hoped she was here. If not, he had a pretty good idea who she was with, if not where.

For two weeks it had been eating at his gut. For two weeks he hadn't been able to look Spence straight in the eye. Ben still wasn't sure why he hadn't told Spence what he had seen that day in the park. Maybe he was hoping he was wrong. He promised himself if he saw her with that man again, he would tell Spence. In the past two weeks, he had almost convinced himself it was all a mistake; the man from the park had been just an old friend. Now, he wasn't so sure.

His knock was answered by Flora, who looked up at him with wide blue eyes. "Why, Mr. Campbell, we didn't expect to see you tonight."

Ben pulled off his hat. "I'd like to see Mrs. Kincaid."

"Oh dear," Flora said, glancing over her shoulder. "I'm afraid she's not here. But she'll be back."

His jaw clenched. "So will I, ma'am."

Ben rode Grady into the alley behind the mission. He had the feeling Torrie would be using the back door. The kitchen was dark. A gas lamp flickering on the side of the back door cast a yellow glow into the wispy fog, lighting the wooden steps leading from the kitchen to the gravel drive.

Following his suspicions, he ducked into the stable. Several horses stood in their stalls; one of them he recognized as Torrie's chestnut mare. The bearded bastard had picked her up at the mission.

Women! A man just couldn't trust 'em, Ben thought as he walked back to his horse. No matter how vulnerable they looked, they were all armed with knives, sharp, steely knives designed to skewer a man's heart.

Ben sat atop Grady in the shadows near the stable and waited, pulling his collar up against the dampness, his anger growing with each passing minute. By the time he heard the rattle of carriage wheels against the gravel in the alley, he was ready to tear Torrie's lover apart with his bare hands. He climbed down from Grady's back and stood beside the stable, his muscles growing tense and ready as the carriage drew near.

In the soft light of the moon filtering through the

fog, he could see the carriage and a single occupant. From the size of the driver, he knew it wasn't Torrie. He pressed his back against the stable as the carriage drew near.

Charlotte McKenzie was driving the carriage. No doubt the little lady was coming back from an evening of preaching and passing out pamphlets. He ducked into the shadows as she drove past him. She climbed down from the high carriage seat, opened the doors, and led the team into the stables.

A few minutes later, he saw her leave by the door near the house. She had her skirts lifted above her ankles as she ran across the drive and up the back stairs. The woman sure was spry for an old gal, Ben thought, watching her disappear through the back door.

He pulled out his watch and moved to catch the moonlight. It was close to ten. It seemed Torrie and her lover were going to make a long night of it. He shook his head and leaned back against the stable. He didn't like this, not one bit.

A half hour later he heard the back door to the mission open. His eyes narrowed as he watched Torrie walk down the stairs.

"What the hell?" he mumbled under his breath, watching her run across the drive and into the stable. A few minutes later he saw her leave through the doors opening on the alley, riding her chestnut mare.

It was time for a showdown, Ben thought. He stepped out of the foggy shadows as she drew near.

"Stay back!" Torrie said, brandishing her riding crop like a sword.

"It's me, Torrie."

"Mr. Campbell?" Torrie lowered the riding crop and peered through the fog, trying to make out his features. "What are you doing here?"

Ben rested his hand on the mare's bridle and looked up at her, filtered moonlight catching his features, illuminating the frown etched into his face. "I've tracked bank robbers across the Mojave. It wasn't too hard to track you."

"I got tired of being treated like a prisoner. As you can see . . ." Her words ended in a gasp as Ben slipped his hands around her waist and snatched her from her horse. He set her on the ground and took a step back as though she were carrying small pox. "Just what do you think gives you the right to treat me like a dancehall girl!"

"You can drop the act. I know all about your little escapade."

The realization hit her like a bucket of cold water. He had been following her. He knew about Charlotte. "Have you told Spence?"

Ben's lips pulled into a taut line. "You're not even going to try to deny it."

"Why should I? I'm sure you've seen everything." Torrie's chin rose. "If you hadn't been following me as though I were some escaped criminal, then . . ."

"I followed you because Spence wanted to make sure nothing happened to you. He was worried Slattery might get his hands on you."

"Oh yes, I know. He was afraid I would be used as leverage."

"Look, lady, I didn't want to be the one to find out your dirty little secret."

"There is nothing dirty about it. It might not be socially acceptable, but if you must know, I'm proud of what I'm doing."

Ben took a step back, looking as though she had just slapped him across the face. "Proud?" He shook his head. "From what I've seen of this city, maybe they just don't teach people to grow up right. But where I come from, you'd deserve a good horse-whipping for what you've done."

Torrie's mouth dropped open. "How dare you! I realize there's some measure of deceit in what I've been doing, but no one has been hurt by it."

"Hurt by it! Lady, you're a married woman. What you're doing is wrong. There's no question about it."

Torrie's hands clenched into fists. "Tell me, what's so wrong about rescuing girls from prisons too horrible to imagine? All right, so I do dress up like an old woman. Maybe that isn't honest, but don't you understand, if I didn't, I wouldn't be able to help. Victoria Granger could never do the things Charlotte McKenzie does."

Ben froze, his gaze fixed on her face. He looked stunned. "Well, I'll be damned," he whispered, his lips curving into a smile. "You and Charlotte are the same person."

"Yes, of course. Isn't that what you were talking about?"

He took her arm. "Maybe we'd better sit down and talk this out."

Torrie tried to break free. "I'm not going anywhere with you."

His grip tightened on her arm. "Either we talk now or I talk to Spence when he gets back."

"You're not going to tell Spence, are you?" she said, grabbing his arm. "He would demand I stop, and I can't. Please don't tell him about Charlotte."

"Damn," Ben mumbled under his breath. "Let's talk."

Torrie nodded and led the way back to the mission. Ben tied their horses to the hitching post and followed her up the stairs and to Charlotte's little room behind the kitchen.

Torrie lit the oil lamp on the desk and turned to face Ben. "Please have a seat."

Ben sank to an oak chair and fingered his dark gray Stetson, sliding the brim through his fingers. Torrie sat on the edge of the oak chair across from him, feeling her nerves crackle with tension. He held her look a moment before he began.

"Torrie, the day after we met, I followed you to the park." The Stetson bobbed in his hand. "Do you remember that day?"

She wasn't sure what he was getting at.

"I saw you meet a man."

Torrie's breath halted in her throat. She lifted her hand to her lips, suddenly remembering that day clearly and the kiss she had shared with Charles. "No wonder you thought . . .Mr. Campbell, you haven't said anything to Mr. Kincaid, have you?"

Ben shook his head. "I kept thinking maybe I was wrong. Maybe what I saw wasn't what it looked like."

"It wasn't." She glanced down at her hands. "Mr. Kincaid knows. He spoke to Charles. You see, Charles and I were engaged a long time ago. He is married now. He wanted to see me. There's nothing happening between us. I wouldn't do such a thing. You do believe me, don't you?"

Ben nodded, a slow smile curving his lips. "I guess that's why I didn't say anything to Spence before. I just couldn't believe you'd pull such a dirty trick."

Torrie released her breath in a long sigh. "Thank you."

"But then, I wouldn't have believed you'd dress up like an old woman and terrorize O'Farrell Street either."

"You can't tell anyone," she said, coming off her chair. "Please promise me you won't tell anyone."

Ben looked up at her. "Torrie, it's not safe."

"I've been doing this for five years." Why did everyone always think they knew what was best for her?

She looked down into his handsome face and tried to make him understand. "I like to think I've helped a few girls return to the world of the living. Please, don't put an end to this."

Ben came to his feet and took her trembling shoulders. "It means a lot to you, doesn't it, pretty lady?"

"I can't tell you how much it means to me."

"All right. I guess you're old enough to decide what's best for you. As long as you're careful."

"Thank you!" She threw her arms around his neck and hugged him, his soft hair brushing her cheek. Ben returned the hug, his hat falling to the floor behind her as his arms closed around her.

"I sure am glad I don't have to tell Spence you've been messing around," he said against her hair. "I have a feeling it'd be like facing an angry bear."

Torrie turned her cheek against his shoulder, hiding her face, feeling like crying. If only Spence did care.

"How did you get out anyway?"

Torrie stepped back in the circle of his arms and smiled up at him. "I dressed up like a chambermaid."

Ben tossed back his head and laughed, the sound deep and rich in the little room. "Lady, Spence isn't ever going to get bored being married to you."

She dropped her gaze to the narrow tie he wore around his neck. Spence was already bored. She wondered who he was with tonight. Perhaps an old flame.

"Are you all right?" Ben asked.

Torrie managed to paste a smile on her lips. "Yes. I'm just a little tired."

"Let's get you home. I always feel better when

you're safely back at the hotel."

And out of Slattery's reach, Torrie thought, shuddering at the thought of what would happen if she should stumble into Slattery's hands.

Chapter Twenty-six

Olivia paced back and forth behind her desk, like a leopard trapped in a cage. Where was the man? She glanced at the clock on her mantel. It was nearly midnight; he should have been here a half hour ago. The man always kept her waiting, and she was getting tired of it. She caught the edge of her skirt on the hinge of a desk drawer and bent to free the ruby red silk.

"You look edgy, my dear."

Olivia spun on her heel and faced the man standing in her doorway. "Must you always sneak up on me?"

Jack entered the office and closed the door behind him. "My, you are edgy."

"Why shouldn't I be!" She watched as he strolled across the room, gaslight gleaming on his shiny, dark head. He sank to the sofa and crossed his long legs, looking as though he hadn't a care in the world.

"It's been two months since that man started his campaign to destroy me. And he's doing a pretty good job of it. Two months and you haven't lifted a finger against him."

He draped one arm over the back of the sofa and pierced her with his dark gaze. "I told you Kincaid might hurt us."

"Hurt us! Look what he did in Chicago. Henri and Genette are ruined."

He dismissed her with a wave of his hand. "Henri and Genette are stupid. They are better off back in Paris."

Olivia lifted her necklace and started sliding the diamonds through her fingers. "What are we going to do?"

Jack released his breath in a long sigh. "What do you expect me to do?"

Olivia came out from behind her desk. "We could kill Kincaid."

"And you think that would stop things?"

Olivia sat on the edge of the sofa. "Kincaid is the one behind this. If we get rid of him, everything will go back as it was."

Jack stroked her cheek with the back of his long fingers. "You really are a naive little thing. Do you honestly believe killing Kincaid will get us anywhere except the gallows?"

Olivia moistened her lips. "Jack, we could make it look like an accident."

"Kincaid has set a wheel in motion, a wheel that won't stop until it has rolled over us." Jack laughed deep in his throat as he grabbed her necklace, twisting the brilliant stones in his hand. "If only you hadn't started this."

"Jack, I'm not to blame." Olivia resisted as he

pulled her near, seeing the brittle anger carved into his face, feeling the diamonds bite into the back of her neck. "It's that woman he married. That Granger woman put these ideas in his head. She's the reason he's trying to put me out of business."

"I suppose trying to kill him had nothing to do with this." His breath touched her cheek as he spoke, smelling of brandy and cigars.

Olivia took a deep breath. "We could kill her."

He dropped the necklace and came to his feet. "And I suppose Kincaid will stand for us killing his lady."

"What if we kidnapped her?" She rubbed the back of her neck, feeling the welts left in her skin from the diamonds, watching as he crossed the room and threw open the liquor cabinet.

Slattery lifted the top from a decanter of brandy and sniffed the rim. "Do you have any brandy that isn't laced with opium, my dear?"

"There's an unopened bottle in the back." She clicked the diamonds of her necklace together, watching him, plotting how she might coax him into doing what she had in mind. "If we kidnapped her we could force him to stop, force him to do what we want."

"The thought has occurred to me." He poured a generous amount of brandy into a glass and turned to face her. "But tell me, my dear, what do we do once we have her?"

She knew what she wanted to do to Kincaid's wife. "We would tell him to leave us alone or we would kill her."

Jack swirled the brandy in his snifter. "And once we returned her, he would only come at us again."

"We wouldn't return her," she said, a smile curving her lips. "We could sell her to someone outside the country." Olivia wanted to see Kincaid's face when she told him his wife was in another man's bed.

Jack stared at her over the rim of his glass before he took a sip. "How long do you think we could hold Kincaid at bay?"

Olivia came to her feet and started pacing. "I don't know."

"I understand his sister was kidnapped once. He was with the group of men who rescued her." He took a sip of brandy. "None of the kidnappers escaped alive."

She kept seeing Kincaid's face, kept seeing him laugh at her. "We should just kill the bitch."

Slattery shook his head. "And if we killed her, I doubt Kincaid would stop until we were both dead. From what I've seen, the man is head over heels in love with his wife."

Olivia stopped and stared at him. "You've seen him with that woman?"

Jack looked into his brandy. "I've had someone following them. From what he says, Kincaid is very much in love."

Olivia's hands clenched into fists, long nails biting into her palms. "So, Kincaid likes starchy old maids."

"Jealous, my dear?"

"Of course not. Why would I be jealous of that woman?"

"Because she has Kincaid, and you want him."

"Don't be ridiculous." Olivia moved toward him, swinging her hips. "You're the only man I want. You know that."

"Do I?" He glanced down into his brandy.

She slipped her hand inside his black coat and ran her fingers downward along the warm silk of his black waistcoat. "Kincaid can't compare to you, darling."

Jack smiled as her hand drifted to the front of his trousers.

"I'll do anything you want, Jack. Just do one thing for me."

"What makes you think I want anything, Olivia?"

Olivia squeezed the rising swell of his arousal through the black wool. "I can feel it."

"All right." He set his glass on the cabinet. "Strip for me."

A smile curved her lips as she looked up at him. "Help me with my gown," she said, turning to present him her back.

His fingers slid against her skin as he slipped his hands into the top of her gown. She felt a tug, heard delicate silk scream as her gown gave way, tiny silk-clad buttons popping, flying in all directions as he cleaved the gown to her waist. "Jack!" she screamed, turning to face him, her gown slipping from her shoulders.

A smile split the center of his beard. "Too many buttons."

She lifted the skirt of the ruined gown and glared at him. "This cost five hundred dollars."

Slattery shrugged. "You're boring me, Olivia."

She felt her anger surge, but she controlled it, knowing she needed his help. A shrug of her shoulders sent the gown billowing to the floor. She stood back to let him get a good look at her. Her black silk corset pushed her big breasts until she was nearly popping from the top of her chemise. She put her hands on her naked hips and smiled as his gaze dipped. Knowing he was coming, she hadn't bothered with drawers, just the corset, black silk chemise, black silk stockings, and black lace garters. That was all she needed to get him to agree to her plan.

She ran her fingers over her belly and brushed the bright curls below. "Still boring you?"

He met her eyes, and she saw the fire flaring in his gaze. "Come here."

A smile curved her lips as she sauntered toward him. When she came within reach, he grabbed her shoulders and shoved her to her knees. She looked up into his dark face and felt flames lick at her belly. He was throbbing with raw power, frightening and exciting.

She unfastened the placket of his trousers and released the heavy swell of him into her hands. With practiced ease, she brought him to within a hairsbreadth of completion, using her mouth, her tongue, her teeth, controlling him. He grabbed her shoulders and hauled her to her feet.

"Bitch!" he mumbled, carrying her to the desk.

She fell back against the desk, her crystal paperweight digging into her back. A low growl escaped her lips as he plunged inside her, taking her with unbridled brutality.

He reached inside her chemise and grabbed her breasts, freeing them to bounce like water-filled balloons as he ground his hips against hers. He took one dusky tip between his teeth, squeezing until she cried with pain.

She sank her nails into his arms as they came together with a bone-shaking fury, the paperweight bouncing across the desk to tumble in a glittering arc to the soft cushion of the carpet. When it was over he collapsed against her, pressing her against the desk.

Olivia smiled against his damp hair, knowing now she had him under control, knowing now she could persuade him to her bidding. "Do something for me," she whispered.

He stirred, biting her shoulder before lifting to look into her eyes. "What?"

She rested her fingers against his throat, grazing

his skin with her nails. "Bring Kincaid to me, let me kill him."

Slattery pulled back, leaving her sprawled across the desk. "Did you really think I would fall so easily under your spell, Olivia? I told you before, killing Kincaid won't help."

"Why not?" Olivia sat up, her legs dangling over the edge of the desk. "He's going to put us both out of business."

"I know Kincaid. I'm sure he has arranged for our funeral if something happens to him or his bride." Slattery adjusted his trousers as he spoke. "I think it's time to get out of this business."

She released a hiss of air between her teeth. "Kincaid has you running scared."

"Maybe I am." He straightened his cuffs and smiled at her. "I don't plan to end up at the wrong end of a noose."

"This was all a game for you, wasn't it? You've made your money, now you're going to move on. Is that it?"

"I have other ventures in mind. I don't need the trouble Kincaid carries with him."

Olivia clenched her fists and let out a scream of frustration as Slattery walked toward the door. "What am I going to do?"

Slattery stopped at the door and looked over his shoulder. "You can still make a living on your back, Olivia. I might even be one of your regulars."

"Like hell! If you won't take care of Kincaid, I will!"

Jack stared at her a moment. "Remember what happened the last time you tried something so foolish," he said, his voice low and smooth as ice. "This time I will not be as forgiving."

Olivia swallowed a curse as he left the room. On her back! She had worked too hard to see everything she had built destroyed by one man. Nor did she intend to end up with a bullet in her skull. "Harry!"

At her shrill scream, the bulldog came running. His eyes grew wide as he saw Olivia sitting half naked on her desk.

Olivia stood and started pacing. "I want you to follow Slattery."

"Mr. Slattery?"

She bent, retrieving her paperweight from the floor. "That's right." Slattery had secrets, secrets she needed if she were going to force him to help her. "I want to know where he goes, who he sees. I want to know everything about the man."

Harry bobbed his head. "Yes, miss." He stood for a minute, staring at her bare breasts.

"Go! I want you to start tonight."

Harry nodded and ran from the room, closing the door behind him.

Slattery was a coward, a coward who had accumulated power. Jack could terrorize women, but when it came to a man like Kincaid, he folded. She would have to handle them. Both of them.

Olivia sat behind her desk and opened a bottom drawer. She stared a moment at the white drawers before lifting them to her cheek. Soft silk brushed her skin as she breathed in the scent of Spencer Kincaid, fires of lust licking across her skin at the spicy fragrance. She would have Kincaid once more before she killed him. A smile curved her lips as she contemplated his fate.

First, she would force him to watch while one of her boys raped his wife, then she would have Kincaid. He would perform or his wife would die.

Yes, she would enjoy him one more time before she killed him. He would die slowly, she thought, imagining the way she would murder him. Poison should do the trick, a slow, painful poison. She wanted to watch him writhe with pain. When Kincaid was dead, she would sell his wife to a particularly brutal man she knew in Paris.

Olivia leaned back in her chair and lifted her crystal paperweight to the gaslight, smiling at the myriad of colors captured in the glass. "With or without Jack Slattery's help, you're a dead man, Spencer Kincaid."

Chapter Twenty-seven

"As far as I can tell," Dr. Wallace said, slipping off his glasses. He cleaned the lenses with his handkerchief as he continued. "From what you say, I'd guess you're a little more than two months into your pregnancy."

Torrie gripped her hands in her lap and stared at the row of books on the shelf behind his desk. Two months. Spence was not only beautiful but potent, far too potent. "Is there anything I should do, doctor?"

Dr. Wallace shook his head. "Just eat well, get plenty of rest," he said, resting his glasses on his nose and slipping the wire frames behind his ears.

Torrie nodded and came to her feet, her legs as wobbly as a newborn fawn. She rested her hand on the back of the oak chair, hoping the doctor wouldn't see she needed the support to keep from collapsing.

Dr. Wallace stood, a wide smile curving his lips. "And tell Charlotte to be careful. Don't let her do anything that might get her tossed out on her behind."

She managed a smile. "I'll be careful. Thank you."

He came out from behind his desk and started to walk with her to the door. "Does your husband know about Charlotte?"

"No." Torrie looked up at him. "I would prefer if he didn't know."

Dr. Wallace studied her a moment, deep lines creasing his wide brow. "Is something wrong? You don't seem very happy with the news."

"I'm just surprised. I thought it might take a while before it happened."

Dr. Wallace laughed. "All it takes is one time." He opened the door and stood aside for her to pass. "Now, don't fret about anything. You're a fine healthy young woman, and I see no reason why you shouldn't have a good pregnancy. With that strapping young man of yours, you'll probably have a half dozen before you're through."

Torrie nodded and walked out of his house, wishing there would be more children, knowing this would be the only child she would ever bear. Sunlight hit her face as she crossed the porch, making her cringe against the brightness.

There was nothing left to do except tell Spence when he returned, she thought, stepping from the porch. How long would he stay after she told him? Her foot turned on the edge of the top step, throwing her off balance. "No!" she screamed, snatching for the wooden banister.

Ben dashed up three steps and caught her in his arms, her weight swinging him back against the banister. "Easy, pretty lady."

"Thank you," Torrie said, stepping back in his

arms, trembling as she looked up at him.

"Are you all right, Torrie?" His brows pulled together over the thin line of his nose. "What did the doctor say?"

Odd; she once thought this would be one of the happiest moments in her life. She was going to have a child. It was a dream come true, and the beginning of a nightmare. "He said I was going to have a baby."

"A baby!" Ben's face split into a wide grin. "That's great! And I was worried something was wrong."

Torrie stared at the black and silver carriage waiting for them at the end of the brick path. Something was wrong. Something that couldn't be fixed.

"Torrie, what is it?"

"Nothing." She started down the stairs, fighting back tears. She wouldn't go back on her part of this bargain. She couldn't.

Ben took her arm as she reached the carriage. "Torrie, what's wrong?" he asked, urging her to face him.

"I'm fine." Ben didn't look convinced. She tried to take a deep breath, but her chest was too tight, too crowded with emotions to allow more than a trickle of air into her lungs. "Please, just take me home."

Deep lines sank into Ben's brow as he looked down at her, but to her relief he didn't prod her for more. He helped her into the carriage and climbed in beside her.

"I feel like a drive," he said, grinning at her. "Would you mind if we didn't go right back to the hotel?"

It didn't matter. Nothing mattered. "That's fine."

Lost in a churning sea of emotions, Torrie didn't notice where they were going. She stared blindly at her clasped hands and tried to come to grips with reality. Spence didn't love her. He wanted his freedom. It was best to end it quickly.

An honorable woman stood behind her word. Still, she wasn't feeling very honorable at the moment. She was feeling needy, lonely, vulnerable. She wanted Spence, wanted his arms around her, wanted to hear him say he would stay with her forever.

A cool ocean breeze brushed her cheeks, bringing her out of her dark reverie. She glanced up and realized they were on Point Lobos Road, just above Cliff House. "Why did you come here?" she asked, glancing at Ben.

"I noticed you like to come here when something is eating you." His blue eyes narrowed against the sun as he looked at her. "You look like you need someone to talk to, and this looks like a good place to talk."

Torrie glanced down at her hands. "I'm fine."

"Sure you are."

Torrie took a deep breath of the briny air, trying to ease the tight pain in her chest. The soft air filled her with memories, sweet memories of a time long past. "When I was a little girl, my father would bring me here every Sunday."

"Just you and your father?"

She nodded, smoothing back a lock of hair that had escaped the neat coil at the nape of her neck to drift with the breeze across her cheek. "Mother never liked the seashore. She was afraid the sun would darken her skin."

She glanced over her shoulder as the carriage bumped on the uneven road, carrying them up the incline to the cliffs. Below them, Cliff House stood tall, graceful, with its white verandas overhanging the water, its bell tower reaching for the sky. Beyond the wooden structure stretched the sea, sparkling in the sun, and the rocks where sea lions congregated, their deep bellows rising with the rush of the surf.

"It was different when I was a little girl. Just a rambling series of buildings standing on that rocky finger of land. But I always loved it here."

"It's a nice place to spend a Sunday."

"Father would buy me a peppermint stick and take me to any restaurant I chose. Always, I insisted we sit near the window, so we could watch the seals on the rocks just off shore. And he always managed to oblige."

"I bet you had your father curled in the palm of your hand."

In that time of innocence she had always thought her father would be there to protect her. Just one more fantasy that hadn't survived childhood.

"Amanda—that's Spence's sister—is like that. Jason adores his little girl. 'Course, she's not so little anymore." He whistled between his teeth. "Truth is, she's grown into one pretty filly. Though she's headstrong as a mule."

She studied the man sitting beside her, wondering how much he knew about his friend's marriage. "How long have you known Spence?"

Ben shifted the reins into his left hand and tipped back his hat with his right, sunlight falling across his face, burnishing his tanned cheeks. "I guess about twelve years. I was working for the Rangers when I got called in to help find Amanda."

"She was lost?"

"In a way." Ben frowned as he looked at her, tiny lines fanning out from his eyes. "Someone kidnapped her."

"That poor little girl. She must have been terribly frightened."

Ben nodded. "Spence's father used to be with the Rangers, so he called in a few of his friends, took his sons and went to get his daughter." He was quiet a moment, staring straight ahead, his features taut as though he were reliving an ugly memory.

"Spence and I got to be friends. He'd just bought an old bankrupt railroad and was trying to turn it around. He hired me to ride the trains with him and help him stop the theft that was putting the company under." He grinned at her. "Spence had that railroad making money in six months. The man is a real genius when it comes to making money."

He was brilliant at other things too. Spencer Kincaid could touch her and make her feel wonderful things. He could hold her in his arms and make her believe in her dreams again. Only dreams didn't come true.

The road became little more than a path as they passed the cultivated acres of Sutro Heights. A little farther civilization faded, and nature ruled supreme. Acres of yellow and white daises spread upward along the hills, nodding their heads with purple wildflowers, filling the air with sweetness, mingling with the heady scent of eucalyptus, cypress, and pine. Ben pulled the carriage under a tall eucalyptus and got down from the seat.

Torrie hugged her arms to her waist as he crossed behind the carriage. They were close to the place where she and Spence had argued. "Ben, I'm fine," she said, touching his arm when he reached to help her from the carriage. "I would just like to go home."

"Now that we're here, let's enjoy the view for a few minutes," he said, slipping his hands around her waist.

She couldn't find the strength to fight him, perhaps because she didn't want to. A part of her needed to talk to someone, needed to release the gate holding back the raging tide of her emotions.

He took her hand and led her to the rocks near the edge of the cliff. Torrie watched the waves rush to the shore below and tried to grip the rising tide of emotions inside of her.

"Spence loves kids," Ben said, breaking the silence. "He'll be real happy with the news."

"He'll be delighted," Torrie said, tears gathering in her throat. This baby was the ticket to his freedom, the end of a distasteful bargain.

"I mean it. You should see him with his nephew. And little Jake adores Spence, why he . . ."

Torrie could see Spence playing with a little dark-haired boy, their boy. With a gasp, the dam broke and tears started to fall.

"Torrie," he said, touching her shoulder. "What is it?"

"Nothing . . . I'm . . . fine," she said, the words choked by tears. She never cried. Tears were for children. Yet, lately, since meeting Spence Kincaid, she couldn't control her emotions, any of them.

Ben took her in his arms and she gave way to the huge raking sobs welling up inside her. She shouldn't be crying, she shouldn't be in Ben's arms, but his arms felt so good, so comforting, and the pain was so awful. She couldn't deny herself the luxury of his embrace.

"What . . . are . . . you doing?" she asked, as he pulled the pin from her hat.

"The little roses are poking me in the chin," he said, slipping off her hat. He stuck the pin in the hat and held it between his fingers by the brim.

Unexpected laughter mingled with her tears. "Sorry," she said, her words muffled against his shirt. She stepped back, sniffing, swiping at her tears. "I really am sorry for this." She pulled a handkerchief from her reticule and dabbed at the damp patches she had left against his light blue shirt. "I just don't seem to be able to help myself."

Ben cupped her chin with his long fingers and

brushed his thumb across her wet cheek. "You'll feel better if you talk about it."

Torrie shook her head. "I don't think anything is going to make me feel better."

He slipped off his dark gray coat and laid it on the scrubby grass a short distance from the edge of the cliff. "Come on," he said, offering his hand, smiling at her. "Let's talk."

She hesitated just a moment before taking his warm hand. In the past few weeks Ben had become more than her guardian angel, he had become her friend. She sat on his coat and dabbed at her eyes with the edge of her handkerchief. He sat beside her, watching her, his eyes the color of the sky that stretched out behind him.

Torrie watched a gull glide on the air currents and pulled together enough courage to tell Ben the truth. After taking a deep breath, she started, her voice so low he had to lean toward her to hear over the rush of the distant waves. When she was done she glanced at him, afraid of the disgust she knew would be in his eyes, surprised by the tenderness she saw. "Do you think I'm horrible?"

"I think you had your back to the wall." Ben tipped back his hat and studied her a moment. "So, why all the tears? Looks like you got what you wanted."

"I know, but . . ." Torrie swallowed back the fresh tears gathering in her throat. "I love him."

Ben grinned. "I kind of figured that."

"I don't want him to go," she said, her throat growing tight.

"Who says he's going anywhere?" Ben asked, slipping his arm around her shoulders.

Torrie shook her head and swallowed back her tears. She rested her head against his shoulder, staring out across the water, sunlight flirting with each rolling wave. "He has lived up to his part of the bargain, now it's time for me to do the same."

Ben gave her a squeeze. "He'd be a fool to let you get away from him. And if he doesn't already know it, I'm going to make sure he does."

She pulled back and looked up at him. "Ben, promise me you won't tell him about what I said today."

"Torrie, sometimes it helps to have someone else . . ."

"Promise me. Please."

"I could just . . ."

"Ben, please." She tightened her hand on his arm. "I don't want him to stay with me out of pity, or out of some sense of responsibility. I want him only if he loves me, only if he wants to stay because of me. I couldn't live with him any other way. I love him too much."

Ben released his breath in a long sigh. "All right, I promise I won't tell him anything you said. But you're wrong, pretty lady. Spence isn't going to let you get away from him."

She only wished she had as much confidence as he did.

Ben did his best to drag Torrie from her black despair, telling her stories about his days with the Rangers, making her laugh. By the time they reached Hampton House, she felt better. Maybe, just maybe Ben was right about Spence. Maybe he would want to stay married.

At the sound of laughter, Spence turned from the windows in his office. He had returned to Hampton House three hours earlier, anxious to see his wife, only to find she had gone for a carriage ride with Ben.

A woman's laughter drew Spence across the room: Torrie's laughter. He stood in the doorway of his office and watched his wife walk down the hall beside his best friend Ben, with his arm slung across Torrie's shoulders. They looked like an old married couple, just happy to be together. Spence wondered if he would ever enjoy that sense of ease with her.

"Nice to see the two of you get along so well," Spence said, something dangerously close to jealousy coiling around his heart, seeping into the tone of his voice.

Torrie spun on her heel, her hand flying to the base of her neck when she saw him. Different emotions flitted across her features: surprise, apprehension, fear. Spence had prayed time and distance would dull the pain of their last night together. One look at her and he knew it hadn't.

"It's nice to see you," Torrie said, her voice barely above a whisper. *Wonderful to see your face. Heaven to hear your voice.* "I hope you had a pleasant trip."

"Fine." God, he had missed her. In the time away from her he had made a decision. For two weeks he had been rehearsing his speech. Yet seeing her had turned his words to dust; he could feel them now, dry and gritty upon his tongue. "Have you been well?" That was brilliant, he thought.

Torrie laced her gloved hands together. "Fine." *Except for missing you. Always missing you.*

"Well, I'm sure you two have lots to talk about," Ben said, glancing from Torrie to Spence. He started backing down the hall as he continued. "I'll just be moving along."

Ben stepped into the parlor, closing the sliding doors behind him. Torrie and Spence stood for a long moment, separated by five feet of gold and white carpet and an eternity of doubts.

"I thought . . ." Spence began.

"I just . . ." Torrie said, her words overlapping his.

"Sorry," they said in unison.

Spence smiled and lifted his hand. "You first."

Torrie hesitated a moment. "I just saw Dr. Wallace."

"Dr. Wallace? Are you ill?"

She shook her head.

His relief was sudden, and short-lived. Spence waited, every muscle growing tense as he prepared for the blow he knew would come.

Torrie moistened her lips. "I'm with child."

So soon. God, he had expected more time; time to heal wounds, time to show her she could love again. "Guess we make a pretty potent combination."

Torrie nodded, slowly lacing together her fingers at her waist. *Too soon. It had all happened too soon.*

A few strands of hair had escaped the intricate coil of thick tresses at the nape of her neck; one shiny chestnut lock tumbled in a long curl, brushing her neck, skimming the front of her powder blue coat, coiling over the swell of her breast. He longed to touch her, to release her glorious hair, to lose himself in the shimmering light of her beauty. Yet, he couldn't move. His body had grown rigid with need, crippled by pride.

"There seems to be only one thing left to do," she said, staring down at her hands. *Tell me I'm wrong, Spence. Tell me you want me. Please tell me you love me.*

She sure wasn't wasting any time, Spence thought. Still, after that last night together, he could understand why she would be anxious to be rid of him. "I can have Billings draw up the papers this afternoon, if you like."

Over. It was over. "Fine." She turned and started to walk away from him. *Don't cry! Get away, hide, before you make a complete fool of yourself.*

Just like that. She could dismiss him with a single word. Well, it wasn't that easy. "What grounds should I give for the divorce?"

She paused, glancing over her shoulder at him. "Grounds?"

"You need grounds for a divorce. Desertion, adultery. What would you like?"

She turned in the column of sunlight streaming through the skylight overhead. Her lips parted as though she intended to speak, yet no words escaped. She just stood there staring at him as though he had grown two heads.

"Of course, we'll need proof. Since I haven't been with another woman, it might be best to choose desertion. Unless, of course, you've been with another man." He aimed the remark like a lance, directing it toward her heart, flinching when it hit home.

Torrie's mouth dropped open, then shut with a snap. "How dare you imply I've committed such a vile act!"

He felt a knife slice between his ribs as he looked at her. She had haunted him every day since the first day he had met her. She would haunt him every day for the rest of his life.

Nothing he had done had penetrated that part of her she kept hidden. Nothing he had done had coaxed her into surrendering her heart. One thing he could do; he could leave without hurting her. "It would make things easier to get the divorce, that's all."

"I do not intend to commit adultery to make it easier." She stood poised in the sunlight, her hair shimmering with unveiled fire, her eyes flashing with anger and hate. "But I doubt it would go against your scruples to oblige us with a little affair."

With her words, she twisted that knife she had buried in his ribs. He was still the barbarian. Only now, she had reason to believe the worst of him. "I guess I deserve that."

She shook her head, her shoulders slumping as though she were suddenly very tired. "I apologize," she said, fixing her stare on the jardiniere sprouting rubber plants on the narrow mahogany table against the opposite wall. "This has been a difficult situation for both of us."

Pain simmered in his chest, a steady burn that would eat away everything inside him if he didn't smother it. Yet he did not possess the means to quench that fiery pain. She didn't want his love, and he wasn't going to force it on her. "I'll want to see the child when I'm in the city."

I'll die each time I see you. Like I'm dying now. "Of course," she said, staring at the tender shoots of dark green peeking above the cut-crystal globes of the jardiniere.

To hell with the bargain. He wouldn't give her a divorce. He wouldn't let her go. Yet he couldn't force her to stay. He could never hold her prisoner. He loved her too much. "There are other arrangements to be made."

"I'm sure it can all be worked out to your satisfaction."

Not to his satisfaction. Never to his satisfaction. He fell quiet, words beating against his throat like moths against a screen, seeking the light, his love keeping them in the shadows. Finally, unable to stand there another minute without touching her, he broke the taut silence. "I've got business to attend to."

He retreated to the solitude of his office, leaning against the door, fighting against the single realization pounding in his brain: It was over.

Torrie leaned back against the carriage seat and stared up at the moon. It hung like a silver smile in the dark sky, crooked and taunting.

Ben pulled up on the reins in front of the mission and turned to face her. "I just don't believe it."

"Ben, please." She swallowed hard, pushing back the tears that hovered constantly in her throat. Lately, all she wanted to do was cry. "Spence met with his attorney this afternoon."

Ben shook his head. "I don't understand. I was so sure he was in love with you."

"Please. I don't want to talk about it any more tonight. I just have to face the fact it's over." And somehow she would face the morning, and the next, and the next, knowing Spence would soon be gone. She would survive. Somehow she would find a way to survive.

She rested her hands on Ben's broad shoulders as he lifted her from the carriage to the sidewalk. He held her a moment, standing in a pool of yellow cast by a nearby street lamp, his dark blond hair curling in golden waves above his collar, his hands lingering on her waist.

"Torrie, if the two of you go through with this divorce—" He hesitated, as though he were groping for words. "I've made some investments with Spence. I'm not as rich as he is, but not many are. Still, I've done well. If you would have me, I'd be proud to marry you."

Torrie stepped back, lifting her fingers to her lips, looking up into his handsome face. Any woman would be proud to be this man's wife. But she couldn't. "That's very kind. But you aren't in love with me."

Ben smiled. "I'm right fond of you."

The sincerity in his boyish smile touched her heart. "And I'm right fond of you. But it wouldn't work." She brushed his lean cheek with her fingers. "You deserve much more. You deserve a woman who is going to love you with every beat of her heart, a woman who is going to make you hear bells when you kiss her."

Ben covered her hand with his, pressing her palm to his cheek. "Torrie, we could make a good marriage."

"What would you do the day you met the right woman and found yourself married to me?" she asked, smiling up at him. "And tell me, what would either one of us feel when Spence came to visit his child? I can't do that to any of us. I love him, Ben. I will always love him." Her voice cracked and she fought her tears.

The time for tears was over. She would face the future with her head held high. She was going to have a baby, Spencer Kincaid's baby. His child would be her future.

"You'll be just fine, Torrie." Ben smiled, and she thought she saw a glimmer of relief in his blue eyes. "I know you will."

She would survive, but surviving and living were two different things. Her thoughts drifted to Spence, and she wondered if he would miss her, at least a little.

Spence stood at the window in his office, his gaze following the street lamps in their march to the bay. He lifted a full glass of bourbon to his lips, then lowered it before taking a sip. He didn't want bourbon. He wanted Torrie.

Instinctively, Spence knew Torrie was the type of woman who loved only once. He also knew she thought Charles had been her one love. His instincts told him she was wrong. But his instincts were colored by his own aching need.

Did he love her so much he was blind?

Time away from her had allowed Spence to examine their relationship with a cool head. Torrie cared for him, he was sure of it. It might not be love, but she cared. No woman could melt into a man's arms the way Torrie had without caring for that man. No woman could pleasure a man the way she had without caring about him. Not a woman like Torrie. And where there was a spark, there could blossom a flame.

He couldn't let her go.

Somehow he had to make her see it, make her realize they were destined for each other. But how? If he held her, if he refused to give her a divorce, the little amount of affection she had for him might dissolve into hatred. He took a sip of bourbon, the liquid cutting a fiery path down his throat.

He had to let her go.

His hand clenched on the crystal. He loved her, loved her enough for both of them. And she was going to have his child. How could he let her walk out of his life?

"Just what should I do about you, Princess?" he whispered, staring into the glass, wrestling with his doubt.

Chapter Twenty-eight

Olivia slipped her fingers around the long, damp neck and twisted the bottle of champagne, ice clinking against the silver bucket that held it. He was late again, but this would be the last time. She laughed as she imagined his expression when she told him what she had discovered.

"You're in a good mood tonight, my dear," Slattery said from the doorway of her office.

Olivia's head snapped up at the sound of his deep voice. She smiled and beckoned him with her hand. "You startled me. Harry was supposed to let me know when you arrived."

"I came in through the back door. You have watchdogs in front."

Kincaid's man and that reporter from the *Examiner*, she thought. Well, she would soon be rid of them. And Kincaid would soon be dead. "My dear Jack, please do come in."

Jack hesitated a moment, a fly staring into the face of a spider. "Where is everyone?"

Olivia smoothed the bodice of her gown, her fingers sliding over the diamonds adorning the snug black satin. "Most of the girls are upstairs, knitting. We haven't had many customers."

Jack glanced around the room. "And your boys?"

"Gone." Her hands clenched into fists at her sides. "It seems they don't like to work without getting paid." But all of that was going to change. She would be rich again, very soon. "Help me, darling, you know how much trouble I have opening champagne bottles."

Jack stared at her. "What do you want, Olivia?"

"Right now I want my champagne opened."

Jack studied her a moment, then stepped into the room. "Are we celebrating something, my dear?" he asked, strolling toward her.

"I am, darling." Olivia leaned back against the desk, her hand brushing the cold bucket.

She studied his face as he moved toward her. It still amazed her how easily he had fooled her. He lifted the bottle from the silver bucket, water dripping, forming small puddles on her desk, shimmering like blood on the solid rosewood. A strange chill slid up her spine as she looked down at the glistening droplets.

He lifted a small white towel from the handle of the bucket and wrapped it around the bottle. "Are you going to tell me what we're celebrating, or should I guess?"

"In time, darling." She followed his long fingers with her eyes as he worked the cork out of the bottle, a loud pop making her jump.

Slattery smiled at her. "You seem a little jumpy."

"Just excited."

One dark brow raised as he looked down at her. "You do want some, don't you?"

There was a tone in his voice, a tone that made her blood burn. She wanted him, but it would have to wait. She raised a fluted glass to be filled. "Are the rumors true? Are you going away?"

"Yes." Slattery glanced at her as he filled the glass. "San Francisco no longer holds the charm it once did."

"You're going to let Kincaid chase you out of town, is that it?"

Slattery smiled as he filled his own glass. "Let's say, I'm smart enough to know when to get out."

Olivia took a sip of champagne, the wine snapping at her tongue. "You're not going anywhere, Jack."

He slipped the bottle back into the ice. "And who is going to stop me?"

Olivia moved away from the desk, her heart pounding against her ribs as she faced him. "I know all about you. Oh, it was a wonderful charade, and so very well played. John Drew couldn't have done better."

Jack twisted the delicate stem of his glass between his thumb and forefinger. "What do you think you know?"

The pulse throbbed so wildly in her throat, she could scarcely draw a breath. Control over Jack Slattery was more than a dream come true. "I had you followed. I know you created Jack Slattery."

She smiled, sending her gaze drifting down the long length of him. Now she would have him whenever she wanted him, on her terms. "And you did a marvelous job. What a wonderful deception. But I know who you really are."

Jack rested his glass on the desk, his fingers bumping against her crystal paperweight. "And now what?"

She sensed the barely restrained tension within him, but her triumph made her reckless. Her laughter filled the room as she moved toward him, swinging her wide hips. "Now, we get on with business. Only this time I give the orders." She ran her fingers over the front placket of his trousers. "And the first one is to get rid of Kincaid. I want the man dead."

One corner of his mouth twitched as he stared down at her. "I won't do that, Olivia. It would be foolish."

Olivia laughed, the sound brittle and grating. "You don't understand. You don't have a choice," she said, setting her glass on the desk. She slipped her hands into his coat and ran her fingers up and down his ribs, his silk waistcoat warm against her skin. "If you don't do what I say, I'll tell the world just who you really are."

The tendons in his neck strained against his white starched collar. Rage emanated from his big body, but lust and power made her blind to any warning.

"I own you." She laughed as she grabbed the edges of his black waistcoat. Buttons sprayed against her breasts as she cleaved the black silk brocade. "Just like one of my girls. You're mine to do with as I please." She ran her hands upward over his white silk shirt, squeezing his nipples. "A slave."

A growl escaped his lips as he lifted his hand. Olivia felt the muscles in his chest contract, saw a flash of colored light as the crystal apple caught the gaslight.

"No!" she gasped.

As if in slow motion she saw the paperweight descend, light dancing in crystal. She, too, seemed to move in slow motion as she fought to escape her fate. A moan slipped from her lips as a sharp stab of pain sliced into the base of her neck. A black pit opened inside her and she tumbled into the darkness, never again to see the light of day.

Jack stood staring down at her, trembling, sweat beading his brow and his upper lip beneath his mustache.

"Olivia," he whispered, bending to lift her lifeless body into his arms. Her head lolled to one side. He slipped his hand behind her neck, something wet and warm soaking his fingers and palm. He pulled back his hand and stared at her blood. "My God! Why did you make me do this?"

At a soft cry in the hall, he glanced at the door. Somebody had seen him. He dropped Olivia to the floor and ran into the hall, the sound of the back door slamming shut ricocheting through the hall. His heart raced as he ran down the hall and threw open the back door.

In the moonlight he caught a glimpse of billowing yellow satin and flying dark curls before the girl disappeared around the corner, driving his carriage. He closed the door and ran down the stairs into the night, his mind churning as he tried to remember if Olivia had used his name, his *real* name. Damn! He wasn't sure; he just wasn't sure.

"Torrie, it's getting late," Ben said, looking across the scarred oak desk to the wrinkled face of Charlotte McKenzie.

Torrie looked up from the ledger on the desk. "The name's Charlotte, me lad."

Ben laughed and leaned back in the spindly armchair. "How many people know the truth?"

Torrie smiled. "Mother Leigh and Flora. But I've been able to keep the truth from most of the girls.

And just about everyone else. So, mind yer tongue, laddy."

"No one is going to hear me. Everyone with any sense is in bed." Ben grinned at her. "How much longer do you think you'll be?"

"Charlotte's been neglecting her work." She sighed and stared down at the ledger. The truth was, she couldn't stand the thought of going back to the hotel, of sleeping in the room beside Spence, of being so close and yet not being allowed to touch him. Right now she wanted to stay here, as Charlotte.

She looked up as she heard a pounding on the front door. "Who do you suppose that could be?"

"I'll check it out," Ben said, heading for the door. "You wait here."

"Someone may need help," Torrie said, coming to her feet. She followed him out of the room and down the narrow hall to the front door.

"Stay back," Ben said, as he reached the door.

Torrie stayed a few feet back, clasping her hands to her waist. As Ben opened the door a girl came tumbling over the threshold and into his arms. She was dressed in a yellow satin nightdress and nothing more.

"Help me! Please help me," she sobbed against Ben's chest. "He'll kill me!"

"What is it, lass?" Torrie asked, moving to Ben's side.

The girl lifted her face from Ben's chest and stared at Torrie. "I saw him! He killed her."

"Easy, little lady," Ben said, holding the girl close to his chest.

Torrie stroked the girl's bare shoulder, the girl's skin like ice beneath her hand. "You're all right. Nothin' is goin' to hurt ye now." She glanced up at Ben. "Better take her to m'room."

Ben nodded and lifted the girl into his arms. She clung to him, throwing her arms around his neck as though she were drowning and he was a lifeline. Once inside Charlotte's room, he lowered the girl to the narrow bed and started to draw away from her.

"Please don't leave me!" the girl said, clutching at Ben's neck.

"It's all right. I'm not going anywhere," he said, sitting beside her on the bed, easing her arms from their stranglehold around his neck.

"I'm Charlotte, and this is Mr. Ben Campbell," Torrie said, kneeling beside the girl. "Now, why don't ye tell us yer name."

"I'm Becky, ma'am." She glanced around the room as though she expected something to jump out at her. "Please, don't let him hurt me."

"We won't," Torrie said, patting the girl's hand. "Who are ye afraid of?"

Becky swallowed back a sob. "That man, Slattery. He killed her. I saw him." She clutched at Ben's hand. "Only he isn't Slattery, he's someone else. That's why he killed her."

"Easy, little lady." Ben patted her hand with his free hand. "You're all right. Now, take it slow."

Becky lifted Ben's hand, clutching it to her chest, just below her neck. "I came down to get something to eat. Miss Olivia's office is right near the back stairs. I heard her laughing, heard her say she knew who he really was. I shouldn't have listened, but I did. There was something in her voice . . . and then, I heard her cry out." Her words ended in a sob. "Please don't let him hurt me."

"Did he see you?" Ben asked.

Becky shook her head, her long, light brown curls brushing her shoulders. "I peeked around the corner and saw them. Then I turned and ran. I took his carriage." She turned, staring at Torrie with wide, fearful eyes. "I remembered you. I remembered you said you would help."

Torrie smiled. "We will."

Ben looked down at Torrie. "Is there a telephone here?"

Torrie shook her head, feeling a chill edging along the column of her spine, prickling her skin.

"I think I'd better go for the police. You should be all right, but just in case . . ." He reached inside his coat and withdrew his revolver. "Do you know how to use one of these?"

Torrie nodded and took the revolver, the silver handle warm from his body.

"Don't leave me," Becky said, clutching at Ben's hand as he tried to break free.

"I'll be back in a few minutes." Ben smiled down at her and gently freed his hand. "Charlotte will take care of you."

Becky hugged her arms to her breast and pressed her back against the wall. She followed Ben with her eyes as he left the room. They heard his footsteps in the hall, heard him cross the kitchen and throw open the bolt on the back door. The door opened and closed a few seconds later.

"It's all right, lamb," Torrie said, pulling a blanket up around the girl. Becky was trembling uncontrollably. "Just lie down, and try to relax." She got her powder blue jacket from the closet and brought it to the girl.

"Thank you," Becky said, slipping her arms into the blue merino wool. "It was so horrible."

Torrie stroked the girl's brow, then pulled the blanket up to Becky's chin. "I know, child." Olivia was dead. Slattery had killed her. It was a nightmare. She glanced down at the revolver and prayed Ben would return soon.

"I'm so cold," Becky said, shivering beneath the blanket.

Torrie smiled. "What ye need is a nice cup of tea. It'll help calm ye."

"Please don't go," Becky said, clutching at Torrie's arm.

Torrie patted the girl's hand. "I'm just going to the kitchen. I won't be far. If ye need me, just call."

Becky nodded and huddled beneath the covers. Torrie glanced at the oil lamp, but decided to leave it with Becky. She turned the revolver over and over in her hands as she walked down the dark hall and entered the kitchen. Slattery wasn't really Slattery. Then who was he?

Soft light from the porch lamp spilled into the room through the thin cotton curtains at the window by the door, lighting her way as she entered the kitchen. Torrie set the revolver on the counter just inside the door and reached to turn up the gas on the kitchen light.

The tiny hairs at the base of her neck prickled. She heard something move behind her. She dropped her hand to the revolver, her fingers curving around the handle. Something heavy hit the back of her head. A burst of pain filled her consciousness.

"Becky," she whispered, pinpoints of light flickering behind her lids. She had to help the girl, but she couldn't command her limbs. Darkness closed around her, stealing her strength, dragging her to the floor.

Jack Slattery tapped the butt of his revolver against the palm of his hand and glanced around the dark kitchen. He waited a moment, listening, wondering if the old woman was alone. When he was satisfied no one had followed her he ventured into the dark hall.

A yellow light flowed into the hall from an open doorway a few feet ahead. Like a jungle cat sensing his prey, he crept along the hall, walking on the balls of his feet, each shallow breath barely disturbing his shirtfront. He paused just outside the door, his palms growing moist. He reminded himself he hadn't a choice. It had to be done.

The girl was lying on a narrow bed by the far wall, huddled beneath the blankets. She glanced up as he drew near, her big eyes growing round with terror.

"Please, don't hurt me," she whispered.

Jack swallowed back the gorge rising in his throat and moved toward her. She opened her mouth to scream and he pounced, bringing the butt of his revolver down against her cheek. She whimpered, and he struck again and again until she whimpered no more.

With the butt of the gun he turned her face toward the wall. He backed away from the bed, swiping at the warm streaks of blood on his cheek: her blood. With a groan, he doubled over and lost the contents of his stomach.

Breathing hard, he wiped the back of his hand across his lips and stumbled toward the door, his gaze falling on the oil lamp burning on the desk. He grabbed the lamp and tossed it at the girl, needing to burn away her image, to make sure no one was left alive who might know the truth. He ran down the hall and into the kitchen, stepping over the old woman's body as he ran toward the back door and freedom.

Chapter Twenty-nine

Spence glanced into a black carriage as it passed, making sure the driver wasn't Torrie. He didn't want to pass her along the way. He wanted to see her, to hold her in his arms, to tell her how he felt. He would be damned before he let her go without a fight. If it meant swallowing his pride, then he could just damn well swallow his pride.

Spence pulled back on the reins as he turned from Montgomery onto Chestnut Street. "What the hell!"

Women dressed in nightgowns ran from the mission, some carrying children, others bundles of clothes. The acrid stench of burning wood permeated the air. Just above the house he saw smoke curling toward the dark sky.

He pressed his heels into the sides of his horse and sent Trooper galloping down the street. He pulled up hard on the reins as he reached the house and jumped from the saddle before the stallion had a chance to stop.

One glance was enough to tell Spence Torrie wasn't one of the women gathered outside the house. He ran up the stairs and collided with Flora on the front porch. "My wife!" he shouted, grabbing the little woman by her shoulders. "Where's my wife?"

"Oh my! Oh dear, there's a fire!"

His hands tightened on her shoulders. "Flora, where's Torrie?"

Flora's blue eyes grew wide. "She was in the back. In Charlotte's room. Oh my, I don't know if she's still . . ."

Spence released her and dashed into the house. Black smoke rolled down the hall, singeing his eyes, ripping past his nostrils to strangle his lungs. He held his arm in front of his face and plunged through the smoke, coughing, fighting for each breath.

Flames shot into the hall from the small room Charlotte used as her office. "Torrie!" he shouted, dodging the flames, trying to see inside the room.

Tongues of fire spread across the floor, licking upward along the walls, devouring all in their path. Through the smoke, he could see a body lying on the narrow bed, flames lapping at a woman's slender figure.

"Torrie!" he shouted, trying to fight his way into the room, heat and flames pushing him back. She couldn't be dead. She couldn't!

"Help me!" A woman's voice pierced the smoke and the crackling flames from the direction of the kitchen. "Please, help me!"

Spence glanced toward the kitchen, then back into the burning room. Flames embraced her, snaking around her still form, igniting her long hair. He drew breath to shout, smoke flooding his lungs, plunging him into a fit of coughing.

"Torrie!" he whispered, trying to push his way into the room, flaring flames pushing him back.

"Please help me!"

A vice closed around his heart as Spence stared through the smoke at the body of his wife. There was nothing he could do.

Instinct alone made him turn toward the cries for help. He stumbled through the smoke, following the plaintive plea, bending below thick gray clouds, smoke etching like charcoal against his tongue, stinging his eyes until tears spilled down his cheek. Through the smoke and the grit in his eyes, in the red and orange glow of the fire, Spence saw Claire kneeling beside Charlotte McKenzie.

"I can't move her," Claire said, looking up at him, her face streaked with tears.

Wood groaned overhead. Spence glanced toward the ceiling. The main beam was sizzling as fire snaked its way across the room. They didn't have much time. He bent and scooped Charlotte up in his arms.

"Follow me, and stay low," he said, starting out across the kitchen.

Sparks rained down on them as they rushed toward the back door. Near the door, his foot collided with something solid. On the floor lay Ben, and in the light from the fire, Spence could see blood smeared from his temple to his chin. He didn't have time to see if he was alive.

Spence forced the door open and carried Charlotte a safe distance from the house. He gulped at the air, trying to force the smoke from his aching lungs. "Stay with her," he said, his voice raising in a husky croak above the roar of the fire.

"You can't go back in there!" Claire said, grabbing his arm.

"I'll be fine." He pulled free and ran across the gravel to the back porch. The beam gave way as he entered the kitchen, falling in the middle of the room, sending sparks flying in all directions. Spence shielded his face with his arm. With his lungs squeezing painfully against the smoke, Spence made his way to where Ben lay. He lifted Ben into his arms and staggered toward the door, praying the ceiling would hold just a few more seconds.

Outside, Spence leaned against the banister and dragged air into his screaming lungs. He heard a crash just beyond the door. They weren't clear. Stumbling, he made his way down the stairs and into the alley behind the house, hearing the roof collapse behind him. He sank to his knees, gasping for breath, cradling Ben in his lap.

"Are you all right?" Claire asked, kneeling beside him.

Spence blinked, trying to focus on her face, his eyes seared dry by the heat. "I'm . . . fine." As fine as he could be, knowing his wife was dead. "Charlotte?"

"She's still unconscious," Claire said, staring at the inferno behind them. After a long moment she continued, sounding like a little girl lost. "Where are we going to go?"

"Ham . . . Hampton House," Spence said, still trying to catch his breath. "Tell . . . the ladies . . . not to worry."

He lifted his head as bells rang out in the night air. The fire department had arrived. Too late. Just as he had been too late to save Torrie. Pain twisted in his chest. God, he couldn't believe she was gone.

Ben stirred, moving his head, coughing, trying to come to a sitting position. "Easy," Spence said, pushing against Ben's shoulder, holding him back.

Ben opened his eyes and blinked up at Spence. "Where's Torrie?"

Spence swallowed hard, the image of Torrie engulfed in flames searing into his brain. "She's gone . . . dead."

Ben groaned and squeezed his eyes shut. "Slattery. It was Slattery," he said, trying to sit. "We have to get him."

Spence forced Ben back. "You're in no shape to go after anyone. I'll get Slattery."

Rage burned through the pain in his heart, filling Spence with the strength he needed to survive. He left Ben in the care of Claire and rode back to Hampton House.

"Jasper!" Spence shouted as he reached his floor.

A few moments later the servant stepped out of his room behind the parlor, tucking his nightshirt into his trousers, his eyes growing wide as he saw his master. "Sir! Are you all right?"

Spence tossed Jasper his coat. "There's been a fire at the mission." He pulled the studs from his shirt as he walked into his room. "Have a dozen rooms prepared and send six carriages to the mission. It's on Chestnut near Stockton."

"Yes, sir. Anything else?" Jasper asked, pulling a fresh shirt from the closet.

He tossed his holster and gun to the bed. "Call Dr. Joseph Wallace. Tell him we need him over here right away."

"Yes, sir," Jasper said, following his master to the bathroom.

Spence tossed his smoke-stained shirt to the floor and turned on the cold water at the sink. "Open the dress shop downstairs. Tell the ladies to take anything they want. And we'll need food." He cupped his hands in the cold water and rinsed his face, his hair, his chest, trying to erase the stench of burning wood, the image of Torrie as he had last seen her, flames licking at her body. God, he couldn't believe she was gone, he thought, squeezing his eyes shut, leaning on the sink.

"Sir, Mrs. Kincaid. Is she all right?"

Spence grabbed a towel from the rack near the sink and started to scrub his skin. "No."

Rage was the only thing he would allow himself to feel right now. The other emotions were too powerful, too crippling for what he needed to do. Right now he needed to find Slattery, needed to kill him, needed to watch the bastard's face contort with pain as he slowly twisted his hands around his throat.

"I'm sorry, sir," Jasper said. "She was a lovely young woman."

Spence threw the towel to the floor, fighting back the pain. "Hurry," he said, shoving his arms into the white shirt Jasper was holding. "I don't want the ladies out in the cold."

"Yes, sir," Jasper said, rushing from the room.

Spence threw open the door to his closet and pulled a black leather holster from the top shelf. He strapped the holster around his hips and slipped the Colt revolver from its nest of leather. He wanted Slattery to see the gun, to know Spence had come to kill him. After checking the cartridges he slipped the gun back into its place at his hip. He shrugged into a black coat and went to find Slattery.

The Golden Hind was quiet, the doors locked. Spence pounded on the front door, then pulled his gun and shot the lock open. Inside, the room was dark except for the light trickling in from the street lamp outside, near the door. The scent of stale whiskey and cigar smoke hung in the room like a specter, stabbing his nostrils.

"Slattery!" Spence shouted, moving into the center of the room. He stared up at the gallery, barely making out the yellow velvet drapes.

"Slattery!" He shot into the air, and still received no reply. The place was truly deserted. He picked up a chair and heaved it across the room. The sound of wood smashing coupled with his footsteps as he stormed from the casino. He swung into the saddle and headed for O'Farrell Street.

Spence arrived at Olivia's house in time to see two men dressed in black carry a stretcher down the front steps. On it, a body lay outlined beneath a black satin sheet. Spence pulled up and stared as the two men shoved the stretcher into a black carriage.

"Hey, boss," Cal said, walking over to Spence. He had been stationed with a reporter from the *Examiner* outside Olivia's, to keep track of the patrons.

"What happened?" Spence asked. "Who is that?"

Cal tipped back his gray Stetson and looked up at Spence. "Miss Olivia herself." He shook his head as he glanced back to the hearse. "I didn't see anyone go in or out, so they must've used the back door."

Spence leaned back in the saddle and watched as the hearse drove down the street. Something told him Slattery was responsible for Olivia's death, as well as Torrie's. Where was the man? "You can go on to the hotel, Cal. I don't think anything more is going to happen here tonight."

Cal nodded and backed away as Spence urged his horse into a gallop. Spence needed to go back to the mission on Chestnut; he needed to get his wife.

Spence pulled up in front of the mission and climbed down from the saddle. He stood on the sidewalk and stared at the blackened shell, the pungent scent of burnt wood heavy in the air, smoke curling from broken beams. A tall figure emerged from the shadows near the house and walked toward him.

"What are you doing here, Mr. Kincaid?" John Samuels asked, his face catching the light of the street lamp, reflecting his grave expression.

"My wife . . ." Spence hesitated, his throat growing tight. He swallowed hard, forcing back his emotions. "She's still in there."

Samuels ran a hand through his dark hair. "I understand. But I'm afraid we can't get into the house yet. Things are still smoldering in there. We probably won't be able to go in until morning."

"Torrie," Spence whispered, moving toward the house.

"Mr. Kincaid, please," Samuels said, grabbing his arm. "You have to wait."

He had waited too long. Torrie . . . was gone.

"Mr. Kincaid, I hope you see the tragedy your involvement has caused." Samuels stared at Spence with cold, dark eyes. "Your wife might still be alive if you had left Slattery alone."

Spence followed a column of smoke as it rose from the ruin, coiling upward, catching the breeze, dissolving into the shadows. "Don't you think I know that, Inspector?" There was nothing here. Nothing to hold in his arms. Nothing but smoke and ruins. He turned and mounted Trooper.

Spence was numb, as though his body refused to let him feel. He rode through the streets like a sleepwalker, music and laughter pouring out of swinging tavern doors to pound against his skull. Instinct guided him, brought him to Point Lobos and the cliffs.

Spence climbed down from Trooper's back and moved toward the edge of the cliff, the ocean's voice drawing him near like a siren. Below his feet, rocks plunged to the beach. Beyond a narrow stretch of sand roared the ocean, waves catching the moon-light and tossing the silvery light in all directions. Quint had told him this was Torrie's special place. Here Spence could feel her spirit, feel the warmth of her breath in the breeze.

She was gone.

God, she couldn't be gone. And yet . . .

Little by little, reality chipped away at his protective walls. As the walls crumbled, emotions hurtled through the cracks, sharp, jagged chunks of pain ripping through his body, cutting into his soul. He leaned forward, dropping his face into his hands, feeling a strange wetness against his palms.

Never to see her face again, never to hear her voice, or touch her hand. Every muscle in his body grew tense as a cry rose within him, primal, naked with emotion, shaking the air around him. Never had he felt such pain, such horrible emptiness.

One step, and the pain would end. One step and he would be by her side. For a lifetime, he stood on the precipice, staring into the dark chasm below, feeling the pull of eternity beckoning. It would be so easy to take that one step. Yet he was a fighter, a survivor. The easy way had never been his way. And he would never rest until her killer was in the grave.

With a curse, he turned away and staggered to the cypress where he had once stood with Torrie. They had argued that day. He had wasted the few precious days they had together. He sank to the ground. "Why?" he whispered, dropping his head back against the tree, closing his eyes. Why had it all gone so wrong?

The steady rush of the waves stroked his pain. In time, sleep raised healing arms and wrapped around him, pulling him away from the shattered ruins of his life. Spence didn't know how long he slept, or what caused him to awaken. He felt something soft against his cheek. He opened his eyes to see a ghost kneeling beside him in the gray light of dawn.

"Spence, are you all right?" Torrie asked, smoothing the hair back from his brow.

"Torrie?" He touched her face, the heat of her skin warming his palm. For a moment he wasn't sure if she were real or some phantom conjured by his tortured heart.

"Spence," she murmured, throwing her arms around his neck. "I was so worried. Thank God you're all right."

If this was madness, then let me be mad, he thought, wrapping his arms around her, clutching her slender body to his chest. He buried his face against her neck, pressed his lips to her skin, roses filling his senses. Through the linen of his shirt he felt her breasts press against his chest, the firm globes burning his skin, heating his blood. "You're real."

"I don't know what I would have done if something had happened to you," she said, pulling back, cupping his face in her hands. She felt his tears warm against her palms, saw his cheeks glistening in the light, and sat back in awe.

In his eyes, she could see the depth of his emotion, naked and vulnerable, shaking her to her very soul. She drew her thumbs over his cheeks. "Don't, my darling. Don't weep for me."

"Torrie," he whispered, pulling her back into his arms. He held her close, as though he were afraid she might vanish like mist in the rising sun. His breath whispered across her damp cheeks before his lips touched hers.

It was a dream, a wonderful dream, and she never wanted to awaken. Warm tendrils of desire curled across her breasts as his lips moved slowly against hers. He tasted so good, felt so wonderful, she wanted to kiss him forever.

He tightened his arms around her, and she felt the passion rising inside him, desire rushing like a raging river in her own veins. She ran her hands up and down his back, feeling the wool of his coat, wanting to feel the smooth skin of his back.

He slipped his hand between their bodies, warmth seeping through her shirtwaist as his wide palm moved over her ribs. She whimpered against his lips as his hand curled around the curve of her breast, his thumb stroking the tip through the layers of fine white lawn.

He deepened his kiss, his tongue slipping between her lips as he freed each button running down the front of her shirtwaist. He pulled back long enough to strip away her coat and shirtwaist, then pulled her into his arms. At one time Torrie had wondered if she would ever feel this good again. Now all she could do was give herself over to the sweet sensations he evoked inside her.

Slowly Spence stripped away her clothes, until there were no barriers between her skin and his warm touch. The wildflowers were cool and moist against her back as he lowered her to the ground.

Behind him the sky came alive with streaks of gold and myriad shades of pink as he shed his clothes. His skin glowed in the morning light, and she ached to touch him. Her gaze drifted from his handsome face to the thick pelt of fur on his chest. Muscles finely etched beneath that glowing flesh beckoned her.

The air was cool against her skin, raising gooseflesh, while inside her curling flames of passion licked at her skin. She longed to feel his skin against hers, feel the rasp of dark curls brushing her breasts, her belly, her thighs. She lowered her eyes, following the hair as it narrowed across his belly to where it grew wide once more surrounding the proud rise of pure masculinity.

She lifted her eyes to his golden gaze. "Come to me," she said, echoing the words he had spoken on a sunswept beach.

Three long strides brought him to her side. She curled against his warm skin as he took her into his arms. He began stroking her body, chasing away the chill from her skin, fanning the flames inside her. They explored each other as though this were the first time. Soft, pleasured sounds escaped her lips as his fingers danced upon her skin and his lips touched her everywhere.

They took their time, fingers stroking, lips touching, breaths mingling, until neither could stand the pain a moment longer. While the sun painted streaks of gold across the blue-gray sky the two joined as one, warm skin clinging, rubbing, creating a wonderful friction. Silently, they pledged vows once spoken in haste, each offering the gift, each taking the pleasure, each holding the other, reveling in possession, complete in the giving.

For a long time they lay entwined, afraid to move, afraid to break the spell. In time, the morning chill forced Spence to gather his coat and wrap it around their upper bodies. He held her close, covering her legs with his, holding her to his chest.

"Are you warm enough?"

Torrie pressed her nose into the warmth of his shoulder. "I never thought I would be this warm again."

His arms tightened around her, and she felt him kiss her hair. "How? I don't understand. I saw you in Charlotte's office."

Reality, stark and ugly, intruded on the dream. For a moment she had forgotten. Torrie closed her eyes and fought against the gorge rising in her throat.

"That poor girl. I said we would help her. I told her she would be all right. She was running from Slattery. Oh, Spence, she was terrified."

"It's all right, sweetheart," he said, holding her closer.

Torrie shook her head. "Her name was Becky. She saw Slattery kill Olivia." Torrie could see Becky's face, so young, so frightened. She could hear Becky's voice, pleading like a terrified child. "Hold me, Spence. Please hold me."

"Torrie, there's nothing you could have done," he whispered against her hair.

"I never should have left her." Tears clawed at her throat. "It's my . . . fault."

"It's not your fault," Spence whispered, running his hand up and down her arm. "Slattery nearly killed both you and Ben."

She shook her head, great sobs shaking her body. "I . . .had . . . a gun."

"Torrie, I'm sure he had a gun, and he wouldn't have hesitated to use it." He ran his left hand up and down her back as he massaged the nape of her neck with his right. "Sweetheart, we have to be thankful both you and Ben survived."

Torrie shook her head. If only she had stayed with Becky.

Spence spoke as though he had read her mind. "If you had been with Becky, Slattery would have killed both of you. You can't punish yourself for his crime."

He pulled back, taking her chin firmly between his fingers and probing her with his eyes. "I was angry, so damn angry with you."

Torrie gulped for air and sniffed. "Angry? For what?"

"For getting killed before I could tell you what I thought of your damn bargain." He brushed at her wet cheeks with the back of his fingers. "I love you too much to ever let you go."

Her heart surged against her ribs. She cupped his face between her hands. "Say it again."

He held her in his gaze, his eyes filled with an intensity that took her breath away. "Do you need the words?"

For too many years she had lived without passion, without love. She needed to hear his words rain down on her, needed to drown in his love.

He seemed to sense her need. "I love you. You are my heart, my soul, my life."

Her arms closed around his shoulders and she pulled him to her, holding him, knowing at last the dream was true, burning the memory of this moment into her heart to cherish for the rest of her years. After a few moments she breathed again, releasing her hold, sliding her hand across his shoulder to toy with the dark, silky waves at the nape of his neck. "It took you long enough to say so."

He laughed and pressed his lips to the tip of her nose. "I thought I had."

"I guess I wasn't listening." With the tip of her finger, she traced the deep cleft in his chin. "When did you know you loved me?"

"I've been in love with you since the first day I saw you." He turned his face, brushing his lips across her fingers. "It would be nice to hear you feel the same way I do."

For a long moment she stared up at him in stunned silence. He needed reassurance from her. This man who always seemed so confident, this man who could have his pick of women, this man needed reassurance. "For the first time in my life, I'm in love. What I felt for Charles was an illusion, a pale imitation of what I feel for you." She pressed her palm against his cheek and slid her thumb over his lower lip. "I love you, Spencer Hampton Kincaid. More than anything in life."

He covered her hand with his and turned his face, pressing his lips to her palm, his breath warm against her wrist. The soft touch sent shivers scattering along her nerves.

"One of these days, I'm going to have to thank Charles for leaving me at the altar."

"Is the past buried?" he asked, his body growing tense against hers.

She could see it would take a while to convince him how much she loved him. What a wonderful gift, to be allowed to show him. She laced her fingers with his. "When I met Charles that day in the park, he felt we could . . ." She hesitated, wondering how best to put his proposition. "Charles thought we could see each other, now that I was married."

A muscle in his cheek flashed as Spence clenched his jaw. "The bastard!"

Torrie tugged on his hand. "He was under the misconception that I still loved him." She drew her upper teeth across her bottom lip, wondering how he might take her confession. "I let him kiss me. I guess I wanted to see if he could send an army of tingles marching down my spine, the way you do when you kiss me. But when he kissed me I knew I didn't love him; I knew I was in love with you."

He grinned. "No tingles?"

"Not one. You were right that day you told me Charles had been the wrong man." She ran her thumb back and forth across his knuckles. "I was frigid with him. I cringed whenever he tried to kiss me. I guess I should have realized it was because it didn't feel right with him."

Spence slipped his arms around her, snuggling her against his chest. "Torrie, I'm not sure I understand how you got out and I didn't see you."

Torrie smiled against his shoulder. "Well now, laddy, ye had a bit to do with that." She felt his breath stop.

"Charlotte!" He shifted her, cradling her back against his arm so he might look into her face. "Why the disguise?"

"Charlotte could do things Victoria Granger couldn't." She smiled and toyed with the dark hair in the middle of his chest. "Dr. Wallace said I was lucky to be wearing a wig. It cushioned the blow and probably saved my life."

He sighed and slipped his hand into the tresses behind her right ear, threading the silky strands through his fingers. "Does Quinton know what you've been doing?"

"No. Neither does my mother."

"That doesn't surprise me. Your mother would howl like a scalded cat if she knew what you were doing."

"I wonder if she will ever forgive me."

His hand tightened in her hair. "Forgive you! Dammit, Torrie! She should be asking you to forgive her."

"She only did what she thought was best for me. My mother has standards and . . ."

"And I'm damn glad her daughter decided to live by her own."

Torrie pressed her nose to the warm skin in the hollow below his chin, breathing in his scent. "So am I."

"How am I ever going to keep you from getting into trouble?"

Torrie pulled back and looked up at him. "Spence, you aren't going to ask me to retire Charlotte, are you?"

He slipped his hand into her hair and cupped the back of her neck. "I think Charlotte better not get tossed out of any brothels, especially when she's carrying my baby."

Torrie resisted as he pulled her toward him. "Spence, I'm serious. The work Charlotte does is important."

"And I'm serious. I think you need to be a little more careful. Charlotte needs to take it easy." Her chin soared, and he smiled. "But if she's careful, she doesn't need to retire until she's damn good and ready."

Torrie's face blossomed into a smile. "You're wonderful," she said, kissing his chin.

His wide hand moved up and down her back, his callused palm warming her skin. "Will you marry me?"

Torrie blinked, her bottom lip dropped, and for a moment she couldn't find her voice. "Spencer Kincaid, do you mean to tell me this marriage isn't legal?"

"Don't get all prickled up." He held her in the warmth of his gaze, his eyes probing hers. "The marriage is legal. It's just, well, you're the only woman I've ever met I wanted to ask, so I figured I should get the chance."

"Ever?"

He grinned. "Ever."

"Yes." She ran her fingers down his bristly cheek. "I'll marry you a hundred times if you like."

"I hope you don't believe in long engagements."

She snuggled against his chest, slipping her knee between his thighs. "When I was a little girl I used to dream of a knight who would scale the castle walls and carry me away. I guess I was always a little partial to an elopement and I never realized it."

He laughed and kissed the palm of her hand before lowering it to his heart. Her cheek rode the rise and fall of his chest with every breath he took. Beneath her palm she could feel the steady throb of his heart. This is where she wanted to be, always beside him.

He pressed his lips to her brow and smiled against her skin. "I guess Charlotte got an eyeful the first time she saw me. In my defense, I'm sure Olivia slipped something into my drink. I really had intended to go home that night."

His words brought reality reeling back to torture her. Into her waking dream, images of death crept like dark specters across her soul.

"You're shivering," he said, trying to hold her closer to the heat of his body.

Torrie snuggled against him. "There's something you should know. Becky said Olivia had discovered that Slattery was really someone in disguise."

"That would explain why we couldn't find out anything about him. He appeared out of nowhere three years ago."

"Spence, you will be careful, won't you? Slattery is an animal."

"Don't worry, sweetheart. I don't intend to let anyone make you a widow."

Torrie snuggled against him, holding him as though someone might steal him from her arms, praying Jack Slattery would disappear from the face of the earth.

"I bought the Chamberlain place."

She pulled back to look up into his face. "When?"

"When I was in New York. I wanted you to have your palace, even if you didn't want me as part of your kingdom."

She pressed her hands to his cheeks. "You are my kingdom."

His eyes grew dark and liquid. "How about a hot bath?"

"In that big Roman tub of yours?"

He smiled, his lips curving into a devilish grin, his cheeks moving beneath her palms.

"Why, Mr. Kincaid, that sounds positively indecent." She tugged his coat from his naked body and came to her feet. "Last one dressed has to mop up the floor afterward."

Chapter Thirty

Torrie spread another towel on the bathroom floor. "It occurs to me," she said, glancing to where her husband was running a towel over his wet hair. Sunlight poured through the window behind her, bathing his naked body in a warm, golden light, making her forget for a moment what she was about to say.

Spence grinned at her. "What occurs to you?"

She felt the warm glow of desire flow through her as she met his eyes. "Every time we bathe together, we end up with more water on the floor than in the tub."

Spence laughed and took her into his arms. "It occurs to me I'm never going to be able to get enough of you," he said, tugging at the towel she wore, sending it to join the fifteen towels soaking up water on the white marble floor.

Torrie slipped her arms around his neck and snuggled against him, brushing her breasts against his furry chest. "Will you still want me when I'm fat with our child?"

Spence groaned. "You'll drive me mad, because there will come a time when I won't be able to touch you."

Torrie smiled, her eyes sparkling with mischief. "Something tells me we'll find a way to feed the dragon."

His deep laughter rumbled against the marble walls as he lifted her in his arms. "What did I ever do to deserve you? It must have been something very good."

Torrie slid her fingers through the damp waves at his nape. "You were a gift," she said, her voice soft and solemn. "A gift to a lonely woman who had almost given up on her dreams."

His arms tightened around her. "Then we both share that gift, my love." He lowered her to the bed and spread her wet hair across the pillow. "A gift we can share and enjoy every day for the rest of our lives."

Torrie felt tears well in her eyes and slip down her cheeks as she looked up at him. A lifetime with this man. It all seemed so wonderful, so very wonderful.

He lowered his lips and kissed one glistening droplet. "No tears, my love."

"You gave me back my tears," she said, smiling up at him.

He lowered his lips toward hers, hesitating as a knock sounded on the door. "What is it?"

"Sorry to disturb you, sir," Jasper said, his voice muffled through the door. "But Mr. Thornhill is here to see you. And he seems quite upset."

Spence frowned and looked down at Torrie. "I wonder what brings Allan out so early."

"Allan probably hasn't been to bed," Torrie said, sliding her fingers down his smooth cheek. "No doubt he heard about last night and wants to make sure everything is all right."

"He has tremendous timing." Spence brushed his lips against hers and gave her a wide grin. "I won't be long."

Torrie sighed as he moved away from her, mourning his loss, craving the heat of his skin, the magic of his touch. She rolled to her side and watched as he shoved his legs into a pair of faded blue denim trousers. "I think I'll check on Ben while you visit with Allan."

"After, we'll have breakfast," Spence said, shrugging into a white cotton shirt. His smile turned devilish as he swept her naked body with his eyes, the heat of his gaze raising a rosy blush to stain the ivory satin of her skin. "In bed."

She nodded and pulled the sheet to her chin before he opened the door. Spence left the room in his bare feet, tucking in his shirt as he walked down the hall. Allan turned from the bay window as Spence entered the parlor. Morning light poured through the lace curtains behind Allan and bathed the room in a soft glow. There was a cut on Allan's jaw where he had slipped with a razor, and his eyes were bloodshot, as though he hadn't gotten any sleep the night before.

"It's a little early for you, isn't it?" Spence asked, wondering when he had last seen Allan look this bad.

"I heard about the fire," Allan said, clutching a glass of brandy between his palms. "Is Torrie all right?"

Spence nodded. "Everyone got out except for a young girl from Olivia's."

Allan released his breath in a low whistle. "Was it Slattery?"

Spence sank to the burgundy-colored silk covering the sofa in front of the fireplace. "Looks that way," he said, resting his arm along the curved rosewood back.

Allan stared down into his glass. "He killed Olivia."

Spence hadn't realized until now just how attached Allan had been to Olivia. He could see the pain in his friend's dark eyes, hear it in his voice. "I know."

Allan rolled the crystal between his palms. "This girl from Olivia's, she must have seen the murder. Was she able to say anything about it?"

"The girl said something about Slattery not really being Slattery. So we can guess the man is using a disguise."

"But she didn't say anything about who he might be?"

"No."

"The poor girl was killed for nothing." Allan set his glass on the white marble mantel, staring into the crystal a moment before glancing at Spence. "What are you going to do about Slattery?"

"Try to find out what Olivia knew."

"Where will you start?"

"The first thing . . ." Spence hesitated as Jasper knocked on the open door.

"Sir, there is a man here insisting to see you. He says it's extremely important."

Spence came to his feet. "Who is it?"

"He wouldn't give his name, sir. He is a short man, stocky, wearing a yellow plaid suit and dirty shoes," Jasper said, raising his brows. "And he seems nervous. He keeps looking over his shoulder as though he is afraid someone is following him. He's waiting in your office, sir."

Spence turned to Allan. "I better see what he

wants. Would you like me to have some coffee sent up?"

Allan shook his head and shoved his hands into his pockets. It looked as though breakfast in bed would have to wait, Spence thought. He could see Allan needed someone to talk to. "I won't be long," he said, turning to leave.

Spence crossed the hall and paused on the threshold of his office. Inside, pacing in front of his desk, was the little bulldog who had once worked for Olivia. "Well, Harry. To what do I owe this visit?"

Harry stopped his pacing and turned to face Spence. The little man took a deep breath, as though trying to summon his courage before he spoke. "I think we can help each other, Mr. Kincaid."

"How is that?"

"I know Jack Slattery killed Miss Olivia."

"Did you see him?"

Harry shook his head, his heavy jowls wagging. "But I know it was him."

"Have a seat, Harry," Spence said, motioning toward the two leather wing chairs in front of his desk.

Harry sat in one and leaned forward. "I figure you're still after Slattery, so that's why I come to see you."

Spence leaned against the edge of his desk and looked down at the man. "What do you know, Harry?"

"He'll kill me, just like he killed Moe and Louie and Miss Olivia. You got to help me get away, Mr. Kincaid."

"You know who he is." Spence felt his heart quicken, sensing he was close to the key to the puzzle, close to putting a noose around Slattery's neck. "You're the one who found out for Olivia, aren't you?"

Harry nodded. "Miss Olivia, she asks me to follow Mr. Slattery. So I does. That's when I seen him, seen who he really is."

Spence rested his forearm on his knee and leaned toward the little man. "Who is he?"

"How much is it worth to you?"

"Name a price."

"Five thousand."

"Sold." Spence smiled down at him. "Now who is he?"

Harry opened his mouth to speak. A muffled pop ripped through the air. A groan escaped Harry's lips. His eyes bulged wide before he fell forward against the desk, exposing a hole in the chair behind him and a rent in the yellow plaid suit.

"Harry!" Spence said, grasping the man's shoulders. He pushed him back in the chair and stared down at his face. Blood trickled from one corner of Harry's parted lips; his little eyes stared blindly, looking like dark polished marbles.

Spence glanced up and found Allan standing in the doorway. He was holding a burgundy pillow from the sofa in the parlor. There was a hole in the center of the pillow where the bullet had ripped through, and goose feathers were floating in the air, like snow in a crystal. Spence stared at his friend, not believing his eyes.

Allan stepped inside and closed the door behind him. "I didn't want it to come to this, Spence."

"You . . . You're Slattery," Spence whispered, reality slowly seeping into his brain. "Why, Allan? Why did you do it?"

A whisper of a smile tugged at Allan's lips. "Money. I didn't know how to live without it."

"But you have money. The bank, the mines. Your father was a rich man."

Allan laughed, the sound harsh and brittle in the

big room. "My father lost everything in the crash. He didn't die of an accident. He put a gun to his head and blew out his brains. I know, I'm the one who found him."

"Why didn't you tell me? I could have helped."

Allan lifted his chin and stared down at Spence. "And what would you have done? Given me a job? Or just given me charity?"

"Dammit, Allan!" Spence said, coming to his feet. "I'm your friend. I could have lent you money, helped you invest."

"That's right." Allan's smile was no more than a grim twisting of his lips. "Spencer Kincaid, the golden boy, could have pulled my little tail from the fire. Well, I didn't want your help."

Spence clenched his hands into fists at his sides. "No, I guess you had a better idea of how to make money."

"I had other friends, friends who gave me ideas."

"Like Olivia?" Spence glanced down at the gun Allan was holding, then lifted his gaze to meet his eyes. "Are you going to kill me too?"

Allan ran a hand across his mouth, wiping away the sweat beading above his upper lip. "Slattery killed her."

"But you're Slattery."

"No." Allan rubbed his temple, looking as though he were trying to gain control of his emotions. "I'm not. I'm . . . You don't know what it's like to be Slattery. He has such power. People respect him, fear him. Not like me. My father didn't even respect me. My father wanted me to be like you."

"You need help, Allan. Give yourself up."

Allan shook his head. "Oh, no."

Spence took a step toward him, needing to close the distance if he were going to rush him. "What are you going to do?"

"That depends on you, old pal."

Spence took another step toward Allan. "What do you want?"

"Just stay where you are," Allan said, waving the gun. "I will shoot."

Spence paused, judging the distance, the few seconds it would take to reach Allan—and the gun.

"I can make a new start in Mexico, and you're going to make sure I get the chance."

"And if I try to stop you?"

Allan stared at Spence with eyes that glistened like ice in the sun. "Don't try. I don't want to kill you. But I will. I have nothing to lose."

Spence studied his old friend and realized Allan was walking a narrow ledge. One wrong move could push him over the edge into complete insanity. "I can't let you . . ." He paused as someone knocked on the door.

"Spence, may I come in?"

Spence felt his heart freeze in his chest at the sound of Torrie's voice.

"My ticket out of here," Allan whispered, smiling at Spence. He stepped back and motioned with his gun. "Come on in, Torrie."

"Torrie, get the hell out of here!" Spence shouted, starting forward.

"Spence, what is it?" Torrie asked, throwing open the door.

Allan turned the gun in Torrie's direction as Spence pounced. Torrie saw the gun, saw Allan pivot toward her husband, pointing the muzzle at Spence's chest.

"No!" She lunged, hitting Allan's arm. The pistol barked, and in the next instant Torrie saw Spence jerk back, as though someone had pulled a rope tied around his waist. He staggered, lifting his hand to his face, looking dazed.

"Spence!" Torrie screamed, rushing toward her husband. She wrapped her arms around his waist and tried to steady him.

"My love," he sighed, his warm breath brushing her cheek as he collapsed in her arms, taking them both to the floor.

She knelt beside him and cupped his face in her hands. The bullet had hit him high on the forehead, and he lay lifeless, blood streaming down the left side of his face. "Spence!" she said, her voice a strangled moan.

"Always a hero," Allan said, from behind her. "Right to the very end."

Torrie pressed bloodstained fingers to his throat, searching for a pulse. His skin was warm, his pulse still beneath her touch.

"No," she whispered, tearing open his shirt. He couldn't be dead! She pressed her hand over his heart and waited, a silent prayer repeating over and over in her brain.

"Is he dead?" Allan asked, his voice emotionless.

Beneath her palm she felt a flutter, a thready rhythm of life. Torrie nearly collapsed with relief. "Thank God."

"Oh, my goodness!" Jasper said, freezing on the threshold of the office.

"Get in here!" Allan said, gesturing with the pistol. "Get in here or I put a bullet in the lady."

Jasper obeyed, sidestepping into the room, staring at Allan.

Torrie pulled the handkerchief from her pocket and dabbed at her husband's bloody brow. "Why? Allan, I don't understand."

Allan tossed her a look, then turned his attention to Jasper. "Who else is on this floor?"

Jasper swallowed hard. "Mr. Campbell."

"No one else?"

Jasper shook his head, his stare fixed on the gun. "Well, let's hope old Ben decides to stay in bed. This time I will kill him."

Torrie stared up at Allan, understanding slowly dawning in her mind. "You! It was you last night, wasn't it?"

Allan's face pulled into taut lines. "Get up!"

"Damn you to hell!" Torrie said, turning back to Spence. He was losing so much blood.

"I said, get up."

Torrie pressed the handkerchief to the gash in his brow. "He'll bleed to death if we don't bind the wound."

"Do you want me to finish him?" Allan asked, his voice low and venomous, not at all the voice of Allan Thornhill.

Torrie glanced behind her at the man holding the gun. Fear clawed at her heart as she realized this man was not the Allan Thornhill she knew, the man who thought only of pleasure and good times. This man was a killer. This man was Jack Slattery. Slowly, she rose to her feet and faced him. "What are you going to do?"

Allan grabbed her arm and pulled her against his side. "You're my ticket to a new life."

Torrie felt the muzzle of the gun hard against her ribs and swallowed back her fear. Spencer's baby. She couldn't let anything happen to his baby.

"Jasper, old boy," Allan said, holding Torrie to his chest like a shield. "Now, you do as you're told or I'll put a bullet into Mrs. Kincaid."

Jasper stared at them with wide eyes. "Yes, I will. What do you wish of me?"

"Sit there," Allan said, motioning toward one of the chairs in front of the desk.

Jasper stepped around Spence's motionless body and sat in the chair, his breath catching as he noticed the dead man sitting in the chair next to him.

"Harry didn't behave," Allan said, moving toward Jasper.

"Mr. Thornhill," Jasper said, "I assure you, I will not try to stop you. I would do nothing to jeopardize Mrs. Kincaid."

"I know you won't," Allan said, raising his gun.

Torrie gasped as Allan brought the butt of the revolver down on Jasper's head. He slumped back against the chair with a groan, his eyes sliding shut, his mouth falling open.

"You're insane," she whispered.

"Keep that in mind," Allan said, jerking her toward the door.

Torrie stared at Spence as Allan dragged her from the room. His blood was already soaking through the cloth she had pressed to his brow. She fought a desperate urge to run to him, to fling herself across his lifeless body. She knew she would only succeed in getting him killed. Allan would put another bullet into Spence without a moment's hesitation. That realization made her shiver.

Allan released her as they neared the stairs. "We're going to take a little trip." He slipped the pistol into his pocket and held it pressed against her side. "If you're a good girl, I'll let you go once I get to Mexico."

She had to pull herself together, she had to maintain some control. The baby, she had to protect the baby.

As they left the hotel, a cool breeze ruffled her skirt and brushed across her damp palms. Her heart pounded, setting her pulse throbbing against her high starched collar. Just what would he try to do to her when he had her alone?

Allan's carriage was waiting on the drive near the

carriage entrance. "Get in, and then move over," he whispered.

Torrie did as he said, cringing as he climbed up beside her. His arm brushed hers as he settled close to her side.

"Take the reins," he said, pressing the pistol to her ribs. "You'll do the driving today."

Torrie glanced to a carriage moving toward them. A young man was driving; he smiled and tipped his derby as he drew near. If she could somehow let him know she was in trouble, if she could . . .

"Don't try it." Allan's voice rasped against her ear. "I'll kill you and him. I don't have anything to lose."

"Where are we going?" she asked, lifting the reins, trying to keep the fear from her voice.

"To the docks." He shoved the gun into her ribs. "And remember, I'll kill anyone who tries to help you."

Chapter Thirty-one

Gulls screeched over their heads, swooping down to feast on the trash discarded by the fish sellers along the wharf. Torrie looked at Allan's ship, the tall masts spiraling toward the sun, and silently she called to Spence. He would come to her. Somehow he would come to her. She had to hold on to that hope.

"Remember what I said, Torrie," Allan whispered, as they walked up the gangplank. "I won't hesitate to kill you and anyone else."

Torrie knew he meant every word. If she panicked, she would get herself, her baby, and who knew how many other people killed.

Captain Hurley met them as they stepped onto the deck. "Mr. Thornhill, I didn't realize you were bringing a guest." The captain's sandy brows rose as he recognized Torrie. "Mrs. Kincaid, this is a surprise."

Torrie tried to smile, but her lips felt wooden. "Captain."

Captain Hurley looked down at her with questioning brown eyes.

"I'm afraid Mrs. Kincaid isn't feeling well, Captain," Allan said. "That's why we're taking the trip."

The captain frowned. "Will Mr. Kincaid be joining us?"

Her throat tightened. Dear Lord, how would Spence find her if they were in the middle of the ocean?

Allan leaned toward the captain and smiled. "Her husband is part of the problem, if you understand what I mean. He caught us . . . well, let's just say we need to get away with all speed."

Captain Hurley leaned back and stared down at Torrie, contempt glittering in his eyes. "Yes, I see."

She felt like screaming. Yet she swallowed her pride. Better to be thought an adulteress than to have the captain's death on her hands.

Hurley drew a deep breath and turned his attention to Allan. "We'll set sail directly, Mr. Thornhill."

She allowed Allan to lead her across the deck, his hand biting into her arm, the wind catching her skirt, whipping it against his legs. He led her to a small cabin beside the one she had once shared with Spence.

"You did very well," Allan said, leaning against the cabin door, staring at her with a smile curving his lips.

Torrie gripped the back of an oak armchair and met his dark gaze. "Why, Allan? Why are you doing these terrible things?"

He ran his hand over his upper lip, wiping away the sweat beading on his skin. "You know, you could have kept me from all of this. If you had married me, I never would have turned to . . ." He laughed and waved his hand. "I might never have discovered my darker side."

"You are Jack Slattery, aren't you?" she asked, voicing what she already knew.

Allan smiled. "At times."

Torrie shivered, her hands tensing on the back of the chair. Allan moved toward her, his movements filled with an arrogance she had never seen in him before.

"You always were lovely," he said, running his fingers from her shoulder to her wrist, his nails raking her skin through the linen of her shirtwaist.

Torrie flinched at his touch. "If you hurt me, Spence won't stop until he hunts you down."

"You're pretty confident old Spence is going to pull through."

She prayed Spence was strong enough, prayed he would survive even if she didn't. "He's a strong man," Torrie said, her chin rising.

"So am I, Torrie." He turned and walked to the door, where he took the key from the lock.

She glanced down at her hands at the sound of the lock clicking into place; they were stained with her husband's blood. *Dear God, let him live.*

After rinsing her hands at the washstand, she explored the little cabin, searching for a means to escape. There was a narrow bed built into one end of the room, with drawers beneath and above for storage, the one door, and two portholes.

Torrie knelt on the narrow window seat and pushed open one of the two small portholes at the side of the ship, salt-tinged air rushing into the room. Twenty-five feet below, gray water lapped against the dark boards at the side of the ship. She placed her hands on either side of the porthole, measuring the width, then brought her hands to her hips. The portholes were too small.

She rested her head on the casement and prayed there was enough of Allan left inside of the man to keep her safe. In a short time, the ship swayed, the snap of canvas mingling with the cries of gulls. Her hands clenched into fists as the ship drifted farther and farther from shore, farther from Spence.

Torrie stared, her hands clenched in her lap as the shoreline became skimming colors of green and brown and gray, sunlight shimmering on the waves separating her from home. In the distance, Cliff House appeared like a white swan perched on the dark rocks. Beyond were the cliffs where Spence and she had made love, the rocks polished slate in the sun.

Had it only been this morning? Would she ever see Spence again? She closed her eyes, feeling the clutch of fear on her heart. *Come to me, Spence. Please come to me.*

The sun arched across the sky, sliding lower on the horizon, the sky bursting into red and gold before fading into darkness. She lit the oil lamp on the wall by the door and returned to the window seat. Her stomach growled, pleading for food. She hugged her arms to her stomach and leaned back against the casement, knowing it was better to endure her hunger than his company, but she wasn't to be that lucky.

Panic prickled her skin when she heard the key scrape in the lock. She came to her feet as Allan opened the door. He was dressed in evening clothes, and smiling at her in a way that chilled her blood.

"Why, Torrie, you aren't dressed for dinner," he said, his dark gaze sweeping her from her prim white shirtwaist to her dark blue skirt.

Torrie stiffened. "It seems my bags were left behind."

Allan smiled and came toward her. "No matter. What man could resist having such a beauty grace his table?"

He offered her his arm, and she balled her hands into fists at her sides. "I'm not hungry."

His eyes narrowed to icy slits. "You will have dinner with me. Take my arm, Torrie."

His voice, deep and menacing, grated, like pointed nails dragged down her spine. Torrie hesitated a moment before taking his arm. She had to play his game. At least for now, at least until she figured out a way to change the rules.

"Do you remember the night we had dinner at Marchand's?" Allan asked, all traces of menace washed from his voice. "You brought your maid as chaperone."

"I don't seem to remember the occasion," she said, as they entered his cabin, the same cabin she had shared with Spence. Red drapes dripped from the portholes to puddle on the floor. Red covered the sofa, the chairs, and the bed, which had been turned down to reveal black satin sheets.

"How you wound me."

"Not as deeply as I would like."

"Shall I remind you?" Allan glanced at the bed, then at Torrie. "Tonight you don't have a chaperone."

Torrie didn't need a reminder. It was all she could do right now to keep from bolting from the room. She had a feeling if she tried, she would feel the bite of a bullet in her back. She fought the fear gathering inside her. This man preyed on helpless women; fear fed his power. She had to be strong. She had to find a way to escape.

"You will find our chef prepares a meal every bit as good as Henri at Marchand's," Allan said as he led the way into the dining room. "But I almost forgot, you already know. You did spend your honeymoon here, on that bed."

She felt him staring at her and refused to meet his gaze. A short, gray-haired man stood by the table in the dining room. He smiled, bobbing his head as they entered. Torrie fought the urge to scream for help. The old man wouldn't stand a chance with Allan.

"We won't need you any more tonight, Browne," Allan said, dismissing the servant.

The old man bowed and left the room, using the door that led directly into the passageway. Torrie broke free of Allan's arm and took a place at the table, not waiting for him to seat her.

"It was very wise of you not to say anything," Allan said, taking the place across from her. "I have a pistol in my pocket."

"I thought as much," she said, glancing at the dishes spread across the white linen tablecloth. Her stomach, once crying for food, now cringed at the sight of it. She sat back and watched as he ate with the gusto of a man with a clear conscience.

He took a sip of champagne and smiled at her. "What's wrong, Torrie? Frightened out of your appetite?"

"Not at all. Perhaps I just don't care for the company."

"Still the Ice Princess?"

"To you." Torrie forced a piece of roasted chicken into her mouth, determined not to show this man her fear. The rich wine sauce nearly gagged her.

Allan smiled as he lifted a small chicken leg. "But not to Spence?"

Torrie didn't answer. Spence would find her. Somehow he would find her.

"Good old Spence," Allan said, before biting into the chicken leg, brown sauce dripping against his palm. He stared at her, his gaze lowering to the front of her white linen shirtwaist. "I should have known if anyone could get to you it would be Spence. He always did have a way with the ladies."

He sounded like Allan. She could almost believe she was with the man she had known since she was a child. But she knew she wasn't safe. Slattery lurked at the edge of Allan's soul, she could see it in the hard glitter of his eyes, sense the evil throbbing inside him. She cut another piece of chicken and forced the moist morsel into her mouth.

"I always wondered what it would be like to bed you," he said, scrubbing at his palm with his napkin.

Torrie's hand tightened on the knife she was holding. "If you touch me, I'll find a way to kill you."

Allan laughed and lifted his glass to her. "You propose an interesting challenge."

She was only making things worse. He liked violence, she could see it in his eyes. She had to try a different tactic. "I never realized I fascinated you so much. I wonder, have you lusted after me for many years?" She forced her lips into a smile and lifted her water goblet to her lips. "Tell me, when you made love to other women, was it my face you saw?"

Allan's lips pulled into a thin line. "You don't compare to some of the women I've had. I've had women begging for me, begging!"

If she could keep him angry, then he might not think about that bed in the other room. He might just toss her back into her cabin and lock the door. "Was Olivia one of them?"

Allan's hand clenched on the stem of his champagne glass. Torrie could see she had struck a nerve. "Was she begging for you the night you murdered her?"

The delicate crystal snapped in his hand, tossing

wine down his shirt, cutting his palm. He didn't flinch. His eyes grew darker as he stared at ·her, his face pulling into taut lines until there was only a passing resemblance to the man she knew as Allan Thornhill. Torrie's heart slammed against the wall of her chest. Had she gone a step too far?

He pushed back his chair and rose. Torrie clutched the knife in her hand and sat ready to strike.

"I think it's time someone taught you a lesson," he said, moving around the corner of the table.

Torrie rose, her chair crashing to the floor behind her. "Stay away from me," she said, holding the knife in front of her.

Slattery laughed, the sound coarse and taunting. "You're like the rest of them." He held her eyes with his as he slid the bolt into place on the door leading to the passageway. "It's time I have a taste of you," he said, moving toward her.

"I'm not a helpless little girl from Kansas," she said, backing away from him.

He kept advancing, smiling, a wild look in his dark eyes. "Stay back," she warned, brandishing the knife.

He laughed and swooped down on her. Torrie thrust out with the knife, hitting his arm, cutting his sleeve, drawing blood. Blind fury filled his eyes. She drew back her hand to strike again, but he was quicker, grabbing her wrist and twisting. Pain shot upward along her arm, numbing her muscles. She cried out as the knife clattered to the floor.

"Let go of me!" she screamed, as he hauled her against his chest, twisting her arm behind her back.

"Go ahead, bitch," he said, grabbing the hair at the nape of her neck. He twisted the silky strands, pulling her head back, forcing pins from her hair. "Beg me."

"Go to blazes!"

He tugged on her hair and smiled down into her face, his eyes chunks of ebony in his flushed face. "Before I'm through, you're going to beg, going to plead for me to take you again and again."

His breath hit her face as he spoke, smelling of brandy and wine and stale cigars. Torrie struggled to free herself, kicking at his shins. He twisted her arm farther up her back. Her breath came in ragged gasps as her tortured arm screamed in agony. She clenched her teeth to keep from crying out in pain. That's what he wanted. He pushed her arm another inch up her back, and she couldn't hold back the sob that escaped her lips.

"I like that," he said, smiling down at her.

The sound of a fist on the oak door thundered in the room. Torrie started to scream. Slattery clamped his hand on her throat. "The gun. One word and you're dead," he said, his voice a strident whisper. "Understand?"

Torrie nodded. His grip slackened enough to allow her to breathe, his long fingers riding each movement of her throat.

"Mr. Thornhill, are you in there?" Captain Hurley shouted through the door.

"What is it, Captain?" Slattery asked, his voice sounding light and unconcerned.

"There's a steamer coming up beside us. They're signaling for us to stop. I think it's Mr. Kincaid."

Spence. She knew he would come.

Slattery frowned. "Don't stop under any circumstances."

"Sir, I think they plan to ram us if we don't stop."

"They're bluffing," Slattery said, his fingers tensing on Torrie's throat.

"Sir, it might be better . . ."

"I said I didn't want this vessel to stop under any circumstances. Is that clear, Captain?"

Captain Hurley was quiet a moment. "Yes, sir. It's your ship." Footsteps echoed through the door as the captain marched down the hall.

"I knew Spence would come for me," Torrie whispered.

"A knight charging to his lady's rescue?" Slattery asked, his lips twisting into a smile. "Well, he hasn't rescued you yet."

Just knowing Spence was near chased away her fear, filled her with a confidence she didn't try to hide. "He will."

"Not before I've had a sample of his lady." He ran his hand over her ribs, spreading the stain of his blood over her shirtwaist. "What have you been hiding under all this chaste white linen? I think it's time I find out."

He held the back of her head as his mouth assaulted hers. Her arm was pinned beneath his arm, but she struck his back with her clenched fist. He ignored her. He licked her tightly pursed lips as he ground his hips into her, pushing her against the table. Desperate anger flooded her veins, giving her strength. She came down with her teeth, tasting his blood before he lifted his head.

Slattery brushed at his torn lip with the back of his right hand, his left still biting into her arm. He stared at the blood, then looked down at her with murder in his eyes.

"Bitch!" he shouted, slapping his open palm against her cheek, snapping her head to one side.

Torrie gasped at the sharp pain that dazed her senses. She heard dishes hitting the floor. Fingers bit into her flesh. She felt him lifting her, tossing her as though she were a rag doll. The air left her lungs in a rush as she hit the table, her head cracking against the solid oak. Pain flared inside her head.

Through the pinpoints of light swimming in her

eyes she saw him lean over her, felt him sliding against her until the back of her knees hit the edge of the table. She lashed out with her feet, hitting his groin. Moaning, he stumbled back. She slid off the table, stumbling toward the door leading to the main cabin.

"Damn you!" he screamed from behind her, grabbing a handful of her unbound hair.

Torrie cried out in pain as he yanked her back against him. She twisted, fighting the tether of her hair, throwing her fists against his back and shoulders. He spun her around and slapped her across her cheek, sending her reeling against the table.

He grabbed her wrists, pinning them to the table above her head. "The haughty, untouchable Ice Princess," he said, his voice cold and sneering.

She twisted, trying to kick him. He pressed her harder into the table. Through gathering tears, she saw him rise above her, his cheeks flushed, his nostrils flaring, madness shining in the dark depths of his eyes. She fought the panic rising inside her. If she were going to survive, she had to reach the man hidden deep inside this maniac. "Allan, you don't want to do this."

"Allan?" He took her wrists in one hand. "That spineless cavalier isn't here."

He leaned forward, pressing her against the oak with his chest, reaching across the table, his arm brushing her cheek. Torrie's breath caught in her throat when she saw the carving knife he retrieved from the other side of the table, the blade glittering in the lamplight.

"All buttoned and proper," he said, slipping the knife beneath the top button of her shirtwaist. With one twist of the knife, he sent the button flying.

She closed her eyes, knowing she couldn't disguise her fear, as he popped one button after the other from her shirtwaist. She felt his knuckles brush the tips of her breasts through the layers of her clothes, and she bit her lip. He wanted her to scream. The man derived the most pleasure from his victim's fear. She wouldn't scream. She wouldn't beg for mercy. Cold metal touched the side of her throat and a whimper escaped her tight control.

"That's it," he said, his voice a satisfied snarl.

With one smooth movement, he plunged the knife into the table near her right ear, the blade quivering, the sound vibrating down her spine. Torrie gasped. He chuckled under his breath.

"I'm going to show you what it's like to have a real man between your legs," he said, rubbing his hand down her ribs. "Once you've had . . ."

The ship lurched.

"Spence," she whispered.

The ship groaned as it pitched and yawed, sending Slattery stumbling back from the table. Torrie slid to her feet and dashed into the main cabin.

"Not so fast," Slattery said, grabbing her arm.

Torrie twisted, trying to break free, but his hand was a vise around her arm. "Let go of me," she screamed.

The door burst open, crashing against the wall. Spence rushed across the threshold, the silver revolver he held catching the lamplight, glowing red in the scarlet room. A bandage covered his brow, a dark red blossom staining the white linen above his left eye. Ben and three other men followed Spence into the room, each training their revolvers on Slattery, who held Torrie in front of him like a shield.

"Let her go," Spence said, moving toward his wife and the man who held her.

"Stay where you are, or I'll kill her," Slattery said, pressing the muzzle of the gun against Torrie's side, just below her right breast.

Spence halted in the middle of the room, staring at Torrie. Her eyes were wide with fear, her pale skin already darkening from a bruise on her cheek. One corner of her mouth was smeared with blood. Blood stained the front of her shirtwaist, the garment hanging open, exposing the lacy edge of her chemise. Something savage stirred inside him as Spence looked at her, pain and anger, a smoldering, killing rage that coursed through his veins in a stream of liquid fire. "If you hurt her, I'll take you apart piece by piece."

Slattery laughed and brushed the muzzle across her breasts. "You interrupted us before I could show her how it feels to have a real man between her legs. But it will be even better with you watching."

Spence moved forward.

"Stay back or she's dead!" Slattery rammed the muzzle into Torrie's side with such force, she moaned in pain.

Her soft moan ripped through Spence's heart like a dagger. He froze, realizing he didn't have a choice. One wrong move and he would lose Torrie forever.

"Drop your guns," Slattery said. "All of you get out of here, except Kincaid."

For a moment Spence hesitated, weighing the risk if he rushed Slattery. Slattery prodded Torrie with the gun, smiling. Spence dropped his gun to the floor, the revolver falling with a dull thud against the blood-red carpet. "Do as he says."

Ben and the other men dropped their guns. Torrie kept her gaze on Spence as the other men backed out of the room. With his eyes he tried to reassure her: *I'll die before I let anything happen to you.* She bit her lower lip, shaking her head in a silent reply.

"Olivia begged me to kill you," Slattery said, smiling at Spence. "You know, I was going to get out of the business. Now, what do I have?"

Spence met Allan's dark, unfathomable gaze. He was surprised by his accent, the same crisp British upper-crust accent that had filled Cambridge. A chilling frost breathed across his blood as Spence realized what had happened: Allan was gone, devoured by the stronger personality of Jack Slattery. And Slattery would kill without hesitation.

Slattery raised the pistol and pressed the muzzle against Torrie's cheek. "Should I kill her, Kincaid?"

"Damn you, let her go!" Spence shouted, taking a step toward them.

"Stay back!"

Spence froze, dragging air into his lungs. My God, he couldn't let her die. Fear pumped through his veins as he watched and prayed the gun would remain silent, prayed he wouldn't lose her. "You can't get away."

The ship lurched and shuddered, tilting to the right, giving Spence a chance. He surged forward as Slattery stumbled back.

"I'll kill her!" Slattery shouted, regaining his balance, before Spence could reach him, pushing the gun to Torrie's cheek, dragging a whimper from her lips.

"Let her go, Slattery," Spence said, calming his voice, fighting the urge to rush him, knowing the man would put a bullet into Torrie. "This ship is sinking. If you want to live, you'll give up, now."

Slattery laughed. "What good will it do? I don't think I'll enjoy swinging from a rope," he said, shifting the gun, pointing it at Spence. "But I've decided you aren't going to live either."

"No!" Torrie shouted, shifting her body, trying to hit Slattery's arm.

"Not this time," Slattery said, pushing her away from his side.

Torrie stumbled and fell. She looked up in time

to see Spence dash toward Slattery and the gun. Slattery fired as the ship lurched, the sharp report of the gun colliding with Torrie's scream, the bullet passing wide of its mark, slamming into the wall behind Spence.

In the next heartbeat, Spence pounced, grabbing Slattery's arm. The two men surged against each other, chests heaving, grunting, both struggling for control of the gun, the silver revolver gleaming in the light from the lamp swaying overhead.

The ship lurched violently. Slattery stumbled back, taking Spence with him. The men hit the floor with a crash and rolled. Torrie came to her feet, swaying, trying to keep her balance on the sloping floor.

"Torrie," Ben said, rushing into the room.

"Help him!" Torrie shouted.

Ben moved forward, looking for an entry into the fray. A foot snaked out, hitting Ben in the ankle, knocking him back into the arms of one of his men. With sudden fury, the pistol barked, the sound muffled between Spence and Slattery.

Torrie pressed her hand to her lips, muffling a moan, staring down at the two men. They no longer struggled. Slattery lay on the floor, smiling up at Spence, an icy look in his dark eyes.

"Spence," Torrie said, terror choking her voice to a strained whisper.

For a moment, neither of the men moved. "Spence!" she shouted, grabbing his shoulder.

Spence glanced up at her, then slowly pulled away from Slattery. As Spence rose to his feet, Torrie saw the blood on Slattery's white shirt. Spence turned, blocking out the horrible sight of the dead man, wrapping his arms around her.

He held her close, lifting her up off the floor when her knees collapsed, burying his face in her hair, absorbing the trembling of her body. "Are you all right?" he asked, his lips brushing her temple.

"I am now," she said, drinking in the warmth of his body, her words muffled against his neck.

Spence stripped off his coat and wrapped it around her, shielding her from the eyes of the other men. A shudder gripped the ship, oak screaming in agony as the vessel pitched and rolled. Spence cradled her against his chest as they slid across the floor.

"We've got to get out here," he said, taking her arm.

With Ben and the other men following, Spence and Torrie made their way down the passageway. A damp breeze ripped at her hair as they rushed across the deck. Near the side of the dying ship a steamship bobbed, smoke billowing from its smokestack to curl toward the smiling moon. Captain Hurley stood at the railing, shouting orders as men scrambled from the deck of the stricken ship across a makeshift gangplank to the safety of the steamship.

Torrie crossed the narrow bridge on her hands and knees, trying to ignore the dark water swirling beneath her. She faltered once, and Spence touched her ankle with his warm hand. Closing her eyes, she crawled to safety.

Once on deck, Spence lifted her in his arms and carried her to a large cabin just off the main deck, far from the cries of the sinking ship, safe from the prying eyes of the other men on board. A gas lamp by the door was lit, casting flickering light across the oak-paneled walls.

"I knew you would come," she whispered as he lowered her to the bed built into one wall.

"To hell, if that's where the devil had taken you," he said, stroking the hair back from her face.

With his eyes he caressed her bruised cheek, her

swollen lips, then he lowered his gaze to where she clutched his coat to her breasts. The memory of her bloodstained clothes haunted him. He had to make sure that bastard hadn't harmed her.

Ashamed at what had happened, Torrie clutched his coat to her chin, resisting as he tried to part the garment.

"Torrie, don't hide from me, love," he said, his voice filled with tender concern. "I need to make sure he didn't hurt you."

"He tried to . . ." She choked on the tears rising in her throat. "He touched me . . . it was . . . horrible . . . he didn't . . . I swear he didn't."

"It's all right, love," Spence said, stroking her hair, wishing he could absorb her pain, suffer in her place. "I'm thankful he didn't succeed. But if he had, my love for you would not be any less than what it is right now. I love you, Torrie, more than my own life, more than I'll ever be able to show you."

"I thought he was going to kill you," she whispered, throwing her arms around his neck. "You looked so fierce . . . I thought you were going to charge at him . . . and then . . . when I heard the shot . . . Thank God. Thank God you're all right."

"Torrie," he whispered, gathering her in his arms, feeling her tremble. "My sweet, adorable Princess."

"I love you so much," she whispered, her tears soaking his shirt.

He held her tighter. "I don't think I'm ever going to get tired of hearing you say that."

Torrie snuggled in his embrace, rubbing her cheek against his shoulder. "Not even after fifty years or so?"

"Not even then." He brushed his lips softly over the red mark high on her left cheek. "If you weren't so bruised, I'd show you just how much I adore you."

Torrie laughed and pulled back to look up into his face. She wanted to make love with him, to assure herself they were both really alive, to erase the horrible images left by Slattery. "Honey, I'd have to be in my grave to be that bruised."

His eyes flashed golden fire. "Are you sure, sweetheart?"

Torrie tugged at the dark curls exposed by his partially open shirt. "Yes, my Lord Dragon, I'm sure." Sure she had at last surrendered her dream to the one man who could make it come true.

Epilogue

Torrie brushed a dark wave from her son's brow and kissed his cheek. Three years old and Quinton Jason Kincaid was already showing every promise of being as handsome as his father, she thought, pride swelling in her breast. "Good night, my darling."

"Tell me a story, Mama," Quint said, grabbing his mother's arm. "Tell me about the Ice Princess."

Torrie smiled and sat beside him on the bed. "Once upon a time there was a princess imprisoned in a dark castle."

"Surrounded by a thick forest," Quint said, looking up at her with big, golden eyes.

"And fire-breathing dragons lurking in the shadows, hiding behind the trees." She tickled his stomach and he squealed with laughter. "One day a handsome knight learned of the princess and made a vow to rescue her. Armed with a mighty sword, the

knight fought his way through the forest, battling
the dragons, slaying each one until he reached the
castle walls. When he reached the castle, he discovered there were no doors, no way to enter except
to climb the castle wall to her window. And when
he found her she was encased in ice. The knight
knew in his heart she was alive under that frozen
coffin."

"So he took his golden dagger and hacked away,
chipping the ice, freeing her," Quint said, brandishing a make-believe dagger.

Torrie nodded, smoothing back a dark lock of hair
from his brow. "But beneath, the princess was cold
and lifeless. For a moment the knight despaired,
afraid he might be too late to save her. Still, the
knight's faith was strong. He kissed her cold lips,
and his warmth melted the ice surrounding her
heart. She opened her eyes and in the first look,
she fell in love with the handsome knight."

"And they lived happily ever after," Quint said,
smiling up at his mother.

"Yes, my darling. They lived happily ever after,"
Torrie said, pressing her lips to his smooth cheek.
She folded the covers beneath his chin. "Now, you
go to sleep."

"Good night, Mama," Quint said, before giving a
lusty yawn.

"Good night, my little darling." Torrie turned and
found Spence watching her from the doorway, their
two-month-old daughter cradled in his arms. In the
light from the hall, she could see the warmth glowing in his eyes, the love shining in the golden depths.

"Is she asleep?" Torrie asked, looking down into
her daughter's face.

"Sound asleep," Spence said, his gaze roaming
over his wife's beautiful face. It had been months
since he had been able to touch her, and he was

hoping to change that tonight. His gaze dipped to the full swell of her breasts beneath her prim white shirtwaist.

Torrie noticed the direction of her husband's gaze and felt her blood grow warm. It had been too long, far too long. "Have my parents left?"

Spence lifted his gaze to her eyes. "A few minutes ago. Your mother asked me to remind you about your shopping expedition tomorrow."

Torrie smiled. Although her mother and her husband were not exactly friends, they tolerated each other. "I thought I would go to bed."

Spence couldn't hide the disappointment in his eyes as he looked down at her. "Are you tired, my love?"

"No. As a matter of fact, I'm not tired at all." She leaned across her daughter and brushed her lips across his. "You look hungry, my Lord Dragon."

His lips curved into a boyish grin. "Ravenous."

"So am I, my love," she whispered, her love for him shining from the depths of her soul. "So am I."